MIKE GRIST

Mike Grist is [illegible] ris Wren thrillers. Born [illegible] lived and worked in tl [illegible] teacher, photographer [illegible]

HAVE YOU READ THEM ALL?

THE CHRIS WREN THRILLERS BY MIKE GRIST

Saint Justice

A biker gang steals Wren's truck in the wilds of Utah.
Now he's going to get it back.

No Mercy

The Blue Fairy hacker group threatens Wren's kids.
There can be no mercy.

Make Them Pay

A billionaire banker is executed live online.
Now all must pay for their crimes.

False Flag

Someone's framed Chris Wren for murder.
He'll kill to clear his name.

Firestorm

A woman burns herself alive online, and others follow.
There'll be no shelter from the firestorm to come.

Enemy of the People

The masses battle in the streets over hellfire and lies.
Only Chris Wren can bring the truth to light.

Backlash

Wren's passenger jet is brought down by twin F-15s.
Let the backlash begin.

Never Forgive

5 dead bodies in Tokyo, Japan, carved with three words:

FOR CHRISTOPHER WREN

BACKLASH

A CHRISTOPHER WREN THRILLER

MIKE GRIST

SHOTGUN
BOOKS

SHOTGUN BOOKS

www.shotgunbooks.com

ISBN - 9781739951177

For Su

1

A380

The Airbus A380's four Rolls-Royce Trent 900 turbofan engines roared in Christopher Wren's ears. At twenty thousand feet above the Pacific Ocean, he looked down through the passenger hatch's window to the black dot of the deepwater oil platform far below.

This was it.

Through wispy cirrus clouds the platform was a barely visible black pinhead on the frozen gray waves. Research had told him it was a floating spar design, lowered into deepwater in the 90s, back when oilfield exploration of the Pacific waters had been a boom industry.

The prospecting company had sunk half a billion into construction and emplacement of the floating platform's mighty 300-foot 'caisson', or hollow screw; the lower two thirds filled with water for ballast, the upmost portion left empty for buoyancy. Within days it had been producing a hundred thousand barrels of crude a day.

The underwater oilfield lasted eleven years before it was tapped out. An investment returned many times over. International law mandated the platform be environmentally disassembled and returned to land, but that had never happened.

Instead it had been bought by a private buyer.

"Any time now, sir," came a voice in Wren's earpiece. That was a new Foundation recruit, Rhonna Tye, a dishonorably discharged Navy test pilot turned Qotl-cartel drug plane pilot. In the wake of the Apex's recent attack on America, she'd turned all the way around and joined the Foundation.

"We are a go," Wren answered. "Prepare to deploy."

"Readying the drop algorithm," Tye answered. "We're on approach, calculations say five minutes to the drop window."

Wren turned to check on his four-strong team, fully geared in tactical suits. They looked completely out of place in the co-opted A380's cabin, surrounded by rows of empty passenger seats. Seatback screens glared back at Wren, all set to the default tracking map, which showed the red blip of their jet way out in the middle of the Pacific.

Only the craziest, most dedicated Foundation members would follow him out here.

They'd launched out of Los Angeles' LAX Airport five hours back, the A380 following a near-standard commercial schedule and route. That should make their approach unremarkable to enemy radar. Three flights just like this one overflew the oil platform every day, capacity 575 passengers, heading from the USA to Tokyo, Japan. So why pay any special attention to this one?

Wren was counting on it.

Mason stood right at Wren's back. It was nearly four months on from his cracked pelvis after the Salt Lake strike, and he looked squat and solid as an obelisk, the old SAINT brands worn into his face. Henry was behind him, Wren's top man with a sniper rifle, a special ops soldier he'd met in

Korengal, who'd backed him on a handful of Foundation hits since.

By Henry stood Doona, once a child soldier for the Lord's Army in Ghana. She'd taken a ricochet of an X follower's bullet in a field outside Medicine Lodge, but she was young and a fast healer, back at full steam already. Behind her stood Alejandro, another ex-Qotl member who'd been with the Foundation ever since Wren had pulled him out of a cartel execution on the banks of the Rio Grande. He'd taken injuries at the Salt Lake strike like Henry, but had been back in full training for a month already.

Four team members Wren trusted with his life. Four pairs of eyes met his own.

"We do this fast," he shouted over the hammering of the engines and the furious skipping rip of the wind. "We take them alive if remotely possible. Agreed?"

Four heads gave him the nod.

He looked further down the cabin, to where a Marine strike squad gathered some hundred feet away, maybe 30 rows of economy-class seating, at the other door.

Ready for the drop.

He switched channel to his Marine squad, where his once-lieutenant Sally Rogers, a CIA asset now seconded to his temporary command, stood at the Marine group's head.

"Ready for deployment?"

"All good here, Boss," came Rogers' shouted reply. "The way I hear it, there's soy lattes down there with our names on them."

Wren smiled. "Make sure mine's a skinny almond milk."

He heard the smile in her answer. "Will do. Now, H4cksl4cker are on the line."

Wren grunted. H4cksl4cker was the internet name his two genius hackers went by, Hellion and B4cksl4cker. He'd hauled them out of some vicious darknet shenanigans a few years back, and now they ran tech support on everything in the Foundation.

"You're ready with the drones, Hellion?" he asked.

"Yes, Christopher," she answered. "This is very special day. Drop 'Big Bad Bird' from Airbus in sky. This is good material for joke, yes?"

Wren stifled a groan. 'Big Bad Bird' was a nickname for him, coined and popularized by some dumb all-day-punditry TV news anchor; a skinny, perpetually puzzled looking guy called Hunter Kason. For the people who liked the Apex still, the followers of X, it was how they made Wren seem small, and Kason was the leader of that brigade.

"I think our Big Bird sounds sickly," B4cksl4cker chimed in with his serious, bass Armenian tones. "Perhaps he needs tweetment."

Rogers laughed. That was annoying.

"Oh, B4cksl4cker," Hellion said, "you really quack me up."

Wren muted the line.

"All ready, so we're a go. Tye, how far 'til the drop."

"Coming up," answered Tye, "nearly at the two-minute count. About to make the course correction."

"Do it."

Wren held the wall handles as the A380 pulled into a gentle left turn, dragging them onto an approach vector above the platform. It was off the standard commercial route, no plain reason for a jet to make that shift, and if the radar operators below were worth their salt, they'd recognize it as an approach vector.

Start alarms blaring. Ready ground-to-air missiles.

"Two-minute count," Tye said. "Mark."

Wren counted the seconds, watching the platform for signs of defensive measures. Everything had been calculated and planned for, other than this narrow span of time. If it went smoothly, Wren and his team would drop like tumbling bombs; their inertia calculated perfectly along with windspeed and resistance to plant them squarely on the platform's deck.

No movement yet. A good sign. Still his heart pounded, mouth drying up. Almost there.

"This is insane!" CIA Director Gerald Humphreys had said, eleven days earlier when Wren had brought him the evidence and the strike plan. "Are you serious, you really want a passenger jet to shoot you out of its belly like God's sickest litter? You do realize there'll be about a thousand people involved in an operation of that scale, any one of whom could rat us out?"

Wren had just stood there. In Humphreys' Pentagon office like the old days, raw beige paint on the walls with the stars of fallen agents in back like nothing had changed, though everything was different. Humphreys had only been released from one of his own black sites a month earlier, on Wren's insistence. The ad hoc US government had listened because Wren was a hero in the public eye, the man who'd brought their national madness to an end. Footage of him marching the Apex into custody had lit up the country's imagination; at least those not already sold to the Apex's lies.

Now he was riding that wave of support hard.

"Unless you feel like authorizing a B-2 Spirit for us, this is the best bet to approach the platform unnoticed."

That had dumbfounded Humphreys. "You mean a Stealth Bomber? Now I know you're crazy. There are only twenty-one Spirits in existence, and they cost a billion five each. There is no chance in hell I'm going to-"

"So an A380," Wren interrupted. "Way cheaper. We go as wolves in sheep's' clothing. They won't suspect anything, and that thousand? They'll have no idea what we're requisitioning the jet for. Nothing to rat out."

Humphreys had stared and stewed, red blooming in his cheeks. Getting renditioned in the middle of the X nationwide terror attacks hadn't blunted his stubborn edge any, but now he glimpsed the negotiation cul-de-sac Wren had steered him into.

"The Apex bought this platform fourteen years back," Wren went on, letting the facts do the work for him. "Eyes high in the sky say there's been movement in the last month. It's got high-spec radar, multiple autocannon machine guns, a standing garrison of twenty or more. No doubt, it's the last bolt hole for any upper echelon Pyramid survivors."

"I don't give a damn where those triangle-worshipping freaks are hiding out!" Humphreys finally boomed. "We've got a hundred-fifty million citizens right here with heads crammed full of jello BS, trying to argue that what you did in Arizona was a war crime, demanding to see their 'Apex' in a live appearance."

"They're never going to see him again."

"Because you burned him alive?" Humphreys countered.

Wren said nothing. There were rumors, sure. "You've seen the court proceedings. He pled guilty, now he's in Guantanamo along with the other terrorists. Job done."

"Except he's not," Humphreys countered. "I actually sent eyes out to Cuba to check. In case somehow you'd backchanneled him in, which is ridiculous since I'm the CIA Director. And guess what? He's nowhere! Also no court anywhere I can find will admit to sitting in judgment of him. It's all a deepfake boondoggle!"

"Go tell it on the mountain," Wren said calmly. "Over the hills and everywhere."

Humphreys stared and fumed. Wren stared back calmly.

"The court videos are definitely computer-generated fakes," Humphreys said. "I've had analyses done, so I know that for sure. So why not come clean about what you really did in Little Phoenix?"

"Never gonna happen."

Humphreys let out a sigh, threw up his hands. "You're impossible. At least tell me why you need the A380. Who do you think's so dangerous on that oil platform that you need our top radar-proof bomber to take them by surprise? Why not just bomb them out of existence from afar?"

Wren said nothing for a moment. He was done explaining himself. The CIA was a sieve now more than ever, with half the populace still loyal to the Apex. Even sharing the platform's location with Humphreys was a risk.

Still, he needed the man on board.

"Someone very bad," he allowed. "Someone who could easily start this whole thing up again. Put you back in jail, Gerald. Break the country on the rack, the whole shebang. I need the A380, because I need to know I really got them. A missile strike's never gonna give me that certainty."

"Kind of the same way I feel about the Apex, then, isn't it?"

Touché. It was a good point, but Wren let it pass right by, simply watching as Humphreys pulled up the A380 requisition papers and signed.

"Thirty seconds," came Tye's voice in Wren's ear.

"Copy that," Wren said, jerked back to the present. He lifted his para goggles into place and focused on the platform far below. Way out in the midst of International Waters. No law out here but the law of the sea and the sky; no one to witness the things that you did or the way that you did them.

The real reason behind the strike flashed through his mind, and he pushed it back down. His kids. Jake and Quinn. They'd been growing up without him, as he'd hunted down his father to keep them safe, and now the job was almost done. Now he just had to make it stick.

Truth was, everything he'd clawed back from his father could be lost in a second if one of the two men on the oil platform started a Pyramid resurgence. Like Napoleon returning from exile on Elba, America would be plunged back into civil war.

Gabriel. Zachariah.

His last remaining Pyramid brothers.

"Drop," came Tye's voice, and Wren yanked down the hatch override, shoved it open wide and let the roaring jet stream rip him out into the air.

2

SPAR PLATFORM

The sky grabbed Wren and spun him like a ricochet bullet, wind ripping at his tactical flight suit. For maybe five seconds he rolled on three axes at once, seeing the ocean below and the sky above, nearly two hundred miles of raw visibility and nothing out there but blue gray waves; not quite high enough to see the curvature of the earth, but it just about felt like it.

After five seconds he was nearing terminal velocity and the pummeling wind resistance brought control; he spread his arms and legs to tailor his angle of descent, working his limbs like the ailerons of a plane, and turned to check the deployment of his team.

Four bodies spun in the air behind him, each spread into stabilizing stars to fall in neat laddered sequence. They'd trained for this a dozen times, dropping onto the deck of a private yacht off the coast of western Mexico. Wren had landed on deck eight out of those twelve times. Doona was a natural at ten out of twelve. The Marines were right there too, with a starburst of tumbling drones behind them.

Hellion's domain. Some fifty individual commercial drones, each equipped with a pound of Semtex and a detonator. The Foundation engineers had been working on the design for over a year, fine-tuning their ruggedness and destructive capacity. This was their first test from 20,000 feet. Their rotors weren't whirring yet and wouldn't until the last minute, and then only just enough to guide them in to any defenses the platform threw up.

Below the platform was growing larger every second, stalky legs emerging from the blot of darkness around its screw-like flotation base, pylons, stanchions and walkways crystalizing like Wren was on a fast zoom from a satellite shot. Few visible weapons at this height, but there'd been plenty of smuggler's tales of this reinforced ocean rig, arms merchants talking up the autocannons they'd sent for installation, enough to shred an F-15 fighter jet right out of the sky.

Mines in the water. Ground-to-air missiles primed to blow anything bigger than a rickety propeller plane out of the sky. The hardened paramilitary remnants of the Pyramid, dreaming of the resurgence to come.

Not if Wren had anything to do with it.

A minute passed in a furious rush as Wren led the pack down; now he could pick out figures on the topmost deck scrambling to the defense. No warning was the key. Eighty-five seconds freefall at terminal velocity from twenty-thousand feet meant some twenty seconds left now, with the platform rushing up toward him.

"You are on target," Tye said from above, tracking the telemetry of her 'bombs' remotely. "Suggest deploy chutes."

"Deploy on my mark," Wren said. Counting the seconds, calculating drift on the sea wind once his rapid insertion chute was deployed. Miss the platform and he'd miss the fight, maybe miss his brothers.

"Boss," Rogers barked.

Fifteen seconds. The first blitz of autocannon fire spun up

below, a hot stream of flaming tracer rounds whipping across the sky like a whip. Deploy too early and they'd be sitting ducks before the drones could reach their targets. Deploy too late and they'd splatter atop the platform's decks.

Ten seconds.

"Deploy!" Wren shouted, gave it two seconds then ripped his cord. The reinforced polymer base-jump chute exploded out of his backpack and hooked the wind like a car crash, jolting Wren through his shoulders and trunk, arresting his momentum and stalling him in the air. All around him black chutes popped like plague crocuses against the blue and white sky, still tumbling fast enough to break a leg if the landing wasn't right.

A hail of bullets ripped toward him, pinged a chute to his left and sent a Marine wheeling madly away from the target. The platform's ground-to-air missiles would be coming on hot now, picking out drifting targets in their twenty-second descent stage.

But the litter of drones hadn't stopped their crazed fall with the chute deployment. Hellion left them until the last possible moment, whirring up their blades just enough to steer and pick out targets, sending each one crashing toward the platform's entrenched defenses like precision kamikaze meteors.

The opening blast erupted from a swiveling box array in the platform's upper gantries, a crow's nest autocannon emplacement that blew first like a perfect fireball and then like a barrel of crackerjacks as the munitions exploded.

A millisecond later another drone steered into collision halfway down the platform's upright comms spine and erupted, then the next blew atop the upper lookout cab's roof beside the radar, then some thirty hit all at once across the top deck in an overwhelming rapture of flame.

Explosive hail from the heavens. Autocannons lit up like

witches at the stake. Sentries blasted to pink mist, body parts blowing out through the air. Black smoke burst up like noxious mushrooms, and Wren pulled his oxygen mask into position, tugged on the para cord to steer himself in, then braced for impact as his feet plunged into the sudden dark.

Three seconds and he hit the deck, rolled to his knees then onto his shoulder to spare his ankles the full inertia of his descent. The impact still crunched up through his core line, knees close to buckling, hips taking a beating, shoulder grinding in its socket as he rolled.

Then he was up. Hit the release to eject his chute, barely able to pick out a thing in the streaming black smoke as flames raced through the cratered wreckage of the platform's topside.

"Clear my route, Hellion!" he called through the comms system, sucked oxygen then started away at a run, pulling his modified FX Impact M3 air rifle from the bracket down his thigh. It was a sleek black dual-grip shotgun-style weapon, .50 cal barrel with a top-loaded magazine carrying ten ballistic syringes loaded with a ketamine-azaperone mix; strong enough to knock out a horse, maybe kill a smaller human.

Not taking any chances.

"On your six," came Mason's voice in back. "We all made it."

A blast rang out in front, maybe thirty yards away, but the smoke was too thick to see the flames. Hellion blowing the door to the command room.

"Almost all here," came Rogers' report. "None dead, two in the drink, securing the perimeter. "

"Copy that," Wren answered, and ran through flames and hot smoke into the command room. He'd studied schematics for days, had run the full layout of the platform multiple times in a wooden mock-up built in a Maine warehouse, and knew the most likely places his brothers would be, in the face of full assault.

Deep down in the structure's belly, taking refuge in a panic room above the caisson screw. No way out, but a place to say your goodbyes, pop a suicide pill and check out before picking up the bill.

"You have them?" Wren asked as he sprinted past monitors and workstations for the stairwell, the smoke thinning the deeper he went.

"Heat trails," Hellion reported. "I have three drones ahead of you scouting."

Wren could hear their buzzing engines more loudly now. They'd run this play in the mock-up too, coordinating their movements so Wren didn't end up blown up by an accidental contact. There should be one off to his left in the parallel accommodation block, one off to the right in the canteen, one down below already.

Wren hit the stairs and rushed down several flights, soon reaching full visibility. Everywhere were raw metal gantries, industrial strip lights held in red V-clamps, no effort made to spruce the place up. He pulled the oxygen mask and goggles off as he turned a sharp corner, watched one of Hellion's drones whizz past him left to right on the lowest deck.

Toward the panic room.

A shot erupted in back; the high-caliber sound of gas explosives ringing through the narrow metal hallways like a cannon burst.

"You missed one," came Mason's voice on his earpiece. "Stopping to clear this deck."

Wren said nothing, saving his breath for the final sprint. He hit the bottom deck and turned left in the claustrophobic corridor, chasing after the drone. It smelled of oil and saltwater here in the platform's bowels, and Wren whipped by rooms either side where naked people were staring back at him through bars.

Women. Men. In green-walled rooms, bloodied and battered, staring back at him in panic. Prisoners and victims both, it looked, but serving no wider purpose than the amusement of his brothers.

Wren's anger surged and he rode it deeper. The corridor zagged through a forest of corroded metal beams and hanging pipework, the drone only five yards ahead now and struggling to navigate the sharp turns.

"Get this thing out of my way!" Wren roared, put on a final burst of speed, and then rounded a steel bulkhead to see the door to the panic room slamming closed ahead.

Too late.

Then the drone swept it, flew into the gap and there was a biting metallic crunch as the door shattered its fragile carapace.

"I will take your gratitude in comedic ringtones," Hellion said, but Wren barely heard, just plunged ahead, slammed his fingers into the gap as someone on the other side of the door pushed it open to get a better swing, and yanked with all his strength.

The metal door ripped clear and swung wide, dragging a slim figure along with it.

Zachariah.

Black buzzcut afro, strange triangular scars dotting his cheeks, dressed in jeans and a white t-shirt sported with blood stains. For a heartbeat Wren only stared; his brother barely inches from his face, so different but just the same as the skinny boy he remembered from his pyramid days.

Zachariah's mouth opened, then Wren's world spun back up to speed and his fist found the slim man's jaw and sent it two inches in the wrong direction. Instant breakage, the temporomandibular tendons unable to take the incredible burst of force and simply snapping to make way. Zachariah's head followed like it was on a time-delayed gimbal, rolling back into the room like someone inside had just called his name.

Out like a light as he stood.

Wren stepped in and Zachariah dropped.

The panic room was small and barely furnished, barely a twenty-foot square space at the heart of the platform that was purely functional. Wren knew all about caissons and flotation now. Like a floating buoy, you could submerge the platform as deep as you wanted up to this watertight chamber. Sometimes they did just that, when working the drill into the plateau a thousand feet below the Pacific's surface. Every inch of extra gain meant a deeper hole dug and more chance of hitting that black gold.

Red-painted curving walls like he was inside a fire hydrant. A bench, two beds, a small bookcase stocked with comics. A TV, a fan, a fridge, and right there in the middle standing on top of the structure's metal plug was his other brother, Gabriel-in-Extremis.

Where Zachariah had always been whip-thin like an ocotillo stalk, Gabriel had been a ball cactus, born with the same heft as Wren. They'd only known each other as boys, but each had recognized in the other the genetics that marked them as different from their shared father, hinting at a shared mother who must've been a giantess.

Gabriel was big and black as the day was long. Obsidian dark, with thick and stubby dreads spiking off his meat-bucket head. Maybe 6' 4", an inch on Wren. His shoulders jutted with oblique muscle, his trapezoids swelled off his neck like cancerous globes, his waist trimmed in from meaty batwing deltoids then broadened out into legs that could deadlift an elephant calf.

Bigger and stronger than Wren.

They stared at each other. In back there came a clattering sound; Wren recognized it as Henry taking up position to snipe around his side. He held up a hand to hold him back.

Gabriel's eyes burned into Wren's. Furious, sure. But there was something else there.

Maybe joy.

"Welcome, little brother," Gabriel said, his voice like coal grinding in a mill. "I've been hoping to-"

"Not going to shoot yourself in the head?" Wren interrupted, scanning the strange metallic space for weapons, suicide pills, the button to start a self-destruct sequence. "All the others did. Galicia blew herself up. Chrysogonus burned. Aden tried, but he choked on his own blood instead."

Gabriel laughed, cracked his big knuckles. "I don't need to kill myself. You'll do it for me."

Wren frowned. "Kill you?" He turned the weapon in his hand. "You're clearly not up to date with your air rifles. This old thing will just put you down for the count."

Gabriel's head tilted slightly to the side. "Will it?" he asked, then charged.

Wren got off two shots before the big man hit. One massive shoulder in the gut drove Wren up against the solid metal wall, blasting the air out of his lungs. Wren was ready for it, already bringing the point of his elbow down hard into Gabriel's back, enough force to break ribs and puncture lungs in a lesser man, but Gabriel had too much meat in the way.

Still, the first blow drew a grunt and dropped his brother a clear foot. Wren brought up his knee but wasn't fast enough to catch Gabriel's face as he pulled away, arms held out like wrestler, starting to circle.

"I've waited for this moment for so long," Gabriel said, "if only-"

"You could've come and found me at any time," Wren spoke over him, circling right with his arms out. "I wasn't exactly hiding. We could've played patty-cake all day long, or, I don't know, a quick game of Apex and Tomb with our father, before he passed on."

Gabriel's expression darkened. "He is dead then?"

Wren laughed. "What do you think, Gabriel? Am I stupid enough to keep that sick old fool alive?"

"He was a great man!" Gabriel shouted. "Now you're going to burn."

He roared and charged. Five steps across the caisson head. Wren just gave a signal, and Henry fired.

Dead into the big man's back. Wren had worked a circle and Gabriel had followed, lost in his vengeance. Henry had closed it out. Four ballistic syringes shot across a ten-foot gap, buried in Gabriel's prodigious muscles and even now pumping their powerful cocktail into his bloodstream, where they joined the two loads Wren had already fired into his chest.

Enough sedative to down an ox.

Gabriel made three steps then sagged to one knee. He looked up at Wren, and his eyes had that faraway look of a man on the wrong side of a long, long drop.

"You're not ready for what's coming." His other knee dropped, his voice elongating as the knockout chemicals finally took effect. "You never were."

His eyes closed and he dropped.

Wren looked over at Henry's bemused expression, was about to say some throwaway line about Gabriel finally shutting up, then Zachariah lolled to his knees. He looked sick, too pale with his jaw hanging slack, eyes unfocused but lit with the burning light of a man possessed, and in his hand...

"No, Henry," Wren shouted, but it was too late.

Henry fired into Zachariah's back, and the ballistic syringe pumped its load into the slim man's bloodstream in half a second. Another half second to travel to his brain, but he managed four slurred words before he collapsed and the dead man's switch clattered from his hand across the metal floor.

"Walk in the fire."

3

RUN

"Run!" Wren boomed, and started toward Henry like a sprinter from the starting blocks, just as the first blast rocked the platform.

Wren missed a step as the floor bucked and heaved, then fell hard and bounced off riveted metal; his hip first, his shoulder second, his cheek third. He skidded until he hit Zachariah, stunned by the suddenness of the impact.

No flames, no blast wave of fire, but still his ears rang from the shockwave.

Henry's hands came on his arm, tugging him up.

"I-" Wren began, reaching for Zachariah, then a second blast came, followed by a third and a fourth.

Henry was toppled and sent tumbling across the space, Wren along with him. The floor tilted at a funhouse angle as the high wail of metal shearing under pressure filled the air. Wren grabbed hold of the screwhead cover as he rolled over it, staring in shock as sheet metal plates in the walls began to warp and ping away like shed scales, each accompanied by a musical plinking sound that didn't…

"Boss!" came the staticky shout in his head. "What's happening?"

Rogers.

He was scrabbling too hard to answer, just getting back to his feet as another explosion came, felt like a mule's kick coming from below. He tumbled like a ragdoll in a rolling barrel. Bodies slipped and slid all around as the panic room roared as the metal strained to its limits. White stress lines sprang up like striated muscle fibers across the floor, fractures promising buckles to come, then another subsonic blast hit and the whole space cracked like an egg.

Freezing water engulfed Wren. From below, from every side, from above in waterfalls pouring through the torn metal panels. He gulped, aerating water into his lungs, then kicked as hard as he could, but couldn't tell which way was up anymore as the level rose far above his head. The world around him rolled on strange and Arctic tides, and he kept kicking for some unseen surface, white electric lights reeling around him like the double 'O' on a roulette wheel.

Too cold. He couldn't think. Not enough air. Kicking madly would get him killed.

Then an incredible pain stung through his whole body. Forced him to suck in water, lose precious air. Blackness tinged the edges of his vision as his limbs worked helplessly, but he resisted the coughing fit that would kill him as realizations stuttered through his mind like objects on a broken escalator.

An electric shock. Carried through the water. Dozens of frayed wires everywhere.

Another shock came and this time he bit blood from his cheek, convulsed for a few seconds, but managed not to expel the little air left in his lungs. Then the lights went out, plunging him into total darkness.

He kicked off metal that flexed, pulled at the water trying to find a way upward. No more explosions came, no more shocks now that the electric supply had voided itself into the

Pacific Ocean, but there was the sense of vast volumes of water moving around him. Jets pouring in under pressure as the spar platform unpeeled, filling every last space.

His fingers stubbed hard into metal; could be the wall, floor, ceiling, and he wouldn't know. For a second, he hung suspended, forcing some measure of rationality back onto his mind.

His brothers must have mined the screw's underwater supports. Five blasts, he'd counted, but no fire. Enough to topple the whole thing, use its own vast mass to shred and dump it to the bottom of the Pacific seabed.

He blinked hard, began to think more clearly. A minute gone, maybe, with barely a minute's worth of air left in his lungs. He hung in the shifting, freezing water, reaching for his bodycam. There was a light attached; he found it, tweaked the dial three times before his numb fingers caught, and a watery cone of wan light gushed out.

A metal bulkhead lay at a forty-five-degree angle ahead, scored down the middle like a T-rex had gouged it. No way through here, but Wren kicked up and away to get a little distance. He took in the bulkhead's shape and size in the faint light, trying to map it onto what he'd seen upon entering.

His lungs convulsed for air, and the image jerkily correlated. He spun to his left, played the light across the slope and saw the circular cap to the screw head nearby, now blown open like a popped tin can.

The floor. That meant the way out was-

He turned, couldn't see far enough to be sure, but kicked off the wall anyway. Powerful strokes swept him across the panic room. As he passed above the ruptured screw cap fresh gushes of freezing water washed up and over him. At the other end near the top, air would be evacuating the structure at the exact same rate.

He had to get out before the whole thing sank, dragging

him too deep to ever reach the surface. Kicking harder, the lamp now held in his left hand as he swam through a school of panicked silver fish, he saw the exit to his left and adjusted his angle.

Hot pangs racked his chest, but he kept on; through the dark entrance, along the hallway now floating with seaweed-like electric cabling. Everywhere the walls were crevassed with deep rifts, spewing water in.

Forty seconds, maybe fifty, and his lungs were close to giving out, the blackness surging like a final tidal wave, when he found the stairs. Leading away at an oblique angle, he grabbed hold of the railing and began hauling himself up. Great whole-body pulls jetted him onward and upward, reversing as the stairs turned back upon themselves, further and faster until finally-

His head broke through into air. He kicked off the steps and pushed on and up, staggering on the tilting stairwell, coughing and hacking out ropey streams of saltwater.

There were lights flickering somewhere above. This was a landing only, several more floors to go. His earpiece crackled but nothing came through. There was no time. Underfoot the water was rising rapidly, now at his ankles, then his calves, then his knees.

He took four big breaths, hyperventilating his lungs, then dived back into the water.

Now he knew the way to go, and pulled himself deeper on the railing like a deep-sea diver on a downline. Three switchbacks, thirty seconds in and he was back in the corridor, kicking off the torn walls and pulling himself forward using clumps of tangled electrical cordage.

Back into the panic room, he broke right into a circling reconnaissance. The scant bodycam light cast ghostlike shadows through the churning water. Bubbles broke everywhere, offering a false route back to the surface.

A shadowy lump lay ahead and Wren beelined for it.

Large, crumpled like a slug at the bottom of the round panic room, now nearly tipped vertical. A body. Wren seized the shoulder, rolled the man and saw his brother Gabriel's face looking back at him, still in death. His throat and chest had been gouged down to the bone in one jagged slash, torn open in the washing machine heave of splintering metal.

Wren kicked away, surveying the 'bottom' of the panic room, but found nothing else. More bodies could have been swept out to sea on the pulsing jets.

Bubbles rose upward, and he kicked away immediately, surfing 'up' on the incoming current through the burst screw head. At the 'ceiling' a thin film of bubbles had gathered into a silvery puddle, and Henry's body hung, floating with his hair drifting across his face.

Eyes open and staring.

Wren grabbed him by his chest strap and swam with all his strength. Down to the doorway out, back along the corridor, pulling back up three, four, five flights of the switch-backed stairs. Far higher than before, until with lungs bursting he broke through the surface and hauled Henry with him.

The big man came out of the water like a landed fish. Wren immediately set to CPR, nose pinched and pumping air into his mouth, pumping his chest. The water rose around them. Two CPR cycles. Three, and Henry didn't budge.

Wren kept on as the water rose to Henry's ears, then dragged him up another flight of stairs and tried again. Two more CPR cycles passed, then the water level suddenly shot up and over Wren's head. Must've punched through some barrier, and he barely grabbed the railing before it swept him ricocheting off the walls like a tsunami tide. Henry was yanked away and careened headfirst into a protruding metal stanchion, coming away in a cloud of blood.

Wren stared. His lungs were burning, down to his last breath after pumping oxygen into Henry's lungs. The big man carried away on the rising flood.

There was nothing Wren could do but swim after him.

4

HOME

Wren stood at the railing of the Ronald Reagan, a Nimitz-class aircraft supercarrier pulled into service as their field hospital, watching the ocean and waiting for the last of the sea rescue missions.

Five hours had passed since the spar platform had sunk beneath the waves, leaving no trace on the surface. They'd sent divers down to collect survivors, but the first three deep dives had produced nothing but the floating dead.

Now Doona was unconscious in the Reagan's sickbay, after the blasts had sent her headfirst into a metal wall. Alejandro was right alongside her, put into a medical coma while the doctors analyzed the damage he'd received.

Henry was missing still, presumed dead. Three Marines were missing too, with no reports of what had happened to them. They'd been clearing one of the lower decks when the blasts hit.

It was a fantasy to think any of them could still be alive in an air pocket, trapped in the sinking hulk of the caisson screw. Even if they'd survived the flooding, the pressure would have long since killed them.

Henry was dead.

His brothers had killed him in a massive suicide blast.

Wren looked at the line delineating the gray-blue sea from the dizzy blue sky. It felt like there was barely an atmosphere keeping all that color in, and all it would take to push through was to reach up and-

"Boss," came a voice at his side.

Wren turned to face his once-CIA lieutenant, Sally Rogers. She looked worn and fractured, like how he felt. There were scratches on her face where she'd been tumbled in the collapsing platform, like everybody else. Bruises were still coming up on her cheeks and around each eye, signifying the pressure wave impact when the water had burst in.

She'd washed up since then, though. The blood was gone, the grime of oil from the platform and the salt stink of the sea. Her blond hair was pulled back tight, and her green eyes fixed on him.

"Reports are in," she said, stepping up to the railing alongside him. "We lost five. They're pulling the search teams; there's nothing in the water now but wreckage."

Wren said nothing, just looked out at the ocean. Somewhere fifty miles to the north a Foundation member had died. Marines had died. He couldn't help but keep seeing Zachariah's face in his final, transcendent moment.

"I'm sorry," Rogers said. Put one hand over his.

Wren turned to her. "I'm sorry. You knew those Marines."

She nodded, lips pulling tight.

They stood in silence for a time. Soon the search helicopters would come back, followed by the boats. The Reagan would move on. There'd be talk of sinking a deep-sea exploration vessel to sift the platform's wreck, but it could take months to put that team together, cost multiple millions, and by that time there'd be nothing left to find. Any paper records dissolved. Electronic records corroded.

"What happened?" she asked softly, after a time.

Wren refocused on the horizon. That was the question.

Together they watched the helicopters come in, then the boats. Dusk drew in across the sky, and the sun set in a furious, almost mocking blaze of oranges, pinks and reds.

"Come on, Boss," Rogers said. One hand on his shoulder. "Let's go home."

He followed.

Mason was waiting beside their Grumman C-2 Greyhound plane on the deck. It stood huge and blocky in slick silver, the Navy's premier carrier on-board delivery plane, high wings boasting twin eight-blade turboprop engines.

Alongside Mason were his unconscious fellows, Doona and Alejandro, strapped into gurneys. The remnants of the Marine squad stood there too, silent and solemn. Mason clapped Wren on the shoulder. No words were necessary.

They boarded together through the large rear loading ramp. Sat along the walls with flight-belts strapping them in place. The turboprops fired up, the shooter on the flight deck crew outside gave the go, and the steam-powered catapult dragged them along the deck and into the air like a stone from a slingshot.

It was a seven-hour flight back to Los Angeles. Wren didn't talk much. Nobody did.

On the blacktop of LAX airport, he thanked his team, as they peeled away to waiting private planes.

"Humphreys sends his condolences," Rogers said. "Says he's looking into everything. Whatever your brother was talking about."

Wren grunted. His Foundation was doing the same. He hadn't spoken to them much, but he'd fired off messages through the darknet, instructing them on preparations. There was nothing yet. Maybe there never would be.

"Stay safe, Sally," he said.

She smiled. "You too, Chris. Call if you need me."

She strode off to a waiting Embraer 300E. Heading straight to Washington for a debrief with Humphreys. Right back into the thick of it.

Mason was next, standing in front of him. They looked at each other a long moment. They'd been through a lot, ever since Wren had turned him around, in the waning hours of the Saints' attack on America.

"Nobody blames you," Mason said. "It's the job. Your brothers are better off dead."

Wren couldn't argue with that. He extended his hand and Mason shook it firmly.

"Say hello to your daughter," he said.

Mason smiled. He rarely did. "Will do," he said, then strode away without another word, headed for his flight back to Nevada, where his wife Wendy and their newborn baby daughter were waiting.

Doona and Henry were taken to Cedars-Sinai Hospital. The Marines went their own way, back to their own worlds. Wren took a light utility helicopter, a Eurocopter UH-72 Lakota, alone.

It was a two-hour flight, and Wren spent it in silence. Soon they were over the bare orange sands of the Sonoran Desert, blurring by a thousand feet below. Wren watched the landscape pass by, barely thinking.

The fake town from his childhood came on fast. It had changed immensely in the past few months. As the chopper came in hot, rotor downdrafts pummeling waves of sand away like a fat, shallow tornado, his heart began to beat harder.

The old fear transmuting to new rage.

Ugly steel fencing encircled everything, now, from the

fake-fronted Wild West buildings at the town's northern edge to the newer buildings spreading to the south. The woman known as Maggie had built a large gymnasium here, a school, a small hospital, a canteen, and many ranks of three-story dormitories for the one thousand Blue Fairy orphans.

Now it was quiet and still, with all the children gone.

The Lakota put down and Wren stepped out. A hot wind blasted his cheeks, and he strode along Main Street, ignoring the empty-eyed windows that watched him.

At the gym he shoved through the swinging glass doors too hard, cracking one pane. A security guard sat at attention. Wren waved his ID and passed through the metal detector, ignoring the beeps as his gun and knife triggered the alarm.

The gym had been cleared of equipment, but full-length mirrors still lined the walls. Wren saw the stranger approaching in the reflection: six foot three and solid with muscle, hair thick and wild, beard knotted and tangled, cheeks and neck peppered with fresh scratches, bruises and welts over older burn scars, eyes burning like Zachariah's at the end.

He scarcely looked like himself. He looked dangerous.

The panel down to the tunnels below had been removed, leaving the access path open and fully lit. Wren passed down, feeling his heartrate ramping up painfully. After several minutes he reached a reinforced metal door, tapped in a code and it swung open.

A wide, ample space spread before him. Some one-hundred-fifty feet across, clad completely in two feet of pale gray cement.

Once this had been a hall dedicated to his father's victims. There'd been hundreds of stone plinths spread around the edge, reserved for the Pyramid dead. Most had boasted a 'triangled' rack of human bones: a pelvic girdle as the base surrounded by leg and arm bones, with the ribcage atop that and the skull bolted through the sternum, empty eyes staring down. To accompany each plinth a self-portrait painting had hung on the wall.

Now the bones were long gone. Repatriated to whatever family members they had left in the world, consecrated and buried. The plinths had been ground up industrially and poured into the concrete mix that filled the chambers below. Wren hadn't had the heart to destroy the self-portraits, though, a record of the Pyramid's last deed before they self-immolated, so he'd walled them off.

Now the space was bright and clean, and contained three interspersed metal cages, each twenty feet square. Within each square was a bed, a chair, a toilet, a shower, a desk, a TV, a cupboard and chest of drawers. Between each cage were various themed zones. One held gym equipment, one served as a small-scale cinema. There was a crafts area, a small library, a few desktop computers with passive Internet access enabled, a tight little kitchen.

Wren's heart beat so hard he thought he might be sick.

She was sitting at the crafts desk, head bent over in concentration, looking just as she always had; dressed in browns, tans and ochres in layers of scarfs and cardigans like desiccated petals around a dried desert rose. Her right arm showed the same burn marks of napalm he wore on his face.

He walked up. She was working on a jigsaw puzzle, looked to be of the White House. Her pale left hand turned a piece thoughtfully. The puzzle was almost done, and after a long moment she found the place it belonged and slotted it in. Then she looked up at Wren.

Her green eyes dug into him. There was no surprise there, only supreme, maybe mocking confidence. She didn't look any different than when he'd last faced her in the chambers below, though her tan had faded from the months spent underground.

X herself. Maggie. Grace.

"Brother," she said warmly. "I've been waiting."

5

MAGGIE

Wren threw the table.

Jigsaw pieces flew through the air, fell in a pattering rain. The table soared twenty feet and hit one of the cages with a metallic clang, crashed noisily to the ground.

Maggie didn't budge an inch and didn't show any sign of fear. Instead she calmly interlaced her fingers and laid them atop her lap.

"I found our brothers," Wren said. The words came hard. "On an abandoned oil platform in the Pacific. The whole thing was rigged to blow."

Maggie tilted her head. "Gabriel and Zachariah. I assume they're dead."

It took everything Wren had to channel his anger into words. "They're dead. These cages," he pointed. "They'll stay empty. You'll be on your own, Maggie, until you die."

Maggie said nothing for a long moment, just regarded him coolly. "I like the silence. I find peace in prayer. Perhaps something you should try, Pequeño 3."

Wren felt himself boiling over. Ever since the platform

blew, he'd been holding it in. Saving it up. Now he wanted to rip her apart with his bare hands, shred the information out of her.

"That's not my name and you know it."

"Neither is Maggie my name."

"So I should call you Grace? Maybe X?"

She studied him. "I can see you're in pain, brother. I assume you lost people in this raid. Our brothers mined the platform to sink, I expect?"

"Don't ask like you don't know. That was your work. It all is. Yes, I lost people."

Maggie shifted her hands on her knees. Perhaps there was a glint of smugness in her eyes. "I'd say I'm sorry, brother, but I'm not. Whoever died on that platform, they were not worth one hundredth of our brothers. I'm glad they will sink to the ocean floor, skulls forever facing down, to serve them even in death."

Wren sucked in a breath, held it. Knuckles whitening, aching to let loose on her perfect, kindly face.

"It won't work," he said.

"What? This transparent attempt to enrage you?" She looked pointedly to the table.

"I'd say it is working."

"You want me to kill you. That way you'll be with him."

Maggie smiled. "I'd prefer to burn. We could go together. Finish the job you started." She looked toward the kitchen. "I've checked very carefully, though. There's not a flammable speck in this entire dungeon."

"I can outsource it."

She turned back. "Would you?"

A fraught moment passed. Wren forced his knuckles to unclench, then found the nearest chair and righted it, sat down.

She looked at him and he looked at her.

"Impressive," Maggie mocked. "What a show of restraint."

Wren ignored that. "Gabriel said something, before he had his head smashed in when the platform toppled. That I wasn't ready for what's coming." He paused, looking into her eyes. "What's coming?"

"A resurrection."

Wren sneered. "Bullshit. Our father's dead, and he isn't coming back. So what has he planned?"

A small smile crept across her face. "We used to sit like this, when we were children. Do you remember? Across a mud pit filled with sand and seeds. We'd look each in the eyes until somebody laughed, then they'd have to dunk in the mud."

Wren barely remembered that. Parts of it, maybe. "The plan, Maggie."

"Call me by my real name," she said, suddenly cold.

"Fine. Grace. Does that make you happy?"

"You take direction well."

"As do you," he countered. "You've settled well into your dungeon. I thought I might find you in a corner, swaying back and forth like some mad animal in a zoo. You're a creature of the sun and the sand, Grace. This has to be killing you."

She spread her hands slightly, a tiny shrug. "On the contrary, it's more dangerous for you, *Christopher*, to keep me here." She emphasized his name. "This is a place of tremendous power."

"Tremendous BS. What's coming, Grace? You ever want to see the sky again, you start talking."

Grace regarded him coolly. "You're afraid."

"Call it concerned."

"I'll call it terror. Of what's out there. Of how our father made you feel. Of losing control like that again."

Wren leaned closer. "So give me nightmares, Grace. Dazzle me with the horrors to come."

Her head tilted slightly. "You always acted this way, in the desert. When you were afraid, you turned to mockery. Our father, our brothers, none escaped your wit." She smiled. "But I know you, Pequeño 3, like nobody else in this world. I know your fear, because I'm right in there with you." She pointed at his head. "Little Grace, trapped in amber. Tell me, do you still have nightmares of me lying in the bottom of that pit?"

He felt the heat rising to his face and tried to push it back. "I tried to save you. I'm still trying."

She smiled. "It's sweet. But there will be no salvation. No escape from the devastation that is coming. The end of this country as you know it."

Wren said nothing.

The silence felt oppressive, but there was nothing to say. Nothing to reason with. Only madness, looking into those bright green eyes. Eyes he'd once trusted implicitly. Eyes he'd dreamed of for decades, staring back at him glassy in death.

"The same old song," he said softly.

"Because it isn't over. Our father's death wasn't the end."

Wren straightened. Shaking off the welter of emotions as best he could. There was no point arguing with her. "You're a liar. You were raised by a liar. Nothing's coming. Doomsday cults always push the date back. That's all this is."

She shrugged. "So go in peace, Christopher. Enjoy these last days. It won't matter. You'll come and beg for my help in the end. We'll sit here again, just like when we were children, and the truth will remain the same as ever: you are not in control. You're helpless. You can't protect anyone."

Wren stood. He looked slowly around the dungeon, at the table and the empty cells and the scattered jigsaw pieces, and finally back to Maggie. He still saw in her the little girl she'd once been, and it broke his heart. He'd known her for weeks only, back when he was just seven years old. After that, the Apex had kept her for decades. This is what you got.

"I was never helpless," he said. "Goodbye, Grace."

6

DESERT

The Lakota was waiting where he'd left it, but Wren was in no fit state to fly. Maggie's chill had bitten into him, and he couldn't just take off and flit away as if that feeling wasn't real.

"You can go," he said to the pilot, and kept walking. At the exterior gate through the encircling fence, he signaled for the guard to open up.

The guy looked up from his comic book, confused. "There's nothing out there," he said. "A hundred miles of nothing."

Wren knew it better than anyone. The Apex had built his town far from the mirror of civilization. Alone out here, his people had no recourse and no escape from his overwhelming presence. Though he was dead, Wren felt him everywhere now; in the sand, in the breeze, and it sickened him.

"It'll be fine," he said, his voice thick and guttural, heart pounding still. The same words he'd said to Henry.

The guy shrugged, then pressed the button. "Just be careful, OK? I hear there's snakes, scorpions, all kinds of lethal critters out there."

Wren almost laughed. The gate opened and he stepped out.

The desert stretched as far as the eye could see. It was vast and baking and empty. No people, no places, no refuge. Always he'd fled to the wild spaces, as a child. He'd never once attempted to leave, though, not even after the Pyramid thousand were left smoking in the ruins, and little Pequeño 3 alone had wandered between them for hours.

It was too far. No one could make it on foot.

He started to run.

The desert barely moved around him, though steadily the town and the fence receded, like a hometown port vanishing over the horizon as the ship set sail. Sand crunched underfoot. The sun beat down on his face.

He ran for hours, keeping a steady, loping pace. Three hours passed, four. Already he'd covered a marathon's worth of distance, twenty-plus miles, but he couldn't stop there. the fire still burned inside him. The anger that he couldn't shake.

He barely watched the sky, the sand, the dirt trail, the sun as it swung overhead. He barely thought. He just ran.

With every mile gone nothing was resolved. He felt no better. No clearer. Henry was still dead. All his brothers and sisters were still dead. He ran until his toes throbbed in his boots, and the sun stung his exposed neck and cheeks, as if he could outrun the tidal wave of the past.

As the sun steadily sank toward the land ahead, it all finally caught up to him. He dropped to his knees in the sand and wept.

He hadn't cried after killing his father. He hadn't stopped once to let the emotions sweep over him; even the time spent with his kids and wife in the fake town had been tight and guarded, because his brothers had still been out there. The threat had still felt very real.

Now they were all gone. Only Maggie remained.

After the fit passed, he lay back in the sand looking up at the sky. Constellations were starting to shine through, as the blue of day turned purple. He just lay there and breathed for a long time, looking around at his surroundings as if for the first time.

Against all seeming odds, life was springing up in the desert. It was April, the thick of spring in the Sonora, and sprays of yellow-headed brittlebushes popped like sea foam off orange waves. Red apricot mallow wildflowers sang a symphony amongst low green fishhook barrel cacti, themselves trumpeting poppy-red blooms.

It was beautiful. It was undeniably, achingly real.

Wren unsheathed his knife, rolled over to a batch of squat hedgehog cacti and set to shaving the spines and outer skin off five of their thumb-like stems. Sticky juice ran down the blade. He sliced the first off at the base then brought it up to his lips, slurping the fleshy meat off the core like corn on the cob.

His palate lit up with moisture and the faint sweet taste.

He ate two more of the cacti thumbs then rose again to his feet. His body ached, but strangely he felt refreshed, like clean air after a storm over their old New York home, blowing away the smog. He began to walk. Soon enough the sun went down, and the chill of night came as a relief. His sunburned skin breathed easier. He took off his shoes and continued barefoot, navigating by the stars.

The desert came alive around him, lit silver by a gibbous moon. Packrats squabbled noisily in the scrub grass, and the eyes of a bobcat glowed in the distance, trying to discern if he was predator or prey. Elf owls hooted. Leaf-nosed bats swooped on fluttering bugs. Cottontail rabbits scampered through the sage bushes.

By sun-up he reached the edge of the wilderness. A mid-sized town awaited him; one he didn't even know the name of. On the outskirts stood a clump of fast-food joints with tall revolving pole signs, a vehicle rental place and a Big Eastern Inn. He checked into the Inn, panting, sweat-stained and dusty.

"You look like you dug yourself out of a shallow grave," said the woman on reception as she took his deposit.

"That's pretty much it," Wren said with a smile.

Via room service he ordered waffles, bacon and syrup two times. He showered, ate, placed an order for a Jeep at the rental place, then crashed out on his still-made bed before the clock hit noon.

He slept long and without dreams. At some point in the night he woke, famished and dehydrated, and drank half a gallon of Gatorade from a vending machine, ordered a two-pound steak with salad and fries, demolished it then crashed out again.

Still no dreams came.

In the morning he felt better. His body ached and his feet were sore, but those were on the surface only. On a deeper level, he felt ready to move on. Not perfect, of course. Henry's staring eyes were a part of him, now. Maggie's, too. But at least the crushing sense of his father's presence was gone, and he could breathe again.

The rental Jeep was waiting for him.

His first stop was the town's Walmart to buy new clothes. He changed in the fitting room, tugging off his stained black strike suit and pulling on blue jeans with a thick-buckled leather belt, brown cowboy boots, a snug red and white check shirt.

In the full-length mirror he looked like a different man. A civilian.

Back in the Jeep he set off, listening to the radio news.

There were no attacks. No viral atrocities. The country was placid, still soothing itself after the events of X. State-wide elections were coming up nationwide, to replace the senators and congresspeople lost in the firestorm, but the campaigns were marked by their decency. The new president was called Jacinda Ablas, the ex-Attorney General, and it seemed she was finding her feet. The country seemed to be standing at her back.

There were no dirty tricks. No foul play. No demonization of the other candidates. It felt like the storm had finally passed.

Wren spun the dial to music, something Country-flavored, and lit out west. He had a curious urge to see the sea. Over three days he took the journey slow, absorbing the sights and sounds along the way. He stopped off at the Grand Canyon and peered down into its depths. He stopped at Bryce Canyon and admired the dam. He piled quarters into slots in Vegas alongside the blue-haired grannies. He drank in a bar off the Strip, avoiding places that showed the news on TV, and sampled his first real R and R in years.

Not recognized. Not feared or cheered. Not racing somewhere or fleeing something.

Still no threats emerged, despite what Grace had said. In an Internet café off the Strip he logged into his darknet, but there was nothing there to worry about, only Teddy's usual clockwork structure, coin meetings, and preparations for future arrangements. They were working on new force-projection tools and techniques, and Wren signed off on something called an Attack Crate 2.0, only vaguely aware of what it contained. Of most interest to him, there were no leads on the Pyramid's funding. No sign of forces mounting in the darkness.

He swapped his boots for sandals and his jeans for baggy cargo shorts, and fit right in with the rest of the tourists in Sin City. He caught a big band show, watched a magic act, then got back in the Jeep and kept on driving until he hit LA.

Grumman's Chinese Theater had always been one of his favorite places. He caught a flick, something about Ragnarok with superheroes punching each other through buildings, then went down to Venice Beach and just looked at the waves for a long time.

The fear was largely gone from people's eyes, he'd noticed. They were uncertain still, but the shifty glances, the double-checking every face as it drew near, that was fading. With his phone gone, no urgent messages streamed in. No barrage of coin meeting requests. It was just Wren and the civilian world. Food, drink, entertainment, rest, and maybe that was OK. For the first time in years, he was starting to feel good about the future.

It was time to go home and see his family.

He drove to LAX, dropped the Jeep off, and this time bought a civilian ticket on a civilian plane headed for New York, onward to Delaware. First class, because why not spoil himself, after all this time? Briefly, at the ticket counter and through check-in, he was worried about being recognized. Even using one of his many fake IDs, with his burn marks and his unkempt hair and beard, he still looked a little like the Christopher Wren who'd been on TV so much in recent months.

It helped that many people were wearing masks. Some kind of pandemic was coming on, though Wren had barely noticed. Wearing one made him feel like a bandit, hidden in plain sight.

Mid-May, three and a half months after he'd burned his father alive beneath the Sonoran Desert, he boarded a 787 at the first passenger call, carrying no luggage except a good book to read, the latest by Stephen King. Heading home to see his kids. To see Loralei. Maybe make a play at winning her back from the guy she'd shacked up with, some kind of 'Dork Squad' multimedia installation guy.

How hard could that be?

He'd think about the rest of it later. Right now, all he wanted was to relax into his spacious seat in his first class-booth, open up his crisp new book and dig in, oblivious to any threats lurking out there in the dark.

7

787

Wren read. It was a great book, engrossing from the start, though nothing much was happening. Small town antics, but wasn't that what King did best? The plane took off and he barely noticed. Out of LA, out of California and heading east, so absorbed in turning the pages that he unconsciously blanked the air steward who offered him champagne, didn't hear the announcement for seatbelts coming off, and only surfaced when a kid poked him in the face with a sticky finger of cucumber.

It took a long second to register.

He looked up from the book just in time to see a mischievous face duck down behind the wall of his booth. Maybe seven years old, couldn't tell if it was a boy or a girl, curly mop of sandy blond hair.

"That's strange," Wren mused to himself loudly. "I could've sworn someone just poked me with a cucumber."

The giggling was audible.

"Guess I better go back to my book, then."

He did. Aware all the time of the cucumber drawing in. The kid shuffling around the booth wall. Taking up position. Preparing to strike.

Strike.

Wren let the cucumber hit him in the temple. Ignored it. It came again, this time more boldly. On the third time Wren nimbly shifted his head, pulled down his mask and neatly bit the cucumber almost down to the little fingers holding it, then went right back to his book.

The hand pulled back, a moment passed, then laughter erupted from behind the screen, followed by two heads popping up over the booth wall. Siblings, both floppy-haired, looked seven and six.

"How did you do that?" the elder asked.

Wren frowned. "Do what?"

"Eat the cucumber!"

"Eat what? I'm just sitting here reading my book."

"Na-ah, you ate it. He ate it!"

Wren chewed.

"There! You're eating it now. Give it back."

Wren swallowed, opened his mouth to show there was nothing. "Sorry, all gone. You didn't want me to eat it, you shouldn't have put it in my mouth."

The older kid looked scandalized. The younger one collapsed into gurgling chuckles.

"Magic," Wren said, did jazz hands.

"Oh my days, there you are!" came a woman's voice, warm Southern accent drawing in fast along the aisle. "What did I tell you about wandering off? Rania you should know better, and Hendrix, you shouldn't be listening to your sister, you certainly shouldn't be bothering some perfectly innocent person, I'm so-"

She breasted the edge of Wren's booth and looked down at him, clearly about to apologize, but something about him stopped her cold. For a long second, she stared at him, the light of recognition guttering in her eyes.

"It's fine, really-" Wren began, at the same time that she said:

"I'm so sorry, they're just-"

They both paused. Wren smiled at the awkwardness. She made a put-upon face, now clutching both her wayward children by their hands. She was mid-thirties, with a fringe of wavy black hair creeping out from beneath a maroon headscarf, freckled tan cheeks and soft hazel eyes, wearing a pale olive blouse with suspiciously grubby palm marks on the shoulders. Wren knew all about kids and their sticky little hands.

"Honestly, it's no problem," Wren said. "In fact, I think I've come out on top in this exchange. One of your kids gave me one of my five-a-day."

Her jaw dropped slightly. "No! He's not been poking you with a cucumber, has he?"

"Not anymore."

Now a blush came on her cheeks, around the edges of the mask. Wren found himself thinking, curiously enough, how pretty it made her look. "That is atrocious. Rania! No ice cream for you. I'm serious. And I'm really sorry, Mr., uh…"

She trailed off. Her kids burbled and kicked by her side, barely visible over the booth's wall. Wren waited for how she wanted to play it.

"It's you, isn't it?" she asked slowly, lowering her voice.

Wren kept his voice low too. "If you won't tell, neither will I."

She kept staring. Then, curiously, her eyes began to mist up. He'd never have seen that coming.

"Hey, it's OK," he said. Not sure what he was comforting her over, but still.

"It is now," she said, then abruptly thrust one hand over the booth's low wall, hand out. "My name's Amira Matheson. I'm not anyone really, but if you're ever in Texas, look me up." She beamed. "I mean, not now obviously, we're going to Washington, big field trip, and-"

"Big field trip!" her two kids called in chorus.

"Right, but if you're in Texas we could have you over to our place, we'd be honored."

Wren just smiled. "The honor would be mine. Thank you, Amira. Maybe I'll bring my own cucumber slices, get some revenge."

She laughed high and loud. "Yes, maybe! Cucumber, ha ha. I'll prepare a dueling ground! Or not actually a dueling ground, that's a joke, you don't want to really duel, I mean-" she stopped, took a breath. Composed herself. Extended her hand further. "Thank you. I don't think you know what you did. Putting that man away? We're grateful."

Wren took her hand and shook it. It was warm, firm and ever-so-slightly sticky. "No one's happier about that than me. Thank you, Amira. I'm Chris. No one special, either, and at least three coins minus in my own Foundation."

She let out a single braying laugh, then pulled her hand back to cover her mouth like she'd just cursed out a sleeping baby. Her cheeks burned red, her eyes turned frantic, and Wren couldn't help but grin like a fool.

"Really, you've made my day," he said. "Please don't feel embarrassed. This was fun." Wren eyed Rania. Extended his hand. "Truce?"

The kid put her hand in Wren's, and they shook. "Truce for now."

"Shake my hand too!" Hendrix hooted.

Wren did so.

"I'm coming back with carrots," Rania said quietly, but not so quiet that her mother didn't hear.

"We are *not* coming back with carrots! Under no circumstances. There will be absolutely no-"

"We have carrots," Rania whispered at Wren. "We've got them in a bag."

"Two of my five a day," Wren whispered back. "Sounds delicious."

"Alright, enough of this," Amira said hurriedly, "we'll leave you in peace. Now come along you two, let's leave the nice man alone."

She gave Wren a long-suffering eye roll as she pulled away. He knew exactly how that felt, and it was nice to be included. Part of their family drama for the moment. The kids warbled their way back down the aisle. Wren sat with an unexpected smile on his face, unable to wipe it away.

Had that been flirting? He wasn't sure. It had been so long. She was pretty, and the whole thing left a foolish grin on his face, but…

"I'm sorry," she said, re-appearing abruptly over the rim of his booth. "I know this is strange, but do you think I could talk to you, later? I mean, of course, if you have time. After we land. Just a coffee. The kids can play their games. I just…"

She trailed off, and Wren saw something different in her eyes now.

"What is it?"

"It's nothing. Just. I'm sorry to ask. Would that be OK?"

Wren smiled softly. Didn't want to pry. "Of course. We'll get a coffee."

The relief that spread over her features stung. He couldn't say why. "Thank you. OK. Well, enjoy your book."

She hurried after her kids.

Wren didn't know what to think. Sat there holding the book, thinking nothing, really. From flirting to something else. He had no idea what. Maybe she was facing a stalker, an abusive husband, something like that. Something he could help with. It left him feeling oddly sad, like he'd just glimpsed something good, and now it was gone.

He was going home to his family, anyway. Except they weren't really his family, anymore, were they? His kids, sure. His wife, technically. She hadn't sent over divorce papers yet.

He looked out of the window. At forty-thousand feet there was nothing but white clouds below and blue sky all around. No answers out there, either. Two hours or so into the flight, three hours remaining to New York. A coffee. A transfer to Delaware. A motel somewhere near his wife's duplex, where he'd wait to be summoned, spending the rest of his days trying not to think about Henry.

Something gray flitted through the cloud cover below, and he tracked it absently. Looked like a bird darting in and out of white cotton candy, but of course, birds didn't fly this high.

Birds didn't get that large.

Wren refocused as the gray shape grew in size. Then a second appeared, flying in formation. Birds certainly didn't do that. All other thoughts fell from his mind. This was something that didn't belong outside the window at all, under almost any circumstances.

A pair of steel-gray F-15 Eagle fighter jets, drawing in fast.

8

F-15

Wren stared at the jets in disbelief. He blinked, but they didn't disappear.

He knew their spec down to the ground. McDonnell Douglas F-15 Eagles, designed for air superiority and bearing that out with no air battles lost, ever. Gunship gray all-metal frames with a semi-monocoque fuselage, the exterior skin supporting its structural integrity. High wings, high speed, high-altitude; the muscle car of the skies, packing some combination of air-to-air Sparrow missiles, Sidewinders or an internal Vulcan Gatling gun.

Now they were here, and it made no sense.

Twin top-end fighter jets flanking a commercial plane over US airspace was almost unheard of. The only other reason to send up jets was to bring a plane down, and the only reason to do that was to get to a passenger on board.

Wren's heart skipped a beat.

Was this what Gabriel had been hinting at? A terror attack from the air?

He stood up and looked around. There was no general alarm yet, but there would be soon. No guys standing up either, holding knives or suicide vests, calling out 'Allahu Akbar' before making a run for the cockpit.

Wren scanned right into the darkened steward's galley, beyond which was the auto-locked door to the cockpit. He considered trying to convince the captain to let him in and use the radio, use his CIA connections to send up a comms flare and find out what the threat was, but there was no way. They'd never open the door for him; he had no authority on this flight, his CIA badge would carry no weight, and he didn't even look like the guy he'd be claiming to be.

He briefly considered force, but dismissed it immediately. After 9/11 all air stewards underwent at least four hours of self-defense training, mandated by the TSA. Not a problem for Wren, but it meant an escalation of violence against the wrong people, just when they'd need to focus on the real problem at hand.

He started walking left instead, along the starboard aisle and swiftly passing through the curtain into Business class, where some ten rows of faces lay ahead. Men and women sat in their seats with the tray-backs down, tapping on laptops or talking on phones, oblivious to the brewing danger.

No eyes rose to meet his. There was no squirrelly looking terrorist-to-be that he could see, none of the tell-tale signs: profuse sweating, obvious vigilance, overly baggy clothes concealing a weapon or bomb.

Fifteen seconds gone already, and soon someone was going to see those fighter jets and raise the alarm, after which point any terrorists on-board would activate.

Wren sped up and pushed through the curtain to Economy. Here the plane's body stretched right back, a nineteen-foot-wide metal tube soaring through the air at six hundred miles per hour. Maybe thirty rows at eight seats abreast, four in the middle block flanked by two aisles, stocked with hundreds of people: all ages, races, types under the dimmed lighting. Couples held hands while they watched seat-back TV, old guys napped under blankets, kids wrestled across their parents' laps, a middle-aged guy drank tequila.

Wren rapidly dismissed people section-by-section as he walked along, using the pattern analysis skills he'd honed over a long anti-terror career. None of the signs here. None of the signs there. He passed Amira and her kids on his left; she raised a hand in greeting with a confused look on her face.

He gave her the slightest nod and kept walking, expecting a seatbelt order to come down any second, with stewards ready to enforce it. The jets would have spoken to the captain by now. The captain would know what or who they were looking for. Most likely the air marshal would have already been alerted.

Strange, then, that there was no movement of any kind, except for the first few people staring out the portholes. Wren reached the rear of the plane and stopped by the toilets, scanning the backs of heads all the way to the Business class divider. Nobody stood up. No weapons were brandished. Wren glanced out the oval windows and saw one of the F-15s dropping low to hang in the 787's shadow.

He turned to the other side, where the second jet was climbing out of sight. Looked like a forced escort formation; no easier way to corral a big plane than top and tail it like that. The 787 couldn't go up, couldn't go down, couldn't make a turn for fear its wingtips would strike one of the F-15s and shear.

Like a sheep in the wolf's jaws.

A minute gone, and now voices were raising in alarm. Wren ignored them and kept scanning as a sinking feeling settled upon him. Nothing about this felt good. The old Paul Newman poker quote came to mind: if you were looking around and couldn't figure out who the sucker was, it was probably you.

Only one way to find out.

He crossed to the port aisle and started back down the cabin, searching for the one person who could shake loose some answers: the air marshal.

The most likely candidate was a swarthy guy he'd spotted by the port wing, matching another set of behaviors: seated either at the front, back, over a wing or by a door; usually somewhere with extra legroom; often a vacant seat beside them and wearing a jacket whether hot or cold, with a conspicuous bulge under the shoulder, if you knew how to spot it.

Wren drew up to the guy, mid-forties with a paunch and a glazed look in his eye, and saw several plastic cups at his feet. A closer look revealed several miniature bottles of whisky tucked in his seatback holder, likely plundered from an LA hotel's mini fridge.

Drunk. Not the air marshal.

Wren turned and fixed on the second-best candidate. An athletic-looking woman in seat 54A, all the way to the rear of the plane. Far from the cockpit, too, but you didn't need to oversee the pilot's security like you used to, with secure door locks. What mattered more now was situational awareness, and there was no better awareness than a place where you could look at everyone from behind.

She was already on her feet, standing out in the aisle. Dark-skinned, shaven head and thin boned, 5' 11" with an elfin face that placed her at no more than twenty-three, barely out of the TSA training center in Artesia, New Mexico. She wore a dark gray jacket with matching suit pants. No noticeable bulge under her arm, but an ankle holster was a possibility.

Wren smiled and advanced toward her, subtly holding his open palms where she could see them. She made no defensive move but waited as he approached. The fasten seatbelts sign clicked on and the pilot came on the PA, gave some milquetoast announcement about being redirected for a mid-flight landing, nothing to worry about and they'd be en route again soon.

It didn't do much to calm people down, but they stayed in their seats and clicked their seat belts; all except Wren and the woman.

He stopped two yards away. Plenty of room for her to feel comfortable.

"They didn't warn you," he said.

"Warn me about what?" she answered. Her voice was husky and tinged with a Texan accent.

"This fighter jet escort." He gestured up then down. "They're F-15 Eagles, must've been launched out of Peterson in Colorado, Altus in Oklahoma or Sheppard in Texas." He checked his watch. "We're halfway into a five-hour flight, so I figure Altus or Sheppard, somewhere over Texas or Oklahoma." He lowered his voice. "You're the air marshal, correct?"

She said nothing. That was a kind of confirmation.

"If you're out of the loop, I'm not filled with confidence about their intentions. But I can help. I'm a CIA agent, Force Recon by training, with connections in the Air Force. If you can get me on the radio up front, I can run a question to the top of the flagpole in minutes, get us an answer about what's going on here. Try to de-escalate before somebody pulls a trigger that can't get unpulled."

The woman just stared. Made no move to pull her weapon from a shoulder or ankle holster. "Sir, I've just watched you casing the whole plane. If anybody's giving me cause for concern right now, it's you."

She reached into her pocket and smoothly pulled out a chunky black smartphone. She raised it up in her left hand, brought her right hand in to work it then in a swift, confounding movement it became a gun.

Wren's jaw dropped a little. She held the 'gun' low at her hip and pointing at his belly. He mentally unpacked the movement she'd just made; with the bottom half swept out, it converted to a pistol grip.

"That's the Cellphone Pistol," he blurted.

He'd heard about this kind of concealed-carry weapon, but never seen one. Looked like twin .38 caliber barrels on a slim but chunky frame. It really had looked like a cell phone, but Wren had no doubt it fired real bullets.

"It's called an Ideal Conceal," she corrected, low and calm. "Now, as the air marshal aboard this flight, I'm going to need you to sit down here, sir, and we'll see what we can do about achieving that de-escalation."

She slid back into her own seat by the window, sat down and waited.

Wren sat down beside her, feeling impressed. She'd gotten the jump on him with the cell phone gun. She had the jump on him still, gun barrel pointed point-blank at his stomach.

"Seatbelt," she said.

Wren pulled his seatbelt on.

"Now turn away from me slowly, hands behind your back, and I'll ensure no triggers get pulled."

Impressive sangfroid. Wren almost laughed, then turned slowly in his seat. Only thing to do when someone had you at gunpoint. "My name's Christopher Wren," he tried. "You might have heard of me. I've got a direct access line to the Director of the CIA." She said nothing, busying herself with one-handedly pulling out a pair of plastic cuffs. "I've got CIA ID in my pocket; you can check it."

The air marshal snorted, slipped the first cuff around Wren's left wrist and cinched it tight. It felt like a modified zip tie, still warm from the heat of her body. "You're saying you're the Big Bad Bird?" She peered at the side of his face. "I don't see it. You're a little too haggard."

She had a real dry way about her. "So I've let myself go, picked up some burn scars, but it's me. I'm not the threat here. I may even be the target."

That took her a few seconds. It didn't produce the reaction he'd expected. Rather than pulling the pistol away, she pushed it into his hip.

"Turn back around," she commanded. He did, and she looked into his eyes, weighing him in the balance. "It is you, isn't it? The ungrateful son."

Wren blinked. 'Ungrateful son' was a term only used by one group of people, and they didn't much like Wren. Of all the air marshals in all the world, he had to bump into one who'd been part of his father's BS cult?

"You're a follower of X?"

She shrugged, eyes flickering with a hint of controlled anger. "Not a follower. He had some good things to say."

"You mean X? First up, she was a woman," he corrected. "And what good things, burn yourself alive?"

The air marshal's eyes widened slightly "She? That makes me like her more, honestly. But no, not the burning." She looked uncertain for a moment. "That was just a metaphor, really, that some people carried too far. There's plenty of good things she said. About the system being broken. About how the only way to force change, sometimes, is being willing to die for a cause."

A tense moment passed. Wren looked in her brown eyes and wasn't sure what he saw.

"I can assure you, it wasn't just a metaphor. People were really burning, because they really believed, and that's really what X wanted. So I'll ask you straight. Are you with these jets? Package deal to bring me in?"

She frowned. "I have no idea what those jets are doing. In any case, it's nothing to do with me."

Wren frowned, recalculating. If she was with them, that was an odd lie to tell. She had him at gunpoint already; villains infamously liked to explain their whole plot, when they had the 'hero' at their mercy. "OK. Then this is all very far from procedure, wouldn't you agree? As the air marshal on board, you should have been notified they were inbound. But you weren't, were you?"

She said nothing, just glared at him.

"That's gotta be setting off alarm bells," he went on. "You want to keep on cuffing me, that's your prerogative, but I may be your best chance to get ahead of whatever this thing is."

Her smooth brows needled together. "What do you think 'this thing' is?"

Wren thought fast. "Right now, I'm concerned they might be here for me. Threats have been leveled against me, and this could be part of that plot. Some faction of our government believes in X a little more than you, and now they're taking that show on the road, going extra-judicial. It wouldn't be the first time." He paused a moment, reading her expression. "Can you think of any other reason you haven't been called on?"

She stared. "You don't know it's extra-judicial."

"Then why weren't you notified? The order to launch those jets most likely went out soon after we left LA. They've had the best part of three hours to warn you. But they haven't."

The moment stretched out.

"Tell me one thing," she said. "X. Is she dead?"

Wren tilted his head slightly, absorbing that change of direction. "I was just with her. She's fine. Doing jigsaws in a black-site jail."

"And the Apex?"

"You saw his trial, like everyone else. He's in Guantanamo."

She nudged him with the barrel of the gun. "Tell the truth."

Wren barely skipped a beat. "He's dead. Burned alive the day it all went down. I saw to that myself."

A long second played out, then she pulled the gun back. "I liked X, not the Apex. It's good you differentiated."

Wren let out a pent-up breath. He'd never been so happy for differentiating. The air marshal folded the gun so it looked like a cell phone again, then slipped it back into her pocket without breaking eye contact.

Just then the 787 banked right, dropping into a sharp dive. Cries called out through the cabin.

"We're entering a dive," Wren said. "They're taking us down. Question is, to where, and what for?"

The air marshal rose to her feet. "Let's go find out."

9

CALL

The air marshal led the way down the port aisle, both of them staggering and grasping seatbacks as the plane's dive steepened.

"This is too fast," Wren said.

She just shot him a glance and kept on.

Passengers clung to their armrests, faces pale. Several children were crying. Somewhere a man heaved his guts into a tiny vomit bag, and the air blanched with the acrid stench. Wren looked over, saw the guy with the hotel whisky bottles clutching the bag to his lips, heaving again.

Off to the right, Amira was half-standing in her seat.

"What's happening?" she called across the central block of seats.

"This is the air marshal," Wren said, raising his voice. "Everything's going to be OK, I promise. We're going to get some answers."

The marshal kept on. Wren followed through the curtain back to Business Class then First Class and right up to the Flight Steward's galley.

The marshal strode confidently up to a steward with bright pink hair, a nose piercing and the hint of a neck tattoo, strapped into the side-facing fold-down seat by the PA phone. The purser, Wren figured, head steward.

"Air marshal," the steward said, eyes uncertain but trying to mask it. "Is everything all right?"

"I'd like to speak to the captain."

The steward gulped. "You can't. The cockpit's been locked down."

The marshal frowned. "On whose orders?"

"All I know is that's what the captain said."

"So unlock it. This is a security matter, and that means I have command. Open the cockpit."

The purser shifted in her seat, clearly uncomfortable. "That's what he said you'd say. I'm sorry. Apparently, we're under DoD control, now?"

The marshal stared.

Wren stepped up.

"Can we at least speak to the captain?"

"I, uh-"

Wren took another step, lifted the PA phone off its cradle. "Don't know why I'm asking, actually," he said, then lifted the handset to his mouth. "Testing."

His voice rang throughout the cabin.

"You can't do that," the purser said. "That's a system for stewards only, you-"

"You realize we're flanked by F-15 fighter jets," Wren interrupted, one hand muffling the handset. "I hate to be dramatic, but that's an unusual situation at the best of times. Unusual situations require communication, wouldn't you agree?"

He turned back to study the keypad beside the phone's cradle but saw no obvious way to link through to the cockpit. That checked out; if the captain couldn't hear potential terrorists on board, he couldn't be swayed by hostage demands.

"Who is this man?" the steward asked.

"He's with me," the marshal answered.

"Cockpit code, now," Wren said.

The steward stared blankly up at him. "What?"

"I want to talk to the cockpit, what's the code?"

"What? I, um, don't have it. Like I said, we're locked down. I can't ring through. They can only contact us."

Wren cursed under his breath. Yes, that made sense too. The stewards couldn't be tortured to divulge something if they didn't know it.

Wren hung up the handset, took a breath.

"None of this is procedure," the marshal said. "There's no such thing as a remote lockdown of the cockpit when there's an air marshal on board."

"Extra-judicial," Wren said, "maybe off-book," then he turned to the steward. "I need a line out. Can you do that for me?"

Her face crumpled. "I can't, we're totally locked down. All the controls are located in the-"

"Cockpit," Wren finished.

A second passed.

The plane swerved rapidly left. Wren braced against the wall then took a few steps to peer out of the nearest porthole. The swift descent was easing off, and they were rushing through cloud cover now. Soon they'd be at ten thousand feet, and then...

The plane shifted again, a rightward jerk.

"We're coming in to land," Wren said, half to himself and half to the marshal. "At this rate we'll be on the ground in ten minutes."

She was watching him. The steward was looking at him too, as were the members of First Class. Wren took a step and pulled the galley curtain shut, the old quote rolling over in his head again: if you don't know who the sucker is, it's you.

He turned to the marshal and the purser. "Where are we right now?"

"Uh," said the steward. "I, uh..."

"Check the seatback system," the marshal offered.

Wren was already pushing back through the curtain, came back to his private booth in seconds. His Stephen King book lay in the footwell; must've tumbled there during their maneuvers. All in a couple of minutes only. He tapped the seatback screen to wake it, tried to page through to the flight map, but couldn't get it to appear.

Instead a single message appeared in white text on black.

Regular in-flight entertainment temporarily suspended.

That was one way to put it. His heart thumped and he pulled out of his booth, took three steps 'up' the steeply slanted plane to the next booth over, where a bespectacled man in a pink shirt was tapping at his tablet computer.

"May I?" Wren asked.

The guy frowned up at him. Some high-powered professional, maybe, perhaps a lawyer from the clipped precision in his eyes. "I hardly think-" he began, then stopped as his eyes darted to the side. The guy's demeanor shifted.

"Yes, officer."

The marshal was standing beside him, holding out her golden badge.

Wren took the tablet and tried to put a call through the guy's phone app. Nothing happened; the Wi-Fi was dead and clearly no calls were going out. Instead he found the maps app and opened it. The topographic map loaded; enough data held in the phone's passive memory to reproduce their last satellite-verified location.

Looked like Texas. The top horn of Texas, near Amarillo.

"Looks they're taking us to Sheppard Air Base," Wren

said, tapping out of the maps app and onto the guy's email program.

"Hey," the guy said, craning his neck to watch what Wren was doing, "that's my personal email."

Wren opened a new mail, typed in an address that would activate his Bullhorn app and send a message to everyone on his emergency list, every minute until someone responded, then typed fast.

AM ON COMMERCIAL BOEING 787 OVER AMARILLO TEXAS, BEING FORCED DOWN BY TWIN F-15 JETS, ESTIMATED TOUCHDOWN AT - he checked the time - 13:25 TO SHEPPARD AIR BASE. PLANE COMMS ARE LOCKED DOWN. GET ME LAWYERS, JOURNALISTS, FBI, GOVERNMENT ASSETS ON BOARD. THINK I'M ABOUT TO BE RENDITIONED.

He clicked send.

"It won't send," the marshal said, peering over his shoulder. "No signal."

"Not yet it won't," Wren said, and walked away, ignoring the guy's protests. He passed through the curtain to Business, opened one of the luggage racks and stowed the tablet securely between two suitcases.

"But it will when it reacquires signal?" the marshal asked, shadowing him.

"Exactly." Wren clicked the rack shut, then nodded toward the front of the jet. She nodded back, and they returned to the front of the plane, pulled the curtain shut and stood by the door away from the stewards.

"You really think these jets are coming for you?" she asked quietly.

Wren made a face. "You're X. Who do you think they're coming for?"

She made a face right back. "I said I'm not X. But if this is about you, I'll agree it looks unlawful."

"Unlawful's an understatement," Wren said. Through the portholes he saw the verdant green of northern Texas stretching away, fields packed with spring cotton, corn, sorghum, rice and wheat. He racked his mind, but he didn't know much about Sheppard Air Base, had never visited and didn't have any contacts there. He knew it was next to the mid-sized city of Wichita Falls, a couple hundred miles northwest of Dallas and right on the state line to Oklahoma, but that was about it. "This is either a case study in what not to do, taught at Annapolis for the next three generations, or it gets hushed up and buried forever, right along with me."

"If it's about you."

"Yeah, if."

The jet shifted angle sharply again, felt like coming in for the landing approach. Wren couldn't pick out clear geographical features, but Sheppard seemed about right.

"So what do you suggest?" the marshal asked.

Wren looked at her. "I'm not going quietly, if they're here for me. Where do you stand on that?"

"With my duty," she answered fast. Hardly an X thing to say. "My plane, my passengers, my responsibility. If they have the goods on you, I'll flip on a dime. They don't, they're not getting you easily. Either way, I'm not going to allow a hostage situation to develop here."

Wren smiled. She was seeing things clearly enough. "Me either. So here's what I propose. I get off the plane and out of your jurisdiction before any of that happens."

Her eyes flashed to the exit door. Widened. "Do you have a-"

"Chute? No. I've jumped out of enough planes recently. I was thinking more along the lines of the cargo bay."

10

E & E

The plane started shuddering madly as their fast descent stressed the superstructure. Wren stepped away from the marshal and looked at the floor in the dim light. The fuselage's underlying metal frame was coated with friction-burn gray carpeting, laid in squares he could just about discern.

"You think you can get into the cargo bay from the galley?" the marshal asked.

Wren dropped to one knee, started picking at the corner of one of the squares. "It's not only cabin crew and air marshals who got special TSA training after 9/11." He looked up. "This is a 787. You and I both know there's interior access to the nosecone cargo space. From there it's a simple drop to the blacktop."

"And if they've got the paperwork for your arrest? What then?"

"Then you say I overpowered you and ran."

She snorted, like that was an impossibility.

"Come hunt me down yourself, if you like," he added. "Show me what you've got."

"You better believe I will."

Wren refocused on the floor and pulled the first gray square away. It came with a ripping sound as tough Velcro strips unhooked, revealing dull iron-colored metal beneath.

"What are you doing?" the purser asked from her seat.

"Looking for the E & E bay," Wren said, and stripped another square, found more bare metal. "Electronics & Equipment. Unless you want to tell me where it is?"

Her eyes bugged. "I can't do that! And you can't go in there either, not mid-flight. The instrumentation is very delicate and-"

"What I thought," Wren said, then ripped another square free.

The pilot's voice came over the PA. "Cabin crew, prepare for landing."

"That's my cue," Wren said, and pulled another. This time the bare expanse of metal had a hatch embossed in the center; rectangular with rounded corners, marked out in red and white duct tape, with a recessed handle in the center.

Wren pushed the handle and it popped up.

"You have to stop what you're doing," the purser said. "You could endanger us all."

"Too late," Wren said, twisted the handle then pulled the hatch up. It released a gasp of cold air. The storage compartments below were pressurized, but on a different system to the main cabin, kept twenty degrees cooler. He rolled the hatch back on its hinge, greeted by an upward flow of cold air.

A white-runged ladder led down into the metal-floored E&E space, walled with blank instrumentation boxes, server racks and fuse arrays.

Wren felt cold steel touch his temple. Looked up to see the marshal had produced her cell phone gun again.

"Remind me why I'm helping you escape."

"You don't need me to remind you. You know why. This whole thing stinks."

She stared a moment longer, then sighed. "Then I go first. Touch one instrument panel down there and you're done."

"Deal," Wren said, and leaned back.

She started down the ladder. He followed her into the compact metal space, a tight fit for the two of them, and looked around.

The walls were a mishmash of dented metal plating, sealed blocks of electronic equipment bolted into racks and heavy fabric screens. Here and there were scrawled Sharpie marks: a couple of illicit comments from happy-go-lucky engineers; a few dated initials alongside notes on temperature, elevation and random hash keys. There were no display screens, but plenty of plugs to dock a mobile unit and interact with the E&E directly. If Wren could rig a hardline to his hackers, they could easily hotwire the whole jet; shame they were so out of reach.

The air marshal was staring at him, the cellphone pistol pointed at his face.

"Contained space," Wren said. "The ricochet could bust this place up good."

"I'll take my chances."

Wren grunted. She already was. "I don't even know your name."

"It's better this way. Just go. Don't make me regret it."

"Yes, ma'am."

Wren turned, searching for the panel he needed.

"It's there," the marshal said, pointing with the gun's barrel. "Slit in the fabric wall."

Wren focused on the sturdy fabric partition snugged neatly between two E&E racks. It was a long time since he'd drilled air terror scenarios, but it was all coming back to him. He reached one hand out slowly, not wanting to give her any excuse, and found the Velcro-ed slit. He brought his other arm slowly around and pulled the Velcro lips apart.

Another chill blast poured through the four-foot aperture. Still pressurized, but that would matter less now they were on final descent. Wren figured a couple of minutes until they were on the ground at Sheppard. He turned back to the marshal, who stood stock still with the gun trained on him.

"Good to meet you, Air Marshal. You're better than X."

"Yolanda Queen," she said. "My name. And I know what I'm worth."

"Yolanda," he repeated, savoring the sound. "From the Greek 'Iolanthe'. It means violet. It's beautiful."

Then he turned back and squeezed through the fabric wall, emerging into the nosecone cargo bay. It was a murky, irregularly shaped metal bay roughly as big as a shipping container, filled with luggage storage boxes in racks. There was barely space to squeeze by at the edges, but Wren started squeezing anyway, as a satisfying clunk and clank came from behind.

Yolanda Queen closing and locking the hatch behind him. Maybe putting the carpeting back in place. It might buy him some time.

He worked his way around the racks as the jet experienced a few rapid drops through air pockets, making his stomach jump like he was on a rollercoaster ride. The racks dug painfully into his ribs and side, then he reached the starboard side directly below the cockpit, beside the large inward bulge of the front wheel well. To his right lay the luggage access hatch. Looked like a whole section of the wall would lift up and out. There was a large red metal handle at both sides, and he tried them. They didn't turn, likely auto-locked until the plane hit ground.

That was OK. From the manic juddering of the undercarriage and the loud whine of the front wheel as it deployed mere inches away from his head, he figured they were about to land any second. He grabbed the nearest rack, dropped flat to his back and braced for landing.

11

SHEPPARD

The plane's rear wheels hit first with an incredible jolt, then there was the sickening three-second drop as the nosecone yawed to earth.

The landing gear crashed down, and Wren took the brunt of it like a hammer, reinforced by the explosion of sound. He bounced on the spot and squeezed the rack as the structure around the wheel-bay flexed, absorbing hundreds of tons worth of inertia.

The stink of burning rubber filled the air as the wheel shredded itself on a runway graded for much-lighter fighter jets. The metal boxes shook chaotically in their racks, the engines roared into full reverse and Wren jammed his hands over his ears.

The plane slowed.

The roaring dimmed.

The great machine came to a tentative halt, and Wren stood woozily in its metal belly, feeling dazed and shaken.

The engines whined down. He resisted coughing as the burned rubber stink filled the bay. Started plotting out next steps.

The red cargo bay door handle was cold and reassuringly

solid in his grip. He pushed, and now it shifted. The auto-locks were off. He swung it all the way to unlock with a clunk, then moved to the second. Turned it halfway, turned it a quarter more, and felt the latch ride the edge of opening. He released it by tiny increments further, and saw black runway through a slim crack.

At once he heard the sound of voices. There was a vehicle drawing up, too, but he couldn't tell direction. The exits were on the port side of the plane, though, and the nosecone cargo bay was on the starboard. That should help.

He opened the hatch a crack wider and dropped his head closer, trying to make out words. There was nothing to see other than the black smoking bulge of the shredded landing gear wheels, but some of the sound came in clearer as his ears adjusted to ground pressure.

Sounded like a big vehicle coming in, beeping loudly. Maybe two, stair cars most likely, for fast access to the cabin. Maybe the sound of booted feet stamping, though that could be his rising pulse. Best not to think about what some remnant X faction would do if they caught him now.

He waited until the beeping halted and the engines died and there was only the clang of footsteps climbing the stairs. He barely breathed, all muscles tensed and ready, until there was a sharp upward suck of wind that slammed the hatch shut, signaling the cabin door above had been opened.

Wren pushed the hatch back open and looked out over the jet's starboard view.

A black asphalt runway stretched away at a diagonal over brown scrub grass. At the edge some five hundred feet away, a metal fence demarcated the line between runway and forest. It looked like an air base. The sky was gray, the air was cool, and a breeze blew the chemical stink of jet fuel backwash across his face.

He scanned left to right. There were no buildings. No

people. No voices called out. No gunfire came zipping his way. He took a firm grip of the hatch edge and leaned his head and shoulders out and down. Directly below him lay the landing gear's twin tires, the rubber shredded and gelatinous, friction-baked heat radiating up. If he could make the drop unseen, there was enough room between the tires to hunker down for a moment.

He curled over further, arms shaking as they held his weight like a gymnast on parallel bars, trying to see beyond the bulbous jet's belly. His entire torso was out of the hatch before he got a partial view of the 787's port side.

Looked like twenty soldiers on the blacktop, wearing full urban camouflage gear. Wren stared. They held rifles at low ready, standing in twin banks between the port side's front and rear exits, where large yellow stair cars now stood, lights flashing.

Beyond them were two MTVR vehicles thirty feet away; bulky 6x6 wheel Medium Tactical Vehicle Replacements for payload and troop transport. Each was capable of transporting eleven Marines, decked in urban gray camo. Vehicles used exclusively by the Navy and the Marines. There was a hint of massed buildings beyond them, surely Sheppard by the scale.

Wren's mind spun.

Ten Marines on the runway. Maybe ten on board already? Massively overpowered, even if they were here to bring in the 'Big Bad Bird'. What was all this? Their camo didn't even look like Air Force. If anything, they looked like Marines.

From above came the first muffled shouts of command, laying down the law to the passengers. Wren couldn't make out the words, but they weren't taken well. Sounds of alarm followed: raised voices, panicked screams, followed by a single muffled gunshot.

The shock of it almost tipped him from the cargo bay.

Instantly bedlam broke loose, shouts and screams of

hundreds of people filling the air, chased by pneumatic rifle fire that raked vibrations through the plane's frame like a jazz drum line.

The squadron of Marines on the runway broke formation, half running for the rear stair car, half to the front. Wren pictured Amira with her kids, holding them tight. It wasn't even a decision at that point, just raw instinct.

He dropped from the hatch and covered the distance to the front stair car in seconds. As the last of the Marines stamped up it, Wren climbed the rear. As they poured into the galley in an eruption of shouted commands, Wren rolled over the railing.

He caught the last Marine in the entrance. The guy flinched as Wren suddenly appeared to his left.

"Wha-?"

Wren gave him no time to bring his rifle to bear, launching a crunching headbutt into his face. It landed like a hammer on a nail, bursting the guy's nose and driving him straight down.

Instant unconsciousness. Not a noise anyone on board was going to hear over the general screaming. Wren lowered the guy, ignoring his rifle but stripping the coyote brown M-18 from a tooled leather holster at his waist.

Then he stepped back into the galley.

He'd only been there minutes earlier, but it felt like a whole new world. The narrow space was vacant except for the purser and her two stewards, still seated in their fold-down chairs, hands cuffed with plastic zip ties. That took a few moments to register, so far from any operating procedure Wren knew.

He rubbed the headbutt blur from his eyes, saw the purser had a nasty welt on her cheek. Looked like someone had bounced a rifle butt off her face; impact bruising starting to come up purple around it. Her eyes were big and round, but there was no recognition as they fell on Wren, only terror.

The air stank of expended cordite. Kids were crying deep in Economy.

Wren took a breath, raised the M18 then leaned in to peer down the port aisle.

Four Marines stood in First Class, two to an aisle, their rifles trained on the passengers. One of the passengers tried to stand, and the nearest Marine clubbed him with his rifle butt.

The guy, mid-forties and dressed in a business suit, dropped cold, head rocking back and spraying blood like an ejected shell. Wren scanned the rest of the booths. Another man lay unconscious in his booth, blood trailing from a similar blow to the head. Put down with extreme prejudice.

"What are you-?" the purser mumbled behind him, and Wren spun back out of the port aisle, putting a finger to his lips.

"Keep your mouth shut!" one of the Marines shouted.

Wren waited ten seconds, then mouthed a question to the purser. 'Where's the air marshal?'

She stared at him a long moment, almost as if she was seeing him for the first time, then raised one slack hand an inch off her lap to point one shaking finger toward the starboard side.

Wren nodded. Took a breath, peered back down the aisle looking for the all-clear, then crossed the gap into the cover of the galley bulkhead. His heart pounded, breath quickening. None of this was close to normal procedure. He edged up to the starboard aisle and chanced a look around.

Air Marshal Yolanda Queen lay slumped in his own vacant booth. Her Ideal Conceal was slack in her lap, deployed but with the magazine stripped, and a clear entry wound in her chest.

Wren stared. She was breathing in low, sharp pants, each

frothing blood around her lips. A shot through the lung; sucking chest wound. Blood soaked a long stripe down her white shirt and sharp gray suit. Her eyes fluttered then loosely fixed on him.

They'd shot her. The air marshal.

If left untreated she'd drown on her own blood, if she didn't bleed out first.

Fury hit Wren's endocrine system like an epinephrine shot. Unacceptable.

Her eyes fixed on him. There was recognition. Her mouth opened, but she couldn't frame words. Instead her eyes glanced to the exit door. Telling him to run. Trying to be the hero.

Not a chance in hell.

Wren stepped into the starboard aisle and fired four fast shots in a little over a second. The nearest Marine took two in the chest, the next along had his back furrowed in a close-knit double-tap. Wren swung immediately across the central booths and fired four more shots before the remaining Marines could react, not the cleanest of hits but enough to put them down.

The plane erupted.

Shouted commands and returning fire surged from Business Class, as the Marines deeper in the plane broke toward Wren. Bullets shredded fabric seatbacks and chewed plastic chunks out of the luggage racks as he ducked into his booth to scoop up Yolanda Queen. He barely felt her weight as she rolled over his shoulder.

He fired blind and high then ran back through the galley, the purser staring vacantly as he crossed the port aisle in a hail of gunfire and out. He raced down the stairs and sprinted over open ground toward the nearest MTVR.

Thirty yards away. After ten he spun and ran backwards, M18 trained on the plane's exit. When the first Marine came through, he fired two shots, no chance at accuracy but enough to force the guy back.

Wren kept up a rain of covering fire until the M-18 clicked empty, then he spun and sprinted the last five yards to the MTVR. By its open door a wall of thunder broke out in back and the blacktop skittered madly as they tried to find his range.

He zigzagged the last few steps, took a thumping hit that almost knocked him off-stride but didn't drop him, then he was at the open door and climbing in. He tipped Yolanda onto the passenger bench, clapped her hand over the wound in her chest and slotted in behind the wheel.

The scene ahead of him was chaos.

A handful of Marines had cleared the stair cars already, firing wildly as they ran, sending sprays of bullets into the front of the MTVR that cracked off its reinforced frame, shattering the headlights and spidering the glass. Others stood braced on the stair car, sighting in.

Wren stayed as low as he could and grabbed the ignition. The keys were there, and the engine coughed to life. He hit the gas, racked the gearstick into reverse and powered the MTVR away.

12

MTVR

The chaos receded fast, fifty yards as the engine strained to something like twenty in reverse, a hundred yards; the Marines gave up chasing and just locked their legs, shouldered their rifles and took aim.

Wren swept the wheel right, fishtailing the truck hard.

Now high-caliber bullets punched divots into the MTVR's rear armored walls. Wren hit the brakes, cranked into first gear and started the truck ahead.

"Hands on the wound, use your jacket, stop that bleeding!" he shouted at Yolanda as he shifted up to second. Caught a glimpse of the other MTVR several hundred yards behind, already racing after him.

He cursed.

Ahead some two hundred yards lay two hangars, to the right the open expanse of runway bounded by metal fencing, to the left a large complex of buildings.

Thirty miles an hour, he shifted to third gear and pushed the pedal to the metal, veering hard left onto the base's main street. He'd been on plenty just like it. Now airmen and women were pouring out of the buildings to watch. The MTVR rocked off a curb, plowed through a few mailboxes then he got it straightened at forty, barreling hard for the double-grilled exit gates, flanked by twin guard towers ten feet tall.

The guard towers let rip.

Wren dropped to the floor, right hand pushing the gas all the way in, left hand steering blind. The windshield fractured then burst inward, bullets raked the driver's seat where he'd been, then they hit the gate and ripped through.

Metal bolts wrenched out of concrete bollards with a tremendous crunch, the MTVR dropped twenty miles an hour of gathered mass, and Wren bobbed back into his seat.

Ahead lay an access road climbing up to a highway, forest to the right, open scrub on the left. The rearview mirror was gone so he looked out the window; the second MTVR was closing on the ruptured gate already.

He rammed the gas home and steamed south onto the three-lane highway. In seconds rifle fire bit at the back end of his vehicle. In his rearview mirrors the MTVR was barely visible, so close to his tail.

Wren looked around the truck's cab. Picked out first aid kit over the left wheel well, heart defib paddles over the right, and along the back wall were racks of ammo. He held the wheel with his knees, grabbed a magazine and slotted it into the M-18, then slammed on the brakes.

The truck squealed and groaned, its huge momentum skidding on a hydroplane of burning rubber. The other MTVR was too close and rammed into his rear like a gut punch, metal screaming under the torsion. Wren held the brake until the truck rocked to a stop, then he leaped out into traffic.

Cars honked and weaved. Wren beaded on the rival MTVR's cab, wreathed in smoke from the wrecked engine. There were three Marines trying to bring their rifles to bear.

Wren shot through the windshield to take out the nearest

in the driver's seat, then ran, jumped, landed on the running board and fired point blank through the window. Half the mag drained into their heads, torsos and upraised hands in seconds. Not a chance of survival. Body armor didn't matter that close, with so many chaotic ricochets.

Wren dropped away from the smoking cab and padded to the rear with the M-18 raised, but the troop supply stations were empty. They'd gone off half-cocked. Likely that had saved his life.

He dashed back to his MTVR. Yolanda Queen lay in the footwell, tossed there by his sudden braking maneuver. He hoisted her back up, saw her eyes rolling in her head, and uttered a swift prayer. Only the faintest breath gurgled up from her lips.

"Hang in there, Yolanda," he urged, checked his rear views, figured he'd covered only half a mile from the base, but she wouldn't last any longer without treatment. At a run they'd be with him in five minutes, but you could do a lot in five minutes.

He scooped the first aid kit from the left wheel well and cracked the tamper-proof seal. Inside the contents were neatly arranged, and he moved without thought. First priority was a wound in her thigh he hadn't even seen before. Must've been that thump he'd felt as he'd made for the MTVR; she'd taken the hit meant for him. Looked like a shot straight into muscle, no exit wound, but bleeding badly.

Recessed into the kit's lid was a SOF tactical tourniquet, really a two-inch band of red reinforced fabric with a hook, loop and long bar of machined aluminum. Wren unclasped the hook and tucked the band under Queen's upper thigh, brought it down closer to the injury then reclasped the fabric and pulled the tightening straps.

She groaned, sweat popping greasily as her leg shifted. The blood flow instantly slowed. Wren took hold of the aluminum bar, four inches long and tooled for easy grip, and twisted it four full turns. Internal bands cinched tight enough to turn her skin below the band white.

"Aaargh!" she cried, then coughed blood.

"We're getting there, Yolanda."

He ripped open a sealed package containing Combat Gauze, pale bandaging infused with kaolin, a fine white clay that helped clot bleeding. He wrapped it swiftly around the wound, then looked up.

She'd stopped breathing. Her sucking chest wound had stopped sucking.

"Not a damn chance," Wren hissed, and tipped out the kit until two thin, firm squares of plastic-backed film shook out. Occlusive bandages, capable of air-sealing her chest cavity.

He hunkered up on the seat and ripped her white shirt away, sending buttons pranging off the roof, to reveal the dark hole between her third and fourth ribs on the left side. He grabbed a fistful of gauze and wiped the area dry, then peeled the first square of translucent plastic and applied it, smoothing it down over the warp of her ribs.

A minute, maybe? She'd be turning hypoxic already. Wren's fingers shook and felt greasy with his own sweat. He wiped them on his shirt, then log-rolled her carefully, pulled her shirt clear to find the entry wound in her back. Looked like a clean through-shot. He wiped with the gauze, sealed with the occlusive film then bent back to the detritus he'd tipped out of the kit.

Found no adrenaline syringe. Maybe too late for that anyway. He spun around the cab once more, caught a glimpse of Marines in the wing mirror, running on foot, then landed again on the red defibrillator case slotted above the right wheel well.

He tugged it out, popped the lid, hit the button to charge the paddles then laid them on Yolanda Queen's chest, low on the left and high-central on the right. The gear whined as it loaded an 800-volt burst, then discharged.

Yolanda convulsed, her eyes jolted open, and she sprayed out a geyser of blood.

Wren rolled her on her left side so her right lung could drain. "You're going to be OK, I promise, just focus on breathing."

Her eyes flared wide, caught on his for second, seemed there was an accusation on that glare, then she started coughing again.

"I feel that," Wren said, and dropped back into the driver's seat. Heart pounding like a mechanical bull. Marines almost up to his tailgate, bullets already cracking off the armored back. He hit the gas and pulled away.

13

IDENTIFY

Wren took the truck up to sixty fast on the open road, pulling easily away from the pair of Marines. His breath came in short, shallow bursts, not unlike Yolanda Queen, laid out on the seat beside him. She needed an operating room immediately, with multiple bags of blood and fluids dumped into her system while a surgeon sutured her busted chest back together and started thinking about triage for her torn leg.

Wren shook himself. Slammed the wheel once, twice.

Yolanda Queen was alive for now, but what about all the others? He'd just left a jet full of civilians in the hands of, who?

He had no idea. He'd never seen anything like it before, not on American soil. He'd been a Marine. He knew the heights Marines held themselves to, and that did not involve battering defenseless civilians with their rifles. It did not involve gunning down a federal air marshal in cold blood.

He looked at the radio, then started twisting the dial looking for a line out. This had to be called in to somebody. Gerald Humphreys, sure, but higher still. The President. This was a brewing terror attack.

Abruptly the radio crackled to life on its own.

"Identify."

The speed dial on the dash climbed to eighty and Wren stared at the radio, his head clearing a little.

"Identify," it said again.

Wren drove in silence for long seconds, trying to figure out some play that could help him here. Of course the MTVR would be lo-jacked with GPS tracking. As long as he stayed in the truck, they'd know exactly where he was. Was there any benefit to letting them know who he was?

He picked up the transceiver and clicked to transmit.

"Put me on with your boss."

A long beat passed. "Hold one."

Wren held. If he could glean any scrap of information about who he was dealing with here, that would help. As he waited, he made a conscious effort to control his breathing, which helped tamp down his racing pulse. To his right Yolanda wheezed low. He took the chance to pat himself down. Cuts and grazes, plenty of bruises yet to come up, but no more serious injury.

Thirty seconds passed. The MTVR rocketed along the highway at a hundred miles an hour, weaving in and out of lanes. Wren scanned the nearby vehicles, looking for an old beater, one unlikely to be fitted with any kind of remote tracking system. His next step was to pull over in front of one, 'requisition it' and fold back into traffic. Hopefully that would get Yolanda Queen to a hospital, and from there he could melt into the country, using any one of a dozen ways to obfuscate his trail.

The radio crackled.

"It's not Mr. Wren, is it?" came an older man's deep bass voice on the radio.

Wren's breath caught in his throat. Instantly the world tunneled down.

"Christopher Wren? I've been speaking with some of your 787's passengers. You were on that jet, weren't you?"

The voice was undeniably Texan, but with hints of an exotic, lilting accent breaking through. Maybe one of the Nordic countries, Sweden or Finland. Wren said nothing in response, thinking fast. Nobody onboard knew who he was other than Yolanda Queen. He'd flown under false ID issued by the CIA itself.

"A beautiful woman," the voice went on. "Wonderful children, so full of life."

Wren's heart skipped a beat, realizing who the man was talking about. Amira, of course. She'd recognized him.

"You're not going to touch her," he said.

"Is that so?" the voice countered. "I believe she thinks you will rescue her, Christopher. Will you?"

Wren squeezed the wheel tight. "Hear this. If you harm her or anyone on that plane, you're signing your own death warrant."

"I've signed many death warrants before," the man countered easily. "I'm comfortable to sign another."

Wren's mind raced. Signed many death warrants? "Who are you? What do you want?"

"Many things. Right now I want you. Stop the MTVR, and the woman and her children will live."

Wren knew how that kind of deal went. Hand yourself over, that was just more hostages. "Not a chance. Let them all go now, and I'll be kind when I come for you. I'll let the federal system take you, rather than burning you alive myself."

The man laughed. "I think I might prefer the burning. You have burned many, haven't you?" A moment passed. "This is most unexpected, I must say. I bring down a plane, imagine my surprise when the ungrateful son himself is on board."

Wren's jaw set. There was that name again, combined

with, what, surprise? "You're loyal to X, and you're saying you didn't target that plane to get to me?"

The voice laughed again. "Not every follower of X is fixated on you, Mr. Wren. We have numerous interests. We are-"

"Going to burn," Wren finished for him. "Every last one of you, just like X, just like my father, if you don't shut this bullshit down, whatever it is."

A silent moment ticked by. Wren overtook a pair of RVs in convoy.

"He is dead, isn't he?" asked the voice. There was an undercurrent of anger, now, beneath the amusement. "Our founding martyr, the Apex. And with your deepfake videos, you robbed us of his death."

"I did you a favor," Wren spat. "It was a pathetic way to die. He whimpered like a three-day-old baby. Begged me. Wept. You should be thanking me I didn't film it."

The man's lilting voice hardened. "I very much doubt the Apex begged. But you will. Your death will take decades. You will become a living symbol of our unstoppable-"

"Unstoppable bullshit," Wren interrupted, spinning ahead. "I've heard it all before, so let's cut to the chase. You've got F-15s and access to Sheppard Air Base, which means you've turned plenty of military personnel already, or convinced them you're acting on legal orders. Now I'm going to come down with the full power of the federal government and disabuse them of that notion. We'll see how you hold up when the F-15s are coming for you."

A silent moment passed. Wren hovered his foot over the brake. They could remote-lock his steering at any moment now, he figured. Just waiting to ride out the maximum distance possible.

"Here is my counter-offer," the voice said. "As of now, a Reaper MQ-9 drone armed with Hellfire II missiles has locked onto your heat signal. I see the air marshal is with you and alive, but barely. It will not even require a direct hit to obliterate you both."

Wren involuntarily looked at Yolanda, then back to the road. It sounded like the kind of threat he would make, oftentimes backed up with nothing but bravado. "I don't buy it. You don't have a Reaper drone."

"Why wouldn't I? I have F-15 Eagles. Unlike you, I do not bluff. Ten seconds."

Wren leaned forward to look up through the missing windshield. All he saw was blue sky, but then that's all he would see, if the Reaper was cruising at over 10,000 feet. An infinitesimal dot smaller than a single pixel on a cinema screen. Five seconds. He pulled the wheel right, racing into the middle lane. Three seconds. Wouldn't make a difference at all, if they really had one.

There was a flicker of streaking movement to the side, then an explosion that blew trees into the air. A blast wave of atomized foliage, surface soil and tiny living creatures burst out of the forest like a tsunami tide, lashing across the MTVR with an audible whomp.

Cars to Wren's right veered into him. He held fast and bore down, letting them bounce off his armored sides.

Not a bluff, then. They really had a Reaper drone, and they weren't afraid to unleash Hellfires on America soil.

"Last chance," came the voice. "Stop the truck, pull over and await rendition. We will find a use for you."

"That's how we took out Soleimani in Afghanistan," Wren said, "and we couldn't even cover that up properly. How are you hoping to cover any of this up here? Jets full of passengers just don't go missing. Every Hellfire missile costs a hundred-fifty thousand, and they're thoroughly accounted for. You can't-"

"Who said your jet is missing?" the voice interrupted.

"Who counts those Hellfire missiles, Mr. Wren? I'd think you of all people would know that there's no such thing as objective truth. It is what we make it."

Wren opened his mouth, closed it. He didn't know what to say. Saw leaves fluttering in the wing mirror, caught on the sucking breath of the blast's after-effect. Twenty pounds of explosive at the head of a Hellfire II missile made for a fifty-foot kill radius, eighty-foot maiming range. He knew no argument that could stand up to raw, brutal force like that.

"Ten seconds until the next missile falls. Stop the truck, Mr. Wren, or you and every person near you is roadkill."

No choice. Except there was always a choice. He glanced at Yolanda Queen, put one restraining hand on her shoulder then slammed the brakes. The truck squealed to a halt. For a millisecond he considered hoisting her again, trying to carry her with him, but he'd never clear the distance with her in tow, and even if he did, the impact of being carried would certainly kill her.

"I'm sorry," he said to her flickering eyes, then flung the door open and leaped out into traffic. He sprinted across the outer lane without pause and down a shallow embankment to the cover of the forest.

Not perfect, but a hundred vertical feet of boughs, branches and spring foliage should be enough to screen his heat signature. As soon as he hit the treeline he picked a forty-five degree vector and ramped up to an all-out sprint. Roots pounded under his feet, red oaks flew by on either side, trying to clear as much of that fifty yards kill distance as he could, all the while counting down the seconds.

Three. Two. One.

The explosion hit to his left and roared through the forest like some giant ravening beast. The blast wave of dust, soil and organic matter punched him in the side like a tidal breaker, almost strong enough to knock him off his feet.

He ran on.

Another blast came directly in back and a second wave washed over him, closer still but not close enough.

Horns blared on the highway from vehicles sprayed with flak. Maybe some injuries, even casualties. Yolanda Queen would have felt the impact rock her in her seat, but not enough to kill her.

Wren hoped.

There was nothing else he could do now but keep on running.

Another impossible decision. Another good person left behind. Another seed of rage planted deep.

14

EVADE

The forest was large, and that was good. Better than a crowded space for shaking off an air pursuit. No way they could know which way he was headed, using infrared tracking from ten thousand feet. Not with a hundred towering feet of live oak, Texas ash and cedar elm boles, boughs and foliage screening his heat signature. No way they could tell where he would emerge.

Wren ran, flanking trails by a good distance and passing unnoticed by the few pairs of ramblers and dog-walkers he saw, unwilling to add more eyewitnesses to his escape vector. It didn't help that he was liberally splashed with Yolanda Queen's blood. Any civilian he approached now would be more likely to call the police than help.

In something like thirty minutes he found what he had hoped for; a parking lot partially under tree cover. He stalked the row of vehicles closest to the forest, picking out a mossy plumber's panel van splattered with bird scat. Sunken tires. Had been there for some time. No clear record of pickup and drop-off patterns, nobody going to report it missing, and no fancy engine wrapped up in motherboards and lo-jacked to high heaven.

He pulled off his jacket, used it to muffle the grip of the M18 and smashed the passenger-side window. Inside, it smelled of molding plasterboard and rotten paint. The seats were torn badly, yellow foam springing through the brown vinyl casing.

No keys in the glove box or sun flap. A picture of a family lay on the dash, bleached almost white by the sun. He scanned the footwells but found no handy tools left lying around. Screwdriver, rasp, pliers. Instead he used the M18 as a hammer again, pounding the sun-warped plastic molding on the steering column until it cracked. He pried it off and found the ignition wire bundle; yellow, brown and red. He stripped an inch of insulation off the two battery wires with his teeth, twined them, then stripped the ignition wire and twined it into the bundle.

Nothing changed on the dash. No lights, no AC, nothing. Could be the battery was long-dead. Wren turned the radio dial, and a pop song stuttered to life. Still good. He isolated the starter wire, stripped it carefully then touched it to the battery/ignition bundle, striking electric sparks.

The engine kicked in and died. Wren gave it a moment then tried again, this time catching the spark with a firm pump on the gas pedal. The engine revved. He edged the old van forward.

He had no map. Instinctively he left the lot and took turns as they came, avoiding I-44. The best place for him now was off the grid. Somewhere he could lay up and figure out what had just happened. There were signs for Wichita Falls downtown district, and he took them heading south.

Eyes on the road and watching the skies. Brain ticking over like the jump-started engine, trying to build sense out of something that seemed utterly senseless.

Why bring down a 787 over home soil? Why drop

missiles, military hardware that was easily accounted for, as if there would be no repercussions?

There would be. Wren would see to it.

He circled east around the city's fringe on smaller roads, through low-density residential and commercial areas, wary that CCTV cameras could be hacked. At some point southeast of the city, he came across an old strip mall in a gentrifying neighborhood, half coffee culture and funky fusion restaurants in bare brick and neon, half homeless folks living out of shopping carts, with acne-ridden Meth junkies hovering in front of the convenience store. He pulled up in the lot, saw no CCTV cameras, took his heart in his mouth and stepped out of the van.

Ten seconds passed by. No missile came searing down like the sword of God from above. Didn't mean they weren't watching him, of course. Didn't mean a missile wouldn't any moment soon.

Either way, his window of opportunity was narrowing.

He strode to a payphone mounted on the convenience store's wall. Gang graffiti decked the interior, loose cards lay in piles advertising lewd services, but there was a working dial tone. He rang an emergency number, expedited by his personal extension, and waited as the line rang.

At last, a familiar voice answered.

"Chris?"

"Sally," he said. Flinched at the sound of a horn on the circular road. At his most vulnerable to missile attack right now. "You are not going to believe the BS I've just been caught up in."

A moment passed, checking his incoming area code.

"I see you're in Texas. Chris, tell me it's not about the hijacked 787."

That shut him up for a second. That she knew about it already. "Yes. Exactly that."

"What do you know?" Sally Rogers followed with fast. "Have you got a target telemetry? Our best intel says these X bastards are going to piledrive the Cowboys' Stadium, or maybe President Bush's ranch, or one of the new downtown skyscrapers. Could be-"

"Wait," Wren said, momentarily overwhelmed. "What are you talking about?"

"Chris, I'm sorry, it's all systems go at the moment. I'm on the targeting team, if you've got something, let me know, or I have to get back to it."

He reeled. Tried to sort what she was saying into his experience of the last hour, but the two didn't seem to map.

"Something's not linking up here, Sally. I was on that plane, the 787, but you're talking about it in the air? F-15 jets grounded us at Sheppard Air Base about an hour back. Some crew of fake Marines boarded the plane, started locking it down. I don't-" he broke off, trying to spin it backward and forward to make sense. "People died already. The air marshal, they shot her in the galley, I guess because she stood her ground. I got her out, shot some Marines, then they tried to blow me up with a Hellfire missile off a Reaper drone over I-44. The air marshal may still be there, in an MTVR truck off the verge, I don't know. She needs help. I barely escaped." He paused, thinking how much to say. "I'm at some mall near Wichita Falls right now. There's every chance they're going to drop a missile on me any minute."

A long moment passed.

"Damn," said Sally Rogers.

"I know all that sounds crazy," Wren said. Reading between the lines, after hearing every crazy thing he'd just said. "And I can confirm, this attack looks to be X-related. But here's the thing. They were after something on that jet. At first, I thought it was me, but they didn't even know I was onboard. If we move fast, we can figure out what they wanted and head them off."

Rogers was silent for a moment, keys clattering in the background. "So you think this terror threat, the 787 in the air as a flying bomb, that's some kind of distraction?"

"Absolutely. This is X, Sally, and somehow they're based out of an Air Force base. They've got F-15s and Reaper drones; they don't need a 787 as a weapon, do they?"

"I guess not," Rogers allowed.

"Have you even had eyes on the jet in the air in the last thirty minutes?"

"Eyes on? Let me check." More keys clacking followed; Wren figured she was pulling up reports. "OK, yes, we have eyes on currently. If they did bring this jet down at Sheppard, it's back in the air now. The threat is real. We just five minutes back scrambled F-15s from that same base for air intercept. Presidential order says we're going to shoot it down before it picks a target. It's half full of fuel still, out of LA bound for New York, but you'll know that already, if you were on board." A second passed. "You're serious that you were really on that plane?"

"I was. And shoot it down? There's got to be five hundred people on board!"

"Trust me, we know, but if it comes down on a heavily populated target with all that fuel in the tank? The death count could be ten times higher, not to mention billions in damage. Right now it's dropping from twenty thousand feet. We plan to shoot it down when it drops below ten thousand. "

Wren spun the wheels of his mind hard. Thinking about Amira and her kids. About the purser's shocked face, and the drunk guy with the hotel liquor bottles, and everyone else on board. "This whole thing's a distraction ploy, Sally. If you end up blowing the 787, it's because that's what these X terrorists want."

"A distraction from what, though?"

"Whatever they wanted on that plane. Someone or something they could only grab in the air. We need to look hard at the passenger and cargo manifests and figure out what that is, or we're going to be blind to the true threat here."

"Because a flying bomb's not a big enough threat," Sally Rogers muttered under her breath. More clacking sounds, maybe calling in her team, trying to absorb the scale of it. "This is all new intel, Chris. I don't know what to make of it, so I'll be guided by you. Do I argue against blowing the plane? What's your recommendation?"

Wren cursed under his breath. Whatever this was, it had multiple levels.

"Do everything in your power to avoid that. The 787-as-bomb is a smokescreen, so you need to figure out what the real target onboard was. At the same time, I'm here on the ground. Activate any and all federal assets you can within range, and get them into my hands." He squeezed his eyes tight shut, trying to see how it would all play out. "Get me trusted assets: not the Wichita Falls FBI resident station. If a whole air base is corrupt, there's no telling who else is." He thought a second longer. "Get me the FBI Critical Incident Response Group out of Dallas, and a wide-ranging federal warrant to match. I want to hit Sheppard Air Base like an ICBM before they can clean it up, start digging some truth from this heap of BS. Can you make that happen?"

"Already on it," she answered. "I have leeway, and Humphreys is eating out of my palm these days. Give me your location and I'll send the Dallas CIRG out to pick you up, should be within an hour by air."

Wren told her where he was. She killed the line.

He looked up at the sky.

Still no missile yet.

15

ROCK

It took ninety minutes for the Dallas CIRG team to arrive; shipped in on twin Bell 407 helicopters to a car rental lot. In that time Wren found an Army Surplus shop and picked up some fresh gear; camo pants, olive shirt. The old lady behind the counter wore a Nixon pin and stared at his blood-soaked outfit.

"Castrated a bull calf," Wren said, by way of explanation. "First time, though, so we made a real mess."

She stared. "Castrated?"

"It's just one of those things," Wren said, laying his new clothes out. "The calf's fine." She rang up the clothes. Maybe placed a 911 call right after he left.

In his new gear he dropped into the convenience store, where he picked up a sandwich, milkshake, an off-the-rack burner phone and a basic Bluetooth earbud. The phone barely qualified as 'smart', but it had a screen, Internet access and a 100GB data deal. The earbud wasn't a patch on the tactical in-ear gear he was used to, likely to wobble out at the first punch, but it would do in a pinch.

Back in his van he forced himself to eat and drink, pushing through the residual shakes from the adrenaline blast of the last few hours or so. He didn't want to think about Yolanda Queen looking up at him on the MTVR's passenger seat, or Amira's cucumber-wielding kids on the 787, or Maggie, or Henry before that. At minimum he'd need to sleep for a week to process it all, but he couldn't afford to rest right now.

Instead he booted the phone to track the news coverage. The guy on the MTVR's radio had scoffed at the notion that the 'media' were going to help.

Seemed he was right.

The major networks were all heavily featuring a twenty-second piece of looped footage showing the 787 in flight. Nothing looked off about it, except maybe if you looked closely, where there were dark dots by the exit door.

Bullet holes, Wren knew, from when he'd laid down covering fire. That realization came as a strangely comforting confirmation that all those crazy events had really happened.

There was no mention of a landing at Sheppard Air Base. In itself, that was incredible. No eyewitnesses disputing the record. A base like that had to have a standing staff of several thousand; could they all really be loyal to X?

It seemed unlikely, but here was the reality, playing live on the news. The anchors were heavily focused on the terror threat the plane represented. According to the scrolling banner along the bottom, the 787 hadn't descended below 10,000 feet yet, so the F-15s hadn't engaged and taken the shot. The FBI's Hostage Rescue Team were working with the Tactical Aviation team and attempting negotiations.

It all looked like BS to Wren.

He moved on to his Foundation darknet. Seemed they had gotten his message, relayed through the First-Class guy's tablet. They were already all over it, but there was nothing to dig clear yet. No way to get eyes-on at Sheppard Base, no source of fresh data, just the same banks of supposition.

Wren tapped out a fast message for the open boards:

AM OK, ON THE EDGE OF WICHITA FALLS ABOUT TO RIDE A FEDERAL INVESTIGATION INTO SHEPPARD BASE. THE BLAST ON I-44 WAS A HELLFIRE MISSILE LAUNCHED FROM A REAPER DRONE. TRACK AND HACK IT IF YOU CAN. I LEFT AIR MARSHAL YOLANDA QUEEN INJURED IN AN MTVR - TRACK HER AND WHOEVER COMES FOR HER.

I SUSPECT THE PLANE JACK WAS A HIGH-PROFILE SNATCH & GRAB OF PERSONNEL OR MATERIEL. GET ME PASSENGER/CARGO MANIFESTS AND FIGURE OUT WHO THEY TOOK. ASSEMBLE A STRIKE TEAM AND GET THEM OUT HERE FULLY GEARED WITH 2.0 ATTACK CRATES.

He sent the message.

The Foundation had been working on the attack crates for months, led by Hellion, the Foundation's lead hacker, and Alli, the highly creative junkyard engineer he'd pulled out of a firm school shooting plan a few years back. Between them they'd rustled up a rough-and-ready range of fast-insertion guerrilla strike gear, capable of leveraging civilian infrastructure to a war footing.

One of their innovations had been the explosive drones used against his brothers' spar platform; cheap commercial models fitted with explosive packs that turned them into pocket-money precision missiles. As for the rest, much of it had yet to be field-tested.

Maybe they'd get that chance today.

Wren polished off his sandwich just as three large black Escalades pulled up in back of his moldy van, fanning across the parking lot. Men in Black. Rogers had sent through their IDs; CIRG specialists all, scooped off an active cartel investigation in Dallas.

Wren stepped out and took up position behind the van's door, hand on the M18 at his waist. A guy stepped out of the front Escalade, stayed shielded by the door too. He was rangy in a black suit, early thirties and laconic-looking, tan-weathered with ruffled blond hair

"Corporal Christopher Wren?" he called.

There was a faint whistle on the 's' of Christopher. His face matched the ID kit set through by Sally Rogers, but Wren had to be sure.

"Who sent you?"

"Most directly, Agent Sally Rogers out of Washington," the guy answered. Sounded Texas down to his spurs, drawling hard. "More indirectly, if you'll excuse the arrogance, I'd say the good Lord himself, as I hear today you've been exposed to travails to rival Job."

Wren grimaced. "Save the patter. Name and provenance."

"Yes sir, I'm Agent Rock Fenner, got my team out of the Dallas FBI field station with me. We're C-I-R-G." He spelled out the letters. "Critical Incident Response Group. I heard you're looking to hitch a ride into Sheppard. I think we can oblige."

Wren grunted. Rock Fenner; it sounded like something out of cowboy central casting. "Tell me, where do you stand on X?"

"No political affiliation here, sir," Rock answered easily. "Just full-blood Americans, shining the Lord's headlights into every sinful crevice."

"And you've got a warrant, Agent Fenner? There's no way they'll accept 'the Lord's headlight' as sanction."

Rock smiled, held up a manila envelope. "Got it right here, and call me Rock, Corporal. Judge is getting his marching orders to step it up to federal arrest for the base commander. That should land about the same time as we do."

A second paused. "And if not, we go balls deep with our badges and see if they shoot to stop us."

Wren nodded. Rock was a hard charger, and Wren always liked hard chargers. Too much testosterone to play the games of a backstabber.

"I faced off with a squad of Marines already today," Wren said. "Could be real, could be stolen valor, but they knew what they were doing. Is your team ready for that? We go in shooting; things are going to get real."

"Ain't that God's ever-loving word, Corporal? Smite the Pharisees, saith the Lord, drive them from the land. Now's as good a day as any."

Wren suppressed a smile. The guy was growing on him. "Then let's saddle up. Call me Wren, Rock. I'll follow you."

Rock looked at the van and frowned. "In that thing?"

"Never mock a man's ride, Rock," Wren said, sliding back into the seat.

"Yes sir, if you say so, sir."

Wren climbed behind the wheel. The hotwire kicked on the third touch of the ignition wire to the starter bundle, and Wren pulled in neatly behind the Escalade convoy; a posse on their way to the corral.

16

CORRAL

Thirty minutes it took to circle back to Sheppard. Wren had the radio on throughout, tracking the 787 in the air. Still no attempt had been made to shoot it down; seemed it was in some kind of holding pattern over Dallas.

Keeping everyone on their toes. Keeping the media's gaze tuned in.

I-44 north was clear, but the southern lanes were still out of order. The site of the Hellfire blast was encircled by emergency services, journalists and white forensic tenting. There was no sign of the MTVR or Yolanda Queen.

He opened up a call to his hackers as he drove.

"Anything?"

"Nothing yet, Christopher, though we have details on base commander."

"Hit me."

"He is one-star Brigadier General, Mads Hellström, executive of Sheppard Base for seven years. Before this, he was in Iraq, Afghanistan, tour in Syria, Ghana. Has a three-star General's home outside rural Cashion Community, seven miles north of Sheppard Air Base."

Wren considered. "Hellström, is that Swedish? The guy on the radio sounded Scandinavian."

"Correct," B4cksl4cker chimed in, "came over at eleven years old from Malmö, Sweden. Second generation, his father was artisan glassmaker, more engineering than art, hired to design ballistic glass for US Air Force. His mother was homemaker. They are retired."

Wren grunted. "Anything on his personal life?"

"Very little," B4cksl4cker rumbled, keys clacking in the background. "Has wife, three adult children. Occasional social media posts. Supports charity, goes to church, suggestion he may run for local government. Nothing unusual."

"And on the darknet?"

"If he is active, it is well hidden. We cannot find it."

Wren ran a quick search on his phone, one hand on the wheel. It brought up photographs of Hellström in his ceremonial whites, standing with his airmen and women. A distinguished-looking man in his early fifties, a jaw so square it was almost a lantern. Wren scrolled down, found an article about the general buying a $2.5 million dollars ranch-style home in the nearby Cashion Community.

"He's rich," Wren observed, scrolling through cached real estate photos. The house was built in the Pueblo Revival style, all squared-off adobe blocks, spotted with dark blots of stained oak beams poking through the terracotta-colored exterior.

"One star Brigadier General makes one hundred fifty thousand per year, base pay," B4cksl4cker said. "This home is far outside his range."

"So he's supplemented his income somehow. Suspicious. Great family home, though."

"Three adult children are all in Air Force," B4cksl4cker supplied. "Different bases, all upper echelon command, all

Texas. Five grandchildren. His wife left him ten years ago, separation, not divorce. It seems he fills gap with work and political campaigns."

Wren frowned. Trying to measure if Hellström was really a traitor to his country. "Campaigns?"

"This man has stood for state senator twice, state governor once," Hellion said. "He did poorly."

"He's too straight-arrow," Wren guessed, looking again at that face. "A boy scout without any charm."

"I know another man like this," Hellion said, but Wren ignored her. On his right the forest gave way to spreading fields, burgeoning with puffy cotton plants. The green growth was broken here and there by the rusted relics of miniature oil derricks, each no more than five feet tall, like modern art sculptures dotting the land.

There'd been an oil boom in the 1930s, apparently. A land grab, and every farmer, councilman and educator in the city had bought themselves a pump and set to unleashing black gold.

That had died away fast.

"Looks like Tinman," Hellion said in Wren's ear. "Many Tinmen of yellow brick road."

Wren grunted, focused on the task at hand. In minutes the Escalades pulled onto the Sheppard approach road.

Seen from outside, the Base was much larger than Wren had realized during his adrenaline-soaked escape down Main Street. Now he picked out multiple blocks within the compound, one toward the center equipped with a tall floodlight rig and satellite gear, had to be the comms center. Numerous roads crisscrossed the blocks of barracks, canteens and offices. Twin runways lay in the distance, with four large hangars fringing their edges. All of it was encircled by a low earthen security hump and twin rows of wire fencing, reinforced with steel cross braces and overseen by more looming floodlights.

Maybe this was a bad idea. Nothing for it, now.

Their convoy rolled up to the central gate, flanked either side by low guard towers. The gate itself had been replaced already, leaving no sign of the damage he'd wreaked in the MTVR. The front guard came up to Rock's vehicle at the lead. Maybe he'd bamboozle them with his Biblical schtick. Paperwork exchanged hands. Wren just squeezed the wheel, waiting for the next Hellfire to drop.

In maybe a minute Rock got the OK. The gate opened and the convoy rolled through.

Wren drove slowly. Eyeing the guys on gate duty. He'd barely seen them on the way out, when they'd been shooting at him. Were these the same guys? He couldn't be sure, but didn't think so. If so, they'd either deny it down to the ground, or claim cover under some unexpected chain of command.

The same went for everyone on this base. Either they were already rotten to the core, corrupted by X, or they genuinely believed they'd been acting under lawful orders. Wren hoped it was the latter. People like that would listen to reason.

Rock rolled ahead steadily, took a right then a left through ranks of low buildings, pulling up in a lot with the runways stretching out ahead. Familiar blacktop stretched in front of Wren, one runway running north-south, the other further off and diagonal, north-west to south-east.

He stepped out of the panel van, feeling the eyes of the base on him. Just over two hours earlier he'd been dropping bodies right here. Four Marines downed in the 787 for sure, maybe a couple others from his covering fire.

"Your rodeo, boss," said Rock Fenner, striding over with the wide gait of a horseman, standard-issue Glock 22 swinging in a non-standard pistoleer's fast-draw holster on his right hip. "What's the call?"

The rest of the FBI CIRG team stood by their vehicles. Eight, all told. A good number, but massively overwhelmed. Time to see how far that warrant would carry them.

"I want everyone out here," Wren said, looking Rock in his blue eyes. "Every last soul on this base, from the big boss at the top to the guy who cleans the toilets. All at parade rest, incommunicado, unarmed, locked down like a man trap, ten feet between them. Nothing in, nothing out. They stand on the runway until they piss their pants for all I care. Interrogations begin. I'll want a tent set up here." He pointed at the grassy verge bordering the runway. "Multiple tents. I'm bringing in my own assets to run the questioning. Forensics, too. Nobody's going home early tonight."

Rock whistled appreciatively. "That'll make for one heck of a mid-game show. I'm outranked here by about three stars, Corporal, and the warrant for the big dog's arrest hasn't come in yet."

Wren gritted his teeth. Mads Hellström. "How far does your warrant stretch?"

"Oversight of everything. Investigative capacity. I can't strong-arm the boss man, though I think I can spook some Pronghorns out of the bush."

"We're after bigger game than antelope," Wren said. "Wield that warrant like a blunderbuss; I'm already working to significantly widen its scope. I want Brigadier General Hellström out here with me, on the blacktop, in five minutes. We're going to have ourselves a heart-to-heart. Think you can wrangle that, Rock?"

"It'll be my pleasure."

"And have your guys walk tall. From this moment on, we own the place. Anyone gives you guff, you spout some hellfire chapter and verse, then you take their names. This is a dick-swinging contest we're going to win from the start then again and again, until they start to feel the weight of our foot on their necks. I want and expect a long, long list of assholes who didn't jump to it. This is going to be a purification by fire."

Fenner grinned. "From your lips to God's ears, Corporal. Fire's the best kind of purification, my momma always said."

"My dad had a similar line."

"So I hear. We're on it."

He started away.

Wren pulled up his phone, placed a call to Sally Rogers. It went through in seconds.

"Chris," she said. "I hear you're on base."

"On base and swinging for the fences," Wren said. "I need you to get me cover for this at the highest level, Sally. Higher than Humphreys. This whole place reeks of conspiracy. It's been cleaned up and sanitized. Gate replaced, bodies gone, no sign of the Marines. Like nothing happened. I need you here, with every trained interrogator you've got." He took a breath, looking around. "We're going to hang these people up by their heels and bleed them dry."

"Copy that," Rogers said. "I figured you'd go bigger. I'm already at work on your federal arrest warrant, wide-ranging powers. As for above-Humphreys' level, I can make a few calls, maybe rope in a couple of rainmakers. I'll be there in two hours, am in the air now, got our old Blue Fairy team investigative with me."

Wren nodded, felt something taking shape in his chest. Not just rage spurred on by the 787 in the air; five hundred-plus souls being paraded for the world's media like a line of dancing showgirls. Not just the thought of Amira and her kids mixed up in this. Call it righteous patriotic fury, spurred on by Rock Fenner's religious talk. At the subversion of the Marine Corps. At the subversion of Habeas Corpus. At the subversion of everything Wren stood for, and the X idiots who thought they could get away with it in the plain light of day.

"I'll be here," Wren said, and ended the call. Paced out over the runway, kicking loose gravel and looking across the expanse, seeing it all come together. Sightlines. Positions. Marking out in his head where it had all gone down. The jet. The MTVRs. The Marines.

All evidence.

He stopped at the place where incoming fire had hit blacktop as he'd climbed into the truck. The air stank of fresh tar. Looked like a fresh, thin surface skin had been laid down across a stretch maybe fifty feet square, enough to cover any residual evidence. The tar was still steaming, must've been laid down in the last hour, now bonded to any bullet fragments or glass shards left behind, leaving a surface that was smooth and clean as a fresh fall of snow.

Wren had no doubt they'd have answers for it. Routine maintenance, they could call it. Air base runways were in constant need of repair, and breaking that story was going to take some work.

That was fine. Wren was planning to dig much further than skin deep anyway. You didn't expect to kill a cancer by operating on the surface. You had to yank it out by the roots.

17

WILD BUNCH

Five minutes passed, and the runway was getting lonely.

Nobody out at parade rest. Not a single soul turfed up by Wren's CIRG team. That just bespoke an abominable lack of protocol.

Rock Fenner came loping across the runway toward him, and Wren ended the call to Teddy, Foundation CEO, after laying out instructions for data analysis on the passenger and cargo manifests. His hackers Hellion and B4cksl4cker had acquired them, were working with the Foundation's man in the NSA, Steven Gruber, to run the names and objects through various federal databases.

Fenner started talking when he was twenty feet out. "Radio room's locked down and the Brigadier General's holed up in his office," he called, sounding halfway apologetic, halfway furious. "Got a squad of armed sergeants encircling both places, I couldn't get in."

Wren nodded. Had figured as much. "You wave that warrant?"

"Like a flagbearer on the 4th of July. The base Secretary wasn't biting, said a one-star General doesn't answer to a two-bit cultist with a fig leaf of temporary authority." Fenner winced a little at that last. "His words, not mine."

Wren nodded. He'd played with all kinds of generals before, and they all thought they were above the law, lords of their own little castles. Here that was turned up to eleven.

"Time for invasive surgery. Pull your team in. This is where we Wild Bunch our way to the heart."

Rock Fenner nodded. One hard charger recognizing another. He nodded at Wren's M18. "That thing loaded?"

"Not anymore. You have a magazine?"

"Always," Rock said, and smoothly pulled one from the back of his belt. Wren slotted it into the M18's grip with a pleasing clunk, racked the slide to feed a bullet into the chamber, then clicked the safety and tucked it into his belt.

"Thanks," Wren said, and started walking.

Off the runway, around a narrow triangle of grass, back to the main street he'd careened down just a couple of hours earlier. Airmen and women were everywhere, standing out in the open or peering through windows and glass doors.

They knew him. They'd seen him. He knew them, too.

Time to weigh their souls in the balance.

The CIRG team picked up from either side, falling in behind. Eight guys in black suits fanned out behind a single guy in camo pants and an olive shirt. Half of a breaking began with the visuals, and the best breakings always began at the top. Cut off the head and the body floundered.

"Left here," Fenner said.

Wren took a left off the main street. Either side lay barracks and amenities; a military library, a training block with floor-to-ceiling windows revealing classrooms with whiteboards. Of such banal stuff was high treason made.

The building lay up ahead.

Office of the Brigadier General. A grand building on a small scale, out of sync with the rest of the base with its white stucco and fake colonnade, like some plantation owner's mini mansion. A couple of cheap plaster statues, the guy's name emblazoned in gold, two topiary bushes, a silver Jaguar XF parked in front.

Six airmen stood before it, M16A2 rifles held across their chests at low ready position; barrel forward but down, butt at the shoulder, finger rigid across the trigger guard and ready to pull. All carried the single chevron of Master Sergeants on the insignia of their dress blues.

Wren stopped five yards out, studying the Master Sergeants before him, as solid as stone blocks. They were expressionless men and women with thousand-yard stares. Wren pulled his burner phone out of his pocket, tapped a few recently downloaded icons, then hit the speaker button.

"Agent Rogers?"

"Here," she answered, the speaker clearly audible, "I have CIA Director Gerald Humphreys, Chief of Staff of the Air Force Mara Holmes, and President Ablas' Chief of Staff Toomey Jimenez on conference call."

Wren grunted. That was pretty good, on short notice. Cashing in on his current brand value.

"Good," he said, then focused his gaze on the Master Sergeants like a laser cutter. "You've been served a lawful federal warrant from Judge Lancôme Grey in Dallas, allowing my team investigatory powers throughout the entirety of Sheppard Air Base." He paused a second. "But you know that already. You've already made a series of choices, here. One, to stand by as my jet was brought down. Two, to stand by while I was hunted out of your base and onto the highway. Three, to stand in my way now." He took a breath. "Thus far, there are two possible explanations. One, you believe you're following lawful orders. Two, you're traitors through and through. In either case, if you persist, you're looking at a lifetime sentence in solitary confinement, minimum. In the latter case, it's more likely to be the death sentence, for aiding gross domestic terrorism. Are we all clear so far?"

They didn't waver.

"We have our orders, sir," one of them said.

"That's what they said at Nuremburg," Wren countered, rounding on the guy. "In case you're unaware, the 'entirety' of my warrant includes this Jim Crow-era monument you're currently guarding. I have the Chief of Staff of the Air Force on the line, and she is not happy."

The sergeants didn't budge.

"Chief of Staff Holmes," Wren said.

Her voice came through the phone. "Airmen. You are hereby relieved of your duty immediately. Stand down. Corporal Christopher Wren is now in temporary command of this air base."

No movement.

"Sir, that could be deepfaked," the same sergeant said.

Wren said nothing. Had expected this. Deepfakes were everywhere these days, and audio was easy.

"I understand that concern. You have your orders, and unless countermanding orders come in from a confirmed superior officer, you can't switch course. Does that sound about right?"

The Master Sergeants said nothing.

"Now I have the highest superior officer in the Air Force on a civilian line, but you won't accept that because it's unconfirmed, and I get it. It's hardly procedure. It could be the President for all you care; rank doesn't matter if it's a deepfake. So you tell me. What's the system for bypassing this situation?"

The Master Sergeants stared. Wren thought he saw the first sign of doubt creeping across their faces.

"Think hard," Wren said. "You know the answer. I'm sure

it was your first thought, when the orders came through to down my 787. There are secure hard lines, correct? Where are they?"

One of the Master Sergeants on the edge shifted his feet. For a second Wren thought he was raising his rifle to fire, but no shot followed.

"Sir, there's one in the radio room," the lead Master Sergeant said.

"That's right. Secure physical lines laid through deep infrastructure, backed with digital and analog cryptography. But I'm hearing your radio room has been locked down, yes? So how is anyone supposed to receive the legal countermand order your Chief of Staff has been sending through for the last two hours, if they can't get in to hear it?"

Nothing came back.

"But there's another secure line on base, isn't there? Where is it?"

The Master Sergeant said nothing.

"Where?" Wren demanded.

"In the Brigadier General's private office," the main guy said.

"Which you're guarding."

Nothing.

"Does that seem like a good system to you? Or do you think, maybe, at least one of you should go in and ask to hear those orders from the secure line? Maybe admit me. I have got the warrant. I'll even hand over my weapon. Whatever it takes, just to get an order from your own Chief of Staff through, before you damn yourselves to the death penalty for refusing to hear a rightful order."

The moment stretched longer. Sweat popped on the Master Sergeants' cheeks. It would only take one, Wren figured. Just one to-

A guy on the left raised his rifle.

A shot rang out.

That guy froze.

Wren turned, saw Agent Rock Fenner with his pistol out and smoking. A warning shot, it seemed. He gave Wren a nod.

Wren turned back, and saw the remaining Master Sergeants were ready to crack. The tide had turned.

"Get out of my way," he said, and strode forward.

18

HELLSTRÖM

Wren shoved through the line of Master Sergeants, through the doors and down a hall propelled by renewed urgency. Upstairs he went, along a corridor carpeted in navy blue with various seals and US symbols worked into the fabric, where the door to the Brigadier General's office lay open.

It was like a miniature Oval Office inside, with a hulking oak desk by the windows that looked like the other half of the HMS Resolute. Facing it were paired sofas, cream-colored walls with burgundy curtains, windows overlooking the road outside, a dome-contoured ceiling painted blue to match the carpet, and a gray-haired man in full dress whites sitting behind his desk, in the middle of a heated telephone conversation.

BRIGADIER GENERAL MADS HELLSTRÖM, said the nameplate on his desk.

When he saw Wren in the doorway, he stopped talking. They stared at each other for a moment.

"He's here," he said, then laid the handset down gently.

Wren felt his anger surge.

Hellström sounded like the guy he'd heard through the MTVR's radio. Had to be. Instinct told him to stamp over, lift Hellström by his lapels and slap him until he sobbed, then parade him back through his own base for all to see, establishing dominance until they all rallied out to the parade ground and spilled everything they knew.

He resisted the instinct. It wouldn't help, not with the base already a tinder keg ready to blow. Instead he strode over and slammed the piece of paper down on the desk.

"I have a warrant for absolute cooperation from every member of this air base, including you. To all extents and purposes, it gives me command for the duration."

Brigadier General Hellström looked up at Wren. True to his photos on the Internet, he was in his mid-fifties, brown eyes with that strong square chin and sharply cut black hair, solid musculature still filling out his snug uniform. He wore a pin on his chest, the lone star flag of Texas.

"Mr. Wren. Your warrant has been canceled."

That took Wren a moment to register. Cut across everything he'd expected.

"What? According to who?"

"To Chief of Staff Mara Holmes." The man's eyes crinkled with something like concern. "While you were giving your speech down below, the world has moved on. Three minutes ago, the 787 which you claim was landed on this air base entered a final descent toward the Dallas City Hall. The moment it breached ten thousand feet in a terminal dive, an F-15 fighter jet from Dyess Base released four AIM-9 Sidewinders that obliterated it. The immediate threat is over. Now the extended threat begins."

Wren just stared. Trying to put the pieces together.

"This air base is now on high alert, wary of another terror attack," Hellström went on, his voice lilting slightly as he spoke. "Our state and national governments are meeting in emergency sessions to address this threat. Five hundred and thirty-four souls just perished. This is no time for anyone to be given investigative control of a key defensive base, especially when the story he tells is backed up by no verifiable facts."

Wren felt himself slipping. Five hundred and thirty-four. Amira. The kids. Everyone lost in a chain of four Sidewinder fireballs. There was no surviving that, and it made him sick. He looked into the General's eyes and saw something far deeper and sicker still.

This was the man.

Wren drew his M18 and leveled it at the General's smug face. "How's this for a verifiable fact?"

"Unfortunate," Hellström said, not missing a beat. Like he'd expected this moment and was disappointed it had come so predictably. "If you shoot me, what will this achieve, other than debilitating our national defensive readiness? Guaranteeing your own immediate arrest and indefinite detainment." He paused a moment, judging the impact perfectly. "You should know I am currently on the line with the President. She wants absolute readiness."

Wren didn't budge. Lots of thoughts buzzed through his mind. Taking the general hostage. Shooting him outright. But in the midst of an air base run by X, he didn't like his chances of getting out alive.

"Let me hear that from the President."

The Brigadier General met his hard stare. Playing his role to a tee. "I am under no compulsion to do that. But out of respect for the man you are, and the things you have done to protect this country, I'm willing to. Please." He pointed to the handset.

Wren picked it up.

"Madam President?"

"Corporal Wren, you are hereby ordered to stand down," came a familiar voice. Not President Ablas, but the deep and resonant tones of Gerald Humphreys. "Whatever you think you experienced within the last several hours, it's not our current concern. We are dealing with the greatest threat to the homeland since 9/11, and you are pursuing an investigative thread that may impede our defensive readiness."

Wren's jaw tightened. It sounded like Humphreys. It could be a deepfake.

He laid the handset down, turned around. The Master Sergeants were there behind him now, along with Rock Fenner. Fenner's gun was in his hand, though he looked confused. The Master Sergeants stood with their rifles at low-ready.

The handset on the desk was still talking.

Wren pulled out his own phone. The rifles raised to high ready, beaded on him. He ignored them, tapped to dial and held it to his ear.

"Chris," came Rogers' voice.

"Tell me it's not true."

Rustling came down the line, keys clacking hard. "It's true, Chris. They want you out of this for now. I'm sorry. The 787 just dived, they blew it, and everything changed."

"What changed?" Wren demanded. "All those deaths, you should be looking even harder at how that came about. The 787 landed here. Everyone here knows why." He spun around. "I'm looking right at the guy who signed the order, but you just cut out my legs underneath me."

A long silence followed. "They're talking about arresting you, Chris."

That hit him like a punch in the face.

"What?"

"I'm against it, but I'm not in the room. They think all the horrors, all the violence and lies with your father, well, there's no easy way to say this. They think you're having some kind of traumatic reaction. That it's involuntary, a need to put yourself in the center of things."

Wren couldn't believe what he was hearing.

"You can't be serious. They think I've gone crazy?"

"Not crazy, Chris. I-" she paused. Wren watched Hellström, but nothing showed on his face. "No one's calling your judgment into question. At least, not at this moment. But the things you're claiming? That you were on board that jet, when there's no record whatsoever of you through ticketing or security? That F-15s forced it down at Sheppard, when there's no evidence from telemetry, radio, radar, witnesses or any single person from the base itself able to corroborate what you're saying? That one of the passengers was possibly abducted, or materiel was taken, when there's no evidence of either of those at all. And now we see the bodies falling from the sky." She paused. "This is a terrible attack, Chris. We have to defend ourselves. We have to react."

Wren glared at Hellström. He met Wren's gaze like a block of iron. There was no hint of smugness in his eyes. To pull something of this magnitude off, he had to be a better poker player than that.

"They have other priorities," Wren said.

"Exactly," Rogers answered swiftly, almost sounded grateful. "The immediate concern right now is defense of the homeland. Five hundred-plus citizens just died, and X forces are the suspects."

Wren blinked. "What? X?"

Paper rustled down the line. "That's right. I shouldn't even tell you this, but I think you have a right to know. There're activist X cells all over the country, and several just claimed this attack. It's not complicated. We're at DEFCON 2 already, extreme high readiness. Answering attacks will be coming within hours, if not minutes. As soon as we nail down these X terrorists, they're going to pay, and..." she trailed off.

Wren read between the lines. "And what I'm saying doesn't play into that narrative."

Rogers said nothing.

"No," Wren corrected, "it's worse than that, isn't it? It's me. Who I am plays into the wrong narrative."

"Chris, it's not like that."

Wren just stared at the Brigadier General. Trying to fathom how this could have happened. An entire base full of airmen and women, all either cowed, following unlawful orders or rotten to the soul. Blacktop covered up within hours. The gate replaced. Now five hundred-plus passengers blown up in the sky, with X taking the blame.

It was immense. Convoluted. He didn't know what it meant.

"You think I'll get pulled in. Because of my father. Because I'm linked to X already. Even though I'm the one that brought him down."

"Right now we want to control as much information as we can," Rogers answered, sounding uncomfortable. "You are one facet of that, yes. You do have fundamental ties to X like nobody else."

Wren's jaw tightened. Damned as his father's son, even though he'd killed him. He turned to Hellström.

"And you're taking the blame yourselves," he said. "Claiming it for X. Why?"

Hellström just stared back at him. "I don't know what you're talking about, Mr. Wren, and frankly I don't much care. I've been polite. Now is the time for action."

Wren itched to pull the trigger. Thinking about what would happen if he executed this man right now, for the deaths of five hundred-plus Americans. No more intel, that was for certain. No path to whatever they'd lifted off the 787. He'd be arrested, if he wasn't shot down on the spot. A true dead end.

"Fire, Mr. Wren, in line with your delusions," Hellström said, utterly impassive in the face of the M18's barrel, "or leave me to do my work and protect this country."

There was no answer. Wren felt the rifle barrels trained on his back. He focused on the phone.

"So am I under arrest?"

"Not yet," Rogers said. "Not if you put your weapon down. You've been through trauma, with no time to recover. There is no outstanding arrest order."

He took a breath. "So you buy the delusion line."

"Not delusions. Trauma."

"As long as I stand down."

Rogers sounded pained. "I know this is difficult, Chris. I still believe you. Something happened, I don't doubt it. You witnessed it. But what I believe doesn't matter. If you stand down, you're free-"

Wren killed the call.

Brigadier General Hellström stood. He was tall, easily had a few inches on Wren.

"Our nation is at risk, Mr. Wren," he said, lilting voice rumbling low. "I've allowed this to continue out of respect for you, but that respect has run its course. Now I need you to leave this base, so I can defend it."

Wren tried to read something in Hellström's eyes, but he couldn't fathom a thing other than darkness and lies.

He lowered the M18 and stalked away. The Master Sergeants spread to let him through. He didn't look at Rock Fenner. He didn't look at anyone as his mind churned a thousand miles an hour.

Down the steps. Out into the fresh afternoon air.

Something terrible was happening. He could feel it. Something bigger than five hundred dead civilians. Something Gabriel had predicted back on the spar platform, and Wren still had no idea what it was.

He got back in his beat-up plumber's van and tore away.

19

DEKE THORNTON

Wren turned left out of the base, heading north. Away from Wichita Falls on I-44. The old van rattled and shook. The fuel gauge was dead. Could be running on fumes, and there was no way to know.

His phone rang and he ignored it.

If it was Sally, there was nothing to say. If it was Hellion, B4cksl4cker, Teddy or any of his Foundation members, he needed time to deal with all of this.

Five hundred and thirty-four people, dead. Blown out of the sky. It was hard to comprehend the scale of it. The loss.

And Hellström had just sat there.

Wren's knuckles whitened on the wheel.

The man knew. Wren had no doubt of it. He'd been right on the edge of unlocking this thing, then it had been washed away in a tidal wave of loss.

He slammed the wheel so hard it hurt.

The timing was almost too perfect. Almost as if the order had gone out to sink the jet just as Wren stormed onto the base. He felt outmaneuvered and outraged. Five hundred and thirty-four souls lost, their deaths orchestrated just to whitewash, what?

Amira and her kids. The purser, the drunk, the pilots, they were all innocent. People he should have protected. It was too many. Too big a loss. The backlash was going to be overwhelming; but against who?

For what?

In his rear mirrors he spotted pursuit vehicles trailing him; looked like twin Escalades. Would they have sent Rock Fenner and his CIRG team? He laughed. Maybe it was no surprise. He felt like pulling over and taking it to them, but then he'd seen Fenner quick draw.

No.

Ahead were signs for Burkburnett, looked to be a mid-sized town. By the time Wren crossed the city limits, the old van was spluttering and dying. He pulled into a big mall with water fountains out front, left the van right by the sliding doors and stepped inside just as the Escalades arrived.

The mall's long faux-marble hall was largely empty. Not many people were in a shopping mood, Wren figured, not after the 787 had exploded. He bounded up an escalator then stopped briefly beside by a crowd in front of an over-stuffed tech shop, watching footage of his 787 exploding on a dozen big screen TVs. It was his first time to see it.

"You believe this?" a guy beside him asked.

Wren watched the screen and the footage looped over as the plane blew again in slow motion: five hundred and thirty-four bodies reduced to wriggles of black dust in four blooming orange fireballs at ten thousand feet. Body parts and wreckage would be set to rain across a dozen counties. Text ran along the bottom in a red chyron bar.

WORST ATTACK ON HOMELAND SINCE 9/11

"No," said Wren.

The guy looked up. "No what? You don't believe it?"

Wren was already gone.

In the food court he took a seat in the center, surrounding

by families, old folks, kids, many of them staring at their phones as they ate, looking numb. Wren knew that feeling well; to be under attack, to have everything you believed in threatened, and not know how to defend yourself.

There was no sign of the team sent to scoop him up yet, so Wren pulled his phone and scanned the Foundation darknet. His hackers had lifted the 787's passenger and cargo manifests an hour ago; now his hackers and his guy at the NSA, Steven Gruber, were running both through various databases. They had nothing otherwise: no satellite footage from over Sheppard or I-44; no sign of Yolanda Queen or the MTVR; nothing on who or what had been taken off the jet.

He tapped out a swift message.

I'VE BEEN KICKED OUT OF THE AIR BASE. WARRANT REVOKED AT THE HIGHEST LEVEL. HELLSTRÖM IS THE GUY - FIND OUT WHAT HE WANTS. SOMETHING TERRIBLE IS COMING. GET ME A TARGET.

He sent it then sat for a moment longer, turning the phone in his hands and waiting for what he knew was coming. They never meant it, when they said you weren't arrested. For optics, maybe they meant it. For show. But in truth?

DEFCON 2. Power spoke to power in one language only, and Wren had made himself a complication. Complications couldn't be left running around stirring up trouble, especially in the midst of a national emergency.

He looked around the food court; still no sign of the team. Maybe he had time. Via the Foundation darknet he set up a secure VPN then placed an untraceable call.

The line rang. He checked the time. 4:34 p.m. on a Thursday afternoon. Back East it would be 5:34. School all done. Maybe the kids would be at soccer practice, or having a pizza treat downtown, or watching TV over his wife's trademark 'fish and chips' dish.

"Hello?" came her voice. The same voice that had haunted Wren's dreams for over a year.

"Loralei," he said, and his voice came out rough. "It's Chris."

A long pause stretched between them. The line was quiet, so no pizza place, and not at soccer. Maybe they were in the guy's duplex while the kids played outside. The Dork Squad guy's house. Tossing a football back and forth with Wren's kids.

"Chris," she said. "Are you OK?"

He smiled as best he could, trying to affect the right kind of manner. "I'm OK. How are you? Jake and Quinn?"

The natural, easy smile came through in her voice. "They're good. They're…" she paused. "Happier, you know? After they saw you, in that town."

He didn't know what to say to that. He'd barely seen his kids before the authorities stepped in, started formalizing everything with debriefs like scar tissue around a wound. He'd been blackened and burned when he'd seen them, hardly the picture of himself he wanted to paint in their minds. But still, it was something.

"That's good," he managed.

"Even though it was awful, you know?" Loralei went on. "In that awful town, with all those awful people. Because you were there. That they got to see a little of what you do, even if it's so terrible. It tells them who they are, and that helps them know who they are."

Wren's eyes stung as a wave of something rose up within him, happiness and sadness mixing together. "I understand that. It's..." he cleared his throat. "It's not a good job, CIA black ops operative, is it? To be a dad."

Loralei laughed. "No shit, Sherlock."

Wren laughed too. Then gulped.

"Chris?" Now there was concern in her voice. He hated

that, even as he wanted it more than anything. For her to care again.

"I'm sorry about this, Loralei. I just want you to know, I was on a plane. Coming home, or at least, to you. You and the kids. I know you're with the guy." He rubbed his eyes, worried it was all coming out wrong. "I'm in some trouble, basically. But yeah. I don't know if you should tell the kids that. Just, that I'm thinking of them all the time."

He heard her breathing. Sounded like the smile was gone. "What happened? Chris, is it about that jet they blew up?"

"I, uh. Kind of. I'm sorry, but I couldn't…" He paused, looked up and scanned the court, but there was still no sign of a black-bag squad coming for him. "I couldn't just disappear like last time. I don't want you to think, for them to think, that they don't matter to me. They do. I was going to show that. I still want to. I'm…"

"What happened?"

He took a deep breath. "I was on that plane. The 787 they blew up. I know it sounds crazy. The whole thing's a mess, Lor. I… they don't believe me. The government. Something bad's going on, and it looks like they're coming for me now. At best they want me to shut up." He caught his breath. "But you know me. I can't just let it go."

There was a snuffling laugh from the end of the line. "I recognize that guy. Sounds like the man who went around to seven different bakeries because Jake wanted a real sculpted Transformer on his birthday cake, not just a picture of one."

Wren laughed, then tamped it down. "Yeah, this situation is pretty much like that."

Loralei laughed, then stopped, then there was silence. "Oh, Chris."

"I know," he said. "I thought with my father gone, things would be different. I would change. But now I'm not so sure."

A beat passed. "You can change, Chris. I believe it. Just

get through this, OK? Get that flight and come back to us, when you can."

He sighed. He didn't know what else to say after that. "I love you."

Now the smile was back. "We love you too, Chris. Not just for what you do out there. I'll always love you, in my way, even if we're not together. The kids talk about you all the time. It's getting kind of grating, to be honest." He heard the amusement in her voice. "But we'll be here, whatever. Now go get that birthday cake."

He grunted. Nothing else to say. He ended the call.

The hand came on his shoulder.

Wren looked up. He'd let his focus lapse. Rock Fenner stood behind him.

"Corporal," he drawled. "I hate to intrude on a tender moment, but it looks like I'm Deke Thornton, today. I hope you'll come in quiet."

Wren smiled. Appreciated that, a Wild Bunch reference. He cast his gaze swiftly around the court, picking out the stations Fenner's CIRG team had taken up on the edges, and nodded.

"They're giving you a chance to prove yourself."

"That's about it," Rock said. "Can't say I rate what they're doing here, though. Riding you on a rail like a hobo. You're not a dangerous man, are you?"

Wren watched the CIRG guys walking tall, like he'd told them. "Not really. I've just got the reload you gave me for the M-18."

Rock grinned. "I've still got my six-iron. Much as I'd love to fast-draw against the 'Big Bad Bird' himself, though, I can't imagine using it here would be a good idea. Pretty much your plan, I'd wager, setting up shop here."

Wren grunted. "So we go hand-to-hand."

"You're a famous man," Rock reasoned. "Or infamous, at least. Figure it'll make my name either way."

"Or we can just not and say we did."

Rock squeezed. "Now where's the fun in that?"

Wren nodded. Laid one hand over Rock's on his shoulder. "This is going to sting a little."

Rock went in fast for a sleeper lock, his long right arm snaking around Wren's neck, but Wren was ready for it and already rising. He shoved back with his hips, caught Rock's incoming right arm at the wrist and elbow, then hoisted.

A textbook judo throw. His hips boosted the slim agent up, his shoulder served as the fulcrum and Rock's trapped arm was the lever. The lighter, thinner agent flew. Up, around, then meatily down to crash into Wren's table, splaying two of the flimsy legs and sending him tumbling away like a one-man avalanche to the floor.

Wren turned.

The others were momentarily frozen. Five guys spread across the food court. He used that moment of indecision to his advantage, picking a vector and charging it hard. One agent stood in his way, hand on his Glock amidst the seated people, but Wren easily scooped a chair and flung it as he ran.

The guy's arms went up, the chair revolved and bounced hard off his shoulder, then Wren barreled into him like a Nickelback on a long QB rush. The guy flew across a table, spraying soft drinks, fries and ketchup into people's laps, while Wren's momentum barely took a hit.

The others gave chase, but through the sudden chaos of panicked shoppers surging to their feet, they didn't stand a chance. In moments Wren was clear and sprinting along the main shopping thoroughfare.

Below he could see the remaining two agents standing across the main exit, weapons in their hands, so Wren swung to an escalator and stormed up to the third floor. No agents up there. He sped through baffled and scattered shoppers, down an access corridor and out into the raw concrete space of the adjoining parking lot.

A car was pulling out of its slot halfway down, a burgundy Ford Mondeo, and Wren ran in front to flash his CIA ID.

"I need this vehicle for an ongoing matter of national security," he barked. "Out of the vehicle now, please, sir."

The driver was a skinny bagel store manager in a baggy white shirt, wearing his name on a badge. He popped out in seconds, bobbing, bowing and gushing nervous questions.

Wren ignored them, dropped behind the wheel and revved away.

20

WE'RE HERE

Wren drove three blocks, acutely aware they had to have aerial oversight of his every movement, or would never have attempted a takedown. He stopped under the underpass where I-44 overpassed Sheppard Road, then approached a lone homeless guy out with a brown cardboard sign.

"You want to make a hundred bucks, you give me that jacket and you drive away in my car."

The guy stared. Had the too-old skin of a user, though his eyes looked clear. Maybe kicked the habit, but still stuck on the streets. The sign said he was an ex-soldier, just trying to get treatment for an old wound.

"What?" he asked.

Wren pulled out his wallet, scooped five twenties and stuffed one in the guy's hand. "Jacket and get in the car. Start driving and you'll get the rest."

The guy stood. Maybe thought he was having some kind of acid flashback. Wren didn't care. The jacket stank, but that would help. The guy pulled it off and Wren shrugged it on. He hobbled over to the car and got in.

"Am I going to be OK?" he asked through the open window.

"You'll be fine," Wren said, and handed him the remaining eighty dollars. "Just don't tell them about the money, OK? Now go."

The guy nodded, took a moment to look at the wheel and the pedals by his feet, then pulled jerkily away.

Wren started off at ninety degrees, remaining under cover of the highway until it sank back to ground level. He pulled the filthy hood over his head, then stepped out over the verge.

Black Escalades flew by. They didn't see Wren. No missiles came down.

He approached a junk food place by the rear, along the trash dumpsters, avoiding any CCTV. In a corner of the lot was staff parking. He found a lime-green Mustang Mach-E, loaded up the near-field skeleton key with his phone, then hit the activate button.

The car unlocked. He left the jacket behind, got inside, hit the ignition, and drove away.

He had no clear destination. Away from Burkburnett, maybe. He switched the radio on, listening to coverage of the atrocity as his pulse steadied out. The terror group claiming the attack was called Al UST. Not an overseas group, the anchors reported. Not a leader hidden away in some distant country no one had really heard of.

This was domestic. Homemade, American Islamic terror.

Al UST. 'The United States Taliban'.

Wren didn't buy it for a second.

As he cruised west on a state two-lane, he opened a secure conference line through his Foundation darknet, pushed the audio through the car's Bluetooth speakers and called four people to an online waiting room.

One by one they appeared. Wren poised his finger over a fifth member. For most of his adult life, he'd kept everyone he knew in separate silos. His Foundation members hadn't known anything about each other. His CIA handlers hadn't known about the Foundation. His wife and kids hadn't known about either, and nobody had known about his past.

That had all changed now. After the Pyramid, they were all in it together. All except one man, and maybe it was time for that to change, too.

He pushed the button. Within minutes the fifth member joined the waiting room. Wren took a deep breath, then activated his microphone.

"Thank you all for answering this call. You're on the line with Teddy, or Theodore Smithely III, CEO of the Foundation. Hellion and B4cksl4cker are here, our genius hackers from Eastern European. Steven Gruber joins us also, he's a Foundation member who moonlights with the NSA."

Wren paused a second. He'd had his doubts about including Gruber; he was barely out of urgent crisis counselling, after attempting to burn himself alive at the Apex's command six months earlier. But he'd been getting stronger. The pain had left its mark, both physically and mentally, but the Apex's death had helped. It also helped that Wren had burned himself too: now they both bore the burn scars of napalm.

Brothers in flame.

"You are silent," Hellion said abruptly, her sharp accent cutting across his momentary silence. "Is this technical issue, Christopher, or mental failure on your part?"

He gritted his teeth. Everyone had to get stronger.

"I'd like you to meet my adoptive father, James Tandrews," Wren said. "He's the one who found me when I was twelve years old, in the fake town." He cleared his throat. "He was FBI gold team leader then, now he's retired, but he's helped us many times behind the scenes over the last year or so." He took a breath. "I think we could use his insight today."

A silence passed.

"I will have words with this James Tandrews," Hellion said. "He has done very bad job with you."

B4cksl4cker laughed low.

"Yes, your son, Mr. Christopher Wren, he is most rude. Did you know he stole billion dollars from B4cksl4cker and I? All gone. Puff. Now we have coins. Three coins each! This is immoral, yes? And poor exchange."

"Isabella," came Teddy's deep, cautioning tones. "Mr. Tandrews, it's a pleasure to meet you."

"Yes, welcome," Gruber added meekly.

"Tell us story from Christopher's childhood," Hellion pressed on. "I wish to hear about his bedwetting. He is champion bedwetter, yes? I see this in his eyes, first time we have met. This man, I thought, has wetted many beds. Correct?"

"A jet just exploded," Wren said. "Hellion."

She coughed. "Yes. Sorry. Inappropriate. For later. Now, welcome."

"Thank you," came Tandrews' response. His voice was deep like Teddy's, but with a raspy burr. Long years of smoking had roughened his vocal cords, and long years of trauma had freighted every word with extra weight. "I am speaking with Isabella, is that right?"

"Yes, I am Isabella," said Hellion, who had never let anyone other than Maggie call her that. "Very quickly, tell me Christopher was lonely child with no friends. This will explain coin system to me. Which person makes coins for closest friends? This is act of feeble-minded child, correct? Child who desires to be Prom King, but is only best friend to school counselor."

At that even Wren smirked.

"Isabella," Teddy rumbled.

"Sorry, yes, this is serious moment. I could not stop myself. Mr. Tandrews, we will speak later, yes?"

Teddy sighed.

"Chris," Tandrews rumbled. "We're here. What can we do?"

Wren took a breath. It was always hard, and never more so than now. "I need your help."

21

BANDING TOGETHER

Wren explained. The plane, the base, the CIRG team, the arrest attempt, now the media gleefully throwing themselves into the Al UST connection. His Foundation members had pieced together much of it already, but Tandrews only knew what he'd seen on television; he hadn't even known Wren was involved.

"I will give you access code for Foundation darknet," Hellion said cheerfully, as Tandrews started asking questions. "Catch up on many selfies he posts. Did you know your son made Foundation website out of wet tissue paper? B4cksl4cker and I broke it in five minutes. He was crying so much."

"James," Wren said, ignoring her. "Can you ask that again?"

"Of course," Tandrews said. "It cuts to the core of all this. You believe Al UST is a red herring, correct?"

"Yes. A red herring to distract us, a false flag to steer us away from whatever's happening at Sheppard Air Base. If all they wanted was to blow up a plane, they wouldn't have needed to grab one mid-flight, bring it down and send it back up."

"And if they had F-15s and Reaper drones, they wouldn't need a 787. They could do far more damage with conventional weaponry."

"Exactly."

"So what are they doing?" Tandrews rumbled. "Motive and objective. You mention distractions and false flags. But to what end? Who will benefit from this attack?"

"Not Al UST," Hellion chimed in. "They will be destroyed. I see many military forces across Texas, nearby states also, readying attacks. It will be tidal wave of bombs."

"Al UST barely even exists," Wren countered. "I've seen them. They're a couple of old hardliners making a lot of noise on social media and a few overheated darknet pages, maybe just a handful of rogue idiots with ISIS sympathies. They don't have the numbers, conviction or skills to pull anything like this off."

"Then they will make perfect scapegoat," Hellion said. "Boom boom, no chance to explain, offer alibi. Rogue idiots gone. Problem solved. This moment is coming."

"Isabella is right," Tandrews said. "This will happen fast. After the Apex, the country's weaker than ever in the eyes of our enemies. Then there's an attack like this, another plane from within our own borders? We look not just weak but incompetent, and we can't allow that to stand. I believe we will see the counter strike within hours."

Wren grunted. "Against Al UST patsies. It's a smokescreen to get everyone to look away for where it started: Fort Sheppard. Hellström. Fake Marines. We need to know why."

"Agreed," Tandrews said. "They're using Al UST as a cover for bringing that jet down. Something or someone was on board that they wanted. Where are you on getting manifests?"

"Analyzing, Mr. Tandrews," Hellion said. "We will have answers soon."

"How long?" Wren asked.

Keys clacked. "Estimate ten minutes.

Wren cruised in silence for a moment, until Tandrews broke the silence.

"What do we know about Hellström?"

"He's a one-star Brigadier General," Wren began, "Swedish, a first-generation immigrant, divorcée in his mid-fifties with his kids flown the nest; all in the Air Force, though, in good positions. Wealthy, but with no clear source for the funds. He's made three bids for public office and failed each time."

"He has political ambition," Tandrews summarized. "Interesting. What about darknet activity?"

"If he is active, it is well hidden," B4cksl4cker said. "We cannot find it."

"Did you run a broad scan of all members of Sheppard Air Base?"

"Yes, large matrix approach," B4cksl4cker said. "Two thousand, three hundred and twenty-one staff. Eighty percent active military, rest are support staff. Many followed Hellström, when he came to Sheppard. Many others turned over during his command. Few remain from before this time."

"That's not unusual," Wren said off-handedly. "Military men and women are always on the move. Any unusual interests amongst them?"

"Again, very clean," B4cksl4cker said, sounding disappointed. "Some drug use, porn, purchases made on Silk Road, bad behavior of various kinds, infidelity, harassment, but no extremist content. No terror activity we can see."

Wren sighed. "But these people brought down a plane.

Two F-15 pilots did that. Someone ordered the Reaper to fire on me. They're there."

"Yes," B4cksl4cker said. "You are not popular."

Hellion laughed.

"Hellström has clearly prepared for this moment for some time," Tandrews said. "We've seen this many times in cults, Chris. A longtime 'sleeper' cell spent readying for some hallowed day. So let's go back a step, look at the long-term planning. You say it's normal for military bases to undergo churn, but to this extent? B4cksl4cker, can you compare the turnover of staff at Sheppard to other bases? Is it unusually high?"

Seconds passed of clacking keys.

"Not unusual. Other bases in state show ninety to ninety-five percent churn in last five years."

Wren frowned. "Ninety-five percent? That does seem high."

"It is normal for Texas data set."

Something was off. "Only Texas. OK, so let's look at other states. The military's a federal body, not state based. Rates of personnel churn should be similar across the country."

"Checking," B4cksl4cker said.

Long seconds passed.

"Back to coin system," Hellion mused. "Is it true Christopher also made coins for imaginary childhood friends, in forest of Maine? I have heard this rumor. Tree friend. Root friend. I would like to see these coins."

"No," said B4cksl4cker. "It is not usual. Christopher, you are right. Churn rates in every other state are lower. Fifty percent, this is common maximum. Some are very low. Hawaii, for example."

Wren considered that. "But the bases in Texas are ninety-five percent?"

"Yes."

Nobody spoke for a long moment.

"This is bad," Tandrews said.

"What does it mean?" Teddy asked.

"They've been consolidating power," Wren said, and a chill ran down his spine. "For years. Banding the faithful together. But together for what?"

22

MANIFESTS

Wren saw signs for Lakeside City and took them, swinging south and east at a steady pace. 4:13 in the afternoon, and the sky was a mottled white and gray above.

"We have manifest analysis," B4cksl4cker said, his voice booming through the Mustang's speakers. "We provided primary analysis then handed to Steven Gruber."

There was a silence.

"Steven?" Wren prompted.

"Oh," Gruber said. "Yes."

There was another silence. Steven Gruber had recovered a long way from his trauma at the Apex's hands, but it had left him with a tendency to space out.

"Yes," he said again. "Sorry. The manifest. I ran it through XKeyscore, FASCIA, MAINWAY, and then I-"

"Apologies, Steven," Tandrews interrupted. "I've been out of the game for some time. What are those databases?"

There was the sound of keys clacking. "They're all monitoring techs; they scoop social media and Internet activity."

"Thank you."

"Similar access to our hacks, but greater range," Hellion said. "Real assets, direct feed from tech companies."

"Yes," Gruber said, the uncertainty in his voice fading a little, "also I borrowed time on the FBI's CODIS, NDIS, FDDU and AFIS. Uh. Those first three are DNA records, the latter is fingerprints and biometric. Additionally various PRISM affiliate databases: MUSCULAR, OAKSTAR and STORMBREW, a range of SIGINT assets, and, um. I think that's it."

"Thank you, Steven," Tandrews said. "That is an exhaustive list. Do you have a summary opinion?"

"Yes," Gruber said. There was an awkward pause. "Oh, you want to hear it. Of course. My conclusion is, the person of greatest consequence on that plane was Christopher Wren."

Hellion laughed. "Person of consequence," she repeated.

Wren frowned. Driving at a stately forty miles an hour, now, through green fields of soy. "I can't have been the target. There's no way they could've known I was on board. Not even the CIA believe I was on that jet."

Hellion laughed.

"Something funny?"

"Of course it is funny. Even now, driving in lime muscle car, you believe you are very clever, outwit everyone."

Wren blinked. "How do you know what car I'm driving?"

"I am more clever. It is simple matter to spin back satellite data, find strange man walking like homeless, watch him steal car."

Wren cursed under his breath.

"But do not worry, we have confused satellite data, scrambled time stamps, infected CCTV databases in area. They will not find you in same way."

Wren let out a breath. "OK, that explains the car. How could they have known I was on the jet?"

"Very simple," B4cksl4cker said, picking up the thread.

"You are creature of habit. Like long road trips across American West. If you do not know where Christopher Wren is, there is good chance he is road-tripping in desert."

Wren frowned. "That's nonsense."

"Is truth," Hellion countered. "Especially after sad news. Mr. James Tandrews, we recently lost good man, strong Foundation member, Henry Bragg. Like many times before, after loss, Christopher takes road trip. Anyone can see this pattern. Wife left him? Road trip in Utah desert. Lost team in Belarus? Road trip in Arizona to fake town. Old friend turned traitor? Road trip all over West. Now Henry is dead, road trip west. Anyone can also see, after this he will fly east. Visit family in New York, Delaware. All road trips end this way. Only question is, which airport will he use? For air intercept, it will not matter. F-15 jets can bring down private jet as easily as 787."

Wren opened his mouth, closed it. Was he really that predictable?

"So you believe he was the target of this attack?" Tandrews asked.

"It is one possibility. At risk of inflating his head further. He is very famous man in your country now. Big Bad Bird. Anything else is big coincidence."

Wren couldn't argue. Still. "I don't buy it. Hellström seemed like he wasn't expecting me. Like I was a surprise. If they really were coming for me, they'd have secured the exterior of the plane better, had the base fully locked down. I never would have got out." He took a breath. "I think they're after someone or something else. What have you got, Steven?"

"Uh, OK," Gruber said. "Well. After you, there were three journalists, one a Pulitzer winner." Papers shuffled. "Four high ranking officials of Fortune 500 companies, including a COO and a CEO. One state senator, a social media influencer with five million followers, an NHL first draft pick for last season, top goal scorer, and a substantial number of avowed X members."

Wren drove, processing that.

"Avowed X members?"

"They're everywhere, now," Gruber said casually. "You can't throw a stone without hitting one."

Wren grunted. "Yolanda Queen, the air marshal, said she was X. Or X adjacent."

"Do you think that's relevant, Chris?" Tandrews asked.

"Perhaps not. I don't know. So let's put the X folks to the side, and posit one of these high-profile people was the target, or they were carrying something Hellström wanted. Each one would make for a very different kind of motivation."

"How so?" Tandrews asked; acting as a sounding board.

"OK. So if it's a journalist, this whole thing could be a revenge attack for bad coverage, like that plane brought down over Belarus, or shutting up some damning exposé to come. If it's the corporate execs, could be industrial espionage, maybe a blackmail situation, overseas interference laundering influence through American companies."

"It wouldn't be the first time," Teddy rumbled. He'd been a Wall Street trader, phenomenally successful, before he'd given that up for the wannabe-vampire life.

"The Senator could mean anything," Wren went on. "A high-power pressure campaign to vote a certain way, or simply taking this person out before a vote could go through. As for the influencer and the NHL guy, who knows, maybe another BS virality push, or shutting down an expose to come."

There was silence for a long moment. Wren took a turn left.

"We need to get up on each of these people," he said.

"Any links they may have. Any crux moments they've faced recently or were about to face."

"We are starting this task," Hellion said. The sound of keys clacking from her line sounded like a kendo training hall, dozens of swords smacking off armor every second. "Thank you, Steven, for hard work. Yes. Already spinning."

Wren hit a red light. Waited in line. Couldn't help but peer up through the windshield to the white sky, wondering if a Reaper was tracking him still.

"James, any thoughts?"

The older man took his time. "Only that we are in the eye of the hurricane here, Chris. This is bigger than Al UST, but they're going to pay the price soon. I believe they're innocent, patsies like you say, but it won't matter, and anything we do to help them will tip our hand." He thought a moment longer, wheezy breath carrying down the line. "We're in the opening gambit still. That can work for us or against us. Any decisive action we take now could be determinative."

Wren nodded. Turned again, pulling into a parking lot. "Such as?"

"All we have concrete is Sheppard Base and General Hellström. As you said, he knows what's going on. He oversaw it. If we could get to him somehow, we could get answers."

"Extra-legally," Wren said softly. "Where's my team, Teddy?"

"Thirty minutes out, Christopher. Private jets inbound, thirty minutes away. Doona, Alejandro and Alli; all we could get on short notice. Alli is bringing several full Attack Crate 2.0 kits with her. What do you have in mind?"

Wren grunted; the attack crates opened up all kinds of new possibilities. He pulled into the parking lot for the air strip, parked then killed the engine. Thinking it through.

Fifteen miles west from Sheppard, isolated on the edge of Wichita Falls, surrounded by verdant green fields.

"Take it to Sheppard," he said firmly. "This time I won't be asking nicely with a warrant, though."

A moment passed. "Repeat, Christopher," Hellion said. "Did you say you're going to attack Sheppard Air Base?"

Wren pushed open the door. Stepped out on the blacktop like an act of defiance. "Attack it. Break it. Leave it reeling."

23

BODY SNATCHER

Alli's private cargo jet, a Beech 1900 twin-turboprop, was first to put down, inbound from Utah. The tires had barely stilled on the scrubby blacktop when she bounced out and straight into Wren's arms, giving him a big hug and peck on the cheek.

She was twenty-two now, six feet tall and no longer as scrawny as she'd once been, boasting red hair that was tied into complex-looking braids woven with white and blue strands. She wore a mechanic's jumpsuit in deep navy, but furred and rimmed with highlight colors everywhere; reflective yellow strips at the wrists, neon orange trim on the back in the shape of tiny angel's wings, with her name plastered across her chest in looping cursive. Around her waist hung a heavy engineer's belt laden with gear: an electric drill on one hip, what looked like a bolt gun on the other, with a hammer, wrenches, pry bar, screwdrivers and more in between.

"This is hardly incognito," he said, when she'd stepped back to look at him.

"Neither is attacking a US Army base, you big lug," she answered. "Let me look at you."

"We've both changed," Wren said, taking in her hair and new style. She'd always leaned toward maximalism, but this was pushing the envelope. When he'd first met her, she was deeply Goth and into suicidal ideation, but festooned in piercings and tattoos. Now, well... "You got a lot brighter. I like it. I got, uh-"

"More scarred?" Alli offered brightly, then her face soured. "I heard about Henry. I'm sorry."

"Me too," Wren said. "I'm wearing all my colors on the inside."

She just smiled. "I wear mine on the outside, so I don't have to get high. It kind of has the same effect."

In spite of their situation, Wren laughed. "Dressing up bright is as good as meth?"

"Better!" Alli cheered. "The wilder I look, the bigger the natural high. It's outrageous, right? You haven't even seen my high heels. Utterly impractical in a mechanic's shop. The boys make noise and it just fires me up harder."

Wren smiled. She'd truly come a long way. "I'm glad, Alli."

"But we're not here for a coin meeting," she said swiftly. "You want your Body Snatchers!"

She led Wren up the rear hatch into the Beech 1900, where three four-feet-square wooden crates were lined up along the fuselage.

"Now, I know you weren't keen on these," she cautioned, plucking a pry bar off the wall, "but I think you're going to be blown away by the developments we've, uh, developed."

She beamed, then jabbed the bar into the nearest Attack Crate and cracked the lid off with a splintery crunch. She leaned in, tossed out some packing straw, rummaged for a moment, then pulled something truly outlandish out.

"Behold, the Body Snatcher," she crooned.

It looked something like an exoskeleton from a science

fiction movie, the kind of thing the Terminator would leave behind after all his flesh was melted off. It had no head, though, and no arms or limbs, more like a long and snaking metal spine. It began with a curved metal shoulder girdle that looked like a bicycle's chunky mudguard. Down from that dangled a four-foot spine of jointed metal stretching down to a heavy-looking metal block fitted with two sturdy hydraulic levers, each a foot long. Near the top there was a large clamp, and all over were smaller ratchets, with wires and cable seaming through and around the spine like nerve bundles.

"Looks heavy," Wren said.

"Yup, a good fifty pounds," Alli said, holding it out like it weighed a quarter of that. Working in the junk yard had worked wonders for her strength. "It has to be. Rugged, powerful enough to withstand some incoming fire, and tough enough to really lock in."

"Like a Body Snatcher," Wren said.

"Yeah. That was Hellion's idea. I guess it looks a bit like it's going to take over your body, right?" She held the rig out, eyeing it like she might a strappy dress in a boutique fashion shop. "This bit goes around your neck and clamps in, couple jack points into the skull, bolt it to your spine. We'll all be living in the Matrix!"

She laughed.

Wren had only seen earlier prototypes, before he'd lost himself in planning the spar platform raid. The design had come a long way since then.

"Show me," he said.

"With pleasure. You have a vehicle to be Snatched?"

Wren pointed to his Mustang.

"Roger that," Alli said, and strode over. She opened the driver's side door, dropped one knee on the seat and began fixing the Body Snatcher into place. The shoulder-like bicycle mudguard slotted almost perfectly over the upper arc of the steering wheel, swallowing it up. She worked a few dials to alter the size and angle of the arc, then it slotted into position perfectly.

"Huh," Wren said. "And that'll adapt to any wheel size?"

"Easily. Couple of brackets, it's prehensile like a snake."

She pulled the electric screwdriver out of its sheath at her hip, spun it like a gunslinger then drove three self-drilling screws through the topmost clamp attached to the Snatcher, locking it solidly to the steering column.

Wren winced as each screw drilled in. "Are there any non-destructive methods?"

"Sure. Powerful magnets can work, if we're dealing with thick metal surfaces. Why, is this your car?"

"No, but-"

"Not to worry, then," Alli enthused, and dropped the Snatcher's segmented spine down the side of the wheel, so the metal block thumped into the footwell. She swapped the drill out for another tool, a bolt gun on her left hip.

"Bolt gun?" Wren asked.

"Yup, your standard chassis is metal, but not too thick. This baby can drive a bolt two inches into solid cement, so it'll be fine. I'd use it on the wheel too, but we wrecked too many mechanisms this way. Worst outcome here, I hit a brake fluid line. But I probably won't." She seemed lost in thought for a moment. "I'd use this bolt gun for everything, if I could. Attaching rivets clasps to jeans? Check. Taking out rats in the junk shop? You betcha."

"Alli," Wren steered.

"On it, Boss man," she said, then ducked down to position the solid block carefully in the footwell, calibrated the two lever 'feet' jutting out of it onto the gas and brake pedals. Then she put the bolt gun to the outside edge of the box, where several brackets emerged.

The bolt gun fired with a loud thunk. She moved around

the box, bolting down each side, then she popped out of the car, smiling.

"Less than a minute, right?"

"I wasn't timing you."

"You should be. I've never seen a pitstop like it. All we need now is the magic touch. I'll let you do the honors."

Wren stared. "What magic touch?"

"Technically there's three magic touches." Alli held up three fingers and counted them down. "Turn the car on, put it in gear, take off the handbrake. It can do the rest itself."

Wren nodded, ducked into the Ford. The Body Snatcher looked like some kind technological parasite, feeding off the Mustang. It earned its name. He pushed the ignition button, put the car in gear then dropped the handbrake.

"Hellion, all yours," Alli said.

Wren waited.

Nothing happened.

"Is it-" he began, but Alli forestalled him with a raised hand.

"Synchronizing wireless," Hellion said in Wren's in-ear device. "Waking Snatcher."

The Body Snatcher rumbled. Wren's eyes widened as the steering wheel turned, first left then right.

"Six skateboard wheels on ball bearing trucks," Alli offered, "rubber-padded for grip, all inside the 'loop'. Call it the Snatcher's hands."

Wren leaned in, listening as the bicycle mudguard kept rumbling. Wheels inside the housing, now braced firmly against the steering wheel by the column-mounted bracket. Forcing the wheel to turn.

"You weren't working with wheels, last time I saw the prototype," he said. "It was steering sticks, drilled into the wheel itself."

"We've come a long way, baby. This mechanism can spin

the wheel as many times as we want, make the sharpest hairpin turns. I'd lean your head back out, Chris, Hellion has a tendency to-"

The Mustang's engine revved and the car jumped ahead. Wren barely pulled his head out in time, felt the wind rush by as the B-column sailed past an inch away.

"Off with his head," Hellion cooed. "Christopher, shall I round you up? Like sheep by sheepdog?"

The Mustang kept driving out over the runway. Wren stared after it. It sped up, slowed down, turned left, turned right, then came back toward them. Alli started laughing. Wren stared down the headlights. It screeched to a hard brake a yard away.

"You hadn't even tested the brakes," he protested.

"I trust Alli, yes? We are very good team. New engineer-hacker collective. Call us Helli."

Wren frowned. Hellion and Alli.

"Or Allion," Alli suggested. "My preference."

Wren walked around the Mustang to look at the Snatcher again. The means of its operation were clearer now. The mudguard arc turned the wheel. The levers bolted to the floor worked the pedals.

"What about reverse?"

"There is no reverse," Hellion said in his ear. "Not yet. Gearstick is very complicated, always different."

He grunted.

"There's probably a way to drill into the transmission," Alli said, "bypass the stick entirely and just work with the underlying gears and cables. It's different for every vehicle, of course, so that's tricky. I haven't cracked it yet."

"And if this thing hits a wall?"

"It must go through that wall," Hellion said cheerfully. "There is no turning around. No three-point-turn. But do not worry. I will not hit wall unless I intend to go through."

Wren peered closer at the Snatcher, looking for the glass dot of a camera lens. "Where's the camera? How can you see where you're going?"

"There is no camera, Christopher."

He looked up at the sky, but it was too dark, and if the drone was high enough he'd never see it anyway. Pictured a camera pointing at them from far above. "You're navigating top-down? We'll all look more like video game characters than ever."

"Yes, it is wonderful," Hellion said happily. "Most familiar for me. Very easy to automate."

"Automate?"

She laughed. "Yes. How do you think I control multiple units at once? Each are assigned target and subroutine programs handle vector. I steer flow of battle, not every unit personally. If it makes you more comfortable, we Allion are working on close-range radar systems, easy for mount to roof. Not top-down view, is the point. Better tactically. Same kind of technology as current parking and lane-change assist. Very easy, can drive vehicle in full dark, inside buildings, in tunnels."

Wren looked at Alli. "You can drive this thing in full dark?"

"There's really no limit to what we can do," Alli said. "Mount an autocannon? Why not, if we have one? It can fire on Bluetooth command. There're any number of James Bond tricks we can attach." She spun the bolt gun, holstered it. "Smoke canisters? Dropping wheel spike strips? Wings, even?"

Wren's eyes widened. "Wings?"

"If you like. I mean, it won't fly, but you can have them if it tickles your fancy."

He shook his head. "She's a bad influence on you."

"She, do you mean I, Hellion? Please, refer to us as

'Them', Christopher. Allion! They are bad influence on themselves. Many wonderful ideas have come from this partnership."

Wren rubbed the bridge of his nose. By blending the Foundation he'd created a monster. "Just tell me how many you've got, and how long it will take you to fit them to all the construction equipment Teddy's been putting into position."

"We have eleven," Alli answered. "It'll take me one minute each to install, if the vehicle has standard gas/brake pedals. If it's non-standard construction equipment, or it's all-metal and requires magnet fittings, then two minutes."

Wren nodded along.

"You've done very well. Let's get to it, shall we?"

"And what is plan, Christopher? Snatch vehicles, then?"

"Set up the strike team to come in on several vectors. We ram the base all at once. Shred the fencing, knock out the lights, overwhelm them with autonomous vehicles they won't be able to stop themselves firing at."

"Excellent show," Helion said, "and objective?"

"Cover me while I grab Brigadier General Hellström. Make enough noise that they don't realize it until we're well out. Then we pump him for all he knows. Bring this bullshit to an end."

There was silence for a moment. "Yes," Hellion said at last. "This is acceptable plan."

"Let's get to it then, shall we?"

"I will drive," Hellion said, and pulled the Mustang forward abruptly. "I wish next, Allion my dear, for pneumatic door-opening capacity. Like Back to the Future DeLorean. This would be excellent power, very practical, most impressive."

"Taking a note, partner," Alli said, and opened the rear door for Wren. "Gentlemen first."

He laughed, ducked into the back of the Mustang.

24

SURPRISE

Three hours later, Wren stood in the forest half a mile from Sheppard Air Base, a five-ton bright yellow construction backhoe loader grumbling by his side and his fists clenched in fury.

Across the state of Texas, numerous buildings were burning. Residential homes. Churches. Shops, offices and restaurants. A horse ranch. A hotel.

Hundreds of people were dead.

Federal forces had attacked shortly after dusk, en masse and irresistible: paramilitary SWAT, SEAL and Marine teams swarming in their thousands. Prisoners had been taken, but more had been killed.

X followers were being blamed for the downing of his 787.

Wren had seen the intelligence behind the decision. In various forms that intelligence was being shilled all across the national media, and it looked solid on the surface; just enough truth in the manufactured 'evidence' to sell it to the American people. But it wasn't true.

The X members who'd died in the federal onslaught were, as far as the Foundation could tell, at about the same level of loyalty as Yolanda Queen. They liked some of what X had said. They held some sympathies, but they weren't going out there burning themselves alive.

They weren't the ones who'd commandeered Sheppard Air Base. They were barely organized, any more than loose affiliations formed at fringe X rallies and on social media. But when the missiles dropped, the soldiers rocked up and the bullets came their way, they'd stood their ground and fought back, which made it look like they were guilty.

Now they were patsies.

The whole thing was a travesty of injustice. A blind and foolish over-reaction, spurred on by fake intel planted by the real perpetrators. Followers of X weren't generally Wren's favorites, but these people hadn't deserved this. Even the news channels were running their breaking updates with a mournful tone, as if on some level they too understood this was all wrong.

Maybe it was a false flag. Maybe it was just violence as distraction. Wren couldn't unpuzzle the purpose of it, and that galled him all the more. Now the Texas legislature were extending their emergency session, in direct collaboration with the federal government.

This thing was far from over.

"On your mark, Christopher," came Hellion's voice in his ear.

He ignored her, too sick with anger to respond. In the last thirty minutes, since the first of the attacks had rained down, he'd tried to call Sally Rogers and Gerald Humphreys to get them to call off the reprisals. Neither had answered. He'd tried others he knew from his twenty-year career in the military and in intelligence, counseling an immediate drawdown and a thorough investigation, but none had listened.

His country had become afraid of its own shadow, firing at ghosts.

Smoke rose over the steeple of a megachurch in Odessa, where the pastor had been an outspoken X apologist. The faithful caught at prayers, now in body bags. Women, children, the aged. There was no good justification for it.

"Christopher," Hellion said.

"Light them up," he answered. "All eleven, for immediate approach."

"Beginning." Keys clacked. "Furthest vehicles will begin approach, will reach inner ring in ten minutes."

"Send me now," Wren said, stepping two feet up onto the wheel ridge of the backhoe. It loomed huge in the darkness, eight tons heavy with a bucket scoop on an excavator-style boom at the back and a large iron blade for the front loader. Resting by a tall gravel heap, left there between public works.

All eleven of the heavy construction vehicles they'd co-opted were circled at various distances around Sheppard Base, either hot-wired in situ where Hellion's drones had found them, or brought in specially from construction rental companies. They had a few bulldozers, some motor loaders, more backhoes, a crane, two dump trucks. All huge, heavy-duty, and capable of taking direction from Allion's Body Snatchers.

Civilian infrastructure, easily repurposed to serve a military end.

"Send you now?" Hellion repeated. "You will be first, alone. Unsupported."

"Element of surprise," Wren said.

"This is surprise to everyone, Christopher! It is not plan. Plan is to strike together. Sow confusion, reap chaos. This plan cannot change now, it is too late. This is your plan!"

Wren gritted his teeth. He had offered the plan, that was true, but things changed. After so many had died, he wasn't about to risk any more of his people if he didn't need to. "I'm going alone. Nobody comes with me. This is not a battle we can win, against two thousand military personnel on highest readiness. The best we can hope is to throw them off their stride for a few minutes, and I don't need bodies on the ground to achieve that."

Hellion spluttered for a few seconds. "You did not say this before. You said twenty minutes. Window of operation. More distraction."

"The Attack Crates will do the job. I'm not risking anyone else if I don't need to, and I don't need to here, Hellion. I go in first and solo. I get to Hellström before their defenses are hardened. When the full blast of our cavalry hits, it'll cover the extraction. That's the way it has to be."

A few seconds of silent air passed, not even any clacking of keys, chased by a small sigh.

"Yes," she said. "I agree. This is indeed better tactic. One-man stealth mission under cover of fireworks."

Wren snorted lightly. If anyone knew tactics, it was Hellion. She'd lived through more battles than any of them, albeit in the virtual world of her computer. Still, the decisions were the same.

"Tell the others I'm sorry. Now start this backhoe up, or I'll drive it myself."

Hellion breathed out audibly. "Yes. Christopher. You will be sole man in lion's den. Odds are poor. This is your decision?"

"Veto-proof. Now fire it up."

Now keys clacked, and the backhoe's engine revved. "You will be in base four minutes before first additional vehicles arrive. And the swarm-"

"Keep the swarm as scheduled. I'll need it to cover my entrance."

"Very well. Good luck, Christopher. I will launch drone swarm now, monitor and relay."

"Thank you," Wren said.

The backhoe started forward, steering its way down the forest path with no driver at the wheel.

25

ATTACK 2.0

The backhoe rumbled forward at twenty miles an hour, through a night that was dark and cool. Fresh winds swept through the forest, carrying the scent of new growth and rising sap. Wren was alone, but it felt like Henry was riding with him, at his shoulder and urging him on.

An old friend. Saved from soul death in Afghanistan, going on to save Wren and the Foundation against the Saints, the Blue Fairy, against countless threats, and now lost.

He didn't speak. He barely moved. But his presence burned hot and terrible at Wren's back.

Soon the fence closed in ahead.

The earpiece was silent. It had been full of protests until he'd ordered Hellion to pull the plug. His team were unhappy he was going in alone, but he couldn't have it any other way. They weren't happy, but at least they'd be alive.

Henry had his Barrett M82 sniper rifle loaded, 7.62mm caliber Special Balls locked in. Wren could almost see him trailing the backhoe in the darkness. In a Humvee, with Abdul by his side, a flash cone tight on the rifle's muzzle.

Beyond the double fence lay the lurid lights of the base:

blinking red beacons along the twin runways; high-power floodlights sweeping across the grounds; the yellowish interior glow from the barracks, commissary and operations buildings; halogen white cones spread from twin hangars; the frequent blast of jets and helicopters coming in or taking off; foot patrols of airmen walking the runway with powerful hand flashlights.

"No jets inbound currently," Hellion said. "I am sending drones in."

"You have tactical control," Wren said.

"Understood. B4cksl4cker will be your operator."

Wren grunted. The digger was about to emerge from tree cover and cross the two-hundred-yard no man's land between the exterior fence and the forest.

"You with me, B4cksl4cker?"

"Always, Christopher," came the big hacker's deep voice. "We will be successful."

Wren knew he would be. With Henry and Abdul in back, he was invincible. "We will. Hellström?"

"In his office. Ten seconds until you hit first fence, Christopher."

Wren drew his Mark XIX Desert Eagle, fitted with an MK-234 suppressor and chambered with .50 AE rounds. In every other regard, he was in uniform as a Senior Master Sergeant, over close-fitting Twaron-weave plate-metal body armor. The kit wasn't a perfect replica, too bulky with the armor underneath, but it should pass in a pinch.

Ten yards out from the fence, perimeter alarms pierced the night.

"Drone swarm incoming," Hellion said.

"Udachi, Christopher," B4cksl4cker said. 'Good luck' in Russian.

Wren braced. The backhoe hit the exterior security ditch and dropped in, then surged right back up again and into the fence, pushing through like it wasn't there at all. The metal crosslinks stretched inward like the band of a catapult, and the nearest fenceposts warped, buckled and ripped from the ground like a string of yanked teeth. The backhoe pushed onward, and the fence kept bowing even as latch posts began ripping off the posts at twenty yards in. The big machine slowed when it hit the interior fence, but not enough. With mass and inertia on its side, within seconds the crosslinks of both fences began to pop.

At thirty yards the popping became a firecracker chain, like a thick swatch of Velcro ripping open. The fence burst and the backhoe jerked forward, its huge wheels trampling the straggling metal under its big wheels.

Now alarms filled the air. Big floodlights tracked in on the huge machine as it rumbled across the runway, Wren hanging on at the back. Figures ran out and gunfire erupted, some bullets ringing off the front blade, many whistling harmlessly into the night.

It meant nothing. Wren saw Yolanda Queen lying in his own booth back on the 787, shot in the lung because she'd stood her ground. Maybe dead, maybe alive.

"You have one patrol group to your seven o'clock, Christopher," B4cksl4cker said. "Hellion is steering drones into primary fire position. Suggest dismount as soon as they hit."

Wren almost laughed. Henry and Abdul would make short work of them. Ahead the base was erupting to life, more floodlights wheeling to pin him down, gunfire breaking out all around. Bullets clanged off the backhoe's front bucket blade, accompanied by the rising buzz of Hellion's drones swarming the air like a shiver of sharks.

"Floodlights," he said.

"On it," she answered.

Already he'd covered half the distance to the central

complex of buildings, coming up on where they'd downed his 787.

"Vehicles coming online," B4cksl4cker said. "Two MTVR trucks to your left, one has anti-aircraft gun emplaced. You must vacate backhoe before it is close."

Wren snorted.

They didn't know what they'd done. They were about to find out.

"Christopher!" B4cksl4cker urged.

Hellion's first drone hit.

The explosion engulfed the gatehouse guard towers far ahead and to the right, pulling Wren's focus like a ground-level firework. Instantly the twin beams of flood light were destroyed, along with the guards, their tower and the gate itself.

A second explosion followed near-instantly, as another drone dropped to blow the floodlight on the comms block. The blast seared afterimages across Wren's vision, blinking over the sudden darkness. Two pounds of Semtex steered down from the sky; unstoppable vengeance falling like the sword of Damocles.

"Go, Christopher," B4cksl4cker shouted. "Hellion will protect you."

He dropped off the back of the backhoe in darkness and ran left over grass siding. The backhoe broke right, ready to lead the air base in a wild chase around its own outer edge, pulling troops from the center like centrifugal force.

Bullets struck sparks off its bodywork. No operator to hit. Wren imagined Abdul driving, Henry in the back, picking his shots. He was in good hands.

Sirens wailed. Cordite smoke hung as wreaths in the chilly air. The first MTVR adjusted its path to track the backhoe, pulling it away from Wren as he reached the edge of the runway and dropped to a fast stride.

Nobody watching him. Somewhere another drone blew, and Wren distantly noted this was an incendiary model, not explosive. Napalm disgorged from a plastic waterskin held under the drone's belly, lit and trickling from the roof of the comms block, lighting up the night.

Bullets flew. People screamed. Orders rang out, even as the ghosts of Henry and Abdul fired up chaos all around.

Chaos was what he wanted. What he needed.

It felt right.

He strode deeper, nodding at the airmen as they raced past him, half out of uniform. Where they thought to, they saluted. He walked the path he'd walked before, took the same left turn as more incendiary drones dropped from the sky like fiery meteors. Buildings lit up. Vehicles blew up. Fires blazed like a battle scene across the Potomac.

"Security are massing at Hellström's office," B4cksl4cker said. "Infrared says he is alone. Suggest stealth attack."

Wren turned left and saw them ahead, clustered in front of Hellström's plantation office. Maybe the same six Master Sergeants who'd been there before. He didn't care. Everybody here was complicit. He had the Desert Eagle ready, but much easier if he didn't have to use it.

"Destroy them, Hellion."

He drew in. The Master Sergeants saw him. One saluted, then they picked out his face and they all raised their rifles. And exploded.

Body parts rained down. There weren't even screams. The raw percussive force of the bomb drone bounced off the blacktop and shredded sideways, blasting the closest to pink mist and disembodying the rest.

The blast left an imminent silence. Wren looked up at the windows, saw the silhouette lurking there, looking down.

Brigadier General Hellström.

Wren broke into a run. Passed through the carnage of the

blast. Soon the base would regain control, soon the drones would be exhausted and the discipline of thousands would win out, but that moment was minutes away yet.

The plantation's statues were shattered and splintered, knocked sideways by the blast. The glass doors were fractured. Wren kicked his way through. The First Lieutenant stood in front of his reception, weapon held out, but Wren was already firing. Two through the chest, one in the head, each discharge suppressed to a hollow thunking sound, like a struck wood chime. The guy dropped like a bad fashion.

Wren raced down the hall, firing where he needed to. Up the stairs he reloaded. More drone blasts rang from outside. Outside Hellström's office he stripped a flashbang grenade off his bandolier and tossed it in, closed his eyes and covered his ears as the immense blast of light and sound washed out, then chased it hard in.

The office was dark, lights blown by the flashbang, smoke hanging like marsh gas in the air. Hellström was on one knee in the center of the grand seal, the whites of his eyes wild and a gun held out.

"You're too late," he shouted, and fired.

Wren fired first. The big AE slug hit Hellström's shoulder and spun him. Something struck Wren in the belly, but he barely noticed. Hellström fired again but the shot went wide, and Wren surged in.

One foot went into Hellström's face, bowling him back. Wren dived for the weapon, but something punched into him from the side as he descended, knocking him sideways.

"Trap, Christopher!" B4cksl4cker shouted.

Wren hit the soft rug hard and rolled, caching sight of figures emerging from a recess in the wall, looked like insectile ninjas crawling on all fours, muzzle flashes bursting from their backs.

Firing automatic weapons.

Several hits landed across the plate armor on his torso and midriff, maybe three; he lost count as he scrambled for cover behind Hellström's desk.

What the-?

"TopDog weapons platform," B4cksl4cker's voice came in his ear. "Invisible to infrared. Three of them, get out!"

Wren's mind jumped erratically as the bullets battered into the desk's edge, striking clouds of splinters inches away from his face. Slumped against the side, and was he bleeding? His ears rang with the cacophony of gunfire. Definitely bleeding. Three streams of unrelenting automatic fire. TopDog? It was a DARPA program, canine-style robots designed to serve in a combat support position. He'd used them himself in the past, for pack carrying and surveillance, but never as a weapons platform.

Weapons platform?

He almost laughed. He had the Body Snatchers, hybridized efforts to turn vehicles into military fighting machines. Seemed Hellström had the real thing.

B4cksl4cker was shouting something, but the sound of it was smothered by a gray wave of pain and shock. Then the bullet rampage halted, and instead there came the thud of metallic feet stamping around the desk. TopDogs on patrol, circling around toward him.

Nothing the Desert Eagle could do against them. At two hundred and fifty pounds a piece, all solid metal and hydraulics, any shot from the Desert Eagle would be like trying to bring down a backhoe with an AR-15.

Were there three? He couldn't remember. His vision blurred. Hit how many times? One hand came up sopping with blood. He cursed.

Five seconds gone already? Ten?

"Move, Christopher!"

He turned to the left. A TopDog was right there, eyeless

face staring into his, the autocannon barrel mounted down its back spinning up.

Wren rolled, barely escaping the laser-like hail of fire as he tumbled behind Hellström's desk.

"Hellion, get in here!"

"Drone cannot pass through window, Christopher!" she shouted back. "I have just one within range, make access!"

Now he did laugh. The TopDog stalked around the desk, vast and black, pneumatic limbs hissing and flexing like metal muscles, its near-range scanners homing in on Wren in a millisecond, autocannon already spun up, letting loose a lightning roar of gunfire.

Wren rolled into the footwell of the desk in time, barely big enough to fit him. A desk as big as a boat, his swirling brain said. A rush of power to sit behind it. Like the Resolute Desk in the White House. Only one way to…

Before he thought about it too much, Wren rolled onto his feet in a deep squat, braced his shoulders against the underside of the desk and pushed.

It hoisted an inch. Maybe two hundred-fifty pounds of solid oak, squat-lifted from an impossibly low position, already leaking blood and compromised. The TopDog circled in, the arc of its incoming fire shredding Hellström's fine carpet. Wren's dimming vision washed to black, but like the TopDog itself, he didn't need to see for this.

With everything he had he thrust upward, surging the desk a foot high, then spun like he was an Olympic shot-putter. The desk swung around hard and clubbed the TopDog in the side. It jogged a slight step sideways, the hail of fire cutting out as it fought for balance, then toppled on its side.

Wren dropped the desk atop it. Not heavy enough to do any real damage, but enough weight to pin it and the autocannon down.

Wren sagged back in the tight leg-space beneath the desk.

Voices screamed in his ear. It seemed like he'd spun a full one-eighty, so now he was looking back over the office. It was dark but for the yellow spill of fire through the windows, now behind him. The air was filled with smoke. Hellström was on all fours in the doorway, crawling away; looked like he wasn't getting far under his own steam.

Neither was Wren.

The giddiness of blood loss settled over him like a numbing fall of snow. He had maybe a minute of decent operating time left. A few minutes more than that, he could bleed out and that would be all she wrote.

The two remaining TopDogs stalked toward him through the smoke, cannons training in. Wren laughed. "Good doggy," he murmured.

"Windows, Christopher!" Hellion shouted.

He needed cover, and reached a blood-slick hand up to the lip of the desk, caught it on the second try and pulled forward with everything he had. The nearest TopDog started firing. Bullets pummeled into the drawers and sprayed sideways like the cutting blade of a can-opener, closing in on-

Wren heaved with everything he had, toppling the desk forward. Hellström's papers and computer and keyboard tumbled as the desk capsized. Wren barely got his fingers out of the way before it slammed down, dropping a two-inch thick screen of hardwood between him and the TopDogs.

Bullets hammered the surface at his back. Wren spun back to the windows, reaching for the Desert Eagle, but it was gone. The only thing nearby was the first TopDog. The weight of the desk had been lifted and now it was kicking at the air, trying to right itself.

Wren rolled up to it, wrapped one arm under its belly and lifted. The autocannon fired upward by his face, chewing into the ceiling. Wren spun in a delirium of noise and exhaustion, the world swirled and he made the best bet he could.

Released.

The TopDog flew and hit the window. Glass blew out like an orchestra reaching the climactic moment.

"Down, Christopher!" Hellion shouted.

Her drone tore in through the shattered window, almost bouncing off Wren's shoulder. The other Dogs were already firing. Wren fell, barely able to keep his feet any longer, and tucked in behind the desk.

The drone blew. The room thundered. The blast drove the desk skating over the rug to hammer into his back and shoulder. Noise and fire chased the room's last oxygen out of the window, looking like an orange aurora borealis against the moonlit sky.

"Christopher!" shouted Henry in his ear. Maybe it was Yolanda Queen? Could be Abdul. He wasn't sure, could be anyone of a thousand lost. Could be little child Grace herself.

"Get up!" the voice shouted.

He saw Henry. Not Henry as he'd been, under the water with blood fountaining from his ruptured skull, but Henry in his prime, atop the Anaximanderian pumping station and saving all their lives with sniper shots through the chalk dust.

"Get up, Chris," he shouted, holding out his hand. Wren took it and climbed to his feet.

The room was in tatters. Dark and garlanded with smoke. TopDog corpses twitched like broken levers, their bodies shredded. Three steps and Wren fell, but now Abdul was there to catch him. Not Abdul at the end, throat slit, but Abdul in his prime too, pinning down the Saints from the desert around their biker bar. Strong and proud. Between them, Henry and Abdul carried him through.

Hellström was in the corridor outside. Crawling and leaving a trail of blood. Another TopDog casualty.

Henry put a boot in his spine. Abdul picked him up by his belt. Together the four of them hobbled to the end of the corridor, tumbled down the stairs and out onto the street beyond, where the third TopDog had been reduced to blacked metal shards by another drone explosion.

Wren weaved on his feet.

In a second a huge yellow dump truck crashed up. Hard brakes. The doors flung open. Doona and Alejandro were there.

Henry and Abdul melted away, while Alejandro took charge of Hellström. Doona helped Wren into the passenger bench of the dump truck, laid out like Yolanda Queen, where she set to work on him at once, as the truck roared away under Hellion's remote control.

Doona ripped his shredded Twaron away. Poured coagulant powder and stanched gauze on the worst of the wounds. Got tourniquets in place, just like he'd done for the air marshal.

"You're going to be OK," Doona shouted over the cacophony, though Wren wasn't sure he believed her. Around them the base was exploding and burning, but all Wren could see was Hellström's face as he kneeled in the smoke, his voice as he shouted the words.

You're too late.

Always too late.

26

DARKNESS

Wren walked in the desert. The sun was a white hole in the acrylic-blue sky, like a welder's spot gun was burning through reality, beating down with heat. The sand was a dried-blood red, and all the cacti were withered and still.

No animals. No growth. No wind.

Ahead stood his father.

Apex of the Pyramid. He was young again, in his prime, blue eyes sparkling with possibility and the raw inferno of belief. The world was going to bend for him, that gaze said. The world was going to burn.

He beamed at Wren.

"Pequeño 3," he said. His deep voice rolling across the desolate land like distant thunder.

"Father."

"Your time has come to choose."

The Apex spread his arms. Wren noticed two shallow mounds of sand, one to either side. Each was ten feet in diameter, laid out in twin clearings, rising a foot above ground level. Wren looked more closely.

Each mound thumped like an aortal pulse. As if dozens of

hands, buried ten feet deep, were hammering up from below. Slowly suffocating. Buried alive.

Thump thump.

"Your family," the Apex said, gesturing with his left hand, then his right. "Your Foundation."

Wren looked.

He'd survived one of the Apex's pits. All his brothers and sisters had survived, but many hadn't. Unknown numbers had died in the desert's embrace.

"Choose." The Apex said.

Wren looked feverishly from mound to mound. "My family's on the left?"

The Apex's beam spread wider. "Or the right. I forget."

Wren stared. Sweated under the heat gun sun. The mounds looked the same. There was no difference.

"There's only time for one choice, son," the Apex said. Came around to stand behind Wren, one hand warm on his shoulder. "I'll be proud of you either way."

Wren tried to move. Tried to run. Imagined himself digging like a dog, windmilling sand out between his legs as he tunneled down to save someone, anyone.

But he didn't move, like there was ice in his bones, freezing him in place.

The thumping of the mounds slowed. Stilled. Stopped.

"The truth is, you were always weak," the Apex whispered in his ear. So close, but Wren couldn't move an inch, frozen to the spot. "My little cactus wren, mewling into the night. There is no help coming, Pequeño. No warmth. No kindness. Only darkness from now until the end of days."

At last the ice in Wren's bones melted, and he bucked forward. Dug until his hands bled, uncovering body after body deep in the pits, faces puffed like Henry's, eyes bloating and red, mouths full of sand…

Wren jerked awake.

Sweating. Thrashing. Frantic and afraid.

"Easy, big guy," came a soothing voice. "Easy, OK, we're getting there."

Cool hands came on his shoulders. He couldn't see anything but blurry colors. He tried to shake himself free, but he was so weak. The ice was back in his bones, and he couldn't do a thing.

"Shh, it's OK, you're through the worst of it now. Rest. Chris, rest."

Exhaustion rushed through him. Maybe drugs, he couldn't tell, and they ushered him back under.

When he woke next it was calmer.

Light spilled in through a window nearby. The walls and ceiling were a cool white, broken by stark blocks of color. Modern art, it looked like. Here was a Dali-esque desert of melting compasses. Here was the clay model of a giant upside-down head on a stick, painted gray.

Wren lay on a white bed. He tried to push himself up, and a pain in his belly laid him flat out and gasping. Nausea followed the pain, and he unpeeled a white sheet, looked down at his bare chest. There was white bandaging on the left side of his abdomen. There were broad purple bruises all across his torso, each as big as a dinner plate.

He remembered Hellström's office. The nightmarish TopDogs, barking bullets that lashed his body. Multiple hits. Looked like his Twaron body armor had handled some of them, leaving those residual bruises, but at least one had bitten through.

Once again, he tried to lever himself upright. His belly throbbed, but he used his arms as props and managed it. Sitting on the side of the bed, legs touching the floor, he focused on pushing back the nausea. Tried a twist, looking over his left shoulder and down the line of his back.

There was bandaging there too. Lined up with the

bandages on his belly. A through-and-through shot, looked like it was two inches in from his side. Likely shredded some intercostal muscles; that was the tightness he was feeling. The nausea could mean the slug had clipped his intestines. The fact he wasn't dead though, bloated with sepsis, meant someone had sewn up the worst of the damage.

He looked out the window.

Saw a cityscape.

Blocks spreading out. Not a huge city. Residential, commercial, a few malls, spreading away into an orange-green heat haze. Maybe he was on the fifth floor. An apartment. He watched traffic flow through nearby intersections, heard the distant sound of police sirens, horns honking, normal life. Maybe the outskirts of Dallas.

He got to his feet, moved carefully over to a sleek white dresser. A full-length copper mirror, leaned against the far wall, and he appraised himself. Dressed in black shorts, bandaging on his belly, another bandage on his right thigh, one under his right arm that he hadn't even noticed.

It felt hot to the touch. His thigh was tight but otherwise all right.

He remembered the escape from Sheppard. Third time in, third time out. A wild race down I-44, glimpsing Doona as she patched him up then passed him off to, who? Going where?

The door opened.

Alli appeared. She didn't run up and hug him. She looked different. It was the hair. It wasn't red anymore. The interwoven tassels of red and blue were gone too, returned to her natural jet black. She wasn't wearing some wild mechanic's jumpsuit either, fringed with riotous colors, just blue jeans and a black Harley t-shirt. Even her eyes were different, and her whole demeanor.

"Chris," she said, sounded flat. "You need to come see this."

"How long?" he croaked.

"Long enough to miss the gunfire, in time for the fireworks," she said, and stepped up. Put her left arm around his waist, guided his right over her shoulders and led him toward the door with an easy expertise.

"That bad?" he asked.

"Worse. You'll see."

27

WORSE

The bedroom led out onto an open plan apartment, with the living room, dining room and kitchen all in one space. It was floored in blond machined wood and framed with bright white walls, broken by more gallery-like sparks of colorful art. Whoever's place it was, they had a nice eye for interior design.

"He's up?" came a voice from the living room, followed by Alejandro rising from a U-shaped sofa arrangement. He wore jeans and a t-shirt too, like a uniform, with his long dark hair pulled back in a ponytail. He had no injuries as far as Wren could see, and that was good. A big flatscreen TV was turned on in the corner, showing a gaggle of reporters crowding a lectern spiky with microphones. The sound was muted, but a banner played along the bottom of the screen:

FORMAL INAUGURATION MOVED UP

Formal inauguration?

"How is he?" Alejandro asked, coming around the sofa to hover nearby as Alli led him over.

"Heavy," Alli said. "A little help."

Alejandro ducked in, took Wren by the other side and guided him down to the sofa. There was a microwave ready meal on the glass coffee table, mac and cheese half-eaten, alongside scattered playing cards.

"Poker?" Wren asked.

"Gin rummy," Alli answered, then grunted as Wren's weight came off. His stomach throbbed as he sank onto the sofa, but he kept enough tension to stay seated upright on the firm cushioning. "Got to do something during lockdown you know?"

Wren looked up at her. She was chewing her lip. Alejandro looked worried.

"What lockdown?"

Alli looked at Alejandro. Like they were deciding who was going to tell him the bad news. Alejandro opened his mouth.

"Texas seceded!" Alli blurted.

Alejandro looked at her. Wren looked at both of their earnest faces.

"Seceded from the Union?" he asked.

They said nothing.

"Bullshit. All right. April Fool's Day, you got me. How long have I been out?"

Alli sank into the sofa beside him and took his hand.

"I'm sorry, Chris. It's true. You've been out for six days. One shot through your lower intestine, it was touch and go with blood loss, we were all worried about infection, but you pulled through. The rest of the hits were grazes and bruises." She squeezed his hand, like she was checking he was real. "We've been waiting for you to wake up since it happened. Um. The doctor comes around to check on you, keeps you sedated so you can heal, but we have to be careful. She's Foundation fringe, but it's getting harder. Everyone's watching everyone out there now, like some crazy surveillance state. Like something out of 1984." She chewed on her lip. "Doona's out right now, it's her turn. Gathering intel, trying for a line out, you know how it is." Her face soured. "Well, no, you don't know. It's..."

She trailed off. Alejandro picked up.

"Six days ago, the Texas State Senate met in an emergency session in Austin. Perhaps you remember this, after the jet blew? Well, it was around then that we found an answer for what they wanted off your 787. Not a flash drive full of blackmail or a suitcase nuke, but a person. A woman, a state senator. She was fleeing a quorum call, an arrest warrant by the state house's bailiffs, trying to enforce her attendance for a particular vote. She'd already fled to California by road with her family, was on her way to Washington to lodge a federal case, or something. She..." he paused, swallowed, went on. "I'm pretty sure she's the woman you met on the 787. Amira Matheson?"

Wren stared.

That was a lot to take in.

"What?"

"Yeah," Alejandro went on. "Amira Matheson. Two kids. Recently elected state senator. Somehow these guys, X, Hellström's people, whoever they really are, they had it all planned out. They snuck her into the state house, must've compelled her with her kids, and she became the deciding vote that tipped the vote to a two-thirds supermajority, twenty-one out of thirty-one. Enough to formally initiate the secession of Texas from the Union."

Wren stared. "If this is a joke, it isn't funny."

"We wish," Alli said, picking up the thread. "Unfortunately not. The vote passed, and they acted immediately. They had everything in place to lock down the borders and secure all military personnel who weren't already loyal. The Internet dropped out within minutes, along with every landline, satellites, everything. They hit the kill switch on all the physical infrastructure, it seems.

Nothing's going in or out, so no Hellion and B4cksl4cker, no Theodore, no Sally Rogers or Gerald Humphreys. We have no sense of what's going on out there, other than what they tell us." She took a breath, gave his palm another squeeze. "There's already a president of Texas. Hunter Kason, his name is. He was a news pundit, a real X shill, on an extremist network. He's already formed his cabinet. The state senators are now senators proper. It's all..." she paused. "It's really f-ed up."

Wren looked at Alejandro, who nodded soberly. Hunter Kason again, the man who'd given him the nickname 'Big Bad Bird'. He looked at the TV news, with its banner about formal inauguration. He looked back at Alejandro, who gave him another sober nod. It felt like he'd passed through the looking glass.

"Not possible. A state can't just secede. This is..."

"Yup," Alli said. "That's pretty much what everyone said. But guess what? It can."

"It can't."

"Wrong again. You know they've been talking about this on the TV constantly. Justifications and explanations of old laws and precedent. We all have them memorized now. How the Constitution enshrines the right to self-determination. Alejandro has this bit down."

She looked at Alejandro. He shrugged. "It was on the citizenship test. The relevant part goes, 'Governments are instituted among Men, deriving their just powers from the consent of the governed - that whenever any Form of Government becomes destructive of these ends, it is the Right of the People to alter or to abolish it, and to institute new Government.'"

Wren opened his mouth, closed it.

"Alter or abolish, they keep talking about that," Alli said. "It's a right we executed in 1776, getting out from under mad

King George. That's the precedent. Then don't even get me started on all the sub-arguments."

Wren felt like he was being smothered under a tide of confusion. "Sub-arguments?"

"About Texas the Republic? How they declared independence from Mexico before, formed up their own government. 1835, right?"

"1836," Alejandro said.

"1836, right. Of course they were part of the Confederacy too, so there was that. 1860. Also, that Texas wasn't even part of the original United States. It was annexed in 1846, after ten years on its own. There's a lot of backfilling going on, Chris, intellectual Zambonis trying to smooth everything over and make it look legitimate."

Wren had to put good sense aside to grasp it. "To make Texas its own country."

"Yeah." Alli sighed. "And you won't like what they're calling it."

"What they're calling it?"

"It's stupid. I can't even. Alejandro?"

"Texas with a small 't'," Alejandro said. "All lower-case, except the 'x' in the middle. That's capitalized."

Wren tried to envision that. It felt like every time they threw him a lifeline, it just weighed him down more. Then his eyes widened. "You mean, teXas?" He emphasized the central 'X'. "Only a capital X?"

"With X at its heart," Alejandro said. "A nation of X-heads."

Wren sat silently, jaw dropped, reeling.

This was worse than the nightmares. It was edging on satire. Amira Matheson was alive, along with her kids, which was good, but she'd been used to cast an illegal vote? teXas was a country of its own, indivisible under X?

Too many pieces didn't make sense. He bulled through the surface and made a grab for something familiar.

"Secession's a declaration of war," he reasoned. "At least, that's how it went last time. Every time, really. War of Independence. The Mexican-American War. The Civil War. Why isn't the United States attacking now?"

Alli heaved another sigh.

"We're guessing, on that front. There's no line out to the USA, but what the media here's saying is all about the vote in the state senate. Amira Matheson pushed them into a two-thirds majority, and with the rest of the US in pieces, barely governed at the federal level and trust in institutions at an all-time low, who was going to push against a supermajority like that? Not any of the neighboring states. They were all Confederate bedfellows, to boot, some with a lot of remaining sympathy for the 'Lost Cause'. To them, teXas is a thought leader. If Washington tries for another round of attacks, they may lose the whole South, the Midwest, maybe the entire middle of the country."

Wren turned that around in his head. It made a kind of sense. What was the United States, after all, but a collection of states? What was the Army, the Air Force, the Navy but a combination of the armed forces from every individual state?

Then he hit on the inciting factor.

"The reprisals?"

Alli nodded. "Bingo. The 787 was destroyed, and early intelligence pointed to X outposts on Texas soil? That was all a setup to force them to overreach. Washington felt backed into a corner, they had to lash back fast and with overwhelming force." She sighed. "They didn't consider the immediate backlash to the reprisal, though. There's X sympathy everywhere, now. It played like massive federal overreach, and they lost the consent of the governed."

More waves washed over Wren. A long and complex plot. Maybe he was starting to grasp it, though. The scale of it.

"They're terrified," he said.

"Washington?" Alli asked. "We figure so. The teXas secession is a spark that could set off a chain reaction. Right now, I'm betting every X-sympathizer in North America is on teXas' side. This new country is the aggrieved party. It's the people here who died. They're the ones standing up for the 'little guy', and President Ablas is King George, lashing out like some dying beast after the Tea Party."

Wren nodded. It didn't sit well, but it made sense. He tried to imagine the conversations taking place in the White House, with CIA Director Gerald Humphreys in place, advising President Ablas right alongside, what the Joint Chiefs would be recommending.

It brought on the unthinkable possibility.

"So they're accepting it. This thing actually might stick. They're not just trying to stop the bleeding, avoid risking more states. They're trying to stem it permanently. This is an amputation."

Alli shifted uncomfortably. "They don't have much choice. Especially when you look at that supermajority. A two-thirds vote, Chris. It's phenomenal. It took folks acting across the aisle together in ways they haven't for decades; the closest thing to political consensus our country's seen in a long time. "

There was silence for a moment.

"Not our country," Alejandro corrected.

Alli grunted.

"When the borders locked up, everyone within the territory of teXas became a teXan citizen, by law," Alejandro went on. "We're supposed to go out and get our new photo ID. We're in breach already. Every time we go out, we're risking importation."

Wren frowned. "Importation?"

Alli stood up. Too antsy to stay still, it seemed. "I'll get you a drink. Some water, right? You haven't eaten or drunk for a week. Yeah. Some water."

She walked off.

Wren looked at Alejandro.

"This is where things get ugly," Alejandro said.

28

IMPORTATION

Wren sat with his head in his hands, watching the television.

He'd heard enough. They'd talked for over an hour, and now he was watching the rest. Alli and Alejandro kept out of his way. Playing gin rummy, maybe. Every now and then they offered him drinks or snacks.

He'd already eaten, a mac and cheese ready meal of his own, a couple of pints of warm water, sipped slow.

"It's a restart to your guts," Alli explained awkwardly. "The doctor said. She said you should wake up today. Took out all the tubes. Said to take it real slow. Mushy food, only. Reawaken your gut biome. Flora and, uh…"

She'd trailed off. Wren wasn't even looking at her.

Importation.

There was nothing about it on the news, but his people had seen it happening. By day, by night. The new teXas special police descending en masse to sweep 'non-citizens' off the streets, into unmarked vans and away.

Shouting. Cudgeling. Doors getting rammed through. Protests getting crushed and the people carried away. Occasionally bodies left in the streets, bleeding out.

"Away to where?" he'd asked.

They hadn't known. Each day they took it in turns to go out. Leave before dawn, try not to let the neighbors see them, try to make connections with other Foundation fringe members, exchange intel and build a picture of what was happening out there, try to get an outside line through radio or a satellite hookup. Then come back after dusk, to this apartment owned by a Foundation fringe member, currently out of state.

Living on borrowed time.

Wren watched the TV, surfing the channels. None of the usual streaming services were available, all cut off when teXas declared independence, but there was no shortage of content. Seemed the teXas leaders had foreseen this situation and stockpiled tens of thousands of favorites, TV shows and movies both, now available for free from a dedicated streaming app. Like the entertainment roster on a plane. All pirated, but who cared? A panacea for the masses, give them something to do while the country changed hands.

Scrolling through the playlist, though, Wren noticed obvious gaps. He wasn't a big TV or movie man, but he knew about the tentpole blockbusters and major franchises. There were obvious gaps, many from within the last few years. Almost as if someone had taken the snipping scissors of redaction to the Hollywood 'agenda'.

He scrolled on. The only fresh content was news, and there were only two offerings in that regard: one was a 24-hour state news apparatus, on which President Kason was frequently seen giving upbeat speeches to adoring crowds about the incredible future that lay ahead.

Kason was nothing special to look at. Dark hair, six-foot-something, lanky build with a perpetually quizzical expression. Maybe he'd engineered this whole X thing.

Maybe he was just the front man selected by the puppet masters in the shadows. Didn't matter. He did the job.

The other news channel was a revamped version of hunter Kason's old network, already adapting perfectly to the X takeover. They had seamless new X-based graphics, the new teXas flag everywhere in their branding, almost as if they'd known in advance that the secession was coming. The new flag was the same as the old Texas state flag, except in one major way: a red horizontal bar along the bottom right, a white bar in the upper right, a blue vertical bar on the left, but with a large white 'X' where the old single star had been.

Just looking at it made Wren's blood boil.

Still, he couldn't stop watching this channel. It was an endless, slick stream of bright and hopeful lies, parroted by cheerful young blond reporters alongside tawny old gray-haired stalwarts, making jokes about the new unity. The things they said weren't important, of course, all BS and fabrications. It was what they didn't say that counted, revealing a wealth of information in the gaps between their lies.

The ghost truth.

The X narrative showed through in the kinds of people who got spotlighted versus the kind who never appeared, unless as screaming, violent mobs. There were sobbing victims of the USA's reprisal attack against X, looking solemn and sincere, versus mobs of raging protesters. There were two-point-four-children families standing gravely in front of churches, mourning their dead, versus a masked troop setting a police car on fire.

It was straight-up brainwashing. No wonder people were cheering along the 'importations'. Reporting their neighbors. You only had to believe a little of this stuff to watch more, and that led you down the rabbit hole to believing more and more.

His head pounded. His stomach throbbed. There was a tightness in his thigh and under his right arm. He sipped his water.

Prevalent everywhere on both news channels was Amira Matheson. They had her out en masse with the other senators. Pretty in her hijab, intelligent in what she said in her quiet, thoughtful tones, clearly under enormous stress but resourceful enough to fake it well. A family-focused Muslim woman who'd embraced X, they said. She was their silver bullet of unity and diversity, proving anyone could embrace the way of X. It wasn't a faith, exactly. It was a call to some form of traditional teXan values.

As he watched her standing by Kason, nodding along with the other twenty-one 'yes' senators, Wren thought of her warm hand in his, back on the 787. Her misting eyes. Her kids and their rabble, and the way she'd hurried back to him after the cucumber incident, asking if they could talk.

Maybe it had been about this. The quorum call, and a vote she'd been trying to escape. He pictured the way they must have threatened her, to get her to vote their way. The way they must've threatened her kids.

The ghost truth.

She'd already been on the run, and they'd just scooped her out of the sky.

"Of course we're not asking people to burn themselves alive!" the pundits would laugh and joke in lighter moments. "That's like Old Testament X. teXas is the New Testament. It isn't hellfire we're fighting, but Queen Ablas of the United States. The war against our freedom is real whether we like it or not, and all have been called to fight."

They didn't talk about how one-sided the battles were. Wren recognized footage of rioters that came from years back, labeled as protest mobs. Still they played on repeat. Disinformation spewed out endlessly.

"Who are they taking?" Wren asked.

Alli jolted in her chair at the sound of his voice, knocking over the card house Alejandro was building. He hadn't said anything in hours, and clearly they were on edge.

"What?" she asked, too loud. "Oh. Who? Uh…"

"The importations. Who is it?"

Alejandro cleared his throat. "From what we've gathered, it's primarily anyone who ever spoke out against X. Could be on social media, in print, on the street, anywhere. We don't have the Internet, but they must have the records still."

"How many?" Wren asked.

Alejandro thought for a second. "Hard to say. I've seen it happen dozens of times now. Doors smashed through, apartments left in wreckage, bodies in their wake. We're trying to build a whisper network of the Foundation fringe, but without the Internet it's a struggle. The people I have spoken to say it's happening everywhere. So thousands? Maybe tens of thousands, across the state. I mean country."

Wren grunted.

Alli chimed in. "I spoke to a guy two blocks over yesterday, Foundation fringe, he says his neighbor never said a single word against X, but he had a real thing for taking down flat-Earthers online. They grabbed that guy on night one."

Wren turned to her. "Flat-Earthers?"

"You know, people who think the Earth is flat?"

Wren rolled that around his head. "So X doctrine says the Earth is flat?"

Alli screwed up her face. "I don't think it's that, exactly. They just don't like too much science or empirical proof. Start arguing for that, it undercuts X, which undercuts their BS freedom schtick, and you buy yourself an importation ticket."

"Importation to where? What are they doing with them?"

They didn't know.

Wren had a pretty good idea. He'd seen mass-scale re-education efforts before, taking place in camps of some kind. Gulags, they'd called them in the USSR. In China they were 'vocational education centers'. In Germany they'd been concentration camps.

Wren sipped his water.

The scale of the changes in six days were overwhelming. They made him want to crawl back into his bed, sleep for another week then wake up and have everything back to normal. The country united. X banished. Henry and Yolanda Queen alive, Amira reunited with her children, Wren in Delaware with his kids and his wife, making a fresh go of it.

Like the early pages of the Stephen King book. A community. Neighbors who cared. Not neighbors who reported each other to the teXas Gestapo. A wave of nausea came over him and he hobbled to the bathroom, flipped the toilet lid and vented.

The kids called through the door, asking if he was OK.

"I'm fine," he managed, lying on the cold white tiles. Everything was white. The ceiling spun. Wren just lay there until the sickness passed.

"We all felt the same way," Alli's voice came through the door. "Sick to our souls, you know?"

Wren didn't say anything. Didn't know what there was to say.

"I was never all that rah-rah about the USA," she went on. "You know me. The patriotic colors in my hair, that was a kind of irony. But seeing this, it puts everything in perspective, you know? We weren't perfect. The union wasn't perfect. We were screwed up in so many ways. But it was infinitely better than this. This just feels like..." she trailed off. "Like a death. Like getting terminal cancer, and the future's been cut off. An experiment that failed. And I can't abide that."

Wren grunted.

"But we're not alone," she said, trying for upbeat. "We have the Foundation fringe. They're out there, laying low, if we can just reach them. Sally Rogers, Hellion and B4cksl4cker, Theodore the third, even Gerald Humphreys. They're all out there waiting, if we can just reach them. Maybe there's something they can do, something we can do. I don't know what. But we have to do it soon, Chris. Before they lock this state down at the inauguration. Before they find us and import us too."

He grunted again. About all he could manage.

"We're out here," Alli said, quieter now. "If you need us. OK?"

He heard her move away.

Everything she said was true.

It did feel like a death.

29

FEAR

Wren lay on the bathroom floor gazing up at the white ceiling tiles, thinking about the inauguration stage back in Washington. His brother had burned alive and taken most of the country's senators and many congresspeople along with him.

From such strange seeds came strange fruit.

Now X had annexed Texas. The USA had been cowed into doing nothing. In twenty-four hours there'd be fireworks and a new national holiday, with President Hunter Kason proudly lauding his new nation on a wave of importations, secession and violence.

It was bigger than anything Wren had faced before. He kept turning this new world in his head, probing for weak spots where an intervention might flip things around, and he kept coming up blank.

They'd planned well. They'd prepared. Wren just had himself and three team members in the middle of a hostile foreign power.

He rose to his feet and padded over to the bathroom window. Outside dusk descended across Dallas; the city getting dark, the streets growing quiet. All the bars had been closed and there was an 8 p.m. curfew now. Occasional sirens rang out, occasional shouts tore through the night; more innocents being imported for their thought crimes.

Twenty-four hours. If only he could bring the federal government in, they could end this thing in a matter of minutes. The nascent revolution would crumble in the face of actual force. But first he had to shake loose the stranglehold X held over the people, and the screen of legitimacy the supermajority vote had provided.

But how?

The wheels of his mind turned, and the window steadily darkened until he could no longer see outside at all, only the reflected image of his own face staring back at him. Scarred cheeks and red-tinged eyes. There were no answers. But maybe there was an idea.

He drank some water and brushed his teeth, clearing out the foul taste from his mouth. He took a cautious, painful shower, swapping out his bandages. The wound in his stomach was knotty and raw, inflamed at the edges still, with blue stitches pulling the skin tight. As he applied a fresh bandage, the idea took on clearer shape and definition. A fresh pair of jeans and t-shirt had been left just inside the door, and he pulled them on.

Back in the den, Alli was sitting with Doona at the table, playing cards again. Another round of gin rummy to while away the dead hours. The TV was on, muted in the background, showing another tearful X interview.

"Doona," he said by way of greeting. "Alejandro's gone out?"

She nodded numbly; eyes glassy. Not hopeful to see Wren. Just worn out. "It's his shift."

"Did you discover anything while you were out there?"

"There was a hanging," she said, her tone flat. "Five blocks south. Looked like regular citizens strung a woman up from the overpass, called her a collaborator. There were children cheering in the crowd."

Wren didn't know what to say. It sounded like something from the aftermath of the Third Reich. "Collaborating with who?"

"The 'Big Bad Bird'. You."

There was a frustrated rage in her voice. He felt it too. "I'm sorry you had to see that."

Doona shrugged. She'd seen worse, in her young life. It didn't make it easy.

"What are we going to do, Chris?" Alli asked.

He looked at her. "It's time I spoke to him."

Alli's eyes flicked to the side, settling on a door next to the bathroom.

"Has he given you anything yet?"

She opened her mouth, then took a second. "I didn't know what to ask. After we fixed up his shoulder, we tried, but…" she trailed off. "He just tells us we're going to die. Calls us traitors. We gagged him, after that."

Wren nodded. That's about what he'd expected.

He walked over and pushed open the door.

The room was around four yards square, bare inside but for a mattress, a bucket and two chairs by the door. The walls, ceiling and windows were heavily padded with soundproof baffling. A bolt had been driven into the center of the floor, from which a short chain led to a figure lying on the mattress.

Tall, thin, wearing gray sweatpants and a hoodie. Left shoulder bulky with bandaging, where Wren had caught him with an AE .50 bullet. Stripped of his rank, hands and ankles bound, wearing a sodden gag.

Brigadier General Mads Hellström.

Wren closed the door behind him. He laid out one chair for Brigadier General Mads Hellström, one for himself, then stripped the gag from the man's mouth and lifted him into the chair.

They both sat. Hellström's face was more lined, his hair less coiffed, but then six days and nights chained to a mattress would have that effect.

They looked at each other for a time, neither speaking. Not a staring contest, but an easing into the moment. In Hellström's dark eyes Wren saw new worlds stretching out. Women hung from Interstate overpasses, men stoned to death in public squares. He'd seen the absence of governance in overthrown states before, as 'regular' people acted on grudges they'd harbored for years, in the name of whatever the revolution dictated.

"Are they alive?" Wren asked.

Hellström's eyes narrowed slightly. "Who?" His voice was more gravelly than before. Mid-fifties and not cut out to be a prisoner.

"Amira Matheson's children," Wren said. "You brought a plane down just to bring her in. Used her to push the independence vote through by a two thirds margin, effect a screen of legitimacy, and I've got no doubt you used her kids to compel that vote." He took a breath. "Their names are Rania and Hendrix. Are they alive?"

The older man's eyes narrowed slightly. "This is what you want to ask me?"

"The first thing," Wren said. "Establish some rapport. Good faith. It costs you nothing to answer."

Hellström eyed him doubtfully. "It sets a precedent."

Wren snorted. "You don't seem a man too concerned with precedent. For one thing, the name of every other state follows grammatical rules."

Hellström took a second. "You mean the X in teXas?"

"You are sharp. Someone should make you a one-star

general, give you an air base, maybe you'll make something of yourself."

Hellström's expression held flat. "There is no precedent to follow in this case. We're not another state, after all. We're a sovereign country."

"I don't see many countries with capital Xs in their names."

"Not yet."

Wren said nothing for a moment. Hellström didn't budge.

"Amira Matheson's children. Let's get the ball rolling. Are they alive?"

Hellström gave a slight shrug, then winced as his shoulder wound twinged. "They were, when we took her. The priority was taking Matheson, as you say. We won't kill her children without good reason."

"Without good reason," Wren repeated. So many atrocities had been committed using mealy-mouthed logic like that. "As if any of this is good. As if the five hundred-plus people on that 787 died for a good reason."

Hellström jutted his chin forward. "They did. For freedom."

Wren clicked his tongue. "I'm not seeing much freedom out there right now, Mads. Curfews. Juntas. People getting killed to settle old grudges, or swept away to concentration camps."

"You know what they say," Hellström countered. "Freedom isn't free."

Wren almost leaped up and pummeled him. He wanted to. Beat him until he couldn't breathe anymore.

"That makes you angry," Hellström noted. "It's always the way with snowflakes. Peel back to the truth and they can't handle it."

Wren forced control back on his animal urges. Hellström was playing from the same hymn sheet as Maggie, it seemed, back in the fake town. "Now you're trolling me. Hoping I'll beat you unconscious, end the interrogation early."

"Perhaps. I've been interrogated before, Mr. Wren. But it is also a fact. You are categorically weak, because you are unwilling to pay the price true freedom requires."

"I suspect we have very different ideas about what freedom is."

"Yes, because you believe freedom is equal to slavery. Your freedom has my people following laws you change at will, has my people outnumbered by freaks and geeks you celebrate instead of shaming. Your freedom is a tax we cannot bear." He took a breath. Wren gave him all the rope he needed to hang himself, and Hellström leaned into it with a sneer. "Tolerance, you'll preach. The togetherness of the 'Union'. Never considering that your togetherness is built off our backs, and shreds the basic structures this country was built around. Faith in God. Family. Patriotism. That is the freedom I believe in!"

Wren set his jaw. He'd heard it all before. "I won't debate you on politics, Mads. Fact is, I'm in the harm reduction business. You go around blowing up jets and tearing up the Union, that makes you the bad guy in my book." He took a breath. "So, let's circle back around. Where are Amira Matheson's children?"

Hellström said nothing.

"You didn't even know I was on that 787, did you?" Wren asked. Trying a different tack. "You were after her, and my presence took you by surprise."

Hellström said nothing, but from the cast of his eyes it seemed Wren had piqued his interest.

"It must have been quite a moment, when you realized it really was me. The 'Big Bad Bird' himself, I hear he's X's greatest enemy? An enforcer for the federal government, the way they're telling it on TV." Wren leaned in. "So I was one hell of an opportunity, wasn't I? And I know you're not a man to let a crisis go to waste." Hellström gave nothing away, so Wren kept spinning. "That's why you tried to grab me instead of just blowing me up with the Reaper. You were seeing dollar signs. Go to the mob with Christopher Wren in your custody, the Big Bad Bird, they would have made you president. Not Kason."

Hellström cracked a small smile. "They still might."

Wren smiled right back. "Now we're getting somewhere. So let's talk turkey. I don't think you really care about teXas with an 'X'. My money says you think the name's just as dumb as the idea." He took a breath. "Truth is, I think you're just in it to win it. Put Mads Hellström first, raise yourself up, and it doesn't matter which myth you nail your colors to in order to achieve that. Whether it's the shining city on a hill or this new teXas, you don't care as long as you have the power. Am I right?"

Hellström's brows pulled together slightly. "It sounds like you're about to make a pitch, Mr. Wren. Either that or you just like the sound of your own voice."

"Probably it's both. But let's go with the former. You're a climber, Mads, and you thought you could climb me. I expect you made a deal with Kason; you deliver him Matheson, he puts you on a glidepath to the vice-presidency. Great positions for your children, too. Maybe you'd be teXas' second President, given time. A legacy, a dynasty."

"Get to the point."

"I am. Now we both know what you want. What I want is teXas with a capital 'X' dissolved in the next twenty-four hours, before the formal inauguration goes global. That's the money shot, right?" He paused, watching Hellström's throat. His pulse was racing. "I want the United States reunified before Kason cauterizes the amputation, and you're going to help me do that."

Hellström snorted. "Not possible, even if I wanted to."

"It is possible. You know it. It's why you're starting to sweat."

Hellström stared.

Wren played his trick card. "You're going to help me invalidate Amira Matheson's vote."

Hellström was silent. It was a different silence now, though. A charged silence, like electricity hanging in the air.

"I find her kids," Wren went on. "I get Amira herself and we talk to the airwaves. With her kids right there, Kason can't compel her anymore. She'll spill that the supermajority vote was forced. Maybe the other state senators were coerced too, and she'll spell that out. In a flash, your legitimacy dissolves. X is exposed. The other states pull back their support. Federal forces storm in and teXas crumbles, while you go on trial as a terrorist traitor guilty of mass-scale murder."

Hellström set his jaw. Maybe the first honest thing Wren had seen from him. "You have to find them first."

"That's where you come in."

"And why would I help you?"

"Because I can make you governor of Texas, Mads." Wren let that hang. "I won't like doing it, and it's not the Presidency, but it's a big step up from black-site prisoner awaiting execution, don't you think? We all have to start somewhere."

Hellström stared at Wren, then looked pointedly around the walls. "This is hardly a black site. We're deep in my country, Mr. Wren, filled with my loyal citizens. You're massively outnumbered. Your people are terrified. I've looked in their eyes and seen it every day."

Wren waved a hand. "You're exaggerating. Worried, maybe. Not terrified."

"Out of their minds with fear," Hellström pressed. "You've been asleep for a week, so how would you even know? First of all, they feared you would never wake up. Then they feared you would, but you'd be just as lost as them, which you clearly are. You think you have something to offer me?" He snorted. "We both know it's only days, maybe hours, before my people find us. You'll be executed live on-air, and your death will become our founding myth."

Wren shook his head. "Never going to happen."

"No? Ask your people how much progress they've made in breaking through our comms blackout. Even if you could find the Matheson brats, you'd never get the word out. We own this country, Mr. Wren, and its airwaves." He gestured toward the door. "They don't have anything but bad news to give you, do they? The only leverage you have is how unpleasant you make these last few hours for me, but I've been tortured before. Do your worst."

Wren felt the pain in his stomach getting worse. Hellström wasn't wrong.

"teXas has a big border," he tried. "When I'm ready, I'll leave with you in the trunk of the car. We'll roll across raw desert into New Mexico, from there to Arizona, where I'll put you in my private black site in the ground, right alongside the original X. You'll never see the sun again. That's my leverage."

Hellström's expression softened.

"The problem is, I don't believe you. I've sent countless men into combat, and I know fear better than any. I can see the terror in your eyes. There is no way out of this for you. Torture or kill me if you like, I don't care; my children will reap the benefit of my martyrdom. At least I have that. And what do you have? Cowards in the room next door, cowards in a fragmenting country that you can't possibly reach, and a family you'll never see again." He took a moment. All the time he needed. "Honestly, I pity you, Mr. Wren. The greatest day of your life was the day you killed the Apex. It will also prove to be the worst."

Nothing Wren could say to that. He had no concrete leverage, nothing more to say than noise to fill the air, and the bluff had been called. His head pounded, and it felt like slivers of glass were slowly being pushed into his stomach.

He stood. "We'll talk again."

"I look forward to accepting your surrender," Hellström answered. "There'll be no mercy for you, we'll make your death into a shining example, but maybe we'll let some of your people survive. Like pets."

Wren opened the door and slammed it behind him.

Doona and Alli were right there, and the fear was all over their faces. Hellström had it right. Wren had just chosen not to see it before. Alli opened her mouth to say something, but Wren forestalled it with a gesture.

He didn't have the strength to reassure them. He just needed air.

"I'm going out," he said, and started toward the door.

"You can't," Alli called. "You're the most wanted man in this stupid country. They'll find you. Chris." She grabbed hold of his arm. "They'll find us!"

He turned. The fear was naked on her face now, but he had nothing to give. He needed more in his hand than an empty bluff.

"So give me a hoodie. I need to see this new teXas for myself."

30

TEXAS

It was cold and dark on the street. March in Dallas, maybe fifty-five degrees, and Wren walked awkwardly in the shadows, hands shoved deep into the pockets of his hoodie, replaying the conversation with Hellström in his head.

Looking for where it went wrong.

He walked along Cole Avenue, north side of the city center, broaching the edge of the Oak Lawn district. On his left rose the apartment complex in moonlit shades of beige and apricot blush, made up of six blocks each five stories tall circled around a swimming pool.

Like a community.

Few lights in windows were lit. Homes for young professionals, looking to become a part of the city's warp and weft, write themselves into its tapestry of life. Now they would be prime targets for X, and clearly knew it; keeping their heads down, respecting the curfew, trying to stay off the radar.

Wren couldn't blame them. You only had to see a neighbor's door smashed down once, see their kids left screaming in the hall, see a protest disrupted with police batons and tear gas and live rounds to know that you couldn't fight against the state.

On his right passed a parade of new-build stores in glass, chrome and stained pine: fancy coffee shops boasting jam-jar glasses in the window, with elaborate, obscure hipster names like Avocado Pumpkin, Jambo Schiaparelli and Sir Clowdesley; boutique tailors where impossibly thin mannequins wore clothes more suitable for children, like bright-red dungarees, skinny capri pants for men that looked to be sprayed on and jackets with mop wigs attached; eateries that were decked out with living green walls, spraying floral scents into the chilly air.

Not the kind of place Wren understood too well. A culture that had risen up around him while he'd been out fighting America's hidden wars, but one he'd happily take part in. Soy lattes weren't that bad, after all. Oat milk. Cashew milk.

A solitary car whipped through the intersection ahead. Out after curfew. To his left a homeless drunk shifted in an alley down the side of a shuttered bar. Wren wondered where he was getting his supply.

He crossed the intersection fast, hands tucked in, head low. The traffic lights blinked meaninglessly on strings overhead, directing nobody. Dallas was a ghost town, and Wren felt like a ghost haunting the fresh corpse of America.

It helped to walk, though. His stomach throbbed hot, but it was a good heat; the inflammation of healing, as the skin sutured itself together.

A multi-story parking lot passed on his right. An indie cinema on his left, boards up displaying the latest movie, some kind of wild fantasy fare with a menagerie of crazy characters. It looked fun. The X forces hadn't gotten around to censoring it yet.

Then he heard a police siren.

He ducked into the awning of the cinema before the

flashing lights spilled across him. The foyer was dark, and he leaned close to the wall beside the shuttered doors, watching as a riot police van wailed down the quiet street. Three figures inside that he could pick out through the armored windows. The sound of its siren Doppler-ed down the register as it went by, then blipped to a halt another few hundred yards on.

Wren peered out from cover.

The van had stopped dead in the middle of the road, the siren silent but the blue and red lights spiraling. The two front doors and right rear door opened in synchrony, three men dressed in police blues emerged, and then Wren saw their target.

A young woman, very slight frame, staggering along the shadowy sidewalk. She was dressed in a strapless red dress, cut short with her shoulders exposed; no jacket and no purse. It seemed like one of her high heels had snapped and she was walking awkwardly, as if she hadn't yet realized. It was dark and she was some two hundred yards away, but Wren thought he saw bruising on her face, a certain glaze to her expression.

Nobody in their right mind would be out in this weather wearing only that, especially given the curfew. There were no bars, no night clubs open anyway. Maybe prostitutes would, forced to work to survive, but they'd huddle in packs, would know better than to come out without a jacket, would know not to lurch closer when the police drew near.

This girl had been drugged. Wren felt it in his bones. A roofie of some kind, a benzodiazepine. Maybe a high dollar escort, picked up and then kicked to the curb after she regained consciousness.

"Help," she said to the three men as they drew near.

By the swirling lights, it was clear they wore no name badges, no insignia, no bodycams.

"You all right, miss?" the lead guy asked. He said it loud,

some kind of charade of kindness, Wren figured, while the other two circled.

The woman said something, still too far away for Wren to hear.

"You're going to be fine now," the guy answered calmly, hands out and open like he was reassuring a skittish animal.

At the same time, one of the two men came up behind her. He put the flat of one hand firmly against her back, delved in with the other between her shoulder blades and pulled down. For a second it wasn't clear what he'd done, then her red dress peeled open, revealing raw gooseflesh beneath; the zipper slit right down to the small of her back.

"Christmas come around again so soon," he said.

The lead guy frowned. "Ma'am, you do know public nudity's an offence?"

She turned. Probably felt the sudden cold breeze on her back, but in her befuddled state would have no idea what it meant.

"Ma'am, I asked you a question," the man said.

The third guy took his turn next, stepping up and yanking on her dress violently. The sound of her flimsy dress ripping carried loud on the still air, and the force of it almost pulled over her over. As it was, she staggered sideways, now wearing only rags, as the dress ripped down the side seam.

The guy caught her.

"Looks like she's my present, Sarge," he said, and finished the job of unwrapping with another hard downward pull.

The dress fell at her feet. She wore only a bra and panties underneath. Give it a few hours like that and she'd freeze to death.

"We'll share, Cam," said the sarge. "Now into the van. You know I hate the feel of cold sidewalk on my knees."

Cam laughed, spun the woman easily and hoisted her over

his shoulder. She barely had the capacity to fight. "I hear that. It's an acquired taste."

Sarge laughed and went around the back to open the van's door. Cam brought her around and carried her in.

"OK, Billings, get your ass back here," Sarge called over the road.

Billings didn't reply. There was a good reason for that. Wren had his knee on the guy's throat, choking him out cold in the gap between a parked GM and a Chrysler. It was a silent piece of work. An easy grab, as the guy had gone in to pick up the woman's torn dress, while the others were focused on putting her in the van.

Snatch him into the shadows.

"Billings, you piece of shit, didn't you piss enough for one night?" Sarge shouted, then went on in a mutter. "How much piss one man got inside himself?"

Wren reached down and pulled the weapon from Billings' waist. A Colt Python. He could tell from the grimy feel of the grip that it wasn't a well-maintained weapon. He wouldn't feel good about pulling the trigger. Fail to clean the barrel after each discharge, and you were setting yourself up for a backfire somewhere along the line. Not only that, but the gunshot itself would doubtless bring on a fresh surge of attention.

Maybe he'd take his chances, though.

"Where's that idiot gone?" Cam asked, emerging from the van. Wren wasn't looking, too busy running low and fast along the line of parked cars, but he could tell Cam's shifting position by the sound of his voice.

"Must be out pissing again," Sarge said. He sounded more riled than worried, and that was good. "Man drinks way too much energy drink. Either that or he found another bitch for himself."

"Could be a nest of them," Cam mused. "Roofie'd whores by the dozen. Like a buy-one-get-one-free kind of deal."

Sarge snorted. "Yeah, like you'd ever pay. Billings, you hot mess of a piss machine! Put your dick in your pants and get back here, or we're lighting out without you."

No answer came.

"Come on, brother," Cam called, striding out toward the sidewalk where the red dress lay. "Share and share alike."

Wren was already seven cars along, moving low and silent, when Billings gave a low murmur as he came back to consciousness. Timed pretty well.

The atmosphere changed instantly.

"What the hell was that?" Sarge asked.

Both men pulled their guns. Cam slowed right down, approaching the spot Wren had left Billings.

"Billings?" Cam called. "You OK, buddy?"

"Maybe he tripped," said Sarge, approaching a few yards behind.

"That didn't sound like a man who tripped," Cam answered, then covered the distance to Billings.

For a second upon seeing his friend laid out in the gutter, snug in between two tall vehicles with his weapon missing, he just stared. Long enough for Wren to lower Sarge to the ground after a five-count sleeper hold.

"Somebody's out here," Cam called, raising his weapon and backing up right into Wren.

Wren sidestepped him easily, caught his gun arm by the wrist and sent a jump knee straight up through his elbow. The arm hyper-extended, the gun flicked free to clatter on the blacktop, then Wren spun a meaty elbow strike into his temple, knocking him out cold standing up.

He didn't even have time to scream. Instead he sagged.

Wren lowered him to the ground.

Now Billings was over to the side scrabbling in the gutter.

Maybe trying to crawl under a car. Sarge was wheezing and about to sit up. Inside the van, the girl tottered to the exit and peered out. "Hello?" she called in a quavering voice.

Not what Wren had been looking for. Maybe what he needed, though.

He got to work.

31

POISON

Wren drove. Cruising the streets of Oak Lawn, looking for the right kind of place to stop. The kind of place the idiots in back might have chosen for their dark business.

He chose the darkened lot around an old thrift store. Parked up, took a breath.

Every bluff was built on a house of cards. Some took more preparation than others. It was all a con, really, and Wren had learned from the best.

He switched off the engine but kept the key turned, so he had lights in the back of the van. Pushed aside the passenger seat and climbed into the back. Three men sat on the park benches along the wall, cuffed wrist and ankle, gagged, hooded and chained to the wall bars.

Sarge, Billings and Cam.

Cam was naked apart from his boxer shorts, and shivering. Maybe he was the worst of the bunch, but Wren wasn't picking favorites. They were all bad.

He'd dropped off the girl already, wearing Cam's clothes. Outside her home. He'd watched her go in. The first deed of a good Samaritan done in this van, he figured, for at least a week.

Now he stood over the men. Cam groaned something. His toenails were turning blue. Fine by Wren. The others sat very still, hoping not to be picked for whatever was coming.

Wren moved slow and deliberately. There was a first aid kit in the front, better equipped than the one in the MTVR, and he kneeled down in the middle of the van, opened it up, started taking pieces out.

The sound freaked out Cam and he started lashing out. Trying to break free, hyperventilating into his gag.

Wren ignored him. Kept on laying out pieces. The clink of glass on the van's steel floor. Syringes. Small bottles containing insulin, epinephrine, the sedative lorazepam. Mix them together in different combinations, you had all kinds of potent, heart-stopping cocktails.

Scary, sure.

Wren waited for Cam to wheeze himself to exhaustion. Sarge was very still. Billings kept on shuddering. When they were still, he stood. Started pulling off hoods. The men underneath blinked and flinched like snails retracting into their shells, pasty and sick-looking in the harsh interior light.

"You were going to rape that girl," Wren said quietly. "Maybe the same thing you've been doing all week. The teXas with a capital X way, right?"

He looked them in their eyes. Savored the moment as they recognized him. That face. Those scars. The man everyone was hunting for.

They all freaked out. Roared into their gags. Lashed out against their chains. The movement bounced the syringe and bottles around on the floor, but they were sturdy, and Wren had time. He waited. Billings pissed himself, yellow liquid spreading over the floor and draining through holes in the chassis.

Soon enough they were quiet, but their faces were deathly still.

"I don't like this new teXas," he said softly. So soft they had to strain to hear him. Letting their fear do the job he couldn't do with Hellström. "Now you're going to help me bring it down."

He didn't say anything for a time after that. Instead he picked up the syringe, started dipping it into the small vials, sucking a little of each clear liquid up. Some insulin. Some knockout sedative. Some epinephrine. He held the syringe up and flicked the needle.

They went into a frenzy again. Begging, Wren knew.

"Stop that right now, or I inject you in the eyes," Wren said.

Cold, calm and they shut right up. Another one vented his bladder. Not bad. The triple would be even better.

"In this syringe I've got a poison," he said. "Special brew. Slow acting, enough that it'll freak you out, make you manic but won't kill you for at least two hours. After two hours, your heart will burst in your chest. Pop. Unless you get the antidote, from me. Are you with me?"

They stared. Their eyes followed the syringe like the crowd at a magic trick followed the card.

"I'm going to need some confirmation here," Wren said.

They nodded. Fell over themselves to nod.

"Good. So, here we go. Like I say, make a meal of it, you get it in the eye."

He went over to Sarge first. The guy's bladder finally voided. Three for three. Wren leaned one knee into his gut. Getting into his space. Put the syringe down into the gap between his neck and his collarbone, for the theatrics of it, and squeezed. Sarge tensed all his muscles, like he could somehow push the liquid back out by force of will, but it didn't help.

In seconds the cocktail hit. Epinephrine sent his already-overworked system into overdrive. The sedative battled it into a noxious confusion, flushing fight-or-flight chemicals through him like a heart attack. Inside his head the fireworks were going off early.

Wren moved onto the next. Cam. Did the same. For Billings he prepared a special dose. More sedative than epinephrine. He took it like a champ. Was knocked out in seconds.

Wren stood back.

"Looks like I over-dosed your friend here."

The other two stared, wheezing hard around their gags.

"Oops."

Wren unclasped Billings' cuffs. Took off his gag. Opened the back of the van and tipped him out onto the blacktop.

They went back into their frenzy. Wren closed the doors. The guy would wake up in a couple of hours. Freezing cold with a killer headache, but he wouldn't freeze to death. Probably.

The two guys in the van didn't know that.

"Do exactly what I say, when I say it, for the next two hours, and you don't end up like Billings out there. I give the antidote. Happy days. Ask anyone for help, though, tell them who I am, fail to act in the spirit of our agreement, you're signing your own death warrant. It'll take them more than two hours to figure out what I gave you, another two to put together an effective antidote, by which point you'll be long gone. So you have to ask yourself one question." He paused dramatically. "Are you willing to die for X?"

They stared at him, maybe only half-comprehending the things he was saying. With their pumped-up systems and attenuated attention, everything would be coming at them in life-and-death shades right now.

Wren waited. Let the moment sink in. They didn't seem

like full-blown zealots to Wren. If they'd truly believed in the precepts of X, at least as Wren understood them, they wouldn't be out raping their way through the populace. They'd be gathering and converting souls for the coming battle, whatever that happened to be.

These guys were just opportunists. Grudge holders pumped up on a little power.

"Are you in?"

They nodded desperately.

"Good. Now, I'm going to take off your gags. First thing you do, you tell me everything you know about the pens. Where they are, how many people they hold, how many guards there are. Lie to me once, out comes the syringe and you join Billings in his piss-pile. Do you follow?"

They nodded so hard capillaries started bursting in their eyes.

"Good. Let's get to it."

32

DEEP ELLUM

Wren seethed in a cold fury, as the riot van rolled down the empty streets of Oak Lawn.

The things they'd told him were appalling.

He'd seen refugee camps on the border of Syria. He'd seen the Blue Fairy's Pleasure Island. Places where people put each other in cages, inflicted pain and depredations for their own pleasure, again and again.

The X pens sounded precisely the same.

According to Sarge and Cam, many were located in existing police stations, spotted through Dallas and across teXas. Some were in fire stations, with cages sprung up overnight, some were in commandeered warehouses. Each followed the time-worn pattern of sites like it across the globe.

Men, women and children all separated, stripped and processed. Given a uniform, scraps of food, a blanket, a bucket, a thin mattress and left to fend for themselves.

Only seven days had passed, but both Cam and Sarge confessed to joining rape gangs over a dozen times. So much they were exhausted from it, they'd said, as they wept. Begging for absolution.

It was so easy, they'd said. Everybody was doing it.

Wren had wanted to stab the life out of them then and there. Instead he'd slapped them until they stopped crying, put one in the driver's seat, one in the passenger seat, and himself in modified cuffs in the back.

The cuffs were jammed, so the bracelets didn't catch on the lock.

Dark streets passed by outside.

Sarge was the only actual police officer in the group. Cam and Billings were his friends. Cam was a laborer, Billings a kindergarten teacher. They'd gone to school together, gone to concerts together, attended X rallies together, and now they were doing this together.

Sarge was not a sergeant in the police, at least not yet, just an officer two years in. A lot of the leadership had been purged across the State, though; long rolls of names that Hellström and Kason and whoever was behind this had prepared in advance. Hundreds and thousands of senior figures let loose or 'imported' themselves, leaving a lot of room for the 'Sarges' of the world to rise up.

Sarge and his C-patrol were based out of the Central Patrol Division in Deep Ellum, just north of I-30. Once carved up into various homicide, narcotics and gang crime divisions, all these sections had now been folded into caging for imports.

In the wake of secession, it seemed the system had largely been tossed aside. Anyone brought in through the building's doors was considered guilty unless proven innocent, and with no lawyer calls anymore, no habeas corpus and no intrusive media reporting on injustices, there was no system for appeals.

Already a gulag.

The van drew in. Far ahead the skyscrapers of downtown

were black monoliths looming on the horizon, lights out and barely visible against the starry sky.

Wren's heart raced. He wished there was a way to contact his team back at the apartment block, but there wasn't. If this didn't pay off, they'd be on their own. If he didn't attempt it, though, it would be much the same.

"We're coming up to it," said Sarge from in front. Forcing more bass into his voice to cover up his terror.

Wren said nothing.

"You don't have to do this," Cam said abruptly, as they approached the turn off. "Just dump us, there has to be another way, I-"

Sarge leaned over from the wheel and punched Cam in the side of the face. Cam whimpered but shut up. Good.

The van turned. The Central Patrol police station appeared through the gloom, a beige brick edifice, low and windowless. Wren didn't want to imagine the atrocities going on within at that very moment. Steeled himself.

Cam began to shudder uncontrollably in the passenger seat.

Sarge pulled the van onto the approach road.

"I can't!" moaned Cam abruptly, and started yanking at the door handle.

"Cut it out!" Sarge barked. "Just quit it, you're going to get us both killed!"

"Stop here," Wren ordered, and leaned forward. He wasn't shackled to any of the bars, could easily reach his hands around Cam's neck and squeeze the carotid arteries either side of his neck.

Cam lashed out, jerking and pulling, but the seat belt kept him confined, and Wren's fingers were like iron, digging in and pressing hard. Sarge sat at the wheel, looking ahead blank-eyed. Already at his max for stress, he couldn't be driven much further.

Soon enough Cam stopped thrashing. His head nodded. Wren unclicked his seatbelt and pulled all two hundred pounds of him into the back. One more jab with the syringe, and he was out for the count.

"Did you just kill him?" Sarge asked flatly.

"Not yet," Wren answered. "Take us in."

Sarge didn't move.

"Your two hours is counting," Wren prompted. "Think about staying alive."

"If I do this, I want you to know. It was never personal. I didn't mean to hurt anyone."

"Didn't mean to hurt anyone," Wren repeated. "It was an accident. Noted."

The guy flinched. "It's just…"

"I can do this without you," Wren said. "It's harder, but I can. Then there's no reason for me to give you the antidote, is there? I don't need you. Or Cam. You have to make me want to save you, and words are not going to cut it."

Sarge sat there a moment longer. Rethinking his loyalties, maybe. All prior plans cast to the wind, replaced by the life-or-death struggle of chemicals in his system.

"I'll do it. You can rely on me."

"I know that. Drive."

Sarge pulled forward into the parking lot.

It was expansive, room for some two hundred vehicles, lit by tall white lamps. Only some quarter of the slots were full. No coaches, which Wren had hoped for, no clear means of shipping the people here out to a concentration camp.

"I don't know where they go," Sarge had insisted earlier, when Wren had pressed. "They just go."

"In a coach? A bus? By train?"

"I really don't know. I haven't seen it. Nobody talks about it."

"But they are moving them out?"

"There's always empty pens. So, yes."

Always empty pens.

Sarge parked three rows over from the building entrance, hit the handbrake, killed the engine and sat for a second washed in the white lights.

"No time like the present," Wren said.

Sarge nodded, unclicked his seatbelt and stepped out. A man resigned to his fate. He yanked the van's slide door open, leaned in and went to pull Wren out, but Wren didn't budge.

"Mime unlocking me," he said. "Think. If they're watching the lot and you pull out a prisoner who wasn't even secured to the rails, that's going to buy us extra attention. It's bad enough two of your partners aren't here. Use your head."

Sarge nodded. Leaned in and mimed unlocking Wren. His hands shook.

"Wipe the sweat off your face, take a second to steady yourself and we'll get through this together."

Sarge nodded. "I'll do my best to keep your hood up."

"You'll do more than your best. If someone recognizes me, we're both dead. Start thinking of it that way. We're in this together."

"Together," Sarge said, and pulled.

Wren followed.

They walked together across the lot. Wren had his hoodie pulled low over his face, but took in a lot. A couple of officers stood by the door smoking cigarettes.

"Drunk, Terry?" one of them called.

"Junkie," Sarge answered.

They'd fouled Wren's clothes in advance; stamping them in gravel and mud, urinating on them, adding some rips and tears.

The other guy cursed, spat, then muttered something about that being 'a real turn-off'. "Put him down the wing,

OK? I don't want to be smelling his stink when I'm hip-deep in heaven."

"Yeah," Sarge said.

They went through the double glass doors. They walked over white vinyl flooring stained with a million different footfalls. Scorch marks from dropped cigarettes, acid stains from vomit, rents where knives or fingernails had clawed in, bubblegum blots hardened to rubber rock, all under harsh white lights. Sarge pulled on the fake cuffs and Wren gave a little resistance, stumbling like he was high.

Officers in blue uniform passed by; Wren saw their legs, the hint of posters on the walls. He smelled strong black coffee, bleach and ripe body odor; the holy triumvirate of the law enforcement system.

They reached the Duty Sergeant's desk.

"One for the pens," Sarge said.

"Name?" came the answer, sounding bored.

"Didn't take a name," Sarge said.

The Duty Sergeant paused, and Wren felt the shift in focus, even if all he saw was the floor. Buying unnecessary attention. Wren had coached Sarge on what to say, a name lifted out of nowhere, and he'd already bungled it.

"Then take it now."

Sarge leaned in. Wren muttered the name they'd prepped.

"Where are your squad members?" the Duty Sergeant asked. "Your recruits. They should be here."

"In the van. He resisted arrest. They're dizzy."

It was getting worse. "He resisted arrest that bad? Does he need to go into solitary."

The exact opposite of what Wren had said. Sarge might as well be babbling now.

Wren began to jerk. Made it as wild and uncontrolled as he could.

"Whoa," said Sarge.

He started gagging. Not easy to fake, but he put everything he had into the performance. Head down, filthy and grunting, it could be convincing.

"Damn it, like this?" the Duty Sergeant said. "That's not fighting. He's having some kind of fit. Get him out of here before he pukes everywhere. Now!"

"Yes, Sir!" Sarge barked and hurried off, pulling Wren with him.

Past the Duty Sergeant. Deeper in the station. Through a turnstile entry area leading into the back offices. The lighting dimmed and the white vinyl gave way to fuzzy gray carpeting. Swiftly the coffee smell faded, replaced by various bodily wastes. He heard babies crying low and parents struggling to soothe them. He heard the grunt of distant violence.

"It's here," Sarge whispered.

"Don't talk to me," Wren whispered back. "Just stick with the plan."

"Right. Right."

Sarge approached a gate. Wren saw feet standing either side of it. A new chain link section of fencing, set up inside the building. Desks shoved over to the side to make way.

The gate was opened. The butt of a rifle slammed into Wren's belly, mercifully catching him on the right side. "Make trouble and you get the shot early," some gruff voice said.

Wren was shoved through the gate. It slammed closed behind him.

And that was it.

He was in.

33

IN

Wren kept his head down and shuffled deeper.

People lay everywhere. Sprawled, disconsolate, terrified, fallen to shock. In the half-light he saw children with saucer-wide eyes, men and women nursing bloody faces, old people and young people, the strong and the weak alike, all battered and broken.

He'd seen people like them before. Go to any war zone and you'd find them. Regular people reeling from the injuries done to them. Not quite believing it. Unable to comprehend the suddenness of the violence perpetrated upon them, or the depths of what they'd lost.

Wren knew all about such transformations, and still it had taken him a day to come to grips with what was happening here. These people didn't have his experience or his skills, and most of them were adrift.

But some were not. One-by-one as he moved through the crowd of hundreds, Wren found the ones he could rely on. They were the ones helping others. Moving about and coordinating as best they could, sharing and rationing what scant resources available. Some food swapped for a blanket here, some water for a pillow, a rudimentary doll fashioned from twine and shreds of sheet to comfort a crying child.

Offering their strength like an umbrella. Only words, sometimes, or the touch of a hand on a fevered cheek, tissues raised to dry the tears.

He reached the edge of the encampment, a fence embedded in concrete slabs laid out across the office's floor, and looked deeper. Toward the cells, where the worst of the cries emanated.

He'd seen rape used as a tool of control before. He'd hated it then and he hated it now. Still, he lingered by the edge, slumped on his side but peering through the chain links, long enough to see and memorize the process. Men and women fetched from the cages and forced down the corridor. Men and women brought back, broken. Nobody fought. There was a regularity to it. This was a system of reward and punishment. Reward for the X peons. Punishment for everyone else.

Wren shuffled to the nearest person on his mental list, staying low and hunched. A woman tending to a pair of old people, laid out on the floor, partially padded by blankets she must have scrounged hard for. There was something about the clinical efficiency of her movements that bespoke rigorous training. Could be battlefield experience, could be trauma ward, could be the floor of the stock exchange. In any case, she knew stress and responded to it by diving deeper in, not retreating deeper inside.

She was short and slight, looked like auburn hair in the grimy shadows. She favored her left side, like she'd taken an injury to her right knee, but she didn't let that stop her. Kept on reassuring and hushing, whispering and adjusting bedding, laying on hands and moistening lips.

Wren nudged into her.

"Sorry," she murmured.

"Don't be sorry," Wren said, taking her by the elbow. "Get even."

That stopped her. "What?"

Wren pulled his hood back a little. Not enough to clearly see his face, but enough to see his eyes. "There's a group of us preparing to take this station back," he said low. "The gates will open. We'll have weapons. Can I rely on you?"

A long second passed.

"Walk on," she said. "Not interested."

She tried to pull away, but Wren didn't let her. Pulled her even closer, spoke into her ear. "You hear what they're doing in the cells. Soon a coach will come and load everyone up. We'll all be shipped out to a concentration camp, where it will only get worse. There'll be no oversight. No protection. No rule of law. The people you're helping now, they're going to die within the first few hours, and if they don't die, they're going to suffer so badly they'll wish they were dead. Stand by now, and you'll regret the decision for the rest of your short life, because trust me, if I can pick you out as an unbroken spirit, they can too. You'll be one of the first made into an example."

She tugged on her arm. Wren didn't let go.

"The only thing necessary for the triumph of evil is for good people to do nothing. You're already doing something here. Do a little more."

That gave her pause. She stopped pulling against him.

"Who are you?" she whispered.

"Best you don't know. Best for everyone. But believe me. Weapons are coming. We have a real chance at this. Succeed here, and we have a chance at turning this whole thing around."

Her eyes widened. "This whole thing, you mean teXas?"

"teXas," he confirmed. "Kason. X. Pull it down. Don't you want to be part of that?"

She paused a long moment. Staring at his lips, his jaw, his scars.

"It is you."

"Don't say it."

"I don't need to. People were saying you'd come. I never thought I'd see it with my own eyes."

"I'm not special. I'm only here by accident."

"But you are going to help us take down this place?"

"Yes. It's just one place, though. There must be hundreds like it across the state. Thousands. After it's done, at least for a while, you'll be on the run. I can't help with that."

"We don't need it," she said. Now a new resilience shone through, like she was feeding off his presence. The Big Bad Bird, here in the flesh. "You said you'd get weapons. I believe it. I believe the gate will open. I don't know much about firearms, but I'll do my best."

"Aim at the bad guy and shoot," Wren said, purposefully light-hearted. There'd be a time to process all this darkness later. "You can't go wrong."

"Sure," she said, then held up her arms, linked by iron bracelets. "Can you do something about these handcuffs?"

Wren grinned, produced a pair of bolt cutters from his filthy jacket. They cut clean through the chain; the shearing sound masked by a rattling cough.

"So what do I do?" she asked.

"Stand ready. When the moment comes, grab a weapon and charge. You might not be prepared to kill the men doing this to you, but-"

"I'm prepared," she said, that resilience burning through brighter still, fueled by anger. "You just got here. I've been here for two days. These bastards deserve everything that's coming to them."

Wren looked at her and felt the heat of her rage. He didn't doubt she'd seen horrors. Already she was burning that for fuel. Good.

"Then spread the word. Keep it quiet. Only tell people you absolutely trust. One traitor looking to save their own skin could blow the whole thing."

"I understand. Good luck."

"And to you," he said, then moved onto the next.

In thirty minutes he'd spoken to a dozen people. Cut their chains. Set them to circulating the dim space, converting others to the cause. Now as he passed, staying low in the shadows, crawling at times, the people he came across were primed. They looked his way, made eye contact. Waiting for the sign.

Not weak people, though many were battered: a young guy with one side of his face so swollen his right eye couldn't open; an older woman with red fingernail weals torn down her throat; a middle-aged man with three broken fingers, roughly splinted, the punishment after he'd tried to protect his son.

Stories of suffering were everywhere. The pain was a miasma hanging like a cloud. But Wren's presence was a kind of accelerant, catalyzing their pain into something else, something simmering with fury and purpose. Maybe the guards at the gate sensed it; something in the movement of these once-broken prisoners, something in the susurrus of whispers spreading like a quiet wildfire, something in the way they looked.

"Quit eyeballing me, you little bitch," one of the guards said.

Staring at a child. She had pigtails and wore a blue school uniform, must've been grabbed up on her way home. Wren couldn't imagine what crime she'd committed at nine years old.

To her credit, she didn't look away.

"All these freaks are coming awake," the other guard said. "This isn't right."

Sarge approached quietly from behind, right on cue. Pushing a crate on a trolley. One of the guards turned to him.

"Terry? What are you doing? You're not on resupply."

"Dinner for the freaks," Sarge replied. "I go where I'm sent."

"They're restive," said the other guard, not taking his eyes off the darkened crowd. "Something's got them spooked. Maybe that new guy. The junkie you brought in. Where'd you fetch him?"

Sarge played it cool. "Under a bridge somewhere? I don't remember. He's a dreg, the only thing off-putting about him is the stench. Now, if anything's riling them up, it's hunger. When did they last eat?"

One of the guards cursed.

"All they do is eat," the other complained. "Eat, piss and whine."

"Until we can kill 'em, we have to feed 'em," Sarge said.

"Fine. We'll open up, just dump the lot. I don't like the way they're looking at me. Think we ought to bring the stun guns into play again, teach some respect, starting with this little whore in front."

"Amen to that, brother," Sarge said.

They opened the gate. Sarge stepped through. Once he was in, he tipped the trolley, sending the crate tumbling. The lid fell open and the contents thudded out, but it wasn't plastic-packed ready meals clattering on carpet. This was the thunk of metal.

"What the-" the nearest guard began, but a bullet took him in the roof of his mouth, shooting his tongue through the back of his head.

It took a long second for the shockwave to rip through the

prisoners and out across the station. Wren used that time to train in on the other guard, fire with Billings' Glock 9mm, and start toward the open gate.

A comet's trail of people followed in his wake.

34

DISTRICT CAPTAIN

Wren scooped a Beretta 9mm on the way out of the cage and started shooting out lights with both guns as he advanced, spreading the darkness of the cages across the station like a crashing wave.

The first shots came back toward him, but they were intermittent and scattershot given the dark conditions. The Central Patrol division was not a standing garrison, ready to take on a sudden attack from within their own building's bowels. Many of the 'officers' in attendance were like Cam and Billings, petty fools with no training, not battle-hardened, stress-tested or capable of doing much more than wielding a big stick from a long distance against civilians.

By contrast Wren had hand-picked his squad. They were beaten-down but fired up, advancing under cover of darkness while shooting at targets in the halogen-white bright of the station front, riding the element of surprise.

Shots rang out all around.

Wren picked out the Duty Sergeant a hundred yards ahead, looked like an old veteran, wielding a crowd control Benelli M4 shotgun. Wren stopped cold, sighted the Beretta and shot the guy in the chest.

He fell back.

Other cops rose up from behind their desks, firing potshots into the darkness. Wren's people surged past him like a zombie horde: climbing over desks and firing into lights, windows, walls and bodies; swinging fists where they didn't have guns. The young guy with the swollen eye had commandeered an extendable baton and was using it to lay waste around him. The woman from before held an M1 pistol and fired wildly, missing every shot but keeping the cacophony of shock and awe rolling over the enemy like an avalanche.

Wren reached the Duty Sergeant, found him frothing out blood from a sucking chest wound, and snatched the Benelli. There was a box of 3-inch Winchester Buckshot shells in the desk and Wren picked it up, spun to take in the battlefield.

The station had collapsed into chaos on all sides. Lights guttered and ceiling panels erupted under gunfire, cordite hung in drifts and screams rang through the darkness, bodies pouring from the depths, thumping and grunting against each other as countless acts of righteous revenge played out.

"Clear!" he shouted, then started back the way he'd come. Prisoners flooded by like spray from a geyser; no weapons now, only teeth and fingernails. Some went for Wren, too pumped to discern friend from foe, and he guided them to either side easily with Wing Chun-style force redirections. Back past the dark mouth to the cages, he found Sarge cowering in a rec room lit only by the backlights of a chip packet vending machine.

"You good?" Wren asked.

Sarge gulped, nodded, swallowed a breath. "Yes."

"Has anyone left?"

He shook his head.

"And you're sure he'll be back there?"

Sarge nodded.

Wren ducked out.

The open hall led away into darkness. At the corner lay a door, the same way they'd been taking the prisoners. It grew quieter as Wren approached, all the noise and gunfire taking place in the foyer. He glimpsed the spark of flames igniting. First would be the carpet, then the desks, then the ceiling boards. Within an hour the whole building would be an inferno.

More time than he needed.

Wren took the cold door handle in his hand and pulled, stepping aside sharply as it opened. Bullets roared out.

"I just want the captain," he shouted into the gap.

The only answer was bullets.

Wren dropped to one knee, swung the shotgun around the door jamb with barely his fingers exposed, and fired four fast shots. Each boomed massively in the contained space, the recoil almost ripping the black metal weapon from his hands. Each shot fanned out in a shotgun halo, distributing the load of buckshot balls a foot wider in diameter for every two yards traveled.

Four distributed impacts spumed crazily back; the clatter of wall ricochets, the crash of glass as lights smashed and rained down, the hard crack off metal and the soft grunts of impact drawn from frail flesh.

The rain of bullets ended. The lights in the corridor fell largely dark. What came instead was a rising welter of shouts and screams.

"I just want the captain," Wren repeated loud. "Stand down or die."

A few desultory shots rang back, but they were unfocused and pointless. Amateurs who'd never been in a firefight before, expending their ammo into the air, hoping the noise and fury would protect them. Wren was a Force Recon Marine who'd grown up in a crucible of violence. He knew how to wield the scalpel where others struggled to swing their machetes without cutting off their own fingers.

"Last chance," he called, and calmly reloaded the shotgun, shuttling shells into the breech with ease.

Someone swore loudly and more shots zinged out.

Wren stood, spun the shotgun once more around the jamb and fired twice. The barrel bucked, the halos of fragging metal roared out, and then Wren strode into the corridor. With the Benelli leveled at his right hip, he zagged to the far corridor wall, dropped to one knee as shots came his way, rolled forward and left to come up on the other side of the corridor, stood and sidestepped, by which time he'd picked out two clear targets in the sickly green light of emergency exit lights.

They'd set up an impromptu barricade of three desks in a pyramid across the corridor, and were clustered behind them, a few bodies slumped either side. The surface of the desks was peppered with tiny divots caused by the Benelli's ball bearings, and the floor was littered with broken glass.

Two guys peered over the desk barricade, firing rifles near-blind. Wren fired twice, caught one in the forehead and threw him back, while the other ducked under cover just as the shotgun bowed a crater into the desk the size of a trash can lid. Wren chased the shot with a sprint; adrenaline slamming aside the pain in his side. Five big steps in two seconds and he vaulted the desk, came down in the viper's nest.

Bodies lay all around in the green-tinged semi-dark, several writhing in pain. The one remaining guy stared at him in horror, tried to swing his rifle into play, but Wren sent a crunching punch into the bridge of his nose, crumpling the cartilage and driving him unconscious into the wall.

A shot suddenly zipped in and bit the vinyl near Wren's foot, and he snatched up the guy's rifle, rolled and fired. His stream of bullets raked the left side of the wall ten feet in, tearing through to drop the man taking cover on the other side.

Wren took a breath.

Silence reigned for an unsteady moment. The cries of the prisoners in back and the squirming of the injured ebbed like low waves beneath Wren's thumping pulse. He rolled to one knee, saw one of the injured figures reach for a weapon, and fired three fast shots: two in the chest, one in the head.

His hand dropped immediately.

Wren surveyed the others. There were maybe four of them, sprawled and clutching their injuries, staring eyes wide like he was the devil incarnate. It might be a mercy to shoot them all. The prisoners weren't going to go easy on them now. The alternative was fire. Wren spared a glance down the long sweep of the station, saw the flames beginning to surge.

"Where is he?" Wren mouthed at the nearest guy, who had his hands out, the gun pushed far away. Looked like a regular working joe. Not a killer. Not a rapist. That was the banality of evil.

"Who?" the guy whispered back. Feverish to please.

"The captain."

The guy nodded. Looked at the others around him. They'd all pushed their weapons away. Civilians, most likely, despite the officer blues. That in itself made Wren angry. More stolen valor. For all people talked about institutional corruption in the police, Wren knew the system mostly worked. The vast majority of bad apples got weeded out before they got off the beat. These were common-or-garden scumbags.

"In back," the guy whispered, then winced as the pain swelled. "Rear office."

Wren absorbed that. About what he'd expected.

"Get out," he said low.

"What?" the guy whispered back. "I've been shot. I can't… the mob, they'll…"

He trailed off under Wren's icy glare. "Get. Out. Leave the weapons. Go now, before I change my mind."

The guy fought to his feet. Looked like he had a belly wound, blood seeping between his fingers. Wren didn't like his chances. He staggered away. The others followed. One of them could only crawl.

Wren stood. Doors extended away on either side. He knew what this space was supposed to be. Night and day rooms for superior officers. It meant some of them were fitted with beds.

In the first on the left, the guy he'd shot through the wall lay in a rictus curl, down to his undershirt and boxer shorts, blood spattered with plaster dust from the wall through-and-through. It was a night room, fitted with a locker, desk, sink and bed. On the bed lay a young woman, cuffed and naked, cheek bleeding, terror and shock making her pupils big as marbles.

It only surged the anger harder.

Wren snatched the keys off the desk, strode over and unlocked the young woman.

"I'm so sorry," he said, as calm as he could. "But there'll be others. Untie them. Wait for me."

He didn't wait for a response and left the room to stride further down the hall, not looking to either side. He didn't want to see. At one point a man charged out firing madly, but Wren simply side-stepped and fired. One shot straight through his temple, dropping him cold.

To the end of the corridor. Corner office. It said, 'CAPTAIN REYNOLDS'.

"I'm coming in," Wren shouted. "Shoot and I'll shoot back. Take your chances."

He kicked the door in.

No bullets came his way.

The captain was a slim man, short, young too. Looked half-Hispanic, half-white, maybe the son of a political donor, leveled up for the X onslaught. He wore his full-dress blues, 'railroad track' insignia on his sleeve as twin gold bars of rank, tear trails running down his cheeks, hands clasped before him in a traditional entreaty.

"I didn't want to," he said, "they made me."

Wren walked up.

"Please," he begged, flinching with every step. "Please, don't!"

Wren stopped in front of him. Chest heaving. Seven inches on the guy, and easily a hundred pounds. It would be so easy to roll him up like a ball. Break his bird bones, smash his buck teeth, shatter his kneecaps and elbows, leave him wailing into the flames.

Wren did none of that. He'd learned the lesson well from Maggie, from Hellström. Control was everything. Instead he pulled back his hood. The guy wasn't even looking up at him. Shuddering on the spot already, like he was out naked on the street in the middle of winter.

"Look at me," Wren commanded. A burring bass that hit the captain like a blow. Slowly he raised his gaze. Saw the scars on Wren's cheeks. Saw the beard tied into a knot. Saw those dark, judging eyes.

A wave of something passed through the captain's body. His eyes flared wide, and his jaw opened like Edward Munch's 'The Scream'. His legs went to jelly and he sagged, barely caught himself.

"No," he whimpered. "Not you. I swear, I swear I didn't want to! It wasn't me, they made me."

Wren reached out. Laid one hand on the guy's shoulder. So easy to squeeze and crush his clavicle. He'd deserve no better. The captain flinched like Wren's hand was on fire.

"Sure they did," he soothed, rumbling like the verdict of heaven. "I believe you. The mob, though?" He just shook his head. "Only two things can save you now, Reynolds. One. Tell me where Amira Matheson's children are. Everything about the operation, how many guards, what kind of defenses. Don't leave a bit out. And two. Get me on a comms line out of state." He paused a long moment, letting that sink in. "Can you do either?"

35

TWO THINGS

The captain stared. For a moment Wren thought he might pass out from fear. To forestall that, he gripped the man's collar in one meaty hand and gently slapped him with the other.

Barely painful. Just enough to center him.

Reynolds spluttered.

"I asked you a question," Wren rumbled.

Reynolds stared. He looked at Wren, and past him, and all around the corner office with its bookshelves filled with leatherbound tomes, walls filled with certifications, awards and photographs of the previous occupant shaking hands with famous political figures.

He found no escape in any of them.

"I don't know," he managed, when his eyes inevitably worked their way back to Wren. "Uh, Amira Matheson's children? She's the senator, the towelhead, right?"

Wren gave him another slap. A little harder this time. "Where are they?"

Reynolds shook his head, spluttered some more, tried to channel indignation. "Why would I know that? Ask her. What's it got to do with me?"

All fair points.

"Then the prisoners here. Where are they being taken?"

He sucked air. "The prisoners? You mean the terrorists?"

Wren didn't have time to take issue with that. Of course they'd have turned it around. "Sure, the terrorists you've been systematically rounding up, abusing and shipping off to concentration camps. Where are they going?"

"Uh, well, it's more than one place, isn't it? Anywhere that has room."

Wren shook him hard. "Where?"

"Sherman!" Reynolds blurted. "There's a big one up there, I heard. One way over in Nacogdoches, another in Junction, that's a ways southwest. Plenty of others."

"What kind of places are they?"

"What kind…? Uh, I, I haven't been there! I don't know. They're terrorists, so it'll be a prison of some kind. Uh…"

"Are they police stations, like here? Warehouses? How do I find them?"

"They're special facilities, as far as I know. Listen, they didn't really tell me much! I know it looks like I'm in charge here, but it's my uncle you want, he's on the new city council, he got me set up here, and-"

"I don't care about your uncle," Wren said softly. "He isn't here. You are, and so am I. The mob's outside. Your fake police are dead in the corridor. There's fires spreading through the building. You give me what I want, or I strap you to your chair and leave you to burn."

Reynolds reached a new layer of terror, eyes rolling like cue balls in his head. "You wouldn't. No, you couldn't."

"Keep wasting my time and we'll find out."

"No, please, I'll do anything! The facilities, yes! They're some kind of warehouses. There was, unnh, they gave me an induction right after we declared independence. Uh, X Boxes, they called them!"

Wren frowned. "X Boxes, like the games console?"

Reynolds laughed high and fluttery. "No, no, sorry that's what we called them. My friends. It's a joke. A bad joke. For holding people. Built up to hold, re-educate, release."

"Show me on a map."

Reynolds made a tight squealing sound, and then his bladder voided. A brief expression of shame passed over his face, quickly subsumed by the terror. Wren took a small step back but didn't relinquish his hold.

"On a m-map?" Reynolds stammered. "I, uh, I don't really know. I can show you the towns, I guess? Not even the drivers know the precise locations, I heard. They pull up to the city limits, then, unnh, someone swaps out, drives the rest of the route. It's top secret."

Wren gritted his teeth. "So you don't know about Matheson. You don't know where these 'X Boxes' are. What do you know?"

Reynolds' eyes did another circuit of the room, still found no escape. Then his face lit up. "A line out! That's what you asked for, right? I have that. Or my uncle does. I can get you a line out. All city councilmen have one. I swear!"

Wren leaned in; his face close to Reynolds'. "Where's your uncle?"

"At home! I guess. It's not even far, in the West End Historic District. A beautiful place. It's-"

Wren was already walking, dragging Reynolds behind him like he was no more trouble than a Chihuahua.

The corridor was a wreck. Survivors from the surrounding rooms were gathering in the dark, half-dressed in whatever rags they'd managed to salvage. Looked like three teenage girls and a boy who couldn't be older than eleven, all of them with shock biting deep into their eyes.

Seeing that made Wren want to rip Reynolds apart even more. He held back. Instead he dropped to one knee before them, slamming the skinny captain to the ground with him. Reynolds' chest hit hard, and Wren looked at the four survivors before him.

They stared back. Swaying from foot to foot. Not certain what was happening, if things had just gotten worse or better for them. For them, he bit the rage back, putting forth the warmest, kindest voice he could manage.

"I am so sorry for what happened to you here. The men who did this are dead. The man I'm holding here will pay. Right now you're in pain. But you will feel better. I swear it. You will be stronger." He took a breath. They were barely taking it in, but that didn't matter. They'd remember it, the empowerment that capped the horror. "For now, I need your help. We need to get out of this building. The front's on fire." He looked up, saw the cages beyond the barricade were already swathed in a frothing ocean of flames. "There has to be a way out. Can you find it for me?"

They stared. Reynolds started to say something, and Wren slammed him into the floor again, silencing him.

"I think, this way," one of the girls said quietly. Pointing back down the corridor, left beside the barricade. "There's an exit sign."

"That's good," Wren said. Showing that even this big, strong man needed their help. "Lead the way."

The girl, her woven hair half ripped out of its braids with one eye swelling up black, took hold of the little boy's hand. She flashed a look at Wren then started away. The other two young women looked at each other.

"It'll be OK," Wren said. "Really."

One was crying silently. The other took her hand and pulled her along.

Wren followed, dragging Reynolds. By the barricade stood Sarge. He looked anxious, was even holding a gun, maybe was thinking about turning it on Wren.

"It's been almost two hours," he whined. "I'm uh, can you…"

Wren stopped in front of him. Took Sarge by the scruff of his chest with his left hand. One sick man in each hand.

"You want your antidote, yes?"

"I did what you asked. Turned on my own people. I did it all. It's only fair."

"Fair's fair," Wren said, and launched a headbutt into the man's face.

He dropped where he stood. Reynolds let out a little shriek. Wren considered leaving Sarge with the other bodies behind the barricade, but realized the kids were watching him from an open exit door off to the left, and what was he but a good role model?

He followed after them, dragging Sarge by one hand and Reynolds by the other, out into the chill of a teXas spring night.

36

UNCLE

The exit led into the senior officers' section of the parking lot, flickering with orange shadows from the rising flames. Guns fired and shouts rang from around the front of the lot.

"Wait here," Wren said to the survivors, dropped Sarge then pulled his hood back over his head and walked along the wall to the main lot, dragging Reynolds with him.

The scene in the lot was chaotic, with multiple cars burning in the midst of a festival-like atmosphere. People were everywhere, here dragging an injured cop and holding him up to the flames so he squealed, here firing weapons into the station's windows, releasing little spurts of hungry flame, there filming a teXas flag as it burned on multiple phones.

Wren hadn't expected this. He'd anticipated the prisoners fleeing as soon as he'd let them go; now it seemed he'd empowered them too much.

"It's him!" someone shouted, pointing at Wren. A guy standing on a squad car roof. For a moment Wren thought his shallow cover had been blown; the fewer people who knew he was behind this attack, the better.

But they weren't pointing at Wren. They were pointing at Reynolds.

The crowd swelled toward him, stolen guns bristling, the thirst for vengeance fuming off them like a fever. Instantly he knew this was a mistake. He'd hoped to find someone to look after the boy and the young women, but that wasn't going to happen now.

"It's the captain!" the man shouted, closing in fast. Wren didn't recognize him, but that wasn't a surprise; he wasn't one of the people he'd deputized for the breakout. He wouldn't have picked a man like this for his team.

"Hand him over," the man said, 6'2" and mid-thirties, maybe a bodybuilder, "we'll string him up from his own flagpole!"

Reynolds flinched, tried to hide behind Wren.

No choice. Wren let Reynolds go for a second and took three fast steps forward, jabbing the noisy guy square in the face. He fell back five steps into the crowd.

"He's mine," Wren growled at the crowd. "No debate. Now get out of here. You want revenge, you have to live through tonight, and I guarantee reinforcements are coming. They'll have military equipment and proper training. Stay here and squabble over cold slivers of vengeance, you're all going to die. This is not the Alamo."

Guns still pointed in his face.

"Who the hell are you?" someone asked; a woman with a blond bob cut, pointing a Glock 9mm at his face. Wren stared right back at her from under his stinking hood.

"I'm the guy who set you loose. Fight me now, it all falls apart. Now turn and run."

"'Dis guy sucker-punched me!" came the numbed voice of the bodybuilder, staggering back through the crowd from where he'd fallen, blood streaming from his busted nose. "Who de hell he think he is?"

Seemed the lesson hadn't been learned. Wren leaped forward, put a front kick in the guy's chest and he flew five feet back, slammed bodily into a white Honda.

"Go," Wren commanded. "Now."

The bodybuilder bounced and dropped forward on all fours.

Wren looked at the woman with the Glock. "Help him," he ordered. "There are four kids around the back, survivors of abuse, and they need your help more than they need your vengeance. Now get out of here."

He spun and grabbed Reynolds, standing where he'd left him, jaw slack. The people in back said nothing.

"Where's your car?" Wren said as he shoved Reynolds on a jittery perp walk back the way they'd come.

Reynolds pointed and blathered them to a Porsche 718 Boxster. He fumbled the key from his pocket and Wren snatched it, opened the door and pushed the captain into the passenger seat. As he dropped into the driver's side, he saw the bob cut woman approach the four survivors. She took two by the hand and led the others, the Glock tucked into her waistband. Wren hoped she wasn't going to need it.

He hit the gas and pulled away. Through the main lot he barely swerved to avoid the escaping masses, flanked either side by burning cars. A brick struck the rear bodywork, rioters acting out, but it wasn't his car, so he didn't care.

Then they were out.

The flames were left behind. The streets were dark but not quiet. Already there were sirens in the air, a fast response team coming from another station over, or maybe the MEPS base, Military Entrance Processing Command. Probably a lot of these people were going to get re-arrested. That was bad, but Wren didn't think many of them knew who he was, at least none who would talk easily. So that was good.

Still, speed was of the essence.

"Direct me," he ordered.

Reynolds was shuddering in the seat.

"To your uncle's house," Wren said, a little more gently. "Where is it?"

He blew through an empty intersection.

"That was a left," Reynolds said. Wren spun a handbrake U-turn and tore back, turned right through the intersection.

Under the I-45 overpass and into the West End Historic district. There were a lot of six-story redbrick blocks with loading arches built into their design; once a warehouse and trade zone. Now interspersed with trees, crosswalks and more trendy coffee shops.

In seven minutes they were there.

Reynolds' uncle, a guy in his mid-fifties by the name of Anson Reynolds, owned a four-floor townhouse wedged into a gentrified block between an upscale dry cleaner's and some kind of hip new co-working space.

"Go," Wren ordered. "Get him to let you in. Give any signal I'm with you, you die, he dies, your whole family dies. Nod your head if you understand."

Reynolds nodded.

"Then move."

Reynolds opened the door. A fire engine wailed by a block over, headed for Deep Ellum. Reynolds limped over to the door. Wren exited the vehicle behind him, tracked wide to come from the side, across the front of the co-working space. He met Reynolds at the door, about to push the button on a video-enabled intercom system.

"Don't look at me," Wren said.

Reynolds gulped. Rang the buzzer. Within thirty seconds an older man's voice came through. Wren was too close to the wall to make out his face on the screen.

"Miguel? Is everything OK?"

"There's something I need to ask you," Reynolds said. Miguel.

"Ask me now, at this time?"

Reynolds' gaze almost broke to Wren, but he managed to control himself. Focused on the video screen. "It's about X. What we're doing here. I'm having doubts."

A long moment passed, then a loud buzzer sounded.

"Come up," Anson Reynolds said.

Reynolds pushed open the door and started through. Wren caught it, ducked under the camera array and followed him in.

Two plush flights of stairs led them to the councilman's door. He was standing in the doorway, wearing a cartoon-like padded maroon smoking jacket, shirt open at the throat, a pipe in one hand. The absolute picture of embedded power.

"Have you heard those sirens, Miguel?" Anson asked, as they appeared up the stairs. "And who's this with you?"

"Judgment," said Wren, and closed the gap in three long strides. He got one foot under the door before the older man could pull it shut, took his hand that held the pipe and easily spun it up behind his back.

Anson the councilman yelped and hopped up on his tippytoes, like he could escape the lock.

"I'm sorry, he made me," Miguel whined.

Wren grabbed Miguel by the back of the head and brought his face down into Wren's rising knee, knocking him out cold instantly.

Anson gasped. "What are you doing?"

"Keeping a promise," Wren growled, as Miguel dropped like a sack of sand. He grabbed the younger man by one arm and propelled uncle and nephew back through the open door.

The door slammed shut behind him. Wren laid Miguel down and took in the entrance hall.

It was grossly opulent, decked out with fine Corinthian

marble flooring, Doric columns lining the split white and teal walls, high ceilings ten foot above, from which a veritable chandelier hung down.

"Anyone else in the premises?" Wren asked. "Think hard about lying, you'll just buy bullets for all of you."

"I, well, no," Anson said. "I'm alone. It's late."

"Let's hope you're telling the truth," Wren rumbled. "Now, your nephew's in trouble. You're in trouble, Anson. I'm having one heck of a night, and people keep getting in my way, trying to arrest me, kill me or set me on fire. Thinking I can be reasoned with would be a major mistake on your part." He pulled his hood back. Bared his teeth. "See, the thing you X people need to learn is, I can't be reasoned with. Your only hope is to do exactly what I say, when I say it. Maybe then you'll survive. Am I understood?"

Anson's tan skin flushed pale and bloodless. "It's you."

"Thought I was dead? You'd voted me out of existence? Can't be done. I'm like a cat, and I've got at least five lives left."

"I-" Anson started, then thought better of it and restarted. "How did you get Miguel? What do you wa-"

Wren stepped up, put one big hand around Anson's throat, the other on the back of his head, and squeezed the two together lightly. "Keep asking questions and I pull your head off like I'm pruning my roses, Anson. Is that what you want?"

Anson croaked something.

"Your nephew out there said you could get me a line out of state. Out of the country, whatever, because you're a councilman. So that's what you're going to do, Anson. Right now, no fooling around, no efforts to warn anyone. The second I let go of your throat, you lead me to that outside line. Anything else is an intolerable sidetrack. We're all on the clock. No questions. Here we go."

He let go.

Anson coughed and made a meal out of getting his breath back, but only for a few seconds, then he straightened up and fixed a bloody gaze on Wren, with anger burning through the fear.

He turned and started walking. Wren followed close behind.

37

IDEALISTIC FOOL

"That's a cell phone," Wren said, looking down at a regular oblong of black glass and plastic sitting on the blotting leather of a pedestal desk.

Anson was restrained, arms tied behind his back with a curtain loop, in a leather-upholstered Bentwood chair. The study around them was richly appointed, all jungle pot plants, dark-stained oak shelving and sideboards stocked with liquor.

"Of course it is," said Anson. His hatred dripped through in every syllable. "What did you expect?"

"All lines in and out were cut. I expected a satellite phone at the least, maybe a special hard line."

Anson scoffed. "You didn't really think we'd cut every cell tower down, did you? Maybe shot the satellites out of the atmosphere, physically cut every single hard line?"

Wren afforded him a wry look. "So what did you do?"

"Locked them. It's simple, apparently. Every phone call and Internet connection passes through an interchange system. Own the interchanges, you decide which signals are allowed to pass. Now we own them, so we decide."

Wren picked up the phone. Just like any other phone. "And this one gets through?"

"Yes. A select number of phones, both hardline and mobile, as well as Internet connections, are allowed access." He paused a moment, lips pursed in a sneer. "Some of us need to know what's happening in the 'wider world'. So we can better prepare for outliers like you."

Wren fixed him with a glare. "Outliers like me? So speaks the X zealot, willing to burn the country down." He tapped the phone's screen, and up popped the familiar lock screen digits. "Give me the PIN code."

Now Anson jutted his chin forward. "You think I'm a zealot? Tell me, Mr. Wren, do you really believe this is about X?"

Wren considered punching the man. One blow should do it, shake him up, shake loose the code, but maybe it wasn't the fastest way. "Your nephew certainly thought so," he said instead. "The commander of Sheppard Air Base believes it. He's got all kinds of crazy ideas. Cap it all, your new President's playing the X theme song across all two state-sanctioned news channels. What else am I to think, other than you're all true believers?"

"I believe in power, Mr. Wren," Anson hissed. "It drives us all, whatever we want, wherever we go. The man who works three jobs to pay for his kids, all he dreams about is power, every hour of every day, because he doesn't have it. A man like myself, I've fought my way up and earned a taste, and it's left me thirsting for more, just to keep myself and my own from being crushed underfoot. And a man like you?" He paused. "A man like you can be bargained with, I believe. Can be won around."

Wren stared at the man. Maybe the punch option would've been faster. If he got unlucky, though, Anson might prove tougher than he looked. That could be a bloody, messy and ultimately unreliable path.

"So persuade me," he said.

"I will. What is X, Mr. Wren?"

"My father's nonsense ideology," he answered fast. "Warped and reconstructed maybe, but the same. Now give me the code."

Anson shook his head, like he was disappointed. "Wrong. X is nothing. X is a gateway only. People open their hearts to X, we can pour anything we want into them, and they'll buy it. Surely you understand this. They're in too deep by then to back out. Chinese communism is good? We can sell it. Camps to re-educate Muslims, or gays, or whomever? Why not? Leave them to live insecure lives in squalor, fear and poverty, little better than indentured servants on a mass scale, and we can make them embrace their lot in life, as long as we stoke their anger and show them someone they hate getting it worse. That's power. We've been doing it for years."

"Get to the point."

"I argued against bringing down the jet," Anson said. "I argued against taking Amira Matheson and compelling the vote, too. We didn't need either, I said."

Wren focused in. "So I'm supposed to say thanks for that? What, you're an X moderate?"

"I'm a man who sees X for what it is. A tool in some hands. A weapon in others. For me it's a lever, a way to open the door wide enough to force myself and my whole family through."

Wren stared at him. Taking his measure. The kind of man he'd known all his life. Take a little. Take a lot. Get yours. "Your nephew presided over a nest of rapists and abusers. Is that the kind of levering you had in mind?"

Anson shrugged. "It's a transition. Violence comes."

Wren gave it up. There would be no shame here, either. "You mentioned Amira Matheson. Do you know where she is?"

"She's with the President. Twenty-four-seven, seven days

a week, as I understand it." Then he smiled. "But it's her children you want to know about, I think, yes?" He read the answer in Wren's eyes. "Yes. We think alike, Mr. Wren. They're the means we used to compel her vote. You hope to take them, take her, reverse this compulsion, yes? But it won't work. The vote's been cast."

"Votes can be over-ruled. You managed it here. After the Civil War, every state agreed the United States was indivisible. It's right there in the Pledge of Allegiance. I'm bringing that back." He put his knee in the older man's belly and shoved. "So tell me where the kids are."

Anson coughed, winced then croaked out a few words. "I don't know. I've had only a taste of power, remember? They won't tell me. I'll be lucky to survive all the pogroms that are coming. I think you know that. Start pouring madness through the door of X, there's no doubt someone's going to push for the 're-education' of my people."

"What people?"

"Hispanics! We're an easy scapegoat, yes? This is why I need power. To show we're not viable targets. So Miguel became a chief of police, or whatever role I buy for him. So I'm here and free to act, not under the President's thumb, like Amira Matheson's children. So I can do the same for you, and your people."

Wren leaned in harder. "And who are my people, Anson?"

"You're black, aren't you?" the man gasped. "Far in the minority in Texas. After this new nation eats its latest litter, the easiest targets first, they'll be coming for you and yours. I can shield you." Now his eyes shone. "Or you can shield me, whichever. We make you a supporter of the regime. They love stories of conversion. Get your own phone, passport, the right to travel. You just need to play the game."

Wren stared at the man. He seemed sincere. Seemed to think his offer might truly hold some attraction for Wren.

"I've listened," he said. "I've weighed your offer. I reject I completely. The world you're describing is empty, Anson Reynolds. Power is an umbrella, that's true, to protect others, but that umbrella should come from the very top, as voted for by the very bottom. It should protect us all, because we all chose it. But any state driven by X will never do that. You just described the system devouring its own. I could never back a worldview like that."

Anson laughed. A difficult feat given Wren's weight in his belly. "You really think your United States is better? You think that system isn't rigged against men such as you and me? Their corruption is institutional, Mr. Wren! It weighs in the balance against us time after time, from the street to the state house to the White House itself. They have their thumb on the scale every day, in every interaction, and they will forever. I've felt it. I know you have. There is no such thing as a more perfect union."

Wren pulled back. Looked Anson square in the eyes. "You're wrong. This year's better than last year, which is better than the year before. No one's ever done this before. There is no more perfect country in the world. We're learning who we are, Anson. Sometimes that's hard. X is a block in the road. It's my job to steamroll it to nothing. Don't get steamrolled with it. Now I've heard you out. Give me the code, or I start pulling teeth."

Anson stared up at him defiantly. "You're an idealistic fool. Wait until you're my age."

"If I live that long. Code, now."

38

LINE

The PIN opened the phone. It was like any other phone on the inside. Square icons for various apps. The one he was looking for was a green block with rounded corners and a phone symbol in the middle.

Wren's heart started to pound.

"I just type in the number?" he asked.

"You've used a phone before, haven't you?" Anson asked, leaning on the sarcasm. "It's a phone. Use it like a phone."

"I mean, there's no more secret codes, special extension out?"

"Special extension out? What are you talking about?"

"All right," Wren said, walking away, "just shush, OK? Stay there."

"Where am I going to go?" Anson called after him. "You tied me to this chair."

Wren walked out of the study, down a richly appointed hall lined with gilt mirrors. The whole place was like a pauper's idea of a wealthy ancestral home. At the end of the corridor hung a large-scale portrait of Anson Reynolds. Definitely a sociopath.

Wren looked at the phone keypad. A week, he'd been out

of touch. Isolated, though he hadn't even known it. He typed in an emergency number from memory. One that would reroute through VPNs around the globe, untraceable and encrypted, and it began to ring.

Long seconds stretched out. Long enough for him to doubt everything the Reynolds men had told him. Maybe this phone was a trap of some kind, summoning X forces right now. Maybe the X 'Marines' he'd escaped at Fort Sheppard were about to burst through the stained-glass windows.

He eyed them suspiciously and the phone rang, until-

"Zdrasti."

Wren blinked. Was about to say 'What?' when he remembered the basic lessons he'd received in Bulgarian. 'Zdastri' was 'Hello'. That meant…

"Hellion?" he asked.

A few more tense seconds passed, followed by a tone of total disbelief.

"Christopher?"

He almost laughed, but didn't, for fear a sob might creep through. "Yes, it's me. Isabella, it's good to hear your voice."

"And very good to hear yours, Christopher," she answered fast. "Especially because you are dead. This is most extreme surprise."

Now he did laugh. "They're saying I'm dead?"

"Yes. Christopher Wren, Doona Joy, Alejandro Gutierrez, Alli Rayler, all forces lost in terrorist attack on sovereign Fort Sheppard. This is tragedy, indeed. So perhaps you are thinking, this is good phone number for exploitation of inside connection? Yes. This means, can you provide proof you are Christopher Wren, and not phishing idiot from CIA, FBI or X-teXas?"

Wren took a second to take that on board. "They're saying I'm dead."

"As dead parrot. Yes. Everybody is saying this."

"And other people have called this number, pretending to be me?"

"Perhaps this is true. None could give particular information, though, which only Christopher Wren would know. Can you?"

Wren nodded along. "OK, I understand. So you want proof?" He thought for a second, something only Wren and Hellion might know. "You hate CIA Director Gerald Humphreys with a passion. You have a ringtone on your phone of him saying, 'How did they do that?' about a basic hack you pulled off. It's one of your proudest possessions."

"Everybody knows this," Hellion countered. "Voice of Director Humphreys sounding like fool, this is popular ringtone, many people enjoy this."

"It's a popular ringtone?"

"Very popular since I released it, yes, top ten ringtones. There is now confused-face emoji to match it, it looks stupid, very expensive to pressure big media companies to adopt this, but they did. So, research is poor in your department. I am hanging up."

"Wait!" Wren blurted, wracking his brain. "It's really me. Hang on a second, I'm thinking. Uh. Something only I would know. OK! The Body Snatchers! I know you pretend not to know that movie well, the original sci-fi invasion story from 1956, you always ask B4cksl4cker what it's called, but I also know you own two copies out of five remaining of the original celluloid canisters they sent out to cinemas, along with three prop body snatcher tails, a dozen signed movie posters and the outfit Dana Wynter wore in the finale, complete with fake blood."

"Memorabilia!" Hellion responded immediately. "This is not knowledge. Everybody loves Body Snatchers. Many people own original canisters of film."

"Only three other people possibly could." Wren offered.

"Many fakes!" Hellion insisted. "Last attempt or I close line forever. Tell me something very true, from dark deep past. Christopher Wren's first love. Name of earliest girlfriend."

Wren's eyes narrowed. He'd a few girlfriends, back in the few years he'd spent at high school, after his days in the Maine woods with James Tandrews. Not something he'd ever talked about with Hellion, though. "OK. You want to know about secret flings? I know that you had a secret crush on B4cksl4cker for years, until the day you met him, and you realized he was way too hairy. Now you have a crush on my mechanic, Alli, but you've said nothing about it to her, too afraid of being-"

"Christopher!" Hellion blurted. "This is open line. Do not say such things!"

Wren snorted. "It's a secure line, encrypted as far as possible. And now you believe it's me?"

"Of course I know it is you from start! How many CIA are so stupid as to call from inside teXas, when teXas is shut down? Only Christopher Wren will do such a foolish thing."

He laughed. That sounded more like Hellion. "So one minute you thought I was dead, the next you were playing with me?"

"Ha ha, Christopher, I never believe you are dead. Bad bet. From beginning, this was game. Very funny, yes, B4cksl4cker?"

"Christopher!" came the big hacker's bass Armenian voice. "Yes, excellent game. We have been waiting for you. You are OK?"

Wren rubbed a hand down his face. Even here, in the midst of Anson Reynolds' apartment, in the depths of X-held teXas territory, his hackers could be as infuriating as ever.

"I got shot, but I'm better now. Listen. There's a lot we need to catch up on. A lot of things we need to do. But first I need to know just how secure this line is. It's the phone belonging to state councilman Anson Reynolds. I'm in his apartment in downtown Dallas, he's my hostage, and I need to know if you can firm up the connection. Ideally, I want you in my ear for the coming twenty-four hours."

"Eighteen hours," B4cksl4cker said. "Until new President is established."

"Exactly. What can you tell me?"

"Easy," Hellion answered. "I can see phone is approved for direct line out. I am in their system now. If they know about me, then I am possible to purge again, as they did the first time. But it will not be easy. I have seen their lockout code kernel. I can hide from them, I believe. This line should remain."

Wren breathed a sigh of relief. "Good. That's excellent. So-"

"What happened, Christopher? Are others alive?"

"Yes. We all are. We made it out of Fort Sheppard, I was shot and unconscious for the past six days, but I'm mobile again now. We've been lying low while the city goes to hell around us. Concentration camps, mass arrests, clampdowns on all kinds of people. It's all happening. Here's what I need you to-"

"So you are alone behind enemy lines? Man with dark past attempting to bring down terrorist control from within, unqualified but using initiative where possible, bringing down bad guys while sending taunting messages, and in touch with one good source on the outside?"

That seemed unduly specific. "What?"

"Is there also your wife being held hostage on top floor, Christopher?" B4cksl4cker chimed in. "Terrorists with unusual Eastern-European accents, asking for money and power?"

Wren thought briefly of Hellström's Swedish accent, but dismissed it. "My wife? What are you talking about?"

"Perhaps there has been scene of broken glass lying on floor, which you must run over with feet bare? Has this happened yet?"

He began to have some inkling of what they were talking about. His hand went back to his face, rubbing his throbbing eyes. "You can't be serious. No, Hellion."

"Yes, Christopher!" Hellion cheered. "This is plot of Die Hard! First movie is building, second is airport, third is, perhaps, a city? It is not so good. Fourth and fifth, B4cksl4cker?"

"I don't remember. Bruce Willis had son. Or perhaps daughter. It is not so good."

"Well, maybe you are sixth, Christopher!" Hellion continued cheerfully. "Rogue agent alone in whole terror-controlled state. This is very epic scale, for Big Bad Bird."

Wren sighed. Right from joy that they were in touch, back to frustration they were such children. "I'm not a bird."

"Of course you are not bird, you are John McClane! American hero. What is famous catchphrase, B4cksl4cker? Christopher, you must say this."

"Yes," said B4cksl4cker, "it is 'Yippee-ki-yay, mother-'"

"I'm not saying that," Wren said swiftly. "I'm not John McClane. What I am going to do is go right back and tell Alli you have a crush on her, then record her reaction on a phone and make that my ringtone. Maybe I'll push it viral, so everyone will know about the schoolgirl crush of the world's second greatest hacker. How does that sound?"

"Perhaps we should move to practical matters," Hellion conceded sharply. "You are right, this is very serious business, of course. Whole state at risk, unity of your country."

"You took the words right out of my mouth. I can

probably fit in a quick coin chat with Alli, though. See how she really feels about Allion."

"Unnecessary, Christopher!" Hellion blurted. "Yes, I think business now is our best step. And do not be rude about B4cksl4cker, poor second-best hacker in world, this is hard fate for him. Now, we must prepare, yes? Tape gun to your back, like John McClane! I am excellent gun taper. Metaphorically, of course. I am in Bulgaria now."

Wren allowed himself a small smile. He'd missed them, really.

"OK. So here's what I'm going to need."

39

NEW TEXAS

Wren left the Reynolds boys firmly tied up in their chairs in the study, facing each other with gags on, listening to low jazz on the antique teak radio.

"It'll help you relax," he said. "And relax is all you're going to be able to do until I call this in. A day or two, as long as it takes."

Anson was red-faced by then, huffing and puffing into his gag. Miguel was only semi-conscious and lolling side-to-side.

"I'd sleep, if I were you," Wren said. "You'll need your rest when the arraignment comes down."

He left the apartment building silently. The street was dark and quiet outside, but for the odd wail of sirens. He could smell the Central Patrol fire on the air, the smoke of insulation material releasing a noxious cloud to drift low across the city.

"You still hear me?" he asked Hellion.

"Very clearly, Christopher," Hellion said in his ear, through an earbud sourced from Reynolds' home. "GPS data is immaculate. Very little traffic through teXas Internet, currently. We have much bandwidth for ourselves."

Wren got in the Porsche, navigated streets hanging with funereal wreaths of smoke lit by flickering blue emergency vehicle lights, and within ten minutes was back on the fifth floor of the Cole Avenue apartment block, walking up to the corner apartment.

A neighbor poked their head out, then ducked back in rapidly when they saw Wren. He considered going in after them, shutting any line leading to the teXas gestapo down, but decided against it.

Let the gestapo come.

He rapped on the door. Alli opened it, holding a shotgun.

"Nice to see you too," Wren said.

Alli breathed a sigh of relief. "Hot dang, Chris. Where have you been? The city's on fire!"

"I know," Wren said, striding in past her.

"On the news they're saying it's you," Alli said, closing the door behind him. "Was it?"

"It was. Now." He stopped, turned so he could look at both Doona, who was holding a pistol, and Alli at the same time. "Get ready to roll out. This whole neighborhood, maybe this whole city is burned. We're leaving just as soon as I get what I need."

Doona tilted her head. "And what do you need?"

"Answers," Wren said. "I should be no more than ten minutes. Oh, and you'll have access to a line out through Hellion. Get a handset and she'll Bluetooth you in through my cell, Teddy can set roles and get things moving. OK?"

They stared back at him, then both spoke at the same time. "You got a line out?" Alli asked.

"Teddy's on the line?" asked Doona.

Wren flashed a smile. "We're back in business, with enough bandwidth for all. Now wish me luck."

They stared. He pushed open the door to the bedroom cell.

Brigadier General Mads Hellström was still sitting on the chair where he'd left him, some five hours earlier.

Wren entered, closed the door then sat down opposite the steely-faced general, just like he'd sat down before. Looked into Hellström's eyes, like he'd looked into them before. The same overwhelming confidence was there, the same arrogance. If anything, he looked more confident than before.

"I've taken a look at your teXas," Wren said.

Hellström snorted. "I can see that. I heard the sirens. You've got blood on your shirt."

"It's not mine."

Hellström sucked his teeth. "It all stacks up, Mr. Wren. Every crime you commit against my country, the punishment will worsen."

Wren smiled again. "I was going to say the precise same thing to you. But maybe I'll leave that to somebody else."

He took out Anson Reynolds' phone.

"Where'd you get that?" Hellström asked.

"It's just a phone," Wren said, then held it up so the general could see the screen. "Hellion."

"Yes, Christopher," she answered in his ear. "Streaming."

Video flashed up on the cell phone. Wren hadn't seen it yet, but he knew what it would show. A woman behind a big desk, not a million miles away from how Hellström's own office had looked.

Hellström's eyes bugged.

"Brigadier General," came the clipped tones of a middle-aged woman, well-known to everyone for her role in salvaging what she could from the battered United States. President Jacinda Ablas.

Hellström's eyes widened. It took a second, then he fixed his gaze on Wren. "That's a deepfake. You don't have a line out."

Wren said nothing, letting the President take the lead.

"I assure you, Brigadier General, you're speaking with the real President." She spoke in precise, clipped tones, but there was a core of constrained anger burning beneath every one. She'd been the Attorney General for four years, after all, with a lifetime of prosecutions stretching back thirty years. She'd brought down killers, gangs and the leaders of vast organized crime networks, facing down death threats and even one attempted assassination, and scarcely blinked an eye. It was one reason she'd ascended to the Presidency near-unopposed. She was the exact kind of fearless, safe pair of hands the American people needed after the Apex. "I suppose I cannot prove who I am," she went on, every word calculated like a knife thrust, "but then why would I need to?"

She let that hang. Wren could only admire her timing. Allowing Hellström to squirm in his seat, like a kid caught with his hand in the cookie jar. He looked at Wren.

"You think this changes anything?" he seethed. "I don't recognize this woman as anything more than the tyrant of a neighboring nation."

Wren said nothing. What he did do was tap the volume button on the phone to the max.

"I've been thoroughly briefed by Mr. Wren here," President Ablas went on. "On what you're doing, on his intention, and what he needs from you. I heard that he offered you Governor of Texas, once your wayward 'nation' is reabsorbed into the United States." She let a tactical pause elapse. "I can inform you that his offer no longer stands. Here is the new one. I am now naming you and your children as terrorists, leaders of the X terror regime. I think you know what we do to terrorists, whether on soil foreign or domestic, don't you, Brigadier General?"

Hellström turned back to the camera, eyes tightening and a snarl on his lips. "You callow bitch. You wouldn't dare."

"Wouldn't dare what?" Ablas countered hard and cold. "Send Force Recon officers to extract your children from their homes, even as we speak? Your nation is a fragile thing, Brigadier General, like a baby bird. I may not be able to strike directly at your leader for political reasons, but you? Your family? Do you think Hunter Kason will go to war over you?"

Hellström's cheeks tinged red. The onset of fury. President Ablas went on.

"Your children will be renditioned to Guantanamo. You will never see them again. They will never see each other again. And you know we have the capacity. Perhaps you doubt we have the will? But you're wrong. I will do anything, anything whatsoever, to heal the wound you've wrought on this country."

"It won't change anything," Hellström said. "As you say, Kason won't go to war over me."

"Hear my full offer, first," President Ablas said. "No governorship for you. No power. Only jail, maximum security, for the rest of your life." She paused. Sirens rang from the street outside. "But not Guantanamo. You can have visitors. Write books, even. And your children? They walk. Keep building your dynasty. Maybe in twenty years, pending good behavior, we'll let you out. You can bask in what they've built. And you will consider this generous, for the man who masterminded the death of five hundred and thirty of my civilians, innocents murdered over American soil."

Now Hellström's cheeks burned red. Fury with nowhere to go.

"The United States is dying," he spat. "A sinking ship tacked together with string and naive stories, and you're the paper tiger presiding over its demise, Ablas. Start a war, attempt to bring us back to heel, and we will rip you apart."

Ablas said nothing. Letting the man vent as his new future settled on him like a fresh fall of snow. She'd seen the same thing hundreds of times in court rooms around the country.

"Take the deal, Brigadier General," she said. "Save your children and your legacy. teXas will fall, I guarantee it. Play your role here, that end comes sooner, with fewer lives lost on both sides, and your children positioned to profit. Defy us, and the war to come will cripple us all. You'll be utterly destroyed. The United States will survive, though, at least long enough for foreign interests to swoop in and finish the job. Is that what you want?"

Hellström was wheezing now. Breath sucking in and out, the cords of his neck prominent as every muscle in his body tensed. Trying to fight the inevitable. Wren had seen it many times, too; the moment reality came crashing down.

His gaze flicked to Wren, burning now.

"You promise. Swear my children will be safe."

"That's not for me to swear," Wren said. "Speak to the lady."

"Not safe from her," Hellström said, his teeth gritted. "From you. I know what kind of man you are."

Wren said nothing for a long moment. He'd never gone after anyone's family, and never intended to. But then these X people had made him into something he wasn't. A boogey-man, the 'Big Bad Bird'. They meant it as a joke, but the joke only worked because the fear was real. They'd lied so many times they'd come to believe it.

"I swear," Wren said. "If you tell me what I need to know, right now."

For a moment longer Hellström strained. Like he could break out of the bonds that had held him for a week, leap for the window, escape into the night and his beloved teXas. Then he just sagged.

"OK," he said. Then again. "OK."

"Tell me where Amira Mather's children are. Tell me everything you know about the facility they're being held in. Don't leave a bit out, Mads. We're all together in this now."

40

SOUTH

They drove into the night.

It was two-hundred-and-forty miles to Houston. Capital of the old Texas Republic in the 1830s, named after its first president, Sam Houston. Rebranded capital of teXas with a capital X.

Wren burned south on I-45; hands hard on the wheel of a boosted Nissan Rogue. Through moonlit fields of surging sunflowers and sugarcane, where bonfires of books burned, through tiny desert townships where crosses flamed into the dark, passing a refugee train of citizens attempting to flee the sweeping hand of importation as the X fever redoubled its grip on the nation.

Mads Hellström lay in the trunk. Doona sat at Wren's right with a pistol ready, Alejandro and Alli were in back packing a shotgun each, and a rotating cast of voices thrummed in his ear, coordinating with their sole actor in the eye of the storm. He listened in turn to Hellion, B4cksl4cker, Teddy, President Ablas, CIA Director Gerald Humphreys, Special Agent Sally Rogers, his father James Tandrews, and more.

Everyone had something to say. Setting up an army ready

to sweep in. Overwhelming force gathering quietly at the teXas borders, waiting for their moment to strike. Every one of them had value, but all Wren could think about was the job that lay ahead.

Hunter Kason.

The man who'd built this thing from the ground up. Decades in the making.

Hellström had regurgitated it all. Kason cutting his teeth in the fake news trenches of the early Internet blogosphere. Spread bullshit lies far and wide enough, they'd eventually find fertile ground and act as fertilizer for a verdant crop. Kason rode that crop like a rodeo clown to a radio show, to a TV show, to a national slot on a major syndicated network, spewing his hateful nonsense into the ears of millions every day.

Wren had seen him before, but never taken him seriously. That smug expression, those perennially spiteful eyes, spouting lies he couldn't back up and making promises he couldn't possibly keep. Smothering his fans so thick in sweet-smelling manure they came to love him more than the real earth and sun they needed to survive. He became their guardian and their leader, and his dreams weren't done with a leading spot on prime-time TV.

Turned out he'd sought out the Apex years back. Looking for funding, looking for tech support, looking for a network. The Apex had connected him to Hellström and a dozen others in high positions who felt the same way. He'd led them all from the airwaves, giving demographic and intellectual cover as his partners in the military, the police, the civil service and the judiciary enacted a long, slow purge of non-believers. Slowly and steadily, they replaced those loyal to the United States and reality with those loyal only to him and X.

So Sheppard Air Base had a total churn of its member

base. The same went for Central Patrol in Dallas. The same story all across teXas.

Enforcing ideological loyalty.

As he drove, the same words rang through Wren's head like a tolling bell. What Anson Reynolds had told him in his third-floor luxury apartment; that X was nothing but a door, a way to pour in whatever you wanted. Anson had believed he could ride that bronco to power right alongside Kason, but now Wren knew different. First, they came for the X-haters. Then they came for the X-protesters. Then they came for everyone who didn't look and think and believe just like Hunter Kason. Those days were coming. Importation on a genocidal level.

The Reynoldses would never have survived the purge.

There was a check point at Decatur. They had warning from Hellion, via a spy satellite redirected over domestic soil. Wren pulled the Rogue over, everyone climbed out and for an hour they circumvented the barricade through claggy fields of freshly seeded milo, orange dirt riding thick and high up their boots.

Hellström marched with his head down. The beaten demeanor of a POW.

On the other side they stole a fresh vehicle, a green Ford Super Duty, and picked up for the next leg.

"We can't cross into teXas without risking war and losing half the other states," Sally Rogers said in his head. Assigned as his point person to the US government, the 'Wren-wrangler', Hellion called her; partly because there was trust between them, largely because cooler heads realized he'd just tear strips off Gerald Humphreys or anyone else they gave him.

"They have an inordinate number of cameras pointing at the border. They've got all manner of birds up in the air, from F-15s to Predator drones to the latest aerial spybots, running constant sweeps. They've got trucks out, patrols out, news crews out; the whole state is ringed with steel and surveillance. We're massing hundreds of teams ready to go on your word, Chris, but the country's on a hair trigger. If we pull that trigger before you get an official recantation of the vote from Amira Matheson, we implode. It won't matter what happens to Kason after that. We've already lost."

Wren knew it. He didn't need to be told.

"Boss, I'm sorry," Rogers said into one of the silences. "I argued for you. I believed you."

He knew it. He knew she had, he believed she'd gone as far as she could, but believing that wouldn't bring back any of the people already lost to the importations, or any of the dead from the 787, or see Yolanda Queen safe, or Amira Matheson and her children delivered from strife.

She didn't push it. It wasn't the time.

He hurtled south and they prepared logistics around him, like the bandaging around a foreign object embedded in the body politic. Ready to rush in with blood-clotting agents, sutures and gauze, but unable to act until the shrapnel was extracted.

Amira Matheson's vote was that shrapnel. Her children were the scalpel. Wren was the surgeon.

Two thirds of the way down to Houston, outside the little burg of Huntsville at 3 a.m. with the skies as black as they could get before they started getting lighter, they were hit by a random traffic stop that Hellion couldn't spot on satellite.

An unmarked Dodge Charger pulled up in back. Another pulled in front. Lights and sirens flashed, and Wren stopped the car.

"What's happening?" Rogers asked in Wren's ear.

"Some people are going to die," he said, then turned to his team. Their faces were set. A random traffic stop, maybe, but they couldn't take any more prisoners, which meant they couldn't leave any survivors.

The doors of the front vehicle opened. Four figures got out, all carrying rifles. The doors of the rear vehicle opened and another four followed. Wren waited, one hand on the wheel, Desert Eagle in his right hand in the shadows of his lap.

"On your mark," Alli said in back.

"We wait," Wren said.

He watched as the four in front and back split, two from each group across the lanes and taking up position at diagonals, rifles raised so they had the Super Duty covered from all angles. Experienced operators, it looked like, working as a smoothly coordinated team. Maybe more flipped 'Marines'. The remaining four approached closer, one to each door.

The lead guy knocked on Wren's window.

Wren wound it down a little. Not enough to pick out Wren's face.

"Where you all going in such a hurry?" the guy asked. Sounded like Rock Fenner. The same folksy down-home accent, the same lyrical confidence, but twisted.

"Houston," Wren said. "We want to see the inauguration."

The guy whistled low, shone a flashlight over the vehicle's interior. "What are you all, family?"

"That's right."

"And what are these two in back, your kids?"

The guy was mocking him.

"Cousins," Wren said. Knew it wasn't convincing, partly because he scarcely wanted to try. "We're all so excited about the rally. Kason's a dream come true."

"Is that so?" the guy asked. "I don't see you flying the flag. No insignia." He looked around at the others nearby. "You think these good folks look like true believers?"

Somebody laughed.

"I'd say we need a better look at you," the guy said. "See if you can walk the line. Step on out, sir."

"You don't need to kill these people," came Sally Rogers' urgent voice in Wren's ear. "You can play this better."

He knew it. He wanted to. He also wanted to burn them down.

"I can't do that," Wren said, answering them both.

"Can't," the guy repeated. Was savoring this moment, clearly. Wren didn't want to give him the rope to hang himself, but couldn't bear the effort it would take to play it any other way. "You sure it's not won't?"

"Can't," Wren repeated.

"What are you, superglued to that seat? All four of you?"

Wren took a breath. Looked at the guy through the slit in the window. It never was enough to warn. They never took your word for how dangerous you were. Sometimes all they left you with was blood.

"Look in my eyes, soldier," he said. "You don't need to have us step out. Best thing for all of us, you get back in your vehicles and go back to harassing civilians. Forget this moment ever happened. Nobody needs to die."

The guy pulled up his weapon. Pointed it at Wren's face through the glass.

"Sir, get out of the vehicle now."

Wren squeezed the wheel. Sometimes they just gave you no choice.

"Alli," he said, and squeezed his eyes tightly shut.

In back she pushed a button. The wireless signal went out from her phone to the flashbang grenade mounted atop a five-inch slab of soundproofing baffles on the Super Duty's roof, instantly triggering a blast wave of light and sound.

Wren saw the flash even through his eyelids, a red lightning strike. He heard the bang despite the baffling, a massive gunshot powerful enough to dislodge the ossicle bones in the inner ear.

He opened the door as the man reeled back. Shot him in the chest and head, then wheeled. They were all sitting ducks. Wren's team deployed as smooth as an oiled axle, shotguns deployed here and here. Wren fired six more times.

It took less than ten seconds to drop them all.

Their weapons smoked. The bodies lay still. Wren's ears rang still from the blast.

Sally Rogers cursed in Wren's ear. He ignored her.

"Alli, can you rig another flashbang?"

She was staring at the dead bodies. She'd shot one of them. Once a woman, maybe full of excitement for her new nation. Now just food for the worms. Alli hadn't ever played an active role in field operations before.

"Alli," he said again, softer but firm. "Rig another flashbang, please."

She jerked, like he'd yanked on a line connected to one of her piercings. Her eyes fixed on him, then she nodded. "Yeah," she said too loud. Trying for normalcy, when none of this was normal. "Yeah, OK, Chris."

Wren looked at Doona and Alejandro. Already they were checking the corpses. Stripping weaponry and dragging the bodies off the road. Next up was driving their vehicles onto the shoulder, leaving nothing untoward, nothing that would be spotted at least until dawn of the new day.

Wren would be well into Houston by that time.

Eight dead. It was no compensation for the 787 dead. It was just necessary.

"Back on the road," Rogers said. "Inauguration's in seven hours."

41

HOUSTON

There was a surveillance ring around Houston three layers thick.

Standard roadblocks made up two layers, at fifty and thirty miles out apiece, while the third was a roadblock accompanied by an aerial flotilla of two helicopters and a dozen drones circling a two-mile-wide sweep across I-45, fifteen miles out of Houston.

Without Hellion's satellite oversight, they would never have made it through any of them. With her, it took two more vehicle swaps to beat the outer roadblocks and a concerted digital blitz to blind the drones, an intricate misdirection gambit to divert the helicopters and a good old-fashioned ruse to bypass the roadblocks.

They were limited by their assets. Fortunately, the federal government had high-altitude drone technology unavailable to teXas. As soon as Hellion had picked out the aerial blockade, she'd requested the launch of an RQ-170 Sentinel, a high-altitude comms platform capable of jamming radio wavelengths within a targeted cone. It blinded the drones, while Doona took to the east on foot, Alejandro took to the west, and started attempting a dragnet evasion through the fields.

They were too recognizable as Wren's closest Foundation members, especially after the Sheppard raid. Facial recognition software would set off alarm bells up and down the new nation at once.

That left Wren and Mads Hellström in the trunk with Alli in the driver's seat; an unknown with zero public profile, approaching the barricade alone.

They'd done a better job since their first roadblock shootout with the cover story, festooning their latest stolen vehicle, a Volkswagen Atlas SUV, with X memorabilia stolen along the way, from cars they'd picked out. Now they had the X teXas flag in their windows, X ribbons in the back, and Alli wore an X t-shirt along with black X's painted on both cheeks.

It was a tight fit in the trunk. Both Wren and Hellström were big men, crushed on their sides and wrapped around each other like the droplets in a yin-yang. Hellström whispered low prayers in Swedish. Wren let him.

Soon the Atlas cruised to a halt. Muted voices addressed Alli, and she bounced back at them full of nervous energy, a high twittering that would hopefully pass for excitement at the prospect of the inauguration.

Wren couldn't pick out much, as a few low questions were asked, a few excitable tweets came back, then the commands began.

"Step out of the vehicle."

"Hands against the side, legs apart."

"Open the trunk."

"Shut up," Wren hissed at Hellström. But Hellström was in a world of his own now, muttering and whispering his prayers in the dark. He'd been locked up in a bare room for a week, locked in and out of trunks for five hours or longer, interspersed by freezing midnight jaunts through the fields. He'd barely slept, hardly eaten, scarcely washed, and now was facing down a lifetime in jail, when he'd once dreamed of the teXas presidency.

Footsteps thudded along beside the car.

"Shut it now, Mads, or your children get renditioned," Wren whispered.

Hellström didn't hear or didn't care. The key slotted into the trunk's lock. Swedish entreaties fumed from the Brigadier General's mouth. Wren did the only thing he could, and wrapped Hellström's neck with his ankles.

He began to thrash.

The key turned.

Wren squeezed. The trunk opened. Hellström kicked a few final times before the neck compression knocked him unconscious. Wren felt the breeze from outside, wisping in between the thin layers of X memorabilia covering his and Hellström's still bodies.

"What was that?" a male voice asked.

Wren's heart skipped a beat. He prepared to explode from the trunk, try and fight his way through the roadblock, but then-

"This old thing is rusty as heck," Alli answered smoothly, her desperation covered by enthusiasm. "It catches like that all the time. Now, look at all this, I've got X flags, rifle straps, enameled lapel pins, t-shirts and signboards." She rattled the list off at a mile a minute, patting the memorabilia that lay loosely right on top of Wren. "I've got my own print shop up in Dallas, you know, 3D printer machines too, so I've also got scale miniatures of President Kason in here, they're fragile but very collectable, and of course a hundred embroidered caps, I've got an embroidering machine too, and-"

"You've been busy," a male voice said. Wren felt the guy

rustling at the surface level of the load, maybe poking with his rifle barrel.

"Yes sir, just doing my duty under X," Alli enthused. Wren had never heard her so spritely, like a cheerleader at a pep rally. "You can have as many as you want, there's also banners, beer cozies and dildos, but-"

The guy's probing rifle barrel froze, prodding into Wren's hip. "Dildos?"

"Yes sir, X-themed, of course, for the lady who dreams of being taken to heaven on the Apex's chariot. Your wife may love one, your girlfriend too, as a gift it's the sign of a truly secure male, I can guarantee-"

"Close it up," the man said. "We've seen enough. Drive on."

"Are you sure I can't tempt you to-"

"Drive on, ma'am."

Wren smirked. The trunk door came down with a slam. Wren released Hellström's neck, and his head sagged. Alli got back in the front and drove on.

"Is Mads Hellström alive?" Hellion asked in his ear. She must have heard the altercation. Wren reached down and managed to get a finger on Hellström's neck. At first, he thought there was no pulse, but it was there, thready and weak. The ankle choke had been indiscriminate, and compression to the jugular was far more dangerous than the standard carotid sleeper hold.

"He is. He may be unconscious for some time."

"Good. He is asset. Now, you will drive for thirty minutes. I am directing Alli. There is no safe place to exit trunk until you are closer, whole city of Houston is swarmed with surveillance. Kason is taking great care."

"Understood. How are we for building a local team?"

Keys clattered in the background. "I have managed to reach several Foundation fringe members. Your cell connection allows me to leapfrog signal to other phones on this network. They will be waiting for you. I am briefing them."

"Not more Chucks," Wren said.

Hellion laughed. Chuck was a non-combat Foundation member, brought in for the confidence schemes he'd run on retirees, bilking them of their 401ks. He'd once managed to talk Hellion into sending him along on an active op in the Nevada desert against an Anti-Fa compound. Wren had grounded him, left standing by the roadside while the fireworks went off.

"No Chucks," she answered. "Only prime T-bone meat."

Wren laughed. "That's a good joke."

"It is excellent joke," Hellion said. "Worthy of ringtone."

He laughed again but it dried up fast. Curled around Hellström's deadweight body, there wasn't much room for levity.

"Are Doona and Alejandro OK?" he asked.

"Of course, OK. Drones cannot see them, thanks to me. Helicopters cannot find them, in forest. They will make their own way to rendezvous, do not worry."

Do not worry.

They drove for the next few minutes in intermittent silence, as Hellion provided updates. She was managing the flow of information in and out, from Sally and Humphreys for the government, from Teddy for the Foundation, from the Foundation fringe members on call.

Wren bounced and rattled in the back, unable to keep the chill of worry from creeping into his heart, despite what Hellion said. Being locked in the dark only made it worse, heading blind into the center of this new state of X Hunter Kason had built. One of the Apex's final bequeathments, an inheritance of blood and atrocity.

It had to come to an end, today.

"Tell me everything you have on the facility holding the kids," Wren said.

Hellion began.

The car rumbled on.

Six hours and counting.

42

TEAM

Soon enough the car halted and Alli's footfalls padded down the side, then the trunk opened. Pale morning light flooded in, and Wren squinted against the brightness even as he pushed up through the thin skin of memorabilia.

"Dildos?" he said to Alli.

She laughed. "It worked, didn't it?"

He smiled, rolled his legs over the edge of the trunk. "Good job."

They were in the shadow of an underpass. I-610, Wren knew, from the updates Hellion had been feeding him. The road was a washed-out gray in the thin pre-dawn light, the sidewalk littered with old trash, the verges mounded with dust and choked with poison oak. Dead ahead lay a bruised gray sky, serrated by the low and distant towers of downtown Houston, like shipwrecking reefs just above the horizon's surface.

A white van rested ten yards further on, the back doors open and three figures standing in front, dressed in nondescript jeans and jackets. Foundation fringe members. One of them raised a hand in a hapless greeting.

"Is he OK?" Alli asked. Wren saw she was staring into the trunk, where Mads Hellström lay still.

"He'll be fine," Wren said, and slid onto his feet, slamming the trunk behind him. "Come on."

He strode toward the van.

The three Foundation fringe members stiffened as he approached, like soldiers at attention. One was a woman, 5' 9" and in her early twenties, with a mop of curly red hair, a profusion of freckles and a button nose. The other two were men; the one on the left was older and taller, maybe late forties but with the lean physique and broad shoulders of a swimmer, 6' 2" and one-eighty pounds, square jaw with a buzzcut head and watchful eyes. The guy on the right was around Wren's age, looked half-Asian, maybe Korean, around six feet tall but built solid like a linebacker. He had feathery black hair raked back by a metal-toothed band, an aquiline nose and a dusting of stubble on the point of his chin.

They looked like models straight out of central casting. Camera-friendly activists, maybe, in another life.

Wren stopped in front of them. "Thank you for coming," he said, trying to keep the gruff edge out of his voice. It wasn't their fault he'd just spent thirty minutes in the embrace of the enemy in the trunk of a car. They were here to help. "I'm Christopher Wren, but you already know that. What are your names, and why are you here?"

They sounded off. The woman was Nancy; seemed she'd flirted with the X ideology for a while in the early days, back when it had seemed a fun and revolutionary kind of game, until one of her closest friends had taken it very seriously and burned herself alive. The fallout from that had sent Nancy first into shock, then grief, then out looking for revenge.

"I'm sorry," Wren said. "Truly."

She shrugged, said something about Wren going through worse.

The older guy was Trent, he was a swimmer, and he'd always wanted to do more for his community. It wasn't until the billionaire David Keller arrived on the scene that he actually got involved. When Keller announced his independent run for the presidency, Trent had been inspired, and went all in. He started knocking on doors, then manning the phones, then was brought in to run a local campaign field office as the presidential election came closer. He'd been in the crowd in Washington, in front of Keller's inauguration stage, when Keller burned himself alive and started the firestorm. He barely escaped with his life. After that, much like Nancy, he'd gone looking for a way to fight back, and he'd found the Foundation fringe.

"We're glad to have you," Wren said, and shook his hand. His grip was solid as a rock.

Last was the Korean guy, name of Jimmy, short for Ji-Myong. His story was perhaps the least likely of them all; turned out he was a cousin of Yumiko Harkness, the woman who'd masterminded the Reparations' attempt to foment class warfare. He'd grown up as a second-generation immigrant in the same south-Texas town as Yumiko, their families growing closer after his uncle married her aunt. His mother had even worked in the very same computer chip factory as Harkness' father, and they'd both lost their jobs together, when outsourcing to China shut the place down. The Harkness family had spiraled into poverty and depression after that, spinning Yumiko off the rails. Ji-Myong's family had fared better, finding work where they could. It had left Ji-Myong feeling wrought with angst and guilt that he hadn't done more to help Yumiko. That frustration had steadily turned into anger for the people who'd led her so astray.

Wren gazed at the three of them, hardly believing his ears as the miserable stories poured out. They were like a full house in poker, all scarred by his father's atrocities.

"You said no Chucks," Hellion's voice came in his ear. "These are not Chuck. You have never taken interest in Foundation fringe, Christopher, but many are people like this. Your father left damage everywhere. Fringe people are invested, have had training in our camps. This is good."

Wren couldn't argue with that. It was good, even if each tale was tragic. They weren't the Foundation's usual members; criminals, hackers, broken souls, the kind of people Wren was used to running and sometimes compelling via the coin system. These were regular people, law-abiding, who'd through no fault of their own been dragged into his father's violent wake. They belonged in the Foundation as much as anyone.

"Again, thank you for coming," he said, no longer having to push the gruff tone down. "If you weren't here, the task ahead would be impossible. Still, I want to be clear." He took a moment, looking into each of their eyes. "By undertaking this task with me, you will be seriously endangering your lives."

He paused a moment. Thinking about Henry, about Yolanda Queen, about others he'd lost along the way. The three waited, and the silence between them felt communal, almost like prayer.

"There are other risks, too," Wren went on. "Short of death, you could sustain debilitating injuries, both physical and mental. The things you see in the next few hours, the things you may be forced to do, will have an impact you may never shake off. You will be different, after today. Sometimes that'll make you stronger. Sometimes it doesn't work out that way."

He thought briefly of Steven Gruber. The man had been a nervous wreck of corrosive, unfulfilled desires from the moment Wren had first laid eyes on him. He'd been easy to bring in and put on a coin, and it really had helped. Under the protection of the Foundation and the guidance of the coin system, Steven Gruber had flourished. Then the Ghost had taken all that away...

"You may become something you don't recognize," Wren went on. "As much as you may be proud of what we do here today, you may also come to regret it." He took a breath. "I want to be as honest as I can."

They were watching him closely now, eyes large and round. That gaze made him feel like a charlatan, like his father on a stage forcing X into people like a wedge into a door, through which anything could be poured. The truth was, though, it didn't matter what he said, because there was no right way to offer a choice like this. They could say 'yes' a thousand times, but they'd never really understand the scale of what they were taking on until its weight hit them.

This was why the Foundation had always been for broken people. They were already damaged when Wren came in, so if they got a little more damaged along the way, well, it was just more scars.

These people weren't like that. They had lives. They had something to lose.

But it was their choice, and there was no doubt he needed them. He sucked in a breath, so loud it startled them.

"I understand you've had training in our camps," he said.

They all nodded.

"Did that include firearms training and crowd control techniques?"

Nancy tilted her head. "Yes. And it's OK. We all understand the risks. There's nowhere we'd rather be."

Wren forced a smile, feeling more like a charlatan than ever.

"Good." Time to sell the charismatic leader they could believe in, someone worth dying for. "Here's what we're going to do."

43

MOB

Ninety minutes later, Wren stood at the intersection of Edwards and Sawyer Streets on the west side of Houston. It was still barely an hour past dawn and below sixty degrees out, but the road was already thronged with a traffic-halting crowd of thousands.

Wren pulled the balaclava snug over his face, both against the cold and the chance of being recognized.

The masses stretched north and south along Sawyer Street, spreading across the parking lot of an indoor driving range on the right and a modern art museum on the left. Power lines crackled overhead, and in back along Edwards Street stood several blocks of new-build five-story apartment buildings, so new the plastic wrapping hadn't been ripped off the cladding wall panels yet.

An area undergoing gentrification and reconstruction. Not a lot of residents so far; no curtain-twitchers to notice the flood of fervent X believers. They carried white-on-black X flags and banners. They wore X masks and beanies and jackets. Some had X bunting striped across their shoulders like ammo bandoliers; others carried real bandoliers, with assault rifles held at patrol carry on straps across their chests. Texas had been an open-carry state for almost a century, and its transition to teXas with an X had only cemented that right more fully.

Wren estimated a hundred live weapons in his vicinity.

"More are coming, but this is perfect timing," Hellion said in Wren's ear. "Shall I signal to begin?"

Wren said nothing; his eyes were on the adult education facility that lay two blocks east along Edwards, now repurposed into one of Hunter Kason's 'importation camps'. According to Hellström, it was where he'd sent Amira Matheson's children, along with some two thousand other 'importees'.

It was three stories tall, housed forty-seven classrooms and was constructed of tin sheeting and steel rebar, surrounded by freshly emplaced metal fencing. The defensive infrastructure wasn't impressive, but that was a byproduct of the rushed timeline, and Kason's apparent need to have Matheson's children nearby. The facility made up for that weakness with its reported garrison of fifty special ops 'Marines'.

"This will not work," B4cksl4cker had said two hours earlier, back when Wren was still in the trunk of Alli's Volkswagen Atlas, outlining his plan.

"Which part?" Wren answered.

"This message. Text messages to thousands of X believers. It will not have effect you think."

"So you can't reach into their phones?" Wren countered. "You can't contact them?"

"Of course we can reach phones!" B4cksl4cker rumbled. "You are in teXas, on private central node, and we have lockout code for servers now. We are claiming further phone towers and servers every second, better access. That is not the-"

"So you can send the message," Wren pressed. "To thousands at once?"

"Yes, to thousands."

"And what won't work?"

"It is not method. It is message. It is obvious manipulation, Christopher. You think X people are this foolish, will really come?"

Wren couldn't help but smile. "Yes. I think they are and they will, because it's what they want to do."

"They want to do what, attack themselves?"

"Attack someone. Blame someone. I'm just channeling that desire."

B4cksl4cker had scoffed, but sent the message, muttering, "Will not work," under his breath.

It had worked so far. Thousands had come, men and women, old and young surrounding Wren. The message he'd sent was simple and direct, and it had galvanized them like nothing else.

UNITED STATES TRAITORS ARE IN OUR MIDST. THEY ARE KIDNAPPING AND BRUTALLY TORTURING OUR PEOPLE RIGHT NOW! THEY MEAN TO STEAL MY PRESIDENCY AND YOUR COUNTRY AWAY. CONVENE AT THE EDWARDS/SAWYER CROSSING AT ONCE, WEST HOUSTON, PREPARED TO FIGHT, OR WE'RE NOT GOING TO HAVE A COUNTRY ANYMORE. I WILL BE THERE, MARCHING WITH YOU.

- HUNTER KASON

Anson Reynolds had said it: X was a doorway through which anything could be poured. On some level Wren hadn't believed it would be so easy.

"Christopher?" Hellion said in his ear, pulling him back into the moment.

The crowds were getting loud and restive. They were only

four hours from the inauguration now, and tension was thick in the air. With no apparent leaders, the people were shouting out questions. Where was Kason? Where were the traitors? Where was the torture?

No one had answers.

"Christopher, stop delaying and harness these people, before they pick targets of their own!"

"Do we have iron-clad confirmation the Matheson children are in this building?"

"There is no confirmation," Hellion answered, sounding frustrated. "We may have cell phone nodes, but that is all. Drone high above, also yes, but little more. Not CCTV, not backup forces. I cannot confirm they are here."

Wren grunted. He wanted to be sure, because the minute he sent these people to the camp, he knew they'd become cannon fodder for the 'Marines' inside. Many of them were going to die.

But that was the plan. He'd made the bed, time to lie in it.

"Put me through to the team," he said. There was a click, and he heard the low breath of his new team members in his ear. Nancy, Trent, Jimmy and Alli. Armed with bullhorns. Trained in crowd control.

"Fire them up," Wren said.

"Yes, sir," answered Trent.

He'd picked Trent as the front man after conducting brief auditions beneath the I-610 overpass. Trent had the loudest voice, was arguably the best-looking, and with his shirt off his swimmer's physique would certainly draw the eye. Alli was behind the wheel of the van, while the other two were plants spread in the audience. Wren had given them the script. Now all they had to do was play their roles.

"Trent is moving," Hellion said.

Wren craned to see. Three hundred yards ahead on Edwards the white van started to move. It covered the distance to the crowd in thirty seconds, accelerating and honking its horn. By the time it braked before the straggling edge of the masses, everyone was looking its way.

Trent got out of the front cab and climbed up onto the roof, making him visible to everyone. He had a mic in one hand, with a sound system fixed to the van's roof beside him, both sourced and fitted by Alli in the last hour. He was stripped to the waist despite the cold air, showing his sculpted musculature, across which had been sprayed twin thick black X's, one front and one back. On his head he wore a black toboggan hat sprayed with white X's.

"Right now in a building near here, United States traitors are torturing our people!" he boomed into the mic. Wren winced at the sound as the speakers relayed it. Trent's delivery was over-sold, too loud and too hot right out of the gate.

"Take it down a notch," Wren said into his phone. "You'll burn them out. You have to build it up". The impact was immediate, as Trent heard the guidance, blinked, and re-set himself.

"Your brothers and sisters," he went on, lowering his volume, "your fathers and mothers, your sons and daughters. United States traitors have them strapped up like animals right now, and they're just destroying them. Ripping off their fingernails. Beating them with batons. Waterboarding and electrocuting them."

Trent paused, looking out over the crowd. That had been one of the notes Wren had most accentuated. Pauses in a speech could be incredibly powerful, giving those watching the time to catch up and get their emotions pumping. Delivered well, a pause could dominate and rile up. In those spaces answering voices could ring out in support, setting the mob to boil.

Trent did a fair job. Holding his gaze, holding his nerve

and projecting strength. Get it wrong and you looked weak and people would disengage. Get it right though, and it was like magic.

"That's good," Wren counseled. "Keep it low-key and crescendo from there."

Trent gave a slight nod and went on, just above normal speaking volume. "You heard me right. There are United States traitors torturing our people right now, only minutes away from here. Humiliating them. Degrading them. Trying to bring our president, Hunter Kason, down into their filth. Trying to destroy our cause and our country, even President Kason himself." His eyes roved the crowd. Another of Wren's notes. "These people will never stop. You know they'll never stop. You know it's because they hate our freedom. They hate our rights. They want to bring us to heel like the dogs they think we are!"

The crowd responded with angry cries. Picking up on Trent's tempo, now. Waiting for his pauses. Wren was impressed.

"They treat us like animals, but they're less than animals," Trent went on. "These traitors are everything that went wrong with the United States. They're every reason we broke away to chart our own path. But they're still here, in our country!" More cries of outrage broke out. "They're here right now, trying to stamp our faces back into the mud. Are you going to let them?"

The crowd cried out a resounding, 'No!' Fists, flags and weapons were hoisted in the air. Some shouted questions.

'Where's the building?'

'Where are the animals?'

"I'll take you to them, my friends, but we have to be ready." Trent made a show of surveying the crowd like he was judging them. He opened his mouth to go on, but Wren interrupted.

"Hold the moment," he said. "Let them really feel you."

Trent closed his mouth. He held the moment like a trooper, staring with that judgmental gaze, driving the crowd to greater heights. They were demanding, now, that he tell them where the building was. Where the traitors were.

"OK," Wren said.

"I see my brothers and sisters have brought arms," Trent called into the mic, silencing the crowd. "That's good, because without weapons we will be destroyed. These animals will not be kind and gentle. They are vicious. They will shoot you on sight just because of your freedom. Are you truly ready to fight?"

The crowd roared out a yes. Trent sustained their cries for a long moment, then dropped his volume, just like Wren had taught him. Time to get any flagging hearts on board. "That's good. Because isn't it as much a crime to stand by as violence is committed against your neighbor, as it is to commit that violence yourself?"

The crowd answered yes.

"Aren't we then complicit by our silence and inaction?"

"Yes!"

"Isn't that the very reason this great nation was formed, to stop the injustice and fight for what's right?"

"Yes," thundered the crowd.

Now Trent smiled. Wren knew exactly how he felt. The right words in the right order delivered in the right way could work a kind of magic on a crowd, and to have that power flow through you was an intoxication like no other.

"These are the precepts upon which our new teXas is built," Trent called across them. "Honor. Righteousness. Responsibility. And we will not fall short so soon, not with the light of the Apex shining down from above. Will we?"

The crowd gave everything they had in a thunderous, 'No!' They were wholly his now. Ready for a moment just like this, now falling into the call and response with glee, guided on by Nancy and Jimmy in the crowd.

"Take it steady," Wren said as the crowd pressed closer to Trent.

Trent kept it steady. His cadences weren't perfect, his pauses not optimal, but after only ninety minutes of practice with Wren, it was impressive. He was a natural, and they wanted what he was selling. They wanted Trent to lead them. Violence was brimming in the air, and it wasn't going to take much more to push them over the top.

"Finish it," Wren said.

Trent gave an almost imperceptible nod, ended his sentence then took a final long pause, looking out over his people with judgment and pride.

"Are you true citizens of teXas?" he boomed.

"Yes!" came back the mass bellow from the crowd.

"Are you willing to fight for your country?"

"Yes!"

"Are you willing to die for your country?"

"Yes!"

"Then fight for teXas!"

"Fight for teXas!" came the reply.

It didn't stop there.

Nancy and Jimmy kept the chant going, growing it louder so that any chance at logical discourse or rational thought was buried beneath the heady release of the mob.

"Fight for X!" they boomed, swiftly eliding 'teXas' to X. "Fight for X! Fight for X!"

"Follow me!" Trent hollered, and reached down to lift up a ten-foot pole, upon which sailed a huge teXas flag. The people cheered as he waved it in the air, muscles rippling. The chant grew louder. Beneath him the van began to move as Alli started reversing back up Edwards.

"Slowly, slowly," Wren cautioned.

The throng peeled east along Edwards, following their leader as he surfed atop the van, waving his flag like a general. Wren fell back as the crowd rolled onward, climbing into his Chevy Malibu. He waited and watched, until Hellion spoke in his ear.

"Time, Christopher."

He started the Malibu and drove south one block on Sawyer then turned left onto a freight rail track running parallel with Edwards. The ride was rough, over iron rails, wooden sleepers and gravel. In thirty seconds he'd outflanked the crowd, and turned the wheel hard left again into an open construction yard. Heaps of sand lay to his right, backhoes to his left.

"Hurry," Hellion said.

He pushed the pedal down and the Malibu accelerated through the yard, reaching fifty as it burst across Edwards barely twenty feet ahead of Trent's white van. Wren glimpsed the crowd off to the left and they glimpsed him; a black car flying X flags from each window, blasting across the road to hit the importation camp's fence like a meteor.

The Malibu ripped through the chain links.

The crowd roared.

Wren braced, adjusted his angle slightly then crashed through the building's yellow double doors. The Malibu skidded across an all-white foyer, wiped out a reception desk behind which a guy was trying to bring his rifle to bear and dead-ended into a back wall decorated with celebratory class photographs.

Wren stepped out and pulled his Beretta 9mm. Outside the mob ravened closer.

The door had been opened. Time to pour X through.

44

CAMP

Bodies flowed in like a sea; through the ruptured fence, into the smashed hole where the doors had been, veering left and right into corridors and stairwells side, as Wren directed them.

Gunfire answered their invasion.

"Marines are responding," Hellion said in his ear, but he didn't need to hear it. He could feel it all around him. Maybe it was the paintings on the back wall, but a disorienting sense of déjà vu filled him, as if this huge oblong warehouse was just a variation of the past.

He felt like he knew this place. Another Pleasure Island tanker ship, beached here in the center of Houston, just like the last redoubt of the Blue Fairy off the Philadelphia coast. Back then he'd stalked the corridors of enslaved children like an avenging angel, bringing an insatiable urge to rain down hellfire and brimstone.

He didn't feel that now.

What he felt now was every impact and every cry. Every bullet finding a target, whether the targets were his people or the enemy. Didn't matter. Every one of them was a patsy.

Used and abused, even the ones who were abusers themselves.

None of this should be happening. None of this should have been allowed, and it made him sick.

Some hundred X believers were in the building now, gung-ho and weapons hot, with more flooding in every second. Enough cannon fodder to mop up the fire of the 'Marines'.

He folded himself into the scrum of their pushing bodies, each so hungry to join the fight, and let them carry him along like a tide. There were stairs and he climbed them, feet barely touching the floor. The chants grew cacophonous, ringing and all-encompassing.

"Fight for X! Fight for X!"

It was nauseating. These people didn't know what they were doing. They truly believed they were righteous, and that total belief made them so easy to misuse and abuse. It was easy to get them to throw their lives away for a lie.

The stairs leveled out and Wren entered a corridor along the spine of the building, hit by a fresh wall of noise. To either side were office spaces, each with internal windows and glass doors, from which a chaotic rush of sounds was streaming, along with staticky flickers of light.

Wren focused on the corridor ahead. Fake Marines jerked in and out of defensive positions, up from behind upended desks and leaning out of doorways, firing defensively. Wren returned fire as if on autopilot, every bullet finding a target. Around him bodies took slugs meant for him, letting out soft oomph's and cries like the hisses of punctured tires, clutching their wounds and dropping.

Wren cleared twenty yards, edging between dying bodies and over spills of spreading blood, then entered one of the side offices. It was dark inside bar a projector screen at the front showing flashes of hectic video accompanied by an onslaught of sound.

It was one of X's propaganda videos. Wren almost recognized it, then a 'Marine' surged out from behind a shadowy column, firing. Three X members beside Wren fell. He returned fire coolly, shooting the man in the head. The other X people nearby cheered, then went back to helping their fallen in that dark, stinking, pounding space.

Wren just stood and surveyed it all. A place like many he'd seen before, but unique in its cruelty. The windows were blacked out with paint. The air was rich with sweat and human waste. There were benches and rows of desks, at which dozens of people were sitting naked, wrists manacled to the wood, many with what looked to be whip marks and welts on their backs.

Their eyes in the flashing wash of the video looked the same as every set of eyes he'd seen in places like it; lost and alone and so terrified they no longer knew who or where they were.

On the screen at the front the X propaganda video rolled seamlessly from one clip to another. The volume was pumped to earsplitting levels. Huge white fonts crashed across the screen in fast progression, superimposed over grotesque images of violence, discord and death. Voiceovers boomed out contrasting parts of the X creed.

As Wren stared, one video about dead babies ended and another began. This one he knew; one of the originals that Maggie herself must have recorded, about how money was a fantasy and the only thing that mattered was your marks of affiliation to X. People were shown cutting themselves with the mark of X. That video swiftly bled into a more recent one, showing the 787 blowing. The lens zoomed in on the falling figures; tiny wriggling bodies burst from the fuselage and tumbling down, down, down.

The videos kept coming, each barely thirty seconds long, and in each X was shown as either aggrieved victim or dominant conqueror. Sometimes both. X was triumphant over his enemies and downtrodden by them at once, was oppressed and victorious, was overwhelmed by enemies while also standing atop a pile of cindered bodies.

"What the hell is this?" one of the X people asked. He stood in the midst of it all, looking around like a man who'd lost all sense of conviction. Nobody answered him. "Who's doing this? Is this us?"

Wren didn't bother to answer. He didn't need to, as a bullet smashed through the nearby window and dropped the man to the floor. Now he was a new and permanent fixture of the audience.

Wren turned to the prisoners, arrayed along their benches with pens and colored pencils in their hands. They were adults and children both, the younger ones in booster seats. Their hands were moving fast like court stenographers, writing onto sheets of paper even as chaos broke out around them, like all this was just one more aspect of the videos they'd been forced to watch.

Wren leaned in, plucked up one of the sheets of paper and held it up to the projector's light. It was covered so thickly in notes it was almost black. He squinted and read a few tiny lines, scribbled into the margins.

'X says hell is a construct we must accept, then there's a woman burning in the center of a bowling alley, and perhaps this is proof, then subtitles claim YOU ARE GUILTY and I don't know of what, but perhaps I burned this woman, or I'm the one in hell, and I don't want to be in hell, and maybe if I listen more and write faster I won't have to go to hell, and they won't whip me anymore, or make me whip the others, and now X is showing us another lesson, but maybe I'm supposed to like the whipping, or accept it, and I just don't know and I want this to stop to just STOP to STOP but it never STOPS and...'

Wren put the paper down.

Maybe every room in the facility would be like this. Some amateur's idea of mass brainwashing. Wren had seen works like it before, and there was no doubt it was effective. Not at persuasion, because there was nothing persuasive about this. At coercion. He could feel the minds breaking all around him. Tried to imagine being locked in this room for hours. For days. Having only this to look forward to, day and night. Beaten when your 'notes' didn't meet some impossible standard. Beaten when they did. Taken aside for private beatings.

The damage would be immense.

He fired a bullet into the projector. The maddening rush of images immediately died. He located the overpowered speakers, mounted to the front two corners of the space, and ripped them down with his bare hands. Sparks flew as the wires wrenched out from the wall, then the cavalcade of noise halted.

Echoes rang in Wren's head. It was just one room out of dozens, so the interminable noise went on. But at least this room knew a little peace. He stalked to the door, found the light switch and flicked it on.

People cried out, tried to shield their eyes from the brightness. In the middle of the space a woman was standing where the man once had, looking around with horror spiking through the certainty in her eyes.

"What is this?" she whispered. "Who's doing this?"

Almost exactly the same question the man had asked. No bullet came to fell her, though. Wren strode over, between rows of desks and chairs, surveying the faces of every man, woman and child in the 'audience' as he went.

There was no sign of Rania and Hendrix, Amira

Matheson's children. Just dozens of people who needed help. He took the woman by the elbow and turned her. "It's a false X factory," he said, just stringing together words that would allow her to function. It was too much to expect her to drop her whole belief system in a second. "Help these people, in the name of the real X. Release them. Get them clothes. Get them somewhere warm. Get them fed. Get others to help. Can you do that?"

She stared at him, then stared around, and nodded numbly.

Wren moved on.

"Team are finding nothing yet," Hellion said in his ear. "Christopher, what is this?"

She sounded like the dead man and the lost woman. "This is X," he answered, and pushed into the next room over. "Nancy and Trent, start shutting down rooms and searching for the kids. Alli and Jimmy, network with Hellion to make sure nobody leaves. We need to find the Mathesons."

In the next room, the story was the same. Prisoners, notes, the all-encompassing video. This time he ripped down the projector with his hands, unwilling to waste a bullet, did the same for the speakers, flicked the light and only then saw the 'Marine' hiding amongst the importees. The man fired, putting two holes through the wall to Wren's left, one hole into an X member to his right, then he reeled back as Wren put a hole in his head.

It didn't feel good. It didn't feel like anything.

He scanned the people. Some were still writing, eyes now feverishly focused on him, trying to capture every moment. Maybe they'd be writing like this for months to come, unable to stop the baked-in compulsion. Maybe they'd be writing in their nightmares for years.

The Matheson's weren't here.

He found another X member, one who looked horrified

and confused at once, and told him what to do, then moved on again.

Every room was the same. Time passed like eggs cooking on a skillet, the yellow running into the white. More rooms, more X videos, more 'Marines' popping up like dynamic cardboard targets in a shooting range, but there were always X members around to absorb their bullets, soaking up the excess.

In room after room Wren repeated the simple procedure; destroy the projector and the speakers, turn on the light, clear the room, survey the audience for the Matheson's, then assign a baffled-looking X member to help and protect them.

Soon he was coming across rooms where the job had already been done, or was half-done, or was in the process of being done. In one the prisoners were being released from their shackles with a thick roll of keys. In another someone had found a pair of bolt cutters and was using those. They all sobbed.

Hellion kept a steady report running through his head: locations of his team; numbers of people in and out of the building; reports on how this attack was playing in the teXas media, which was to say, not at all.

Wren stood at the end of the long corridor, breathing hard. The windows had been shot through in numerous places, letting a harsh wind blow through. Twitching bodies littered the vinyl floor in smears of blood. Good guys. Bad guys. People were wailing and wandering like ghosts, children were crying, X members were running back and forth with horrified eyes, trying to do whatever they could to stem the tide of suffering.

"Any sign of the Matheson's?" he asked Hellion.

"Nothing yet, Christopher," she answered. "Team are still checking, and-"

"I've checked every room twice," Wren said, flat and cold as lead. "Anyone got out?"

Keys clacked through the earpiece. "Uh, no, few, not children. I do not think-"

"They're gone."

A moment passed. There was moaning, and crying, but at least the godforsaken videos had stopped.

"Are you sure?" Hellion asked.

"I'm sure." He'd looked into every single face in the whole facility multiple times. He'd seen them all. The Matheson children weren't there. "He must've moved them. Kason."

"Kason? But when?"

When. It seemed obvious, now he thought of it. Mads Hellström had been the one who'd captured the children. Mads Hellström had sent them to Houston. It made sense that, when Mads Hellström himself was captured by Christopher Wren, the children would be moved.

Hunter Kason was no fool. He knew his new nation hung by the thinnest thread of legitimacy. Expose the Matheson's to oversight, and that legitimacy would be swept away.

It left Wren with nothing. No clear way forward. Only three hours and counting until Kason locked teXas down.

45

EMPTY

Wren wandered east on Edwards Street, away from the sound and chaos of the importation camp, not really thinking. He'd warned his team about the impact they might experience in the strike, but hadn't thought of the impact it would have on him. The cold helped, but just enough to keep him on his feet and walking.

He felt numb.

Throughout his life he'd seen a lot of dark things. As a child in the Pyramid he'd survived cages, pits, boiling vats and the firestorm. As a grown man he'd looked into the ugliest corners of humanity and beaten back the devil time after time.

It had never felt so pointless before.

Everything he'd just witnessed, everything he'd been dealing with since his 787 came down, felt empty. People dying for lies, spun by liars who wanted, what, power? Was that all? A state to rule as their own nation. The ability to punish anyone they wanted, according to the whims of the moment. In the months since his father died, his complex ideology had been twisted into something incredibly shallow, vapid and self-serving.

Just power. Power without any real purpose attached. Power that existed only to reinforce itself.

He laughed. Imagined what his father might say, if he were here right now.

"You miss me, Pequeño 3."

That thought cracked Wren up.

"It's true," his father's voice continued, as if they were walking side-by-side now into downtown Houston, past a hipster waffle place and a designer coffee table shop and an Italian dry cleaner's. "They're making a mockery of my legacy."

"There should be no legacy," Wren muttered to himself. "No sign of you. No hint of you at all."

His father smiled. Wren didn't need to turn to see it. A sparkling grin crammed with white teeth, overtopped with those dazzling blue eyes. "Both of us know that was never going to happen. What I did *mattered*, son. It mattered to me, and it mattered to you, and it mattered to the people who died. They believed in something, and that made it real. Their deaths gave it value."

Wren shook his head, arguing with a ghost. "It's the same. Maybe you spun some impressive BS for them to lap up, hellfire and pyramids, but it still came down to power. You just dressed it up better that Kason does. It didn't *mean* anything."

"So why does this feel so empty, then?"

Wren stopped in his tracks.

He was standing in the middle of an empty street. No cars, no people. The curfews were still in place, keeping all good teXas citizens indoors and glued to their TVs, lapping up the two state-approved news channels. Kason's inauguration would have a full audience, no doubt, but only comprised of carefully selected zealots. The right kind of audience. The right kind of sycophants.

Here on the edge of downtown Houston, Capitol of the old Texas Republic, there were just empty spaces, and an empty sky, and people peering back at him from empty windows.

He turned to his father. Of course he wasn't there. But it felt like it.

"It feels that way because I'm broken," Wren said. "I suppose you did that.'

"The country's broken," his father countered. "Maybe the world. Did I do all that?"

Wren started walking again. "Not yet."

The Apex laughed. There was no joy in it, though, only mockery. "So what will you do to stop it this time, little cactus wren? Are there more vehicles you can turn into battering rams? More people you can sell out for cannon fodder? More deepfake lies of your own, spreading to stop my lies? Surely you have to ask yourself, at what point does the cure become worse than the disease?"

Wren didn't say anything. He didn't have to justify himself to a ghost. Ten minutes passed as he walked on. Twenty.

He'd slipped out of the building as the X followers began to argue amongst themselves. While most of them were horrified by what they'd found, some seemed to think that the treatment of the prisoners was necessary, even deserved. Maybe the enforced videos were a good thing, they argued. It seemed extreme, they accepted, but sometimes extremes were required.

Perhaps the two sides would come to blows. Wren had no intention of sticking around to find out. He told his team to save anyone they could, especially the children, and get out, then he'd taken out his earpiece and started to walk.

No Rania or Hendrix. Without the Matheson children, without any way to find them or fetch them in time, he had no backup plan. Maybe they were dead already, and there was nothing he could do about that. He couldn't bring back Henry, or Abdul, or any of the other people he'd lost. In this life there was no resurrection from the dead, no matter what Maggie insisted.

He sighed. Memories of the 787 came back to haunt him. Amira's kids and their cucumbers. The look of pride in her eyes, spiked by the fear. He should have realized something was wrong sooner. Maybe he would have been more ready for what was coming.

"You shouldn't give up," came a voice by his side.

He turned but saw nobody, only new-build shops and terracotta apartment blocks.

"Down here," came the voice again, and he looked down.

Her eyes were so green. Her small, nut-brown face so angelic. Maybe she was eight years old again, and as innocent as the day was long.

"Grace," he said.

"Don't cry," she said, and took hold of his hand. Her little palm was hot in his. "I said we'd be speaking again, didn't I? It'll always be you and I, at the end."

He laughed through his blurry vision. Maybe it was the smoke, or the exhaustion, or some concussion, but it felt like she was really there. Little Grace, little Maggie, the seed of the original X right by his side.

"Maggie did say that," he agreed, thinking back to her cell under the fake town. "I don't think her vision of that final chat was quite as pleasant as this, though."

"Maggie's broken," said the little girl with a shrug, like it was obvious. "She spent decades with that man. Who wouldn't be broken after that? And why wouldn't you be, too?"

Wren's eyes blurred more. "I didn't spend decades with him. He didn't impact my life at all after the fires."

Grace was silent. Wren had to turn back and look at her to see the judgment in those sharp green eyes. Even as a child she knew him.

He laughed. "OK. You got me."

"He's shaped everything you've done," she said, with the sternness only a child could muster. "You know this. You built yourself in opposition to him." She paused a moment, looking up at him. "Maybe it's time to stop doing that."

Wren sighed. "I want to. God knows I want to. But I don't know how. He's everywhere, now. He's in everyone."

"So stop trying to ignore him," Grace said casually, like it was the most obvious thing in the world. "Killing him wasn't enough to stop his legacy, obviously. Tainting that legacy with deepfakes wasn't enough, either. To truly move past his legacy, you need to reclaim it."

Wren laughed, but there was a fraught edge to the sound, and he forced himself to stop. "I was trying to do that, but they're gone. Amira's children. They were the key, and I couldn't find them. I'm sorry, Grace. I couldn't save them and I couldn't save you."

Her little frown deepened. "I'm not dead yet. Neither are they. It isn't over."

He smiled. "It will be soon. Kason's getting crowned in two hours."

"So stop the inauguration."

"I don't know how."

"You do," she said sharply, "you just can't admit it." She sucked in a world-weary breath. "So your father's gone, and the world feels thin without him hanging over everything. I understand that. But you're looking at it all wrong. This is not a crisis, it's an opportunity. You get to take what he did and reshape it."

Wren rubbed his eyes. "Right, by reclaiming his legacy, got it."

"You think I'm joking. So tell me, was it a joke when we made strooberry mud pies together in the desert? Or was that the greatest thing we ever did, the thing that kept us alive through the darkest times?"

That almost cracked him. He barely squeezed out words. Every day back then had been a battle to survive. "The greatest thing."

"Precisely. It was real. I'm real. So don't quit on me, Chris."

He turned to her. She was eight, but she sounded older. "You never called me Chris before. I didn't even have this name, then."

She made a face. "Of course you did. You think you weren't always Christopher Wren to me? You think this moment wasn't always coming? It was. You were. I never once doubted it. And I've seen what's coming next, too."

He laughed. "More strooberry pies?"

"If that's what it takes. You and me hand-in-hand, last survivors of the Pyramid, looking in each other's eyes and talking. Just talking, Chris. Not persuading, not trying to convince. Just being there, like we always were for each other. You want to save this country? You have to save me."

He took a slow, raspy breath. There were a lot of words, a lot of images roiling in his head. People lost; people found. He blinked, and when he looked again the little girl was gone. His father was gone. The emptiness was gone, too, and in its place something new was growing. Something he hadn't considered before, too big for him to fully grasp.

Reclaiming his father's legacy.

Maggie had started that herself, though she'd twisted it. She'd turned the fake town from a burned-down ruin to a place of healing. She'd brought the families of the dead back and helped them move on. Even if it was a lie, she'd been showing him the way. Something he'd never attempted to do himself, back when all he could think was to destroy everything his father had built.

Heal the wounds of the Pyramid. Salve the trauma his father had sown.

Maybe now was the same.

The Foundation had always been his best effort. Taking broken people and giving them something good, a coin system of accountability. It was a starting point that led to self-sufficiency, then pride, then finally decency.

Now he saw he had to go bigger. Open his umbrella wider. Shelter more people, save more people, even protect his enemies from their own madness and make things right. That was how he reclaimed his father legacy. Not by burying it in concrete and locking it behind steel fences. By making it good again.

In a flash, he knew what he had to do. He took the earpiece from his pocket and slotted it into place, started making calls.

46

LIVE BY THE SWORD

Ten minutes later, Wren waited for his new team in a bowling alley parking lot. Twenty blocks north lay Houston City Hall, designated as the teXas state capitol, and site of Hunter Kason's inauguration. He sat on a step under the shelter of the alley's car port, looking out at the blue and cloudless sky.

It buzzed with helicopters and drones. Off to the west a cluster of black aircraft hovered like a swarm of flies over the Edwards Street importation camp. Trying to pick out the route of the Big Bad Bird, most likely. In the chaos, though, they hadn't found him yet.

He swept his gaze north. The sky was thick with oversight, with dozens of manned and unmanned aerial vehicles circling like buzzards over city hall. Hellion had reported back to him already, sharing footage from her MQ-9 Reaper surveillance drone. He'd seen the layout of Hunter Kason's stage, between the impressive limestone bulk of City Hall and the long rectangular reflecting pool.

There were fences encircling the area for an approved audience, and checkpoints where that audience was being admitted through metal detectors. There was a white-roofed network of marquee tents adjoining the stage and stretching out across McKinney Street to City Hall's south, where black-clad Secret Service agents moved in and out constantly. There were police and SWAT forces manning roadblocks in all directions up to ten blocks out.

"This is craziest plan yet," Hellion said in Wren's ear. "You are crazier than X. It cannot work."

"Are they almost here?" Wren asked.

"Almost there. Thirty seconds. Crazy."

Wren stood as the white panel van rolled up and under the car port, shepherded by the MQ-9's drone-blinding capacity. The team piled out of the van; Trent, Nancy, Jimmy and Alli. They were all intact, and rather than looking horrified or distraught, they seemed to be riding high on adrenaline. Trent had found a shirt and rubbed the Xs off his cheeks, still glowing with the fire of his impassioned speech. Nancy's eyes were wide, and she wore twin pistols in gun belts around her waist. Jimmy bounded out of the van first.

"Mr. Wren, thank God, we're so glad to see you! I can't believe what just happened."

Wren smiled kindly. "Call me Chris."

"It was amazing," Jimmy went on, "and so horrible. Those poor kids. It's-"

"I kind of get what they were doing in there," Nancy said, picking up Jimmy's thread. Her face was flushed with the aftermath of excitement. People had died, but the weight of that clearly hadn't settled on his team yet. That was good, as he needed them operational. "Brainwashing all those people en masse. But does that really work?"

Wren shook his head. "Not in the way you might think. Techniques like that, they aim to overwhelm rather than persuade, destroying the sense of self. It's mental torture. If it's prolonged, the effects can be very real and long-lasting. People come out severely compromised."

Nancy shuddered. "I'm glad we shut it down. That was the right thing."

Wren nodded. Looked at the four of them. On the surface they were dusty and blood-spattered, panting and wild-eyed. Give them a day and the shock would bed in. The reality of the deaths they'd caused, both directly and indirectly, would begin to weigh them down. Better that they keep their certainty; killing was so much easier when everything was black and white.

"Absolutely, we did the right thing," Wren said firmly. "Without a solitary doubt. You saved people today, and I'm very proud of you. We couldn't find Amira Matheson's children, though, so it's not over yet." He took a breath, letting them absorb that. "But I've got a plan, if you're still willing to help. You might not like it, though."

Alli laughed. "When he says that, it means we're going to really hate it."

Wren smiled. It was good to have Alli around. "Not you, at least not for this first part. You're probably going to love it. As for the rest of you…" He looked at Jimmy, Trent and Nancy. His new team. "I need you to beat me up."

They stared back at him.

"You need what?" Jimmy asked.

"Beat me up. Lots of cuts and bruises. Really obvious. No deep damage, though. I've got some of that already."

They surveyed him for a moment, looked amongst themselves, then Jimmy spoke up. "Honestly, Mr. Wren, you look pretty beat up already."

"Call me Chris."

"OK, yes, sure. Forgive me for prying, but we can see you've got bandages on your stomach. Front and back. Uh. I think that means you got shot?"

Alli laid a proprietorial hand on Wren's shoulder. "He did. A week ago. We had a vet come in and sew it up."

"A vet?" Trent blurted.

"All we could get on short notice."

A silence played out. The sound of helicopters whirred closer overhead, and his team ducked instinctively.

"It's OK, they can't see us here," Wren said. "Can they, Hellion?"

"Probably not, Mr. Wren," she answered.

Wren gritted his teeth. This was no time to chide her. "There's a reason," he said to the team. "The new plan is, I'm going in as a prisoner."

Alli laughed again. "Of course you are! You already pulled this trick once."

"This time I'll do it better.'

Alli looked at the confused expressions of the others, enjoying her 'seniority'. "In Dallas, he got himself fake arrested by fake cops, then he bust up their fake police station from the inside, which was really more of a rape factory than anything." She beamed. "So yeah, why not run the Dallas play again?"

"Alli's simplifying somewhat there," he smoothed.

"But that's basically the plan, right?"

"Basically," Wren allowed. "Now, we haven't got long. Who's going to punch me in the face?"

Alli's hand shot up.

"Not you. I need your hands and fingers in good condition."

The others avoided meeting his eyes.

"Easy answer, you all are," Wren said. "I'll give you ten minutes to get ready. I need to be run ragged. Only cautioning point is, avoid the gunshot wound. Now, is Hellström awake?"

"He was," Trent said.

"Good. Open the door."

Trent opened the slide door of the van. Mads Hellström

lay inside on the raw metal, looking sickly, his once-immaculate dress unform filthy and rumpled. His eyes darted and blinked in the sudden light.

Wren stepped up to the open door. "How are you, Mads?"

The brigadier general tried to spit in Wren's face and failed. Instead the liquid dribbling down his own chin.

"We'll have to fix you up. I think we've got some methylphenidate in here somewhere, that ought to put a spring in your step. Have you eaten at all? Had any water?"

Hellström's gaze sharpened slightly. "I will never help you."

"You might think differently once you've had a burger and fries," Wren said, and clicked his fingers to Alli. She re-focused. "Or at least a microwave meal from a convenience store, a milkshake perhaps, some Tylenol?"

Alli nodded, looked up to the sky and saw it was clear, then darted across the parking lot to a nearby convenience store. While Wren held Hellström's gaze, there came the sound of shattering glass.

"Never," Hellström said.

Wren leaned in. "What if I put the governorship back on the table? Help me get close to Hunter Kason, as your prisoner, and I promise you will run Texas once it's returned to the fold. I'll even come to your campaign rallies, if you like."

Hellström stared. "Campaign rallies? You're lying."

"I could be, but I'm not. I need you, Mads, and I may bluff, but I never cheat. It's all approved with the President. The real President, of the United States, Jacinda Ablas. Help me now, and you will be governor. That's ironclad. Your children will be safe. Sell this fully, and Kason will fall while you rise." He paused to let Hellström take that in. "It's a good deal. You're not going to get a better one."

It didn't take Hellström long.

"I want to hit you," he said. He must've heard the conversation. "I hit you now. I speak with your President. Then I'll decide."

"I'll take a punch with pleasure," Wren said. "Just know one thing, Mads. Drop the ball here, and you go to jail forever. Your kids go to jail forever. It all comes crashing down. Get it right, though, we all win big. You with me?"

Hellström stared. "You have my word. And the same goes for you. Double cross me, and I will come for your family."

Wren's eyes hardened. Live by the sword, die by the sword.

"Deal."

"Now I will hit you," Hellström said.

Wren climbed in to uncuff him.

47

THE DALLAS PLAY

Nearly two hours later Wren lay in the back of the white panel van, cuffed wrist and ankle just like Mads Hellström, breathing in air tainted with old, dried dirt and oil. The cold steel bed of the van was crenellated with shallow channels; for grip, he figured. Maybe there'd been a courtesy carpet here once, something musty and battered, but it was long gone now. Now his own blood puddled in the channels, smelling of iron and cold.

His whole body ached. Once Hellström had got them started, his team had gotten involved. Mostly fists, some knees and elbows to bring up bruising on his torso and thighs. They'd apologized a lot. He'd insisted they continue.

It came out looking good. He'd seen how he looked in the bowling alley's reflective glass, and it was convincing. It had even put some color into Mads Hellström's gray cheeks; at least that and the methylphenidate tabs.

The van rumbled onward. Not too fast, not too slow. Jimmy was at the wheel. Mads Hellström sat by his side in the passenger seat. Wren in the back, while Nancy and Trent made their own way to City Hall.

"Route is clear to first roadblocks," Hellion said in his ear, as Wren steeled himself for what was to come. The first roadblocks were ten blocks out from the inauguration stage.

"Any sign of Amira Matheson?" Wren asked. Still hanging on to the shreds of the old plan.

"I cannot see her. Assume she is unreachable."

Wren grunted.

"Inauguration is very lively," Hellion said, sounding faintly amused. "They are playing music that I could like as a ring tone. This is new national anthem, perhaps? There is marching band, marching around reflecting pool. Very pretty."

That figured. If Hunter Kason was anything, he was a showman. Every detail would have been considered with his international television audience in mind. Wren had seen the early feeds going out, before they'd locked him in back. The new Capitol building was festooned in teXas flags. A large screen had been erected behind the stage, so close-ups could focus on the moment Kason swore his oath on the Bible. There were cranes erected in various positions, set for optimal camera shots. There were speakers dotted everywhere to offer cinematic surround sound.

Everything about the moment was big.

"What's the music?" Wren asked, shifting slightly to alleviate the pain in his left side.

"I do not know. B4cksl4cker?"

A moment passed. "It is very jaunty song," B4cksl4cker said. "Much snare drum. They are singing about 'Yellow Rose'. American marching band is very fun."

Wren smiled. He knew the song. Elvis had sung it once, about love and longing and redemption. It didn't hold much in common with what this new teXas stood for. He hummed it quietly to himself as the van rumbled on, and it helped a little to stem the fear building in his belly as they headed defenseless into enemy territory.

"First roadblock in one minute," Hellion said in his ear. "Christopher, may I say once more, this is crazy plan."

"I know," he said. He pressed his hot forehead against the cold steel floor, enjoying the brief balm.

When the van made a ninety-degree left turn, he slid slightly along the metal.

"You are on McKinney Street," Hellion narrated. "City Hall is ahead, straight shot now. First roadblock can see van and are responding. Very broad and thorough blockade here, five trucks, many police."

Wren could picture it. He could almost hear the fading trails of the 'Yellow Rose of Texas' in the air, almost taste the anticipation in the swollen crowd.

"How many guards?"

"A dozen. This is unbreakable blue cordon, Christopher, as we thought. It is good we did not try to ram City Hall."

He laughed low, but it hurt, so he stopped. "We would've had to hit it with a plane, and I'm never going to do that."

"Yes, that is bad memory. Now, thirty seconds."

The van rolled on, and Wren heard every tick of the engine, felt every burr in the road vibrating up through the metal. Maybe he could hear the crowd, now, surging like a restive ocean.

"Closing in, they are waving to halt. Yes."

The van slowed and stopped. Wren's heart slammed against the metal flooring. He'd be in the limelight soon. Voices barked demands outside, and the passenger-side door opened, slammed closed. Wren heard every word that came next, filled with just as much righteous pomposity as he'd hoped for.

"My name is Brigadier General Mads Hellström, commander of Fort Sheppard, and I have a prisoner that President Hunter Kason needs to take possession of immediately."

Wren grinned.

The Dallas play, an oldie but a goodie. It had worked with the Central Patrol Division, after all. It could work here, too.

"Do not grin, Christopher," Hellion chastened. She couldn't see him, but she knew him too well. He wiped the grin from his face and went back to looking justifiably pained.

The guard at the gate was arguing. Demanding ID. Calling in his superior.

"Call whoever you want, son," Hellström said, "but do it fast. I don't think you want to rob the President of his greatest triumph, at the most vital turning point in our young nation's history, do you? The moment he unveils, judges and executes Christopher Wren himself, for all to see."

There was a silence for a long moment. It was understandable. From their perspective, Wren was the boogeyman. Popping up and causing chaos wherever he wanted, leaving death in his wake. They would have heard about the raid on Edwards Street by now. They would have their suspicions it was Wren.

There was some kerfuffle outside. A fast and noisy phone call made, authorization requested, voices rising in volume as the urgency set in. Wren could imagine Mads Hellström standing there imperious as ever, a puppet who'd been properly motivated.

"They are coming to open door, Christopher," Hellion said. "Look broken."

That was easy.

The slide door rammed open. Light flooded in, and Wren clamped his eyes shut against the sudden bright light, curling his body away.

"You, you, let me see his face," someone commanded.

There was a thump as booted feet stamped into the van. Two men. They grabbed Wren and spun him, seizing his head and roughly orienting him to the light. He could hardly see a thing in the white glare except the tall thin figure of Mads Hellström, standing beside a stocky man.

There was silence for a long moment before the stocky man spoke again.

"My God," he whispered. His hand went to his chest. "It's him."

Wren tried to spit and failed on purpose, dribbling it down his chin. He'd seen how pathetic it looked when Hellström did it.

"It's really him," the man repeated. "How did you…" he trailed off, turned to Hellström. "You've been missing for a week, Brigadier General. Assumed taken." He spread his arms to encompass the van. "What is this?"

"This is what it takes to become vice president," Hellström said coldly, and jabbed the thick man in the chest with his index finger. "It should be obvious to everyone that I allowed myself to be taken. Do you think there could be any other way, from within my own air base? My team tracked the Bird to Dallas, where he perpetrated terrorist acts they were not able to stop. They tracked him to here, where you were unable to stop him from committing more terrorist acts. Now I have seized the moment and taken him back, to prevent any more such vile atrocities. Now," he paused a moment, leaning back, "if you wish to keep a shred of your rank or your self-respect, then from this moment on you'll stop wasting my time and let us through. This man belongs to Hunter Kason. Do not stand in his path."

The men holding Wren's head squeezed harder, grinding his ears on purpose. Enjoying the petty pains. He didn't give them the pleasure of crying out, just focused on the thickset man as his eyes adjusted to the light. The man was dressed in police blues, maybe another fresh intake to the service, this time at the rank of major, as signified by the gold oak leaf on his sleeve.

He looked at Wren, at Hellström, then nodded once, and again more firmly as he came to his decision. "Of course. Yes, of course." He turned and started shouting. "Let them through! Radio ahead. This man must be taken direct to Hunter Kason, on my order, and with my escort!"

Hellström looked at Wren. Wren looked back. Of course the major was going to try to get involved with this windfall too.

The men holding his head let go but didn't step out of the van. The door did not slide shut, but Hellström did get back in the passenger seat. Jimmy put the van in gear, a siren started to caterwaul as the major got into his escort vehicle, then they were away.

"Very smooth," Hellion said. "Kason is about to come onto stage."

48

MARQUEE

They passed through two more roadblocks without any trouble. Wren lay on his side looking out of the open van door, watching the faces of police and soldiers as they passed by. All were staring in at him, hungry for a sight of this prisoner that had so swiftly broken through their dragnet.

"He doesn't look so tough," said one of the guys standing behind Wren.

The other toed the back of Wren's head. "If that old man up front did this, you're damn right."

"How about if I-"

Wren felt the kick coming before it landed, something in the guy's breathing and the shift of his weight, and rolled onto his belly as it came in. Instead of taking a punishing toe jab into the kidney, he took a swipe across the hip.

"Slippery bastard," said the other, already teeing up a kick of his own.

Wren let this one land, hammering into his belly. Bruised abdominal muscles were a much easier burden to carry than a ruptured kidney.

"Got him!" the guy crowed.

The other one dropped to one knee and went to punch Wren in the side of the head, but Wren was ready for it and already rising, thrusting a headbutt into his face. Cartilage crunched and the guy yelped and fell back. Another kick came into Wren's back, sending him sprawling sideways.

"Stop playing, Christopher," Hellion said in his ear.

He rolled onto his knees just as the bloody-faced guy came in for one more go, a big kick to Wren's face. It was an easy duck, leaving the guy off-balance and spinning. Wren hopped off his knees to his feet and surged upwards like a jack-in-the-box, catching the man's groin in his shoulder and hoisting him straight out of the moving van.

There was a meaty smack as he hit the blacktop accompanied by another yelp, then he was gone.

"Put yourself back down, son, right now," said the other man.

Wren turned, looked down the barrel of a gun.

"Christopher," Hellion chided.

Wren kneeled back down. The guy was panting, panicked at how badly that had just gone, while Wren felt perfectly calm.

Outside the streets changed as they drew closer to City Hall. Where they'd been empty but for police sawhorses and cruisers, now there were crowds spilling outward, covered in teXas gear and symbols of X. Their faces stretched away as far as Wren could see, hollering slogans and craning to peer into the open van.

They were left open-mouthed. Their nation's greatest enemy in chains, right in their midst.

"Is that the Bird?" they shouted.

"It's the Bird! We got the Big Bad Bird!"

Cheers broke out. People chugged beer and waved flags. The air was wild. The guy in the van with Wren went to close the door, then paused with his hand on the lever, like he was reconsidering. He looked at Wren, maybe imagining himself alone with the Big Bad Bird in a dark contained space, and pulled his hand back again.

Wise choice.

Soon the crowds peeled away as the van passed through a final checkpoint and into the giant white canvas marquee. That positioned them to the south of the stage. The van passed parked black Escalades and several men in Secret Service gear, wires behind their ears, speaking into their wrists. They went past a metal detector arch leading north, toward the stage, then the van stopped.

Figures approached holding under-vehicle search mirrors, each like a rectangular dust-trough on the end of a long stick. They quickly swept the underside of the van, then surveyed the two figures inside; one cuffed in bloodied rags with another standing over him, dressed in police uniform.

Seemed like the OK was given. There were raised voices from far-off, croaky walkie-talkies replies, the sound of running feet.

"Kason is not on stage yet," Hellion said in his ear. "Must be very close. I think he is in that tent with you."

Wren grunted.

"You're not going anywhere," the guy beside him said. "Stay right where you are."

Hellström's door opened up front and the tall general appeared moments later by the open van door. He looked in, surveying the scene.

"Where's the other one?" he asked, sounding faintly amused. "Weren't there two of you?"

"Sir," the cop replied, "the Bird threw him out of the van."

Hellström shook his head. "Of course he did. Tell me, is that why you're holding your weapon on a man who is, I assure you, securely restrained?"

The guy babbled something. Wren just stared into the middle distance.

"Get out of there," Hellström commanded, then turned and pointed. "You, where's the President?"

Answers came. Secret Service agents, or their teXas equivalent, appeared to look in at Wren. Some spoke into the wrists and others ran. Wren waited. The big moment was coming. Agents climbed in and lifted him under the armpits, hauling him out of the van and giving Wren his first clear look at the marquee.

It was long and large, fifty yards in length at least, some thirty wide, with parked vehicles and men in black everywhere. Entrances and exits led off to either side. Wren had seen the layout of sites like it before; likely there was a dedicated 'Situation Room' tent for SWAT forces to manage overall event security, an A/V space to run the big screen and cameras, probably a green room for Kason to get his makeup done, maybe even a holding cell to keep Amira Matheson secure.

A commotion broke out back near the metal detector. Everyone turned, as aides and Secret Service agents spilled out from an adjoining corridor into the main thoroughfare.

"This had better be worth it," came the unmistakable voice of Hunter Kason.

He was a tenor with a reedy edge; like if he pushed just a little harder, he'd start to whine. His Ivy League education came through in his unconscious intonation, though everything he said sounded carefully calibrated to target middle America and position him against the 'elites'.

Wren had heard his voice a thousand times before. For years it had been everywhere across the country, an opinion pundit who led the docket of one of the country's biggest syndicated 'news' channels. Wren had watched him on the television in the Dallas apartment, as he stood beside Amira

Matheson and brayed about what a victory this was, coming in the midst of the United States' savage and unwarranted attack on X.

Finally he appeared.

He was too tanned for the season, clearly bronzed over for a 'healthy' TV sheen; tall but not overbearing, maybe 6' 3", with a shy chin and crooked nose and eyes that were a mite too close together to class as striking. He wore sleek black pants and a white shirt with the sleeves rolled up and the collar unbuttoned; a look that said he was just another regular Joe, and this was going to be a whole different kind of Presidency. The kind of guy you trust at the levers of power, because he was like you, and had your best interests in mind.

He strode through the metal detector with a long, almost ungainly stride, forcing those around him to canter to keep up; aides and security operators hurrying sideways and backwards, clipboards and tablet computers in their hands, coming on until at last Kason's eyes settled on Wren.

He stopped dead in his tracks.

Seconds passed.

Wren saw everything he needed to know in those narrow-set eyes. They didn't have the sparkling, far-seeing glint of his father. This wasn't a man enlivened by some all-encompassing vision. This was a man driven by the same old mixture of fear and greed, assessing every person that crossed his path as a means to his own further greatness; were they someone he could co-opt or someone he had to crush.

The aides went silent while the boss considered.

"Hunter Kason," Wren said easily. "You look smaller in person."

That helped Kason figure it out. His face broke into a fake grin and he strode over; always a show for his people. He stopped looking at Wren and focused on Mads Hellström instead, putting both hands on the Brigadier General's shoulders.

"Mads," he said, sounding like this was the great relief he'd been hoping for. "Thank God you're alive. Are you responsible for bringing this terrorist in?"

Hellström shook his head. Now came the crunch.

"I'm afraid not, Mr. President. What I am is loyal, despite every effort by the Bird to corrupt me." He pointed right at Wren's face. "Our appearance here at the onset of your reign is not by chance. This is his plot, Hunter. To reach this point he has threatened my family and my life. He wants to get on that stage with you, pull the knife in his pocket and slit your throat live on stage."

Wren was already moving; popping the clasp on his cuffs, reaching down to the knife hidden in his ragged pants. He almost got it clear when the first Secret Service agent hit him. He came in at full extension, a flying body tackle direct into Wren's floating ribs that hammered him to the side.

Wren hit concrete hard, and the knife spun away. He scrambled to get his feet under him, but more agents piled on top; in seconds flat they'd wrenched his arms behind his back and shackled him afresh, ankle and wrist with a hog-tie bracelet linking the two like a daisy chain down his back. He tried to shout out a warning, but they cinched a gag into his mouth so tight it cut into his lips, pried a slim metal tool into his ear to wrench out the earpiece, then left him wheezing and bleeding on the floor.

It all happened in less than a minute.

The blacktop was cold against his cheek. He faintly heard Hellion squawking from the disembodied earpiece, before one of the agents crushed it under his boot heel.

Wren was on his own.

Mads Hellström and Hunter Kason stood over him.

Hellström was shuddering, now, and that was no surprise. He'd just signed the death warrant on his children.

Kason patted Hellström's shoulders. From where Wren lay it was an utterly transparent show of empathy, a show for everyone to see. "We'll keep your family safe," he said solemnly. "I swear it, Mads. What you've done here will go down in the history books. This level of personal sacrifice, the loyalty to teXas? I never expected less of you. We will keep them safe."

Hellström nodded, though he couldn't stop himself from shaking. He couldn't meet Wren's furious glare.

Kason could, though. He turned his beady eyes down to Wren, and now the uncertainty was gone, along with any hint of fear. All that remained was that greedy look of appraisal; each man as a steppingstone to be used. He'd figured out how he was going to use Wren.

"He wanted to come on stage, slice my throat you say?" Kason asked. Not to Hellström anymore, not even to Wren, just to the air at large. Saying the words for posterity to take down, marking the moment his legend would soar on the shoulders of a dead Christopher Wren. "Fetch me his knife."

It was brought over.

"Ceramic," the Secret Service agent said. "It would've passed through the detector."

Kason took it and knelt down by Wren with the easy fluidity of a man who'd rehearsed every move he'd ever made. He held the knife's beige blade up in front of Wren's face, letting its high gloss catch the light.

"I think you're going to make it onto my stage after all, Mr. Wren," he said. "Though it may not end the way you'd hoped."

49

STAGE

Hunter Kason went first, while five Secret Service agents held Wren on his knees in the wings of the stage, as secure as the nuclear football. Each of the agents kept a hand on him at all times, two on each of his arms, one with a fist squeezed tight in his hair.

Wren's mind spun even as tears welled up from the tightening of his scalp. Shackled, hog-tied, there was no chance of escape. These men were unyielding. This was it.

The crowd outside roared. They were only one layer of white canvas away from Wren, and the raw sound of their bellowing lungs struck him like the heat off a blast furnace. They adored Hunter Kason. Wren watched through fuzzy eyes as he strode out before them with that lanky, arrogant stride, bathing in their adulation, arms up so their voices could better wash over him.

The cheering became rhythmic as Kason stood at the podium, voices merging and spreading until they devolved into one lusty, resounding chant.

"Fight for X! Fight for X!"

"How you like that?" asked the agent with his fist in Wren's hair, tugging so hard the roots began to pop out.

It wasn't the visual Wren would have gone for, but then he wasn't a medieval warlord. There could be no argument, though, parading Wren in his current state onto this stage was undoubtedly a power stroke. Strike fear into those who would come for Kason with an unforgettable visual message: this is what becomes of my enemies.

It also put Kason and teXas at large into company with the Dark Ages. It boiled down to a public lynching, no two ways about it. The people might lap it up, but the backlash would come after Wren's death. His martyrdom would begin small but spread, because while people loved blood, they also loved the rule of law. And nobody, not even the Big Bad Bird, deserved this kind of end.

That was one hell of a plan B.

Kason was speaking. Wren could barely hear him over the hurricane tide of his pulse. His heart beat so loud it felt like it would burst from his chest at any minute, like his veins would erupt and geyser out across the stage. A man going to his execution, though he wouldn't be the first. Many had died in far worse ways before. Kings and queens had walked to the gallows with their heads held high, holding their water until the moment they swung.

"Watch him, you terrorist scum," the agent said, yanking Wren's head up by the hair, bracing his face so all he could see was Hunter Kason. The man glided over the stage like a natural. "You could never beat a man like that."

Wren couldn't help but smile through his blurry vision. Out there he didn't see Hunter Kason, latest pretender to greatness, walking a walk he'd copied from others and practiced in the mirror to perfection, like some latter-day pop act replicating the moonwalk. Instead he saw his father in his prime.

The Apex. Striding the stage or the dusty side of some two-horse Texas town, shilling for the locals to send him their sick and their lame, their wayward children and their fallen women. Promising them the Earth and the Heavens and dominion over Hell.

He'd been so grand, then. Such a towering figure in Wren's child's eyes. Time after time he had worked genuine magic, proving himself to be the miracle worker he claimed to be as he 'saved' his own followers planted in the audience, redeeming the lost and faith-healing the sick, sending these 'converted' believers into fits in the desert grit.

In those moments little Pequeño 3 had grasped it all and felt right; from the role he played at his father's side to how everything added up to one beautiful whole. He understood the necessary beauty of all the pains that followed, in the underground pits where people choke out their last, in the vats where they slowly boiled and smiled for the cameras, in the cages where they baked in the beating desert heat. It all made sense and came full circle in the Apex's blazing blue eyes.

Heaven. Hell. Purpose.

"He's crying," someone said. "Look at the Big Bad Bird, he's sobbing like a baby!"

"Looks like he's laughing to me."

"Wait, the bastard's laughing? Not on our watch."

They struck him. Fists across his cheeks, into his stomach, leaving him sucking madly for air around the gag, eyes streaming, but still nothing could shift the angelic vision on the stage ahead, or alter the sickening truth as it dawned in the pit of Wren's palsying belly.

He still loved his father. Despite everything. Moments like this had cemented that love in wonder and awe, because Wren was a part of it. He could still feel his father's tousling touch on his unruly black hair. The pride with which the great man introduced little Pequeño 3 to the crowd.

'This is my son, and he's a believer!' he would boom.

And they would buy it. Wren had bought it too. He always had. That was what made it so hard to bury his memory.

Kason hit a crescendo. The last few blows rained in, but Wren barely felt them. All he felt was the small, hot hand holding his own. He couldn't turn but didn't need to, to know the tiny figure of eight-year-old Grace was right there at his back, with him at the end, just as she'd promised.

"Just think of strooberry pies," she whispered in his ear, as the men lifted him up. He couldn't even walk, with his ankles pulled up by the hog-tie, so they carried him out onto stage like a stuck pig. "Think of you and me," Grace whispered. "I'll be right here the whole time."

Now he was out before them all, Pequeño 3 once again on display for the crowd, and how they roared. He couldn't see a thing but their shifting colors stretching back and back, broken by the reflecting pool at the center, catching the blue sky like a doorway into heaven. It was all so beautiful.

They dropped him to his knees beside the podium, and the crowd cried like a hard wind across the Arizona desert.

"Let's skip stones across the sand," little Grace whispered urgently in his ear. "Come on, Pequeño 3, skip stones with me."

"You can't skip stones on sand," he mumbled into his gag, as he'd protested once some thirty years ago. "Don't be silly."

"Of course you can, if you believe it," Grace whispered. "Come on, Chris, keep count with me."

She spun stones out into the crowd, and they bounced over faces and heads and shoulders just like they'd once bounced over sand, and she counted every one. "One, two," she guided, "three, come on, Chris."

Chris. Pequeño 3. He didn't know the difference. What did any of it matter, now? A good death, maybe, the kings and queens of old. He straightened up as best he could and counted, barely shifting his lips.

"That's good, little Pequeño," Grace whispered, her hot warm breath smelling of strawberries and sand. She was always like this after she'd come from the Apex's cabin, so feverish for something, for anything. Wren hadn't known about the Blue Fairy back then, about what it had meant. He hadn't known what his father was doing with the other children behind closed doors.

"I'm sorry," he whispered to Grace, words only she could hear under the storm of the crowd. "I'm sorry I loved him. I know what he did, and I'm sorry he did it to you. I'm sorry I was so helpless."

"Count the skips now, Pequeño!" Grace called over the rush of the wind. "Count them with me!"

Strong hands turned Wren's body to the side, to face Kason at his podium, and he caught a glimpse of his swollen, bloodied, tear-stricken face blown up across the big screen. It showed these people he was nothing to fear. He was no boogey man, no awesome terrorist lurking in the shadows. He was just a man brought low and broken.

Kason held up the knife, and the crowd went apoplectic.

Wren could feel the bloodlust fuming off them like a hot, dusty wind. This was a dark delight none of them had anticipated. The end of the Big Bad Bird at their leader's hand. It made everything right, confirming their every choice leading up to now. Together, they could dominate even the greatest of legends. Together they would emblazon their name across the annals of history, a brand forever stamped across the flank of the United States.

The knife came in, and Grace threw herself tight around Wren's broad shoulders, as if she could somehow shelter him from the blow.

"I'll protect you," she whispered in his ear. "I'm not going anywhere."

"I know," he whispered.

The knife touched his throat. Maybe Hunter Kason had practiced this movement too. A confident lean. A few final words in the ear of the condemned, like some two-bit jihadi in a beheading video, standing at the pivot point of a nation.

"This is your moment," Kason whispered. "Enjoy it."

He pressed the knife in.

50

PIVOT

But the cut didn't come. No opened jugular vein. No blood streaming out to splash over the exultant faces of the tight-packed crowd.

Nothing.

At first Wren didn't know what it was. The knife pressed still and chill at his throat, and there was a certain cold in the breeze, a difference in the sound of the crowd.

Then he remembered, and arched his head back as far as he could, away from the knife and the crowd and past Hunter Kason's confused eyes, to the big screen in back of the stage.

It was showing CCTV footage. Wren blinked to bring it into focus. The interior of a plane, taken from the galley and pointing back down one of the aisles, through an array of first-class booths. The resolution was crisp; Wren could tell that even through his bleary vision. At the front on the port side sat a figure clearly recognizable as Christopher Wren. The same man on the stage.

Wren felt the eyes of the crowd darting back and forth like saw blades, working across Hunter Kason at the center. They gasped as a pair of children scampered into frame. A boy and a girl clearly up to mischief, they consorted briefly between booths, whispering in each other's ears, then settled on a target, reached a little hand over the booth wall and poked a stalk of cucumber into Wren's cheek.

The scene played out, and the crowd watched rapt. Hunter Kason was whispering into the ear of an aide, now, Wren forgotten for the moment. Wren couldn't hear, but he knew what he was saying.

What is this? Get it down! Pull the plug.

Wren watched as State Senator Amira Matheson came into sight, matched by fresh round of gasps from the crowd. There was no audio, but as she approached the Chris Wren on the screen, it was clear the exchange was pleasant. Almost flirtatious, Wren was glad to see. It was how he'd felt at the time.

"Shut it down!" Kason was shouting now. The crowd were calling their own questions, the bloodlust fading like they'd been hit by a cold shower. This was the 787 that had started it all. The departure point after which teXas had become a real possibility.

Wren strained against his shackles, trying to pull himself upright.

There were drones hovering above the crowd now, transmitting their own live feed of this moment out of teXas and to the wider world. They saw Hunter Kason feigning command in the face of losing control, Christopher Wren straightening up like he'd planned for this to happen.

The tide of the crowd changed as the footage on screen sped up, and the first of twin F-15s was just visible through the starboard window.

In two hours his team had worked magic. The 787 had already transmitted every bit of its onboard camera footage a week ago. teXas had locked it down, but with the keys to their network in hand, Hellion and B4cksl4cker had unlocked it.

Alli had commandeered the hardline feed into the big screen, with the help of Alejandro and Doona, who'd finally made their own way into Houston. With all eyes on Wren and the stage, they'd slipped through the Secret Service and spliced in a second feed. Wren heard the crashing of gunfire from behind the stage as they defended their work.

Just a little longer. Kason's head spun like a spectator at a tennis game, from the screen to the crowd to Wren and back again. Two hours back Trent and Nancy had led a squad of Foundation fringe into the audience, plants to guide the mob in the direction they wanted.

The direction they wanted now was silent and watching.

The footage raced forward, while a gun battle went on in the background. Kason went back to holding the knife at Wren's throat, but no one was watching. He gave up, resorted to yelling again.

On the screen Wren dropped into a hole in the aisle. The screen raced forward, through the landing, through the arrival of fake Marines in the galley, to the moment the air marshal pulled her Ideal Conceal on them and they shot her.

The crowd cried out their displeasure.

Just as Wren had hoped. So when he appeared in the galley again, magically transported from the baggage below, some actually cheered. The Foundation fringe in the audience drove the moment on. They cheered louder as Wren on the screen took out more Marines and scooped up the injured air marshal and risked his life to flee with her.

Chaos was breaking out. The crowd's unity was broken. The stage emptied of everyone but Wren and Kason, as all Secret Service agents flooded to the battle behind the stage, until at last the silent movie flickered and disappeared.

Cries went up for more.

Wren stood. Mads Hellström stood beside him, bolt cutters in hand. Nobody had seen him approach. Nobody had stopped him. Now he went to the lectern and plucked a spare microphone and handed it to Wren, who took it and said the first words these people needed to hear, amplified outward for the world to hear.

"I am not who you think I am."

Kason charged on stage with a group of Marines, weapons leveled at Wren and Hellström at the center, but neither budged. The crowd stared. The world watched, and Kason felt it.

Wren saw the change happening in his eyes. the confidence fading as he dialed back through the stages of his assessment. Starting to doubt everything. Re-evaluating and looking for the next route out and up. This was what happened when you sought power without any kind of vision, when you emptied peoples' heads so completely that you could pour anything in and have them believe it.

Anyone could just reach in and pour them full of something else.

Wren rode the moment.

"You've been told I'm your enemy," Wren boomed over the crowd, "but I am not. You've been told I'm an outside invader trying to bring X and teXas down, but this is not true either. If I'm fighting for anything, it's for you. It's for teXas. I am my father's son, after all."

That sowed all kinds of chaos.

Kason sent his Marines in. They came at Wren en masse, weapons down, and that was their mistake. Even wounded and battered, Wren was a match for any of them.

They came in hot, pumped on adrenaline from the gunfight behind the screen, and Wren met them with cold, hard efficiency. The lead Marine came in with a haymaker right that Wren strode into, taking the curl of the guy's bicep in the shoulder even as he sent an elbow uppercut into the man's jaw.

His momentum dropped out in a heartbeat, like a car hitting a semi-truck. His jaw rocked back, his body rolled around his hips like he was attached to a hinge, and he swung flat back. The next man in dived for Wren's legs, and Wren was already dropping; one elbow across the man's back, his thigh coming down on the Marine's head. They hit the stage together, the guy tried to roll but Wren had already grabbed his trailing left foot and twisted hard, breaking his ankle.

He screamed and rolled from the fight.

Hellström tackled the next one in, sending three short sharp punches straight into his face. With that cover, Wren rolled to his feet and grabbed the mic, turned to the crowd and began.

51

WHAT IS TEXAS?

"What is teXas?" Wren called across the crowd, momentarily silencing those who were booing and those who were cheering alike. Strength won converts like nothing else, and the people loved an underdog story.

"I'll tell you what teXas is," he went on, "it's freedom. Freedom to live your life as you choose. Freedom to life, to liberty, to happiness. Most of all, it is freedom from the interfering, domineering, tax-and-spend federal government of the United States of America."

The crowd stopped short of any kind of response Not agreement, not protest. They clearly didn't know what to make of him, and Wren leaned into their silence. This was exactly the kind of thing they believed but coming out of the mouth of a man they thought they despised.

"teXas is about freedom," Wren repeated, "but you know that freedom isn't free. Freedom requires strength. It requires a leader who's been battered a hundred times and always comes out on top. Someone who's faced down the federal government and won time after time." He paused, then pointed at Hunter Kason. "Is that the kind of man you had in mind?"

Kason was staring daggers at Wren now. Desperate to get his microphone back, to reclaim the moment he could feel slipping away from him, but how could he? No way he could charge the stage, not while his security guys lay groaning across the stage.

"Do you really want to be led by a man with the fragile ego of a desktop warrior, co-opting a mission he doesn't understand?" Wren asked. "A man who's a keyboard jockey at best, spraying bile and lies instead of bullets? A man with resting bitch face that half the continent laughs at? The kind of guy you would've wedgied at school and would avoid in real life? Is that the kind of leader you want? Because when has that man ever truly fought for anything?"

The crowd remained silent, their eyes big and disbelieving. They saw Wren throwing insults, and they saw Hunter Kason doing nothing. Get the right words in the right order, delivered in the right way, and you could work magic.

"That man is a charlatan," Wren went on, "with my father's legacy wrapped around him like a protective blanket, and on some level, you know it. He's faked his way to this stage. He's faked his way to this position, and he's never once got his hands dirty." Wren stared, challenging any to disagree with him. "Where was he when I was fighting jihadis in Afghanistan and cartels in Mexico? Where was he when I was battling violence across the country, keeping us safe while cowards like him twittered away for profit? He's an Internet troll amped on the amphetamine of your attention, and you know it." He let a pause open up. "You're teXans, like I'm a Texan, born and bred. You know he's not from here. You know he's an East Coast elite, went to the Ivy Leagues by birth right, only taught himself in his thirties to talk like us, thinking we were easy marks. But we're not easy marks." Another pause. "I ask you, is your life measured in social media likes and video streaming views? Do you count fans and sign autographs to earn your keep, or do you get in there and work with your hands, day after day? Do you sit behind a fake desk and fight from behind a camera lens, or do you actually fight every day for what's yours?"

The crowd remained silent, but the quality of that silence was shifting. At first, they'd been stunned. Now they were leaning in to listen.

"No one handed me anything on a silver platter. My father put me in a cage on the day I was born. My brothers and sisters have been trying to kill me for years. The US federal government sent me out to defend the nation so many times that it broke my family in half, then they turned around and stepped on me every chance they got.

"Still, I stopped the Saints, and the Blue Fairy, and the Reparations and the Ghost. You know this. You've seen this on the news for years. It wasn't the US government who saved this country. It wasn't X, and it certainly wasn't Hunter Kason. It was me." He took a breath. "Now you want someone to protect your freedom? To hold back Uncle Sam while you get on with living your lives, and you think Kason has the balls to get it done?"

Wren shook his head, then dived in with gusto. "Bullshit he does! This selfish fool has you running scared from me. The Big Bad Bird, right?" He cracked a smile, maybe got a few laughs as the crowd began to warm up. "You know how many times US politicians kicked me out of Force Recon, all because I broke some stupid rule while I was out there protecting the country? Five times in total. And you know why they asked me to come back, each time? Because the bad guys are afraid of me. Because they needed me. Now they're the bad guys. Not you. I'm on your side. So use me for what I'm good at. Set me loose like they never would."

He could feel them shifting before him. All the techniques he'd learned from his father and spent a lifetime refining were put into play now: his cadence, his delivery, his pauses.

"I want to protect teXas. I am able to protect teXas. And I will protect teXas, from backstabbers who would demonize their greatest asset just so they can put their boot on your necks next. Men like Hunter Kason."

He pointed again. Standing there across the stage, the contrast between Wren and Kason couldn't be clearer. One battered but vibrant, bloody but unbowed, and the other paling and fading before everyone's eyes.

"That man engineered the blast of the 787 jet. Five hundred and thirty people died to put him on this stage. He blackmailed State Senator Amira Matheson by threatening her children. Now ask yourselves, what kind of person blows up planes and kidnaps children? I'll give you a hint, it starts with a 't'."

The crowd started making some noise at that. Some angry and protesting. Some clamouring to hear more.

"We should be hunting him down like we hunted bin Laden. An ocean burial and a black mark forever against his name. He sought to divide us. Well, now we're divided. teXas is a nation, and I ask you, who do you think can keep us this way? Who's the United States government afraid of most, is it Hunter Kason, or is it me? I'm the one picking up the pieces. I'm the one with the strength. I say string this piece of crap up from the nearest lamp post. Here's to teXas!"

The crowd ruptured, stray cheers erupting through cries of protest.

He had them.

"He knows it," Wren called, pointing again. "It's over for him, false idol trying to claim my father's legacy. If anyone's going to claim the mantle of X, it's going to be me!"

The crowd were getting into it now. As if on cue, the big

screen came back on, showing Wren in close-up. He looked strong. All he had to do now was hold it.

He turned to Mads Hellström. A figure everyone knew, after media coverage had played up his kidnapping. Open the door wide with X, and you never knew what was going to get poured through.

"Arrest that man," Wren ordered.

Hellström responded. He walked right up to Hunter Kason. The Marines didn't stop him. Kason was white with shock. The cameras lingered on his clean-shaven, milk-pale skin. Next to the rough and rugged closeup on Wren, the choice was obvious.

Hellström produced cuffs and put them on Kason's wrists. Kason didn't know what to do. Finally they'd found a maneuver the man hadn't practiced in the mirror.

The crowd roared their approval.

Wren faced them and spread his arms wide, "teXas, you're free!"

That really set them off.

52

UNITED STATES

52. UNITED STATES

Wren commanded the stage like a firebrand preacher.

Arms wide. Voice loud. Pacing up and down before the crowd gushing promises like an oil well blowout, and the crowd lapped it up and shouted themselves hoarse.

At some point his team splashed highlights of his past exploits across the big screen: the moment he jumped a monster truck flying huge US flags over an LA River dam; dizzying dash-cam footage of him shredding the Anti-Ca arena with a Jeep Wrangler; the moment he talked down a rioting crowd by kneeling in front of LA's Wilshire Building.

The crowd responded, and Wren kept on feeding them more red meat, even as in the background Hellion and B4cksl4cker cemented their control over Kason's command infrastructure. At some point a Bible and a judge were brought out. When Wren laid his hand on the book and gave the oath of office, the crowd went ballistic. Black and white baseball caps scrawled with X's flew in the air, accompanied by a new chant.

"Big Bad Bird! Big Bad Bird!"

It was a good day's work.

After an hour, Wren finally staggered off the stage, feeling more drained than ever. His body was failing him. Someone caught him in a chair. He saw it was Doona Joy. Her eyes shone with enthusiasm.

"Christopher, I never expected to see this."

He managed half a laugh. People were running everywhere. A new regime coming into power would cause that. Old orders getting canceled and new ones rolling out, as Hunter Kason's grip on teXas dissolved.

The importation camps were being closed even as Wren sat there sucking down a bottle of water and gasping for air, head spinning. The police who'd been fired for too much loyalty to the old system were all being called back in while the ones who'd been hired since were kicked out. At Teddy's direction, the National Guard, Army and FEMA resources were being directed to help the survivors of the importation camps as a measure of absolute urgency.

Wren had the voices of Hellion and B4cksl4cker in his head giving updates and asking questions. He answered them all, as some measure of order descended across Houston.

"Christopher, I have President of United States on line for you," came Hellion's voice. "Jacinda Ablas."

Wren laughed, then sobered. Of course the President was calling. Everything on the stage had just been transmitted globally.

"Put her through," Wren said, closing his eyes and dropping his head into his hand, putting all his energy into focusing.

The line clicked in his ear, then he heard her warm, confident tones.

"President Wren," she said, sounding amused. "Congratulations. I'll admit, few people here believed you could get it done. You have proved them wrong."

"Thank you, President Ablas," he countered. "And the work's only just beginning."

"Indeed. I am readying troops at the teXas borders as we speak, if you'll just stand down your forces, as we agreed, then-"

"I'm afraid I can't do that, Madam President," Wren interjected. Took a breath.

A long pause stretched out between them, broken by discordant chants from the people on the other side of the canvas tent.

"Excuse me," Ablas said. "It sounded like you just said you couldn't stand down your military."

Wren took another deep breath. He'd promised a lot of things to get to this point. "The situation's changed. I'm sorry. I can't stand down, and if you ever want teXas back in the fold, I need you to accept that for the time being."

She said nothing. Probably her microphone was muted, conferring with her advisors. Wren cracked his eyes open and saw Doona staring at him with wide eyes.

"Mr. Wren," President Ablas came back. He noticed his title was now missing. "That is not what we discussed. We provided you with communications amplification. We have backed your coup. What good was that to us, if you're going to go ahead with this harebrained independence scheme anyway?"

"I understand why you'd feel that way," Wren allowed. "Here's the truth as I see it. The second I give the order to stand down, I get overthrown from within. Whatever authority I have right now is on a tightrope a hundred feet high. Same goes for if you cross the border anyway. You saw my speech. The whole point of it was that I can protect these people from you. You breach our borders now, you ruin me, and you ruin any chance I ever had of getting them to listen. They'll pick up their weapons and turn guerilla, if that's what it takes. It'll be your military battling these people in the streets. Is that the visual you want for reunification?"

Now he heard her breathing. No need for mute anymore. When she spoke again, any hint of amusement was gone from her tone.

"So what you're telling me is, you just took teXas, Mr. Wren."

"President Wren," he corrected.

Another silence.

"You knew this was coming. You planned this."

Wren snorted. "Don't kid a kidder, Madam President. You knew this was coming too. I know how the federal government thinks. You're hoping to get my people all tied up in overthrowing me, while you sweep in with a thirty-minute push to Austin. I understand that. But I'm here on the ground and I can tell you, it'll never work. It won't be like securing Iraq, a fast sweep followed by a 'Mission Accomplished' sign on some aircraft carrier. It'll be more like trying to hold Afghanistan. These people will fight you building-by-building if you try to force your way in. The only way you ever get Texas back is to stand down right now."

"So I cede Texas to you for my own good, is that what you're saying? Are you serious? That can never work. I'm giving the order-"

"Do not attack, that's advice and it's also a warning, Jacinda. Any attempt to retake this nation by force will be met by the full weight of our military, which you'll know is sizable and loyal. I think you'll also find the neighboring states will join us. In minutes you'll have yourself a civil war. Give that order, and you precipitate the very crisis we're trying to avoid."

Now she was breathing heavily. Wren leaned lower over his knees, head spinning.

"Tell me this is more than a land grab," President Ablas said at last. "Tell me I haven't just swapped one dictator for another."

"I promise you, Madam President, I am loyal to the United States. I want teXas brought back into the Union as much as you do. I don't want to be some tin-pot dictator. But it can't happen today. Today and going forward I am President of teXas, and I'll play my role to the full." He took a rattling breath. "At the same time, we'll be leaking evidence like a sieve. The blackmailing of Amira Matheson, and any other state senators who were coerced, will come out in an unstoppable trickle. We'll dig into the conspiracy behind the downing of my 787. We'll empty out and expose all the importation camps, and everyone involved in them. We'll chip away at the legitimacy of this whole thing until we prize back the support of the neighboring states. Pretty soon there'll be embargoes against us, and our economy will crash. The people will feel every bite at the kitchen table and realize what they're missing." He took a breath. "That's the only way this can work. We are the example you set. teXas on its knees and begging for annexation is the message you send to every would-be seceder state: break the union and you will lose everything. No other will risk it again for a century."

Silence followed.

Wren's head swam. In the last few hours he'd said so many words, spun so many concepts back and forth, that he hardly knew where he was or where he was going. He stared down at raw blacktop underfoot. To think, just a week back he'd been trying to leave it all behind. He'd been reading that Stephen King book, with its lovely evocation of American neighborliness.

"How long?" Ablas asked, startling him.

Wren blinked back to alertness. "Three months. Just as soon as I can. I want to go back to my family, Jacinda. I don't want this. Six months, at the outside. I think the economy will be in freefall by then."

She sighed. "Freefall, like that's a good thing. Look what you've done to us, Christopher Wren." She pulled in a fortifying breath. "They warned me about you, you know. Said you're an egomaniac."

Wren managed a chuckle. "What president isn't?"

"Three months," she said, changing direction as sharply as a hammerhead shark. "I need to see a drop-off in support by then. The polling has to shift. Six months at the outside, with your own people calling to come back. You achieve that, maybe I can keep you from swinging as a traitor. Any longer, and at the minimum we'll have to imprison you. It's the only way."

Wren laughed. No good deed shall go unpunished. There was a backlash to everything. "You can try."

He took the earpiece out of his ear. The call was done anyway.

Doona was looking down at him. "What do we do now?"

Wren stood. He was shaky, but this thing was just getting started. They had miles to go before they slept.

"Get out there and press the flesh. Shake hands. Be seen. Don't shoot anyone."

She nodded seriously. "We can try."

53

ONE HUNDRED DAYS

One hundred days later, Wren took his first day off. The UH-72 Lakota helicopter descended swiftly out of an acid blue summer sky, kicking up a whirling torrent of ochre sand. Wren leaned out to survey the Arizona landscape. On all sides lay barren, wind-scoured scrub and withered cacti, shooting with pops of desert flower color.

Apricot-orange desert globemallows. Yellow-orange Mexican gold poppies. The lavender spears of desert lupines.

It was beautiful.

The helicopter put down with a soft thump. He stepped out and looked across the fake town.

The metal fences and guard towers were down. That was one of his first orders to the Foundation, given in the initial rush of his teXas presidency. Life was returning to Little Phoenix now, as construction crews bustled over buildings, making them safe for the impending return of the Blue Fairy orphans.

Reclaim X, little Grace had told him. Make it your own.

This was the lesson he should have learned a long time

ago, maybe. The more you fought the enemy, the stronger you made them.

Hammers clanged on nails. A buzzsaw ripped through the air. Men and women shouted instructions. Nobody remarked much upon his arrival, and that was good. Here he wasn't President of a breakaway nation. Here he wasn't anything but a wayward son.

He'd left the teXas Capitol Building, the old Houston City Hall, two hours earlier. Already his new country was starting to flag. With its importation camps disbursed, many thousands of fresh legal cases were working their way up to the Supreme Court from the victims, claiming all manner of horrific, amply documented abuses. One of those was Yolanda Queen, after the screening at Wren's inauguration had raised her profile. She'd largely recovered from her injuries and was proving to be a powerful witness. As a result of her testimony, the investigation into Hunter Kason's role in the downing of the 787 was making fast progress. Just a day earlier Brigadier General Mads Hellström had been arrested.

"You said I'd be Governor," he'd whispered furiously at Wren, who was there in person. "You promised."

"I promised," Wren said. "But the law didn't. Five hundred and thirty people is beyond my ability to forgive."

The border with the USA held secure, but nobody was looking to cross over anymore, except for those trying to flee. In the first few weeks, there'd been a mass influx of X followers drawn to the new 'promised land'. But as footage of Amira Matheson's tearful reunion with her children achieved saturation play across the Internet and TV, and the underlying conspiracy to coerce her independence vote was spelled out bit by bit, the flow had slowed.

Now the X brand flagged under the weight of a thousand cuts. Teddy masterminded the rollout, with help from Hellion and B4cksl4cker using botnets to amplify the message on social media. The evidence was all there. The economy had yet to take a substantial hit, but that was due to government deficit spending to bridge the crisis. Wren was about to cut off the bailout faucet and present the tax bill to the people. He anticipated a rapid drop-off in real, take-home pay after that. Give it another three months and teXas would be on its last legs.

Sand crunched underfoot. The early morning air was fresh and blooming with the aroma of raw sap.

He walked along Main Street alone, admiring the buildings he'd once despised. Once scarred by rifle fire and soured by the dark secrets Maggie and the Apex had built underfoot, they no longer looked so inhospitable. He found himself yearning for the day the orphans returned, and along with them all the teachers, counselors, custodians, nurses, shopkeepers, cooks and everyone it took to run a small town. Little Phoenix would bustle again.

The new-build gym was there, standing at the edge of town. Wren nodded to the guard at the security desk, passed through the metal detector, and walked back through the empty space where all the weights machines had been. In the full-length wall mirrors he saw a different man from the one he'd been when last he'd come this way.

His scars were healing. His eyes were brighter. He still felt a slight wince in his side, from the bullet that had shot him through-and-through, but that was more a phantom pain than anything. The loss of Henry was three months removed, the loss of his father half a year away. He hadn't seen his children in person since the town was reclaimed, but he felt more ready than ever.

Ready to be a father, ready to let it all go.

The secret door through the mirrors hung open, and he descended down the long passageway. Back under the earth, to where the cicadas remained buried for eighteen years at a time. Back into the past.

A few hundred yards along and twenty feet deep, he passed through the secure metal door and entered the same temple-like space as before, now clad in a foot-thick layer of concrete. Behind these concrete walls lay the paintings he and every member of the then-Pyramid had made of themselves, the day before they'd burned.

Now he saw the error of walling those paintings away. You didn't move on by covering up the past. You moved on by airing it out. For now, though, the three cage cells remained. They had been intended for his brothers and Maggie, but with Gabriel and Zachariah dead, Maggie alone remained.

She was sitting at her table, just as she'd been the last time he'd come. A desiccated desert orchid, wrapped in brown and tan layers, head down and working on a jigsaw.

Seeing her brought up a welter of emotions in Wren. Not anger anymore. Not pity, either. Maybe empathy. They were so similar, in so many ways. She'd committed atrocities, there was no denying that, but the atrocities committed upon her were every bit as egregious and had lasted most of her life.

Maybe there could be forgiveness. He wanted that.

He walked over to her table. Just as before, she did not look up. Perhaps waiting for him to start shouting, making demands, even toss the table through the air, as he had the last time. Instead he sat down. Reached a hand out toward her.

She looked up at him, then. X herself. He could still see the hint of who she'd been in those startling green eyes, each a lychee in full bloom, buried in the pale earth of her face.

"Something's different," she said, studying him.

Wren smiled gently. "I thought you might like to go upstairs for a spell. There's something I want to show you."

She stared at him. There was no trust there at all. No belief. If anything there was just deep suspicion and hate.

"You're not here looking for answers," she said. She sounded surprised. "You're not begging."

He nodded. "That's what you predicted, isn't it? I remember. That I'd come back cap in hand, we'd be sat here together at the end? Well, at least I'm here. It's not the end, though, right?"

She tilted her head, like she was trying to make sense of that. "Not the end. So they failed?"

"You mean Texas? Or teXas with an 'X', I should say."

Maggie said nothing.

"I'm actually President of that new nation, believe it or not."

Her brows beetled slightly closer together. That passed for shock in Wren's book.

"I know, it's crazy. I can hardly believe it myself, and I've been serving for three months, just passed my hundred-day honeymoon period. It's a temporary thing only, though. I'll be handing control back to the United States soon, when teXas is annexed back in." He paused a moment, watching her eyes. "But that's not what I wanted to talk to you about."

She stared. "teXas was hardly the limit of our father's plan. There are many-"

Wren raised a hand. "It's OK. Maggie. Grace. Really, I'm not here for that. Just to show you something. Will you come see?"

She glared. He felt her resistance battling her curiosity. That was how it worked, when you didn't come head on. When you stopped making demands. When all you did was show respect, empathy, even love.

Abruptly, she stood. The brown and tan layers of her customary uniform rustled like sun-dried petals. She didn't take his hand, but that was all right. "Lead on," she said.

So he did. Out of the temple with its cells he went, up the passageway toward the light, into the gym where Maggie spent long moments blinking in the sudden light. She hadn't seen the sun in half a year, Wren realized. Like Persephone emerging from the underworld.

He gave her time to adjust. He'd felt much the same, when he'd emerged after burning their father alive, and he'd been underground then for less than an hour.

"I don't see anything," Maggie said.

"You will." He led the way out of the gym, out onto Main Street and walking west. Maggie trudged along behind him, no cuffs or restraints in place, blinking like a newborn.

"Where are the fences?" she asked, peering into the distance.

"I took them down."

She absorbed that silently for a moment, eyes flickering over the town that had once been hers. "And what are they building?"

"They're rebuilding. Little Phoenix will return to what it was, under your stewardship, Maggie. A home for orphans, cult survivors, people who've suffered." He turned to her. "And your cell? We'll take down the concrete walls and it'll become a museum to the lost, with all the original portraits on display, even little Pequeño 3." He smiled. "This place will go back to healing, in line with your vision."

She said nothing.

Wren kept walking. The sun beat down. They went past the old saloon where once babies had cried out in their cages, past the hotel, the brothel, all props from some forgotten Western film that was never made. He kept on until the street turned to dust underfoot and by either side there lay only low concrete slabs, each as large as the foundation to a home, each carved with hundreds of names in a large, elegant font.

Maggie stopped and stared. Wren stopped with her, reading the unspoken question in her eyes.

"This is our memorial to the victims of the Pyramid," he said.

The names stretched on and on, filling slab after slab. Maggie led the way, and they walked and read. Wren knew most of the names by heart; not just the first victims of the Pyramid, those who'd burned themselves alive thirty years ago, but every one of his father's victims since: those lost to the Saints, the Blue Fairy, the Reparations and the Ghost; to David Keller's burnings and the X-apoc attacks; right up to the five hundred and thirty souls lost over teXas as the 787 was shot out of the sky.

They stopped at the last of the slabs, where there were only five names.

Chrysogonus-With-Bared-Arm.

Galicia-In-Her-Mother's-Heart.

Aden-Of-The-Saints.

Gabriel-In-Extremis.

Zachariah-Of-The-Marsh.

Maggie let out a little gasp. "Our brothers and sisters."

"I couldn't find remains for many of them," Wren answered. "Chrysogonus burned on his stage, Galicia blew up in her zoo. Gabriel and Zachariah sank into the depths of the Pacific. I was able to retrieve Aden, he died in Mexico. It's the best I could do."

Maggie gazed at the engraved names for a long moment, her expression inscrutable. Sand had gathered in some of the valleys of the letters, making them stand out all the more against the gray stone slabs.

"This is your scorecard against the Pyramid," she said at last. Not looking at him, though her voice trembled with quiet rage. "All the souls the great Christopher Wren has taken. So you can stand over them forever. So you can possess them, like you now possess me."

Wren shook his head slowly. Sad that this was what she thought of him.

"How is it my score card, Maggie?" he asked gently. "I didn't kill any of these people. Not one of them. To a person, they killed themselves. They burned themselves, or they shot themselves, or blew themselves up, all on our father's orders." He let those words hang. "This is the record of a long tragedy. They were all victims of our father. Like me. Like you."

Her gaze snapped up to him, blazing emerald. "I am not a victim. Neither are you. You killed our father."

"He's the only one I killed. But his name will never be written here. He may have been a victim too, in his own way, but I can't go back that far. I can only forgive so much. And this place is for victims, Maggie. For survivors, and even forgiveness, if they can manage it."

Silence reigned over the low tombs. A whispery wind rustled sand across stone, dropping more grains into the freshly carved lettering.

"I will never forgive you, Pequeño 3," Maggie said. Now her eyes shone with tears and her cheeks were flushed with emotion. "No matter how many tombstones you lay. For causing their deaths. For killing our father. You will burn for this."

Wren just nodded. "Maybe. Maybe you'll burn me one day, Maggie. Grace."

"If I could burn you now, I would."

"I know," he said softly, "and that's OK. Really. Your days will be different now, I promise. You won't be underground. You'll have a generous cell above ground, and you'll see the sun. You'll be able to hear the children. They'll let out you to walk in the desert every day. I don't want you to die, but any time you want, you could walk out there and just keep walking." Wren pointed into the wilderness. "The guards won't stop you. Your life is your own, to lead as you wish."

She stared at him like her eyes could cut him in half. He'd seldom seen rage like it. But then what was rage, except the other side of love?

"I loved you, Grace," Wren said. "The little girl I couldn't save. Maybe you're the foundation for this hero complex I've got." He smiled. "I loved Maggie too, I think, or I was coming to. Maybe I still do, in some way, and that's enough for me. So take all the time you need."

She began to tremble. Maybe that was rage. Maybe it was the first crack in the edifice of faith she'd built over the decades.

"There are more attacks coming," she said. "This isn't the end."

"It never is. Now, I'll come and visit. I hope you'll agree to see me. I hope you'll find forgiveness and peace here too, Grace."

She said nothing. He nodded and started walking away.

"There are greater forces by far arrayed against this country," she called after him. "Devastation and destruction will come, and…"

It didn't matter. Wren wasn't listening anymore. Instead he was thinking about finishing up his time in teXas and heading east once more. Taking a civilian flight to Delaware and closing out the King novel on the way.

Going to see his family.

Going home.

CHRISTOPHER WREN WILL RETURN

THE NEXT CHRIS WREN THRILLER

NEVER FORGIVE

Vengeance never forgives.

Tokyo, Japan. A city thrown into uproar, with five members of the Japanese elite murdered. The killer is a ghost - leaving no trace except for three words carved into the bodies:

FOR CHRISTOPHER WREN

Wren's in semi-retirement. Enjoying some well-earned time with his kids. But there's more at stake here than five dead power-players.

The tally's just getting started.

Some crimes can never be forgiven.

AVAILABLE FOR PRE-ORDER NOW

www.shotgunbooks.com

HAVE YOU READ THEM ALL?

THE CHRIS WREN THRILLERS BY MIKE GRIST

Saint Justice

A biker gang steals Wren's truck in the wilds of Utah.
Now he's going to get it back.

No Mercy

The Blue Fairy hacker group threatens Wren's kids.
There can be no mercy.

Make Them Pay

A billionaire banker is executed live online.
Now all must pay for their crimes.

False Flag

Someone's framed Chris Wren for murder.
He'll kill to clear his name.

Firestorm

A woman burns herself alive online, and others follow.
There'll be no shelter from the firestorm to come.

Enemy of the People

The masses battle in the streets over hellfire and lies.
Only Chris Wren can bring the truth to light.

Backlash

Wren's passenger jet is brought down by twin F-15s.
Let the backlash begin.

Never Forgive

5 dead bodies in Tokyo, Japan, carved with three words:

FOR CHRISTOPHER WREN

TRY MIKE'S OTHER BOOKS

WRITTEN AS MICHAEL JOHN GRIST

The Last Mayor series - Books 1-9

When the zombie apocalypse devastates the world overnight,
Amo is the last man left alive.
Or is he?

Learn more at www.shotgunbooks.com

JOIN THE FOUNDATION!

Join the Mike Grist newsletter, and be first to hear when the next Chris Wren thriller is coming.

Also get exclusive stories, updates, learn more about the Foundation's coin system and see Wren's top-secret psych CIA profile - featuring a few hidden secrets about his 'Saint Justice' persona.

www.subscribepage.com/christopher-wren

ACKNOWLEDGEMENTS

Thanks to Barb Stoner, Julian White, Monte Montana and Sue Martin.

- Mike

Printed in Great Britain
by Amazon

83511611R00212